# The Book of Goodnight Stories

# The Book of GOODNIGHT STORIES

*Written by*
Vratislav Šťovíček
*Illustrated by*
Karel Franta
*Translated by*
Stephen Finn

Exeter Books

NEW YORK

First published 1982 by
ORBIS PUBLISHING, LONDON
Illustrated by Karel Franta
Translated by Stephen Finn
Graphic design by Roman Rogl
© ARTIA, PRAGUE 1982
Published in USA 1983 by Exeter Books
Reprinted 1984, 1985 and 1986
Distributed by Bookthrift
Exeter is a trademark of Bookthrift Marketing, Inc.
Bookthrift is a registered trademark of
Bookthrift Marketing, Inc. New York, New York
ALL RIGHTS RESERVED
ISBN: 0-671-05963-7
Printed in Czechoslovakia by Svoboda, Prague
1/99/29/51-08

# JANUARY

# 1 JANUARY

## The Owl King

Long, long ago, the birds were far wiser than men. They needed no king to rule over them, or ministers to tell them what to do. Nor did the council of the birds lay down foolish laws, but when they met there the birds would tell each other one tale after another, and speak about who had been born, who had died, what young bird had been orphaned, and altogether concerned themselves with much more important matters than orders and prohibitions, rules and regulations. The birds lived by the one wise law of love and friendship. They knew neither hatred nor anger. But one day a wicked man wandered into their realm. He looked around him, and was envious of the birds' happiness. "Why do you not raise yourself up above the rest?" he asked the peacock. "You are far more beautiful than the other birds." The peacock was flattered by these words, and began to

look at himself proudly in the pool. "Why do you make friends with the humble quail?" the man asked the eagle. "Are you not far stronger and more noble? Why, you can fly to the very clouds: you could tear the quail's lowly head to pieces with your powerful beak!" The eagle was so filled with conceit when he heard this that he went and ripped the quail's nest apart with his sharp talons. And so, slowly but surely, the evil man went about sowing seeds of contention among the birds.

# 2 JANUARY

## The Owl King

Before very long the realm of the birds began to look like a Turkish bazaar. The birds squabbled and abused each other, shouting one another down, until at last the stronger ones among them began to hunt the weaker ones and kill them. Each was proud of his own kind and did not have a good word to say for anyone else. "We cannot go on like this," the

brilliant little humming-bird said to himself one day; he called together all the small birds, and they flew off in a great flock to the mountain peak where the mighty eagle had his nest. "We want justice!" they cried. "You are the strongest of us all; you must take power over the birds, and see to it that they do not harm one another." The eagle was flattered at being chosen in this way, and would have taken up the sceptre at once. But the wicked man told him, "Eagle, you are a fool to want to be king. The king is only the slave of his people. He must constantly see to their well-being, decide their ridiculous quarrels, and protect the weak against the strong. It would be better to make the owl your king. He has eyes like precious stones; he can see at night, but in the daytime, when the other birds are flying about merrily in the sunshine, he is quite blind. He will not interfere in your affairs, and each will be able to do as he pleases." The eagle decided it was a good idea, so the birds made the owl their king. During the day he sleeps, and at night, when the other birds are tucked away in their nests, he holds sway. So to this day peace has not returned to the kingdom of the birds.

merriest, a faint tapping was heard at the door, and a strange voice croaked, "Princess, you have given your word: now you must grant your frog his wishes." And there stood the ugly frog himself. The princess was horrified, and turned to her father for help, but the king said sternly, "The royal word may not be broken: what you have promised, you must fulfil!" So there was nothing for it but to take the frog on her knee and eat with him from her golden plate in front of the whole company. How loathsome he was to her! She quite lost her appetite. When the frog had eaten his fill, he croaked out: "Now I am sleepy. Take me with you to your bed!" What do you suppose happened next?

## 3 JANUARY

## The Frog Prince

A princess was once playing in the garden with her golden ball, when it rolled down the well. At once there emerged from the water a hideous frog, who said, "Do not cry, princess. If you promise that I may sit with you at table, eat from your golden plate, and lie beside you in your bed, I'll give you back your golden toy." The princess gave her word gladly, and before long the frog came out of the well, holding in his mouth the golden ball. Snatching it from him, the princess hurried home as fast as her legs could carry her, and her promise was soon forgotten. That evening the king held a great feast for some honoured guests. When the royal banquet was at its

## 4 JANUARY

## The Frog Prince

Well, the princess ran ahead of the frog to her chamber, hoping to slam the door in his face, but the frog slipped through her legs and leaped between the sheets. The princess nearly fainted with horror, but she managed to overcome her loathing and, taking the vile creature in her fingertips, she hurled him onto the floor. Then, wonder of wonders—whom should she see standing before her but a handsome prince? "I was under the spell of a wicked fairy," he said. "Only the girl who fulfilled my wishes could set me free. I thank you with all my heart for breaking the evil spell." The stars had grown pale in the sky before the joyful princess heard the end of the

frog-prince's tale. No sooner had dawn broken than the sound of a carriage was heard beneath the chamber window. "My faithful servant, Henry!" cried the prince, joyously. "He shall drive us to my palace, where you shall become my wife." The princess and her father willingly agreed, but the carriage had scarcely set off when a terrible crack was heard. "Henry, a wheel is breaking!" called out the prince. But the faithful servant replied:

> *"Nay, master, this was far a gladder sound,*
> *For while you were accursed,*
> *With golden bands my grieving heart*
> *I bound: 'Tis one of these has burst."*

And before the prince's carriage reached his palace, all the remaining hoops which bound the faithful Henry's heart had cracked with sheer joy at his master's return.

## 5 JANUARY

## Prince Bajaja

There was once a poor king who had an only son. One day he called the young prince to his throne and said, sadly, "Hard times are come upon our land, my son — why, even the mice in the royal palace go hungry. Saddle my trusty white stallion, and go out into the world to seek your fortune!"
The prince did as he was told. On and on he rode and, so as not to feel homesick, he kept up his spirits by singing to himself. "Your song comes from a pure heart, and keeps time with my hooves," said his mount, suddenly. "Clearly, you are a stout-hearted young fellow, and I would serve you faithfully for that. If you follow my advice, good fortune shall be yours." The prince wondered greatly that his horse should speak in a human voice, but he asked no questions, and promised to take his steed's advice. After some time they arrived in a strange kingdom. The stallion stamped the ground with his hoof, whereupon it opened up beneath them, and the prince and his horse found themselves in a secret, golden cavern. "Here we must part," the horse told him. "Go to the royal city and enter service at the palace. But you must pretend to be quite dumb. Whatever they ask you, simply answer 'bah-yah-yah'. When you need me, return here and stamp three times!"
The prince set off obediently. He walked, and walked, and it seemed he would never reach hig goal.

## 6 JANUARY

## Prince Bajaja and the Three Beautiful Princesses

The royal city to which the prince was

"bah-yah-yah". So he came to be called Bajaja. His smile allayed their grief, so that they almost forgot the cruel destiny that awaited them. But on the last evening before the full moon, amid weeping and wailing, the prince slipped out of the palace and set off to consult his wise friend, the horse.

"In the chest by the wall you will find a suit of magic armour," the white stallion told him when, in the golden cavern, the prince had related the whole sad tale. "Before sunrise we shall ride into battle. But now it is time to sleep."

## 7 JANUARY

## How Prince Bajaja Fought the Nine-Headed Dragon

The next day before cockcrow the old king and his unhappy daughters made their way to the dragon's lair. They were greeted by nine fierce roars, and from out of the rocks nine hideous heads appeared. The princesses almost fainted with terror, but—out of nowhere, it seemed—a strange knight appeared on a fine white horse. Vizor lowered and sword drawn, he rode full tilt at the monster. Who would have thought that this bold deliverer might be the dumb page Bajaja? The monster roared furiously, its nine throats hurling fire at the prince; but Bajaja never flinched. He felled the dragon heads bravely, until the blood spurted out. But scarcely had one head rolled to the ground, when another grew in its place. Bajaja was growing weary, but just as it seemed it was all over with him, the youngest princess tossed him her white rose, whereupon he suddenly found new strength, and took up the fight again. Dragon heads tumbled like corn beneath the scythe, and before long the last of them was lying bloody on the ground. The prince cut out the tongue, pushed it into his saddle-bag and, without so much as a word of farewell, was gone as swiftly as he had come. When the joyful princesses arrived back at the

travelling was a sad sight to see. Black flags hung from the windows, and the sound of lamentation was to be heard on all sides. An evil nine-headed dragon had moved into the once-happy land, and had threatened to destroy the entire kingdom if the king did not bring his three daughters to the dragon's lair the morning before the full moon. Only the boldest of the knights had dared to challenge the fearful monster, and not one had returned alive. All this the prince learned from the citizens as he made his way to the royal palace. In the palace gardens he came across the three hapless princesses. The most beautiful of them was the youngest, Princess Rosalinda. He plucked her a white rose, and smiled at her. "Your smile warms the heart," she whispered. "What is your name?" "Bah-yah-yah," replied the prince. "Oh, you poor mute. Stay here with us in the palace until we go to meet our fate. You will cheer us with your smile." The prince willingly agreed. The girls often asked him who he was and where he came from, but he would only say,

palace with their father, the dumb page Bajaja was at the gate to greet them with a happy smile.

"Oh, you ungrateful wretch," Rosalinda scolded him, playfully, "to leave us at our time of greatest need. But for your smile I forgive you." "Bah-yah-yah," replied the prince, smiling broadly. That evening the princess found a white rose on her pillow. Now, who do you think had left it there?

## 8 JANUARY

# Prince Bajaja and the Golden Apple

The youngest princess could not forget her saviour. Day after day she languished, until at last the king called his daughters to the throne and told them, "Our land has seen grief enough. The time has come to find you husbands." He ordered the most handsome princes from all around to be invited to his palace, and thrust a golden apple into each one's hand. The dumb Bajaja crept among them and he, too, put out his hand for an apple. The king declared: "Whoever rolls his apple to one of my daughters shall have her for his wife." For a long time the noble princes tried in vain. Then at last the apples of the two most handsome princes found their way to the feet of the elder sisters. Then Prince Bajaja threw his apple, which rolled to the feet of the youngest and most beautiful of all. The poor girl burst into tears. How she had dreamed of her bold deliverer, and now she was fated to marry the dumb Bajaja! But the page disappeared as if the ground had swallowed him up. They asked after him in vain. Then, one day, a fine prince on a spirited white stallion came riding with a flourish into the palace courtyard. "I am Bajaja, your

bridegroom and saviour," he proclaimed, drawing the dragon's tongue from his saddle-bag to prove it. "If you do not want me for your husband, then I release you from the promise given by the king himself!" But Rosalinda threw herself at once into the arms of her deliverer. Thus it was that Prince Bajaja found his fortune in the world. And his faithful white stallion? He disappeared like a puff of smoke. Perhaps he is in his golden cavern to this day, waiting for someone to ask his help.

## 9 JANUARY

# The Little Shepherd Boy

Have you ever heard of the clever little shepherd boy? His sheep were so inquisitive that he could scarcely keep up with their questions. Soon he knew the answer to every question in the world. The king himself heard of his wisdom. He summoned him to the palace and told him, "If you can answer three questions, I shall adopt you as my own son." And right away he began with the first question: "How many drops of water are there in the sea?" — "A difficult question indeed, Sire," replied the boy. "But if you were to have all the rivers of the world blocked up, that the sea might grow no larger, then I should count them for you." The king said nothing, but asked again: "How many stars are there in the sky?" The shepherd boy took from his tunic three bags of poppy-seed and spread it over the ground. "There are as many stars in the sky as there are poppy seeds here, and you may count them yourself!" he said. The king smiled. "Very well, but now you must tell me how many seconds there are in eternity." The shepherd boy replied, "Sire, at the end of the Earth stands a diamond mountain, an hour's journey high, an hour's journey deep, and an hour's journey broad. Once in a hundred years a bird flies to the mountain and sharpens its beak on it. When the whole mountain has been worn away, the first second of eternity will have passed. Why do we not, Sire, wait

together for all eternity, so that we may count the seconds?" The king broke into laughter. "You wise young fellow," he said. "I will adopt you as my own."—"But you must take my sheep, too," replied the shepherd boy. And so it was. The shepherd boy ruled the land, and the king watched over his sheep.

## 10 JANUARY

# The Two Hens

What do you think? Two hens quarrelled over a grain of corn, and hurried off to complain to the cock. "Bring me the grain!" ordered the cock. The hens obeyed, the cock gave a quick peck, and the grain of corn was gone. "How unfair!" shrieked the hens, and they scurried off into the forest to tell the fox. "Bring me the cock," said the fox, smacking his lips. "He is surely plumper than you are. The grain will lie heavy in his stomach for nothing." The hens returned home and lured the cock into the forest. The fox's jaws snapped shut once or twice, and that was the end of the cock. "How unfair!" grumbled the hens, and off they went to complain to the wolf. "Bring me the fox," snarled the wolf. The hens enticed the fox into the wolf's lair, the wolf bit and chewed a few times, and that was the end of the fox. "How unfair!" clucked the hens, and scampered away to see the bear. "We quarrelled over a grain of corn, and the cock pecked it up. The fox swallowed the cock. The wolf ate the fox. How unfair it is!" they complained. "Bring me the wolf!" growled the bear. A couple of mouthfuls, and the wolf was in his stomach. "And now be off with you, before I eat you up too!" he threatened. Away they ran, as fast as their legs could carry them. "Well, there's a fine thing," grumbled the hens. "One little grain of corn, and see how many animals have eaten their fill! Only we, who quarrelled over it, have gone hungry. How unfair it is!"

## 11 JANUARY

# The Fox and the Cat

The fox was known for her airs and graces. There was not a ball in the forest that she did not attend; she went about dressed up like a courtier, and held her nose higher in the air than any princess. "I am the most beautiful of all the animals," she would boast to all she met. One day a poor cat saw her and said, admiringly, "My, my, dear fox, how fine you look today, as always! How do you come to do so well for yourself? How I wish I could be as well-to-do as you." The fox nearly burst with pride. "He who has a bad time of it is a fool," she said, haughtily. "Can you do anything clever at all, you good-for-nothing cat?"—"No, indeed," replied the cat. "It is enough for me that I can jump into a tree whenever I catch sight of a dog."—"Well, there you are, then," sneered the fox. "For I have a whole sackful of tricks, ruses and clever ideas up my sleeve for any dog that comes along. Come with me, and see how I put dogs in their place!" Just then a group of hunters and their dogs came into the forest. As soon as the hounds picked up the fox's trail, things looked black. Without more ado

the cat jumped into a tree. "Quickly, cousin fox," she called. "Open up your bag of tricks!" But the dogs soon caught the proud fox, and throttled her to death. "There you are, you see, madam fox," purred the cat. "My one little trick was worth a whole sackful of your cleverness." And she curled up in the tree and slept, and slept.

## 12 JANUARY

# The Goose Princesses

There was once a king who had two naughty little daughters. He didn't know what to do with them—even a sound beating did no good at all—so he simply sat on his throne and shook his head, saying, "Children, children, whatever will you grow up into!" One day, down by the palace lake, a wild goose appeared with her goslings. The moment the princesses saw them they started throwing stones at them. "You'll be sorry, just you wait!" cackled the goose. But the princesses only laughed at her. The next morning, when they woke up, they found to their horror that they were covered all over with feathers, and had bright orange beaks where their mouths should be. "Heavens, we are turned into geese!" they gaggled. What a weeping and wailing there was throughout the kingdom! Wherever he went, the king asked, "How are their Highnesses the princesses?" His unfortunate servants would reply, "Begging your pardon, Your Majesty, they are, one might say, in high feather, if Your Majesty will pardon the expression." One day a certain scatterbrained housemaid wished to stuff

a pillow. She caught hold of the first two geese she came across, and began to pluck them alive. The geese cackled with pain till they were blue in the face, but all to no avail—the girl soon plucked them quite bare. No sooner had she torn off the last little feather than—what should she see but, there, standing before her as bald as two coots, the naughty little princesses. "Begging your pardon, Your Highnesses the geese . . . er, Your Highnesses the princesses," she stammered, "but I wasn't to know you were geese . . . er, I mean princesses." But the princesses just burst into tears and hid under the bed. They may very well be there to this day—or do you suppose their hair has grown by now?

## 13 JANUARY

## The Devil's Bride

There was once a clever piper who had a beautiful daughter. The fame of her beauty spread to hell itself. Now, there happened to be in hell at the time a stupid devil who had thoughts of marrying, and it occurred to him that such a wife would be the envy of all who set eyes on her. So without delay he set out to visit the piper. He flew down the chimney straight into the parlour, and, paying no regard to formalities, shouted at the musician: "Give me your daughter for my wife, or I shall carry you off to hell!" As it happened, the

beautiful maiden was not at home, having gone down to the well on the village green to draw water, so the wily piper just went calmly on filling his pipe, and said: "And why not, my friend? But she is not here just at the moment. She was disobedient, so I locked her up in the shed out in the yard." As soon as the devil heard this, he rushed into the back yard to do his courting. A bearded billy-goat's head appeared from the shed. He was getting on in years, and was grumpy and didn't have much time for jokes. "By Hades, a truly devilish beauty!" exclaimed the demon with satisfaction. "Horns like Lucifer himself, a chin as hairy as a tinker's—how the other devils will envy me such a bride." And at once he begged a kiss! The billy-goat bleated angrily and butted the devil so hard that he flew all the way back to hell. Just then the sky clouded over like doomsday, and a passing shepherd called in to the piper, "This must be the devil's wedding day!" —which is what the local people say when the sky is very black. "Indeed it is, neighbour, for he is marrying our old billy-goat!" replied the clever piper. And with a smile of satisfaction he stretched himself out in front of the fire.

## 14 JANUARY

# The Magic Flute

Over nine rivers there lived, until not very long ago, a proud princess. Nothing was to her taste; she turned her nose up at everything. One day a little vagabond passed by, and he had a magic flute. He played to a white rose, and out of it stepped a white doll, which bowed three times and pirouetted three times. He played to the blue forget-me-not, and out jumped a little knight in blue armour, who waved his sword three times and raised his lance three times. "Oh, what a beautiful toy!" cried the princess from the palace window. "I must have it, whatever it costs!" — "You may have it for nothing," smiled the vagabond, "if you promise to play for the joy of people and flowers." The princess promised, but she did not keep her word. She wanted to play the

flute only for her own amusement. She played once, and out crawled a black spider, which bowed three times and three times spun her a black web. She played a second time, and out flew a yellow wasp, which circled three times and then stung the princess three times. She started to cry and, throwing down the flute, ran indoors to complain. "The flute's magic is only for those who have a good heart," the little vagabond called after her, picking up the flute and setting it to his lips again. Wherever he went, the flowers danced; wherever he turned, all the birds of the air flew after him. Perhaps one day he will come your way.

## 15 JANUARY

# The Musicians of Bremen

There was once a donkey who had toiled away all his life in a mill. Now that he was old and weak the miller wanted to have him put down. "What an ass I should be to wait for such a reward," the poor creature thought to himself. "I shall instead run away to Bremen to join the musicians." And so he did. On the way he was joined by an old dog, a homeless cat and a lame goat, all of which had been condemned to die. They walked and walked, and as they walked they made music. The donkey brayed, the dog howled, the cat mewed and the goat bleated until your ears would have split. On the fence of a farmstead a cock was crowing for all he was worth, singing his last song before the farmer's wife slit his throat. "Come along to Bremen with us, for it is a fine place, and we shall be musicians there," the donkey told him, and the cock did not wait to be asked twice. Night had fallen by the time they reached the cottage of a band of

robbers. The donkey peeped in at the window and saw the robbers feasting at a richly-spread table. "Let us play these good people a tune: surely they will not turn us away hungry from their doorstep," he said, and he began to beat time with his hoof. What a racket! The animals' music was enough to set the robbers' hair standing on end, and without more ado they fled the cottage like bats out of hell. So our fine musicians scampered over each other towards the table, where they ate, drank and made merry, and then dropped contentedly off to sleep.

16 JANUARY

## The Musicians of Bremen

The robbers had run away from the cottage as if the devil himself were at their heels. Their ears were so sore from the music that they thought their heads would burst. But in the end they came together again in the forest to discuss what they must do. In time the pain in their ears subsided. "Who were you running away from, you oafs?" demanded their leader, angrily. "We?" the others retorted. "We were running after you!" And they began to argue so fiercely that they nearly flew at each other's throats. In the end their leader crept back alone to see what was going on. The cottage was now as dark and as quiet as the grave. On tiptoe, the robber stole inside and made straight for the hearth, where two bright embers were still glowing, to blow the fire into life. Alas! They were not glowing embers, but the cat's eyes, and, hissing and spitting in the dark, she tore angrily at his beard with her claws. Startled out of his wits, the robber chief once more took to his heels. But as he crossed the doorstep he trod on the sleeping dog's tail. The creature was far from pleased and, howling and whining like the devil himself, he sank his teeth into the robber's leg. The noise woke the donkey as he lay outside on the manure heap, and he began to beat a tattoo on the robber's back with his hooves, which in turn brought the lame goat hobbling along to

butt the intruder. Then the cock flew up and attacked the robber with his beak. "Cock-a-doodle-do!" he crowed. "Thieves, robbers! Beat them! Beat them!" Battered and bruised, the unhappy bandit ran into the forest, calling to his men: "Run for your lives! The cottage is full of demons. They chop and tear, spear with pitchforks and beat with clubs." As soon as the robbers heard this they turned tail and ran, and this time they did not return. And the musicians of Bremen? They never reached that town. Maybe they are still keeping house in the robbers' cottage.

17 JANUARY

## Snow-White and Rose-Red

Once upon a time there was a little cottage; beside the cottage was a little garden, and in the garden were two rose bushes. One of them bore white roses, the other red. In the cottage lived a poor widow who had two beautiful daughters. The first of them was called Snow-White, because her skin was as white as the whitest rosebud, and the second was known as Rose-Red, since she ran about so tirelessly that she was always flushed like a scarlet rose. The two girls and their mother worked hard, and when their work was over

be afraid, my dears," their mother reassured them, "the bear will not harm you." The girls took heart, brushed the snow from the poor animal's fur, and made him a bed by the hearth.

They were soon great friends, and the bear stayed with them in the cottage the whole winter.

the sisters would go into the forest to play with the birds and animals, often sleeping among them in the soft green moss the whole night through. There was not an animal in the forest that would hurt a hair of their heads. When the first roses of summer blossomed in the garden, Rose-Red would carry whole armfuls of them into the parlour, till the entire cottage smelt like a bed of roses. And each bunch of roses would have a white rosebud for Snow-White, a red one for Rose-Red, and one, the loveliest of all, for their mother. They lived together happily in the little cottage. One year there was a particularly hard winter, and on an evening when the frost chilled to the marrow and the wind thrust snowy fingers through every crack, there was a sudden thumping at the door, and a huge bear pushed his head into the parlour. "Let me warm myself by your fire, good folk!" he begged, in a human voice. The little white dove cooed with fear and huddled into a corner, followed by the sheep, followed by Snow-White and Rose-Red. They shivered with fright. "Don't

## 18 JANUARY

# Snow-White and Rose-Red

What a merry time they had in the little cottage! How Snow-White and Rose-Red played with the bear and teased him — they almost smothered him with love, so that from time to time he had to scold them mildly:

> "Snow-White, take care —
> Rose-Red, by gentle in your play,
> 'Twere sad to slay the husband
> before the wedding day!"

The girls laughed gaily at this. But when spring came the bear could not be persuaded to stay. "I must guard my treasure from the wicked dwarfs. While the ground was frozen, they could not dig, but now they will again steal whatever they can lay their hands on," he explained, and took his leave of them graciously. As he passed through the door, he tore his skin on an old nail, and for a moment they saw a gleam like pure gold under his fur. But before the girls could ask about it, he was gone.

One day Snow-White and Rose-Red went into the forest to gather kindling-wood. In a clearing they came across an ugly dwarf, jumping about and screeching angrily. He had got his beard caught in a crack in a tree stump, and he could not get it out again. The girls ran willingly to his aid, but though they tugged and tugged they could not pull him loose. In the end Snow-White had to cut off the tip of his beard. "Oh, you horrible children, to disgrace me so!" he hissed, and without even bothering to thank them he snatched up a pot of gold from the grass and disappeared beneath the ground. Another time they found the ungrateful manikin down by the river. This time his beard was caught up in his fishing line, and a great fish was dragging him into the deep water. "Help!" he called, desperately. Again the girls took pity on him, and, since they couldn't untangle his beard, they had to cut it off right at the top. The dwarf insulted them at the top of his voice, grabbed a sack of pearls from the reeds, made a rude face at them, and once more the earth swallowed him up. "That's the last time we help him, ungrateful fellow," resolved the girls, and they went home to bed.

## 19 JANUARY

# Snow-White and Rose-Red

One day Snow-White and Rose-Red were on their way to town to do some shopping. All at once they saw the thankless dwarf struggling vainly with a huge eagle. Forgetting their resolve, the girls prized him out of the bird's claws. "Fie! You horrid little wretches, you've ruined my tunic!" he hissed at them, throwing a sack of jewels across his shoulder and disappearing as before. Towards evening, as they returned home, they spied him playing with diamonds on a patch of ground he had cleared. "What are you staring at?" he squealed, angrily. Just then a huge bear emerged from the forest, making straight for the dwarf. "Eat those horrid girls, not me!" pleaded the little man, but the bear struck him a great blow with his huge paw, laying him dead in the grass. Snow-White and Rose-Red took to their heels, but they heard a voice call: "Do not be afraid, it is I, your friend the bear!" They turned around and, lo and behold! The black bear skin had fallen away, and there stood a prince dressed all in gold. "The wicked dwarf once stole all my treasures and turned

me into a bear," he said. "Now that he is dead, the spell is broken." As he spoke these words a golden coach appeared by magic; the three of them sat in it and set off for the cottage to pick up mother, the sheep and the white dove. Then they all drove together to the prince's palace. The prince took Snow-White for his wife, and Rose-Red was married to his brother. They brought the two rose bushes from the little cottage garden and planted them in front of the palace. And whenever a rose-bud blossoms on them, a little child is born at the palace. Sometimes it is as white as snow, sometimes as red as a rose.

## 20 JANUARY

## Thumbling

In a cottage on the hillside lived a peasant and his wife. It was a sad household, for they had no children. "If only we could have a child, even if he were as tiny as a pea," the woman would sometimes sigh to herself. Now, what we say and think is sometimes not as unlikely as we suppose. And so one winter's day it happened that a little boy was born in the cottage. He was no larger than your thumb, and though he ate enough for two, he never grew so much as a hair's breadth taller. He wore a tunic sewn from a single mouse-skin.

But he was soon all over the parlour, and was full of fun and no trouble to anyone — in short, as lively a lad as ever you saw! They started to call him Thumbling. One day, when his father had gone to collect firewood, towards midday Thumbling said to his mother: "Harness up the horse, I shall take the cart to meet father." His mother clasped her hands in dismay. "My poor child, you will never hold the rein!" But Thumbling begged her to set him in the horse's ear, and as soon as she had done this, hey-up! Off went the horse at a trot. Oh, what a ride! They went like the wind. On the way they passed a couple of rogues, who stared in wonder and said: "A cart without a carter, but still someone is shouting the horse on. What wonder is this?" And they ran after the cart curiously, until it reached the clearing. What should they see there? Out of the horse's ear popped a tiny boy, and leapt into his father's palm. You can imagine how proud the peasant was of his little son.

## 21 JANUARY

## Thumbling

The moment the two rogues set eyes on Thumbling, it occurred to them that they might make a good living for themselves by showing him at fairs, and they at once begged the good-natured peasant to sell them his son. "Not for the world," the peasant told them, but Thumbling crawled up his sleeve to his shoulder and whispered in his ear, "Sell me, father: you shall not regret it!" The peasant hesitated, but in the end he agreed to sell, and made a tidy little sum out of the deal. One of the travellers then stowed Thumbling away in his knapsack. It was packed full of gold pieces! The clever Thumbling threw one ducat after another out onto the path where he knew his father would go on his way home. When the knapsack was empty, he demanded to be let out of it, saying he had had enough of sitting in the dark, and asked to ride on the brim of the man's hat. There he strutted up and down like a squire, and gazed merrily around him at the passing countryside. But as soon as they had gone some distance thus, the lad began to cry out, "Help, let me down, my stomach hurts me so!" The moment the travellers put him on the ground, he slipped into the nearest mousehole and made his way to safety through the underground passages. When he finally came out into the sunlight again, he curled up in an empty snail's shell and slept like a tiny log.

## 22 JANUARY

# Thumbling

The sparrows on the fences were already chattering nineteen to the dozen when Thumbling woke up. He could hear voices not far away. Two robbers were arguing over how best to rob a nearby parsonage. "Take me with you, I shall help you!" called Thumbling, in a thin little voice. When the startled robbers saw him crawling out of a snail shell, they burst out laughing. "What use to us are you, little man?" they jeered. But Thumbling offered to squeeze through the grille on the parsonage window and throw the booty out to them. The robbers liked the idea. When night fell, one of them took him in his coat pocket, and when they got to the parsonage they pushed him through the window-bars into the drawing-room. The boy began to shout, "Do you want everything that is here?" "Quiet, you fool!" called the robbers, softly. But Thumbling pretended not to hear, and went on yelling. This woke up the cook, who went

to see what was going on. The robbers fled. And Thumbling? He slipped through the cook's legs into the yard and buried himself contentedly in a haystack, where he went to sleep again!

## 23 JANUARY

# Thumbling

Early next morning the servant-girl went to feed the animals. She gathered up an armful of hay with Thumbling inside and dropped it in the cow's manger. The cow munched hungrily, and before you could say Jack Robinson Thumbling found himself in the cow's stomach. How dark it was there! "They must have forgotten to put windows in this room," he thought to himself, but as one mouthful of hay after another came tumbling down on his head, it was a wonder he did not suffocate. The clever lad began to shout at the top of his voice, "Enough, enough! Feed me no more!" The girl was frightened to death. "Save us, our cow can speak!" she called out, and ran to tell the parson. The parson crossed himself, and called the butcher to slaughter the possessed animal. When he had done so, the butcher

threw the stomach with Thumbling inside it on the manure heap. A passing wolf, being very fond of tripe, was not slow to devour this titbit, little boy and all. But Thumbling soon had a bright idea. "Brother wolf," he called, "why do you not go to our cottage, mother's larder is full of good things to eat!" The wolf needed no further persuasion; he slipped in through the larder window, and ate and ate until he was so bloated he was unable to get out again. Then Thumbling began to shout, "Father, help! The wolf has me in his stomach!" When his father heard this, he slew the wolf with an axe, slit open its stomach and set his son free. What a joyful reunion it was! The boy related his adventures over and over again. But from then on he was content to stay at home.

## 24 JANUARY

# The Sea-Princess's Gift

Far out on the open sea, a young fisherman cast his nets. Drawing them in, he caught sight of a strange fish, with lovely human eyes, and a golden key hanging round its neck. All at once, it spoke: "I am the sea-king's daughter: if you set me free, I shall take you with me to his palace beneath the waves, where you shall be richly rewarded." The fisherman agreed; he took hold of a fin, and the fish plunged beneath the surface, dragging him along. He was quite unharmed by the water, and they swam past placid underwater scenes, through shoals of merry fish, gliding by dancing octopuses and grim-faced sharks, till they came to a palace built of pearls and red coral. No sooner had they passed through its gates, than the fish changed into a beautiful princess. She led him through mother-of-pearl chambers, where people like fish were dancing, and into a golden hall, filled with riches of all the seas. "Choose what you wish," said the princess, handing him the golden key to the treasure chests. The fisherman did not know which way to look first, but just then

a lovely young girl, set all over with silver fish-scales, danced up to him, and whispered in his ear: "Take only one old mussel!" The fisherman did as he was told, and when the sea-princess learnt of his wish, she only smiled at him kindly, and took him to the palace gate. From there the girl with the silver scales accompanied him to the shore: but scarcely had they passed through the gates, when she changed into a silvery fish.

## 25 JANUARY

## The Sea-Princess's Gift

The fish-girl was so kind and beautiful that the young man fell in love with her before they reached the shore. "What a pity you may not live on land," he mourned. "I should like you to be my wife." But the fish only smiled, and

answered: "Trust in your mussel, it will fulfil your every wish!" So the fisherman told the mussel his wish and, lo and behold—when they reached the shallows the silvery fish again changed into a beautiful girl, and she stepped out onto the shore with him. But the fisherman looked around in vain for his cottage home. While he had been in the palace beneath the waves, a hundred long years had passed in the world above. The young man was startled. "If only my old mother and father were here," he exclaimed, bitterly. The moment he had said this—wonder of wonders—the family cottage appeared before his very eyes, and on the doorstep an old couple began to wake from a deep sleep. "How soundly we have slept," they yawned in wonder, and at once they warmly greeted their son and his bride. From then on they all lived in happiness and

contentment. The magic mussel fulfilled their each and every wish; and when, one day, the envious king of that land heard of their riches, and tried to steal away the magic mussel by force, a great wave from the sea swept the king and all his soldiers into the depths of the ocean. Then the poor fisherman became ruler of the whole country, and the beautiful fish-girl his queen.

## 26 JANUARY

## The Old Woman and the Mouse

In a little paper house on a little paper hill lived a kind old woman. One day a cheeky

little mouse moved in with her. "I'm going to stay here and live with you, granny," he told her coarsely, "and if you don't like it I shall chew your little house to pieces!"—"I don't mind," smiled the clever old woman. "At least I shan't be lonely here on my own. If you like, we can ask each other riddles." The mouse agreed, and perched haughtily on the woman's outstretched palm. "I shall begin," he squeaked. "Tell me, old woman, tell me, how many steps does a sparrow take, to cross an acre field?" "An easy one," replied the old woman. "None at all. A sparrow doesn't step, it only hops. But now listen carefully to my riddle! Ears like a mouse, claws like a mouse, whiskers like a mouse, but it isn't a mouse. What is it?"—"I give up," said the mouse. "No, no," said the old woman, shaking her head. "You must keep guessing. Let's try it another way. What is it? Eyes like a cat, legs like a cat, tail like a cat, voice like a cat, and right now it's getting ready to jump on your back!" "C-c-c-c-cat!" shrieked the mouse, and was off and out of the little house in a flash. "Dear me, wherever would a cat appear from in my house—it was only a riddle," smiled the old woman, thinking to herself how glad she was to see the last of the silly little mouse.

## 27 JANUARY

## The Master of the Robber's Trade

Once upon a time, a cottager was out in his garden planting trees, when a stranger rode by. He had the look of a gentleman, but there was something roguish about his eyes. "What, have you no son to help you in your work?" he called out to the cottager. "Indeed, I have a son," said the cottager. "But he was good-for-nothing, and ran away from home." The stranger smiled, and asked if the cottager's wife might cook him some simple peasant food. "I have had enough of fine delicacies," he said, with a sigh. While the woman was cooking him a dish of dumplings, he stood in the porch, watching the cottager tying back young trees. "Why do you not tie up that old, crooked tree?" he asked in surprise. "It is clear that you are no nurseryman," replied the cottager. "Old wood cannot be straightened. If you wish to have straight trees, you must tie them back from the start." At this the unknown traveller pushed his hat to the back of his head and said: "So is it also with people, father! I am your long-lost son. Had you bound me to honesty from the very start by using a firm hand, I might have been an upright man. As it is, I have learnt the robber's trade: mind you, I am master of it now, and make a good living by it."
The cottager and his wife were filled with horror. "What would your godfather, the noble duke, say to all this?" they cried in despair. "He would surely have you swing

22

from a gibbet!" But the wayward son only smiled, and said, "What of it? He, too, is grown rich otherwise than by honest work. Tomorrow I shall go to visit him." And he did.

## 28 JANUARY

# The Master of the Robber's Trade

The next day, when the cottager's son had himself announced at the mansion of his godfather, the duke, and told him what trade he had learnt, the stern nobleman frowned darkly. "I should hand you over to the executioner without delay," he said, "but since you are my godson, I shall be merciful to you if you fulfil three commands. First you must

steal from my stables my favourite horse. If you succeed, then you shall enter my bedchamber and steal the ring from my wife's finger and the sheet on which she lies. If you manage this second task, then you must steal from the parsonage the parson and his sexton. If you are able to perform all these feats, then you are truly a master of the robber's trade. If you do not, then you will be shorter by a head!" The clever thief was not dismayed. That evening he dressed up as an old woman, took a skin of wine, added to it a strong sleeping draught, and hobbled off towards the duke's stable. The duke's soldiers were on guard there. One sat on the horse, a second

held its rein, and just to make sure, a third was holding it by the tail. "Hey, old woman, where are you going with that bottle?" they called. "To you, my dears," the old woman croaked. "The duke sends you some of his own wine to warm you." The soldiers needed no encouragement; they drank, and drank, and soon were sleeping soundly. The one who sat on the horse, the robber tied to a beam; the second he gave a piece of string to hold instead of the rein, and the one who had held the tail snored on contentedly, grasping a bunch of straw. When the duke came into the stable the next morning, he could not help laughing at the way the robber had fooled them. "But just you wait, you rogue! Tonight I shall keep watch a good deal better!"

## 29 JANUARY

# The Master of the Robber's Trade

That evening the duke sat by his wife's bed with a blunderbuss in his hand and his eyes peeled for the robber. But the young man had hurried off to the execution yard, where he cut one of the victims down from the gallows and carried him off to a spot below the mansion windows. When midnight came, he placed a ladder against the wall and dragged the hanged man's body up it, pushing its head in front of the bedroom window. Scarcely had he done so, when the duke let fly from his gun, and then rushed off to see the results of his marksmanship. He found the body beneath the window. "Poor fellow," he thought to himself, "he brought about his own undoing in the end." And he began to dig him a grave. In the meantime the robber had entered the bedroom, where he whispered to the duchess: "Do not be afraid, it is I, your husband. You need fear no more, I have shot the robber dead. But he was, after all, my godson, and he deserves a Christian burial. Give me your bedsheet to wrap him in, and your ring, that he may at least take with him to the grave that for which he died." The duchess obliged, and the clever thief was gone like the wind. When the duke returned to his bedchamber, he could not believe his eyes. "Is that rogue a wizard, too?" he wondered. "Did I not bury him with my own hands?" The next day the robber brought him the ring and the sheet, smiling beneath his beard. "Just you wait, my clever lad, the third time you shall not be so lucky," warned the duke. But what can one do with robbers?

# The Master of the Robber's Trade

Late that night the robber made his way to the parsonage with a bag of crayfish he had caught. Onto the backs of the crayfish he stuck lighted candles, and set them among the graves in the churchyard. Then he dressed in a black smock, and, holding a large sack at the ready, climbed up into the pulpit. He began to shout, "Hurry, hurry; the end of the world is at hand! See how the dead leave their graves on their way to the heavenly kingdom! I am Peter, who guards the golden gate. Whosoever wishes to enter the kingdom before the end of the world, let him climb into my sack!" The parson and the sexton heard this and, looking towards the churchyard, saw the strange lights moving to and fro among the gravestones. Without more ado they jumped into the robber's sack, anxious to be the first. The robber dragged them down the steps until their heads banged this way and that, calling out to them: "Now we are floating above the mountains!" Then he dragged them through a puddle, and cried: "Now we are passing through rainclouds!" When he had given them another good shaking on the steps of the ducal mansion, he shoved the sack into the dovecote. "Can you hear the beating of angels' wings?" he whispered. "Why, of course," replied the parson. "I beg your pardon, St. Peter," said the unhappy sexton, "but it stinks here in heaven like some pigeon-house!" The robber laughed till he almost dropped. When, the next morning, he showed the duke his night's booty, his lordship was forced to laugh, too. When he untied the sack, the two foolish prisoners thrust out their heads and said in surprise, "By all the saints, Your Lordship, are you in heaven already?" What was the duke to do? He gave the clever robber a chest full of gold coins, and told him, "You are indeed a master of the robber's trade; but be gone with you from my dukedom, never to return, or it will go ill with you!" The rogue thanked him, left his parents money enough to live in comfort, and disappeared into the world. Who knows what has become of him since. Perhaps he has retired from robbery, and turned his hand to playing the lute and singing robbers' songs!

## 31 JANUARY

## The Bowl of Milk

A cat and a pig set off together into the world one day. Soon both of them began to feel quite hungry. They met an old goat. "Give us a little milk, mother goat!" they begged her. "If you first dig my garden," bleated the goat. The pig set to at once, but the cat mewed that she must first take a rest. She lay down in the sun, stretched herself out, and spent a long while cleaning her fur with her pink tongue. When noon came, the goat brought along a bowl of cream. "This is for the one who has done the most work in my garden," she said. The pig, who was covered in earth, rushed towards the bowl. "I have dug the whole garden on my own," he grunted. The goat shook her head. "You have the manners of a pig," she said. "Is that any way to come to lunch?" Then she looked at the cat. "And what did you do all morning?" she asked. "I?" said the cat. "Why, I washed myself instead of the pig." The goat thought for a while. "The cat shall have the cream," she said at last. "For she has worked for both." And that has been the way of the world ever since. While one does all the work, another laps up the cream. And all because of the stupid goat.

# FEBRUARY

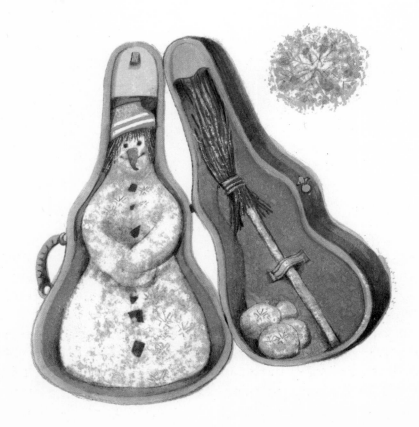

# 1 FEBRUARY

## Ali Baba and the Forty Thieves

In a land far away to the east, where the sun blazes down like a huge red jewel over the glaring white cities, there lived, long ago, two brothers, called Kassim and Ali Baba. Kassim was a rich merchant, but Ali Baba was as poor as a church mouse. He was just able to support his family by gathering dry sticks to sell as firewood. One day his work took him far beyond the city, where the sand and scorched rocks of the desert begin. He was just tying the last armful of sticks up in his bundle, when he heard in the distance the thunder of a great troop of horses. Ali Baba hid himself in the bushes, and waited to see what would happen. A band of robbers came riding up in a cloud of dust. Not counting their leader, there were exactly forty of them. They leapt down from their horses and gathered around one of the rocks, and in a fearful voice their leader called out, "Open, sesame!" In the twinkling of an eye the rock face opened up before them, and the robbers poured into a secret cave. Ali Baba waited, and watched. After a while the rocks again opened up; the robbers came out, mounted their horses and galloped off. Ali Baba could not contain his curiosity; he went up to the cliff and called out, "Open, sesame!" To his surprise the hard stone wall parted to let him into an exquisite cave, filled with gold and precious stones. The cliff face crashed shut behind him.

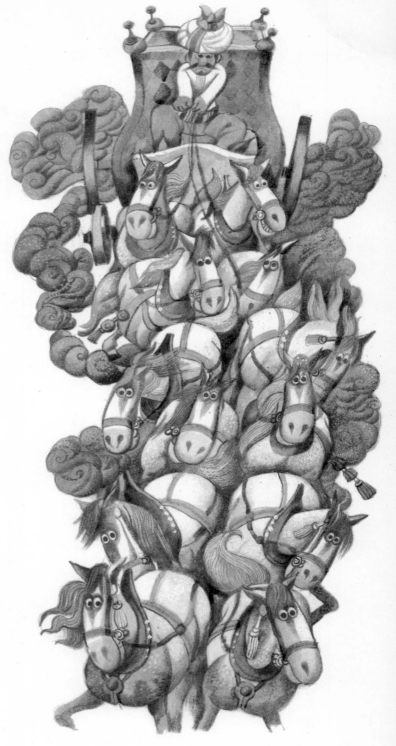

# 2 FEBRUARY

## Ali Baba and the Forty Thieves

Ali Baba was dazzled by the beauty and richness of what he saw, but he wasted no time, caught up as much gold and jewels as he could carry, and ordered the rocks to release him again. He shoved the treasure into his bundles of firewood, loaded them onto his donkey, and hurried home. His wife could not believe her eyes when she saw the riches he had brought. She ran off at once to her sister-in-law, Kassim's wife, to borrow a grain measure, in order to measure their new-found wealth. But Kassim's wife was curious to know why the poor folk needed a grain measure, when they scarcely had enough to keep body and soul together, so she spread a little honey on the bottom of the measure. When she got the measure back again, she found a tiny gold coin stuck to the honey. As soon as Kassim heard from his wife that Ali Baba the pauper had been using a grain measure to take stock of his gold coins, he went off and demanded that his brother should tell him where he had come by such wealth. The good-hearted Ali Baba told him everything, and the greedy Kassim rode off at once towards the secret cave. "Open, sesame!" he called out to the rock face, and it opened to let him in. The miserly merchant could not bring himself to go away and leave such treasures. He played with the tinkling gold pieces for so long that the robbers, returning to their cave, found him there and cut his throat.

## Ali Baba and the Forty Thieves

When Kassim did not return for a long time, Ali Baba went out to the rocks to look for him. But in the cave he found only his brother's lifeless body. Sadly, he slung the dead man over his donkey and carried him back to the city, where the family buried him. He and his wife and children then moved into his brother's house. Meanwhile, the robbers had returned to their cave from another expedition, and when they saw that Kassim's body had disappeared, they realized that someone else must also know their secret. Their chieftain ordered one of his cut-throats to go into the city and find out who had dared to enter their cave. The robber stood in the market-place asking questions, until at last he heard how a poor man called Ali Baba had recently buried his brother, and had come by mysterious wealth. The robber made a chalk cross on the door of Ali Baba's house in order to remember where he lived, and went to report to his leader. But Ali Baba had a clever servant-girl called Morgiana. She noticed the chalkmark at once and, suspecting foul play, made crosses on all the doors in the street. When, that night, the robbers stole into the city, they could not find Ali Baba's house. The robber chieftain was so angry with his spy that he had the poor man's head cut off on the spot.

## Ali Baba and the Forty Thieves

The robbers' leader stayed behind in the city himself, until he had again found the house he wanted. He went back to his men and ordered them to load forty skins and jars onto a train of mules. He filled one of them with olive oil, but in each of the others he hid one of his men. They agreed on a signal, at which they would leap out to attack Ali Baba's house. Then the

forest to gather wild strawberries, and there she met an old woman. "Give me at least a poor crust of bread, my girl, for I am so hungry I can scarcely stand," the woman begged. The kindhearted girl shared with her the little food she had, and for her generosity the old woman made her a present of a cooking pot. "It is magic," she explained. "If you say to it 'pot, cook gruel', it will cook as much gruel as you could wish for." The girl thanked her kindly and went home, and she and her mother cooked sweet, wholesome gruel until they could eat no more. From then on they were never short of food. One day, the girl had gone on some errand or other, when her mother began to feel hungry. She put the pot on the hearth, so that the gruel would be nice and warm, and told it, "Pot, cook gruel!" The pot cooked and cooked, until the gruel ran out of it and onto the floor, then out of the door into the garden. The girl's mother was so upset that she forgot how to stop the pot from cooking. She took a broom and brushed the gruel out of the hallway, but to no avail: soon the parlour was full of gruel, then it flowed out of the window, down onto the village green. At that moment the girl came running in, and told the pot, "Pot, enough!" But by that time there was so much gruel on the village green that the farmers and their horses could not get by, and had to eat their way through the sweet morass.

robber chief disguised himself as a merchant, made his way with his caravan to Ali Baba's house, and asked for a bed for the night. Ali Baba willingly took the stranger into his house. While they were talking together, the lamp in the kitchen went out, and the servant-girl Morgiana went to fill it with oil. She remembered that the merchant had left his jars of oil in the courtyard, and she went up to them. When the hidden robbers heard footsteps in the yard, they asked in a whisper: "Is it time, master?" The clever girl suspected a trap, and whispered in a deep voice: "No, not yet!" She felt the skins until she found the one which was full of oil, which she then boiled in a cauldron and poured into all the other vessels, scalding the robbers to death. Then she called the soldiers, who recognized the robber chief and executed him on the spot. Thus it was that once again the clever Morgiana saved Ali Baba and his family, and he rewarded her richly for her courage and faithfulness.

## 5 FEBRUARY

## The Magic Pot

Once upon a time a poor girl went into the

## 6 FEBRUARY

# Primrose

There once lived a poor, but hard-working young girl whom everyone called Primrose, for though she was very beautiful, she was as humble as that lovely flower. Whenever she went into town she would hide her face behind a veil, being too modest to show her beauty. One day the king's son himself saw

her, and he asked the people why she did not show her face. "She is beautiful, but modest," they replied. The prince was burning with curiosity and, determined to see the girl's beauty for himself, he sent a servant to her cottage with a golden ring and a message that she should meet him at sunset beneath the great oak tree. Thinking that those in the palace were going to give her some work to do, she waited beneath the tree at the appointed hour. When the prince saw her without her veil, he was so enchanted with her beauty that he wanted to take her off to the royal castle without delay. But Primrose refused to go with him, saying, "I am a poor girl, and your father would surely be angry to know whom you had chosen for your bride. Let me have at least a few days to consider." Unwillingly, the prince agreed. Soon afterwards, he sent a servant to her cottage with a pair of silver shoes, and again asked her to meet him beneath the old oak. She went to meet him, but again he was unable to persuade

her to go with him, try as he might. And when the prince sent her a present of a golden gown, she did not even go to the tree to meet him, because she was so afraid of the king.

## 7 FEBRUARY

# Primrose

One day the king did indeed hear of his son's meetings with a poor peasant-girl. His anger was truly great, for he had chosen the daughter of a powerful neighbouring king to marry his heir. So he ordered his soldiers to burn down the roof over her head. "Let her burn along with her cottage!" he thundered. The soldiers went and carried out his command. Primrose was busy sewing, her beloved songbird beside her in its cage. Suddenly, flames licked at her from all sides. She ran to the door, and saw that the cottage was surrounded by the king's soldiers. So, without more ado, she caught up the birdcage and leapt straight from the window into the old well. There she lay hidden for many days, crying her eyes out with grief. She was sad to lose her little cottage, but she was even sadder to think that she might never see the prince again. In the end she took heart again, dressed herself in boy's clothes, and set off for the royal castle to ask to be taken into service. The comely page at once caught the king's eye. "What is your name?" he asked. "I am

called Misfortune," the girl replied. "That is not a pretty name," said the king, shaking his head, "but I shall take you into my service if you sing me a pretty song." Primrose and her songbird sang a song so beautiful and so sad that the king's heart was moved. From then on the new page was treated like the king's own son.

## 8 FEBRUARY

# Primrose

When the unhappy prince heard that Primrose had gone up in flames with her cottage, it was a wonder his heart did not break, such was his grief. When at last his suffering eased a little, the king decided that his wedding with the princess should be delayed no longer. So he set off with his entire court in a magnificent procession to the neighbouring kingdom. At the rear of the royal train came Primrose in her page's dress, riding on a horse. She felt very melancholy, so to cheer her heart she began to sing: "For Misfortune, Prince, to wear, tie a primrose in my hair."—"Who is it that sings so sad a song?" asked the prince, in surprise. "It is Misfortune, my servant," his father told him. Unable to resist the plaintive refrain, the prince plucked from the wayside a primrose and rode up to the page. He recognized his gold ring, gleaming on the girl's finger, and knew she was his chosen love. He smiled at her, but said nothing. When all had taken their seats for a great feast at the palace of the neighbouring king, their host said to them: "Come, let us tell riddles!" The prince was not slow to pose one: "Sire, in my castle I have a golden casket, from which I lost the key. They promised to make me a new one, but now I have found the old. Tell me, my lord, which key should I keep—the old or the new?"—"Why, the old, of course," replied the king. Then the prince took Primrose by the hand, and proclaimed, "You yourself have decided the matter, my lord! I cannot marry your daughter. For here is the key which I lost, and have found again." When

all had seen the lovely Primrose and heard her tale, anger was forgotten, and a magnificent wedding prepared. When the celebrations were over, the prince returned to his palace with his happy bride.

## 9 FEBRUARY

# The Three Wood-Elves

Once upon a time there was a widower who had a beautiful daughter. Not far from them lived a widow who also had a daughter, but she was ugly and selfish. The two girls had known each other since they were little, and from time to time they would visit each other. One day the widow told her neighbour's daughter, "If your father were to take me as his wife, you would not be sorry. You could bathe every day in milk, and drink good wine; I should treat you better than my own

daughter. Perhaps you might speak a word in his ear." The girl did as the old woman told her. But the old man did not too much like the idea of marrying again, and he said: "We shall let Fate decide." Thinking to make an end of the matter, he took an old shoe, hung it from a beam in the attic, and filled it with water. "If the water remains in the shoe until morning, it shall be a sign that I am to marry again," he said. The old shoe was full of holes, so he thought he had nothing to fear. But the water made the shoe swell, the holes closed up, and in the morning the water was still there. What could the old man do? He had to marry the widow, as he had promised. The first day after the wedding his new wife treated her stepdaughter like a rare gift from heaven, but it was not long at all before she had changed her tune. Her own daughter she spoilt endlessly, but the old man's child began to wish she had never been born.

## 10 FEBRUARY

## The Three Wood-Elves

Winter came, and the frost bit deep. The cruel stepmother sewed a dress from paper, put it on her stepdaughter, and ordered her, "Go out into the forest, and bring home a basket of strawberries; otherwise you need not return at all!" What was the poor child to do? She wandered through the snowy wastes, icy tears running down her cheeks. Somewhere in the

depths of the forest, where she no longer knew her way at all, she came across a little cottage. It was the home of three little wood-elves. The hapless child begged them to let her warm herself by their fire. They frowned at her, but let her in. She crouched gratefully in front of the flaming logs, and took out a crust of dry bread. "Give us some too," said the elves, quite sternly, and the girl was only too willing to share what little she had. Then she told them how she came to be in the forest in such cruel weather. "Take the broom and sweep away the snow behind our cottage!" the elves ordered her. She did as she was told, and when she went out, the elves discussed how they might reward her for her obedience. The first of them said: "My gift shall be for her to grow lovelier day by day." The second said: "My gift shall be for gold pieces to fall from her mouth each time she speaks." And the third declared: "My gift shall be for a king to come and take her for his wife." Meanwhile, the girl had swept away the snow as she had been bidden, and what do you suppose she found buried under the snow? Ripe red strawberries! She thanked the elves for their kindness, and hurried home.

## 11 FEBRUARY

## The Three Wood-Elves

The girl had hardly reached home with the strawberries and spoken a word of greeting,

when a shining gold piece fell out of her mouth. And when she told them of all that happened in the forest, the kitchen floor became littered with gold coins. The stepmother and her daughter were quite green with envy. And to make things worse for them, the good child grew more beautiful every day. One day the ugly sister resolved that she, too, would go off into the forest in search of strawberries. She put on a warm fur coat, took a basket of cakes for the journey, and made straight for the wood-elves' cottage. Without a word she sat herself down in front of the fire and began to eat. "Give us some too!" called the elves, but she did not even look their way. When she had finally eaten her fill, the elves told her to sweep away the snow from the garden path. But work was not to her liking at all, so she decided it was time to go home. The elves were furious. "My gift shall be for her to grow uglier every day!" scowled the first. "My gift shall be for a toad to fall out of her mouth every time she speaks," said the second, and the third added: "My gift shall be for her to meet a cruel fate." And so it happened that when the ugly girl came home, with the first word she spoke a toad leapt out of her mouth. In a short while the parlour was thicker with toads than a woodland pond.

# The Three Wood-Elves

It was then that life really became difficult for the girl with the golden tongue. But one day, when the stepmother had sent her down to the frozen stream to wring out the washing, the king himself passed by. The girl greeted him politely, and gold pieces fell from her mouth as she spoke. "Such a beautiful and rich bride deserves to marry no less than the king himself," he said, and took her off to his castle to be his wife. Before the year was out a child was born to the young queen. The moment the stepmother heard this, she hurried off to the palace with her own daughter to visit the royal mother. But when the king left them alone in the bedchamber, the wicked women dragged her from her bed and threw her from a window into the river below. The ugly girl climbed into bed in her place, pulling the sheets up over her face. When the king

returned to the chamber, the stepmother told him his wife had suddenly become ill. The king was deceived, but when she did not rise from her bed the next day, he went to inquire after her health. The moment she spoke, toads began to drop from her mouth instead of gold. "It is on account of the fever," the stepmother declared. But that evening a small duck waddled into the royal kitchens. "How is my child?" she asked. The cook recognized the young queen's voice, and he replied, "He is asleep in his cradle." He hurried off to tell the king, and led him into the kitchen to see the wonder for himself. The duck begged the king to pass his sword three times over her head, and no sooner had he done so, than there in front of him stood his golden-tongued wife. And what of the stepmother and her ugly daughter? So afraid were they of the wrath of the king that they leapt out of the window of their own accord, and drowned in the river below.

## 13 FEBRUARY

## The Ugly Duckling

Underneath a burdock leaf a duck was sitting on her eggs. She could hardly wait for the ducklings to burst out of their shells. Then at last they began to hatch. "Peep, peep, peep," they said, as they pushed their little heads out into the big world. But there was only one strange, large egg that somehow refused to hatch. "Sure to be a turkey's egg, my dear," whispered a neighbour to the mother duck.

"They once gave me one of those. Better leave it be and teach your dear little ducklings to swim." The mother duck decided not to abandon the last egg, and at last the strange egg hatched. But what was this? Out of the shell came such an ugly, gawky duckling that the mother duck was quite dismayed. "Perhaps it is a turkey chick, after all," she said to herself. "But we'll soon see." And she took the whole family off to the pond and went splash! into the water. One by one, the ducklings plopped in after her, the big, ugly one as well. "That's no turkey, dear, it's one of your very own," said the old goose. "See how beautifully he swims," the mother duck said proudly, and she led her family off to meet the other ducks, especially their queen. She was a noble duck with a ribbon on one of her legs, and had Spanish blood in her veins. She looked the ducklings over for a long time.

## 14 FEBRUARY

## The Ugly Duckling

When the queen had had a good look at the duck family, she said, "You have indeed pretty children, my dear, except for the last one, that big one; he is terribly ugly. Never in my life have I seen such an ugly little thing!"
When the other ducks heard this, they began to peck the poor duckling, and pinch him, and the geese and the hens joined in; and the old turkey, who thought he was emperor, charged at him, crimson with rage and gobbling fiercely. Even the poor creature's brothers and sisters laughed at him, and his mother cried. She secretly wished he would wander off somewhere and never return. One day, when the ugly duckling could stand it no longer, he

a flash. "Oh dear," said the duckling to himself, mournfully, "I am so ugly that even a dog shrinks away from me!" And he flew away. Towards evening he reached a little cottage. In it lived an old woman who had a cat and a hen. The cat could arch her back and purr, and if you stroked her the wrong way she could even give off sparks. The hen laid beautiful eggs. Both were very proud of themselves, and thought themselves the most intelligent creatures in the world. The old woman took the duckling in, thinking he would learn to lay eggs. But he soon seemed not only ugly, but also quite useless, and the cat and the hen made so much of his stupidity and of their own wisdom and skill that one day he was forced to run away again. "It serves you right for being so ugly!" they called after him.

## 16 FEBRUARY

## The Ugly Duckling

The unhappy duckling again wandered

ran away in a flood of tears. He flew over the fence, and on, and on, to the great marshes where the wild ducks lived. "Oh, how ugly you are!" they said to him. "But we don't mind, as long as you don't marry into the family." Just then a pair of wild ganders flew by. "You are so ugly that we quite like you," they cackled. "Wouldn't you like to come along with us and be a bird of passage?" But the ugly duckling just hung his head sadly.

## 15 FEBRUARY

## The Ugly Duckling

The two wild ganders did not get far. A shooting party was lying in wait in the marshes and, bang! bang!—the ganders plummetted into the water. Then retriever dogs came charging through the rushes, medals around their necks. The duckling hid in the bushes, but it was no use. Suddenly a huge dog was standing over him, tongue hanging out and eyes glinting threateningly. He touched the duckling with his nose, licked him with his tongue, and then was gone again in

# The Candle-Flame Fairy Tale

In a certain little cottage lived an old woman who had a magic candlestick. A candle burned there day and night, and never burned down. Whoever gazed into the flame of that candle would dream a fairy tale at night. And which fairy tale? Why, this one: Once upon a time there was a little prince called Rini. He lived inside a hazel nut, in a diamond chamber inside a golden palace. The silver flowers beneath his window were watered and cared for by a little gardener-girl called Lini. The two of them were always quarrelling. One time it would be over which of them was taller, another time who was smaller, another who had more freckles, how to make doughnuts, or whatever. They quarrelled so much that in the end they fell in love with each other—but please don't tell anyone, or they would be terribly ashamed. One day the little prince went out hunting. What was it he

aimlessly through the world. No one wanted him, and all the animals despised him for his ugliness. Summer passed, and autumn, and then cruel winter came along. The duckling shivered with cold. Words cannot describe his suffering during that harsh winter. It was a wonder he did not freeze to death on the frozen lake.

But then spring arrived, and with a strength which surprised him the duckling took to the air. One day he alighted on an ornamental lake in a beautiful garden. On it there swam magnificent white birds with long necks. They were swans, although the duckling did not know it. He felt only a great joy, and a wish to join the lovely creatures. He swam shyly towards them. He was afraid they would drive him away for his ugliness, but they leaned towards him and welcomed him. Suddenly, the duckling saw his own reflection in the water. It was not that of an ugly duckling, but of a splendid white swan. Just then some children ran up to the lakeside, calling out: "There is a new swan—look, it is the most beautiful of all!" The young swan was so happy he burst into song. "Never did I dream of such happiness, when I was an ugly duckling!" he thought to himself joyfully, and proudly swam about the lake with his companions.

went to hunt? I can't remember exactly—it was probably mosquitoes. But just as the chase was at its most exciting, from out of nowhere two giantesses appeared. One of them caught the prince in her hand like a butterfly; the other lifted the first onto her shoulders, and off they went! The king proclaimed to the whole world that he would give half his kingdom and a quarter of a curd tart to whoever brought the prince back home; but to no avail, for no one could find him. "I shall bring him home," declared Lini, the little gardener, one day. "Simply because I have no one to quarrel with any more." And she put on her gossamer shoes and set off.

## 18 FEBRUARY

# The Candle-Flame Fairy Tale

Do you know where Lini went? Why, she followed her nose, of course, so as not to go and get lost. After some time she came to an ice-cave. Inside were golden icicles, and in the middle a cot. There were paintings of flowers on the front of it, and on the back two white swans, and beneath the swans a magic inscription, written upside-down so that no one could understand it. In the cot lay little Prince Rini. He was sleeping like a log. Little Lini pulled his nose, then his big toe, but Rini did not move, or so much as bat an eyelid. Just then there were thundrous footsteps outside the cave, and in came the two ugly giantesses.

Lini just managed to hide behind an icicle in time. The giantesses leaned over the cot and called out, "Swans, within whose cot he lies, Sing, that sleep may leave his eyes!" The swans sang, the prince woke up, and the giantesses growled at him, "Will you take one of us for your wife?" The little prince put out his tongue and said, "Pigs might fly!" At this the giantesses flew into a rage and shouted: "Swans, within whose cot he lies, Sing, that sleep may close his eyes!" The prince fell fast asleep again, and the giantesses left the cave.

## 19 FEBRUARY

# The Candle-Flame Fairy Tale

As soon as the giantesses had disappeared from sight, Lini ran up to the cot and ordered the swans to wake the prince. When he had opened his eyes, he and Lini embraced, then quarrelled a little, and then made up again. Then Lini told him that next time he should pretend to promise that he would marry one of the giantesses, but only if they told him what they did when they were not in the cave, and what the secret writing on the cot meant. At that moment they heard the giantesses coming back, and Lini slipped behind an icicle again. As before, the giantesses asked him roughly if he had not changed his mind. "I shall take one of you for my wife," answered the little prince, "but you must tell me where you go when you are not at home, and what is written on the cot." The giantesses were pleased, and they revealed that they went to a nearby wood to play with a golden egg. "If anyone were to smash the egg, we should turn into a couple of black crows," they told him. Then they read him the inscription on the cot. It said: "Magic cot, without delay, Carry me off wherever I say!" Then they put the prince back to sleep, and hurried off to the wood to play with their golden egg.

## 20 FEBRUARY

# The Candle-Flame Fairy Tale

Lini stayed hidden until the giantesses' footsteps had died away. Then she ordered the

swans to wake the prince, jumped into the cot beside him, and called out, "Magic cot, without delay, Carry us off to where I say!" And she ordered it to take them to the giantesses' wood. The cot soared into the air, and flew and flew until they reached a black wood. There Rini and Lini hid in the crown of a tall tree. Rini broke off a thick branch and made himself a sturdy spear. Before long the ogresses arrived. They sat down beneath the very tree in which the prince and the little gardener were crouching, and began to throw the golden egg to each other. Prince Rini aimed his spear carefully and, smack! The golden egg was shattered to a thousand pieces, and the giantesses were turned into black crows. Without delay, Rini and Lini ordered the cot to take them back to the cave; there they filled their pockets with gold and precious stones, and then ordered the cot to take them home. What a celebration there was, when they both returned safe and well! The king prepared a grand wedding for them, and gave them his whole kingdom, leaving himself only the curd tart. And Rini and Lini? They have stopped quarrelling. Lini sits on the throne ruling the kingdom, and Prince Rini does all the sleeping for her in the little cot.

## 21 FEBRUARY

# The Dumb Child

A son was born to a farmer and his wife. He grew into a fine young lad, but, sad to relate, he did not speak a word. Hither and thither they took him, to see doctors and herbalists, sought the advice of the parson, the schoolteacher and the old woman who cast out devils, but the boy spoke never a word, and went on being as dumb as a fish. When he grew up, his parents looked around for a wife for him. Since they had a good-sized farm, they did not have to look far. In the end they chose a scatterbrained girl who spoke very little herself. "At least they will not quarrel together," they thought to themselves. Then there was a wedding the villagers recall to this day. The young bride baked basketfuls of little

## 22 FEBRUARY

# The Seven Swabians

There were once seven cowards from the German land of Schwaben, who never tired of boasting of their bravery. One day, the most talkative of them all, Schulz, said to the others, "Bold Swabians, why do we not set off on our travels, that we may show the world what fine fellows and heroes the men of Schwaben are?" All agreed enthusiastically. So that they would not be afraid, they made themselves a lance, so long that all seven of them had to carry it at once. Out at the front was Schulz, followed by the biggest of the Swabians, then the next, then the next, down to the smallest at the back. This last was almost lost among the clover, but judging by his words, he had

cakes and carried them to the table. And, as was the custom in that part of the world, she also cooked a pot of millet gruel, so that folk would not forget everyday things even at the wedding. She put a bowl of this gruel in front of the dumb bridegroom. But the moment he tasted it he cried out in disgust, "The gruel is not sweet enough!" All the guests gathered around him. "How do you come to speak now, when you have never before so much as murmured?" they asked, excitedly. The dumb husband wiped his mouth on the back of his hand and said, "What reason had I to say anything, when the gruel was always sweet enough?"

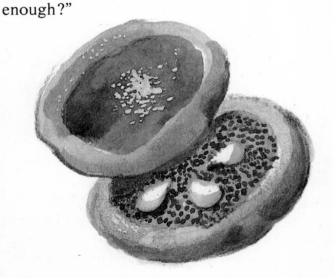

courage enough for three. They came to a great meadow, and there they disturbed a hornet, which buzzed angrily around their ears. "Halt!" cried Schulz, startled. "Can you hear? The enemy's drums are beating the advance!" Just then the wind blew the smoke from a chimney in a nearby village towards them. "You are right, Schulz, for I can smell gunpowder!" cried the second hero. "Forward to battle!" yelled the seventh, the smallest, hidden behind the others' backs. His knees were knocking with fright. Schulz got such a shock that he jumped so high that we shall have to wait till he comes down before going on with the story.

## 23 FEBRUARY

## The Seven Swabians

By a piece of bad luck, Schulz came down right on a rake which happened to be lying there. The handle flew up and hit him right between the eyes. "Help! I surrender!" he cried with a will. When the others heard this, they leapt head-first into a hayrick and called out, "We surrender too, mercy, mercy!" When nothing happened for some time, they cautiously stuck their heads out of the hay. The enemy was neither to be seen nor heard. "What a glorious victory we have won," the

Swabians congratulated themselves, and went on their way. They stamped and swanked along like a whole army. Under a wild rose in the hedgerow a fine, fat hare was sleeping. "Halt!" called Schulz. "What creature is crouching there in the bushes?" The hare had his ears pricked and his eyes wide open. To the Swabians he seemed like a monster. "It is a dragon," stammered one of the heroes. "Dragons are not hairy," squeaked another. "Lord save us, it is the devil himself, or at least his grandmother!"—"Forward, upon him!" yelled the smallest, from the rear. "Hack him to pieces!"—"Then you go first," they told him. "No fear," the little fellow replied, "let Schulz go first!" What could he do? Step by step Schulz, the leader of the heroes, went up to the hare, his valiant rabble following behind. As he drew near, his legs almost gave way beneath him with fear, and he cried out "Oh, oh, oh!" This woke up the hare, who ran off as fast as his legs could carry him. Again the bold Swabians celebrated a great victory!

## 24 FEBRUARY

# The Seven Swabians

After their triumph over the hare, the Swabians went in search of further adventure. Soon they came to a field of hemp, which was in flower. "What is it?" cried Schulz in amazement. "It is blue, it is large, and I cannot see to the end of it!"—"It is the sea!" shouted the others behind, pleased at having answered their leader's riddle. Schulz took a couple of gingerly steps into the sea of hemp, but soon found it was only up to his knees. "How foolish people are!" he laughed. "They build great ships just to cross the sea, and we wade across it as if it were nothing. What heroes the Swabians are!" When they had made their way safely across the field of hemp, they came to a deep river. "How can we get across?" they called out to a ferry-man over on the other side. "Wait for me!" he called back, but the wind made it difficult to hear, and they thought he said "wade to me". So the brave Swabians set off into the deep water. "We waded across the sea," they said to each other, "so why should we not wade across an ordinary river?" And one after the other they

drowned. But for this unfortunate accident they would surely have conquered the whole world.

## 25 FEBRUARY

# The Mighty Tailor

Once upon a time there was a tailor who grew tired of pricking his fingers with the needle, so he took his grandfather's old sabre out of the chest, dressed up like a general, and set off into the world. "Something will turn up," he said to himself. He walked for a long time and, since he was not used to such treks, his feet began to hurt him. He took off his shoes, sat down on a bank, and began to cool his blistered soles in the wet grass. Soon a swarm of gnats flew out of the grass, and began to bite him on his bare feet. The tailor took a swing at them and squashed a round two dozen. "Gracious, how many other men could kill so many with a single blow?" he said proudly, and he took his tailor's chalk and

wrote on his tall hat: "Killed twenty-four with one blow!" Then he set off again. Before long he came to a strange town. The people looked at him queerly; they didn't want anything to do with such a strong fellow, and when he asked the way to nowhere in particular, they sent him on purpose to the dark forest where a wild boar was known to roam. They thought the beast would tear the mighty stranger to pieces. No sooner had the tailor gone into the trees, than the old boar came charging at him. The strong-man took to his heels and ran, and ran, and ran.

## 26 FEBRUARY

# The Mighty Tailor

The wild boar had almost caught up with the tailor, when they came to a little wayside chapel. The tailor just managed to hide behind the door before the bloodthirsty creature came hurtling in after him. Before the animal was able to stop and turn around, the tailor dashed out again and slammed the chapel door. Then he went back to the town and told everyone he met how he had taken the boar by the ears and flung him into the chapel so that he would not escape. The people were amazed to hear what a courageous fellow he was! Before long the king himself had heard of the tailor's brave deed. He sent for him and said, "My strong fellow, a terrible unicorn has come to my kingdom, and is causing great damage. If you kill him, you shall have my daughter for your wife." "Why not?" replied the tailor. He asked for a gold piece or two for the journey, and looked for the quickest way out of the palace. He had not the slightest wish to pick a quarrel with a unicorn. Swatting flies was much more in his line. But he had scarcely left the palace gate when there was the monster itself, making straight for him! He just managed at the last moment to jump behind a huge oak tree. The angry unicorn stuck its horn so deep into the tree trunk that it could not move from the spot. The tailor

was not slow to tie its legs with his belt, and he hurried off to boast of his success to the king.

## 27 FEBRUARY

# The Mighty Tailor

The tailor told the king a fine tale of his courage; how he had caught the unicorn by the tail and flung it against the tree with such might that it was a wonder the creature had not been killed at once. And right away the hero was anxious to marry the princess. But the king had other ideas. "If I were to have such a strong fellow about the place, I should not be king for very long," he thought to himself. And he told the tailor he must first deal with three wicked giants who were wreaking havoc in his kingdom. He supposed he was sending the tailor to a certain death. The tailor did not hesitate. He tied a couple of cheeses up in his bundle, threw in a few gold pieces, and as soon as he got out of the palace set off quickly, so as to be clear of danger as soon as possible. He did not give a thought to any giants. As he walked, he heard a rustling in the bushes. A little bird had got caught among some twigs and couldn't get out. The tailor put the bird in his bundle. "Perhaps I can sell it to some bird-catcher," he thought to himself. Before he had gone a hundred paces, he heard a roar of thunder. But this was no thunder! A giant was stamping down the road, until the trees cracked beneath his feet. "Little man," roared the giant, "let us try our strength! If you lose, I shall swallow you like a raspberry." What was the tailor to do? He thought it was the end of him.

## 28 FEBRUARY

# The Mighty Tailor

The giant said to the tailor, "Let us see who can throw the highest!" And he picked up

a great boulder as if it were a pebble, and hurled it into the sky. It was a quarter of an hour before it came down again. But the tailor took the little bird from his bundle and threw it in the air. "The devil take me, if that stone ever comes down again," he said, jauntily. Nor did it. "Very well, you win," said the giant, gruffly, and, picking up a stone, squeezed it until drops of water fell from it. The tailor only laughed. "That is nothing, my friend," he said, and he squeezed one of the cheeses from his bundle until the whey poured out of it. The giant could not believe his eyes. "Then let us see who can jump higher," he said. And with one great leap he reached the top of the cliff on which the giants' castle stood. But the clever tailor caught hold of the tip of a tall fir tree which the giant had kicked over as he jumped, and it sprang him to the very battlements of the castle. "I see that you are indeed a strong fellow," said the giant. "Come into our castle and meet my brothers." The giants sat and feasted with the tailor until late into the night, then made up a bed for him in the hall. But the tailor did not lie in it; instead he hid behind the stove. Soon the giants crept up to his bed. "Are you sleeping?" they asked, and when the tailor did not answer, they dropped a millstone on his bed in the dark. "What a trick to play, laying such a hard eiderdown on me!" cried the tailor. The giants were so startled that they leapt out of the window, straight into the abyss, and broke their necks. The tailor returned proudly to the royal palace, and the king was so afraid of him that he handed over his throne to him. The little tailor rules there to this day.

# MARCH

## 1 MARCH

# The Clever Potter

Beyond the blue horizon and the black sea lived a great and wise sultan. There was no rarity in the whole world he did not already own, but most precious of all to him was his beautiful daughter. One day, he had it proclaimed the world over that he would give his daughter in marriage to the man who brought him a gift of something he did not have. Before long suitors began to arrive at his palace with caravans loaded with gold, pearls, fine carpets, diamonds and ivory, but the sultan laughed at them all and said, "These gifts are but a drop in the ocean compared with what I have long ago received from others." One day a poor potter craved an audience with the sultan. "I give you something you have never yet received, noble sir!" he said. He bowed graciously and, before the startled potentate knew what was happening, gave him such a slap in the face that it echoed around all the chambers of the palace a hundred times over. All the servants and slaves fell flat on the ground with fear of the sultan's rage, but their master just laughed sourly, and said, "Potter, you have fulfilled my condition! I see that cleverness means more than riches: therefore shall you rule the land when I am gone." And so it was to be.

## 2 MARCH

# Old Sultan

There was once a peasant who had a faithful dog called Sultan. But when the dog grew old and toothless, the peasant decided to shoot him. Sultan overheard his plans, and right away he set off into the forest to ask his friend the wolf's advice. "Have no fear," the wolf told him. "When the peasant and his wife go to the fields and place their baby in the shade of the bushes, as they always do, I'll snatch the child up and make off into the woods with it. You

run after me, and I'll give you the baby. The peasant will think you have saved his child, and out of gratitude he is sure to spare your life." Everything went as planned. From then on Sultan had everything a dog could want. Then, one day, his friend the wolf came to see him. "Time for you to pay your debt to me," he told the dog. "Tonight I shall come to steal a sheep. Pretend to be asleep — your master will suspect nothing!" But the dog would have none of it. "I am faithful to my master — I cannot let you take a sheep," he said. And when the wolf, who did not believe his friend would give him away, came in the night to take the sheep, Sultan barked so loudly that the whole family was aroused, and they drove the wolf off. "You have used me ill for my friendship," called out the wolf. "I challenge you to a duel. Bring along a second, and meet me in the forest at dawn. There we shall settle our score."

## 3 MARCH

# Old Sultan

The next day at dawn the wolf brought along the wild boar as his second, and himself climbed up into a tree to keep watch. The only assistant old Sultan could find was a lame cat.

She had only three legs, and limped heavily, but she held her tail proudly erect. When the wolf saw her from afar, it seemed to him that she was constantly stooping to pick up stones; her stiff tail he took for a drawn sabre. His teeth chattered with fear. When he told the wild boar, the latter burrowed among the fallen leaves, until only his ears stuck out. When Sultan and the cat arrived at the appointed place, there was no one to be seen. Then there was a rustling among the leaves, as the boar pricked up his ears. The cat thought he was a mouse and, pouncing on one of the ears, sank her teeth into it. The boar fled in panic, calling behind him, "I meant no harm — he is the one! He is up the tree!" The dog and the cat gazed up into the tree and saw the wolf shivering among the branches with shame and fear. They began to laugh. "A fine hero you are!" cried the old dog. "Come on down with you, we had better be friends!" So Sultan and the wolf made up their quarrel.

## 4 MARCH

## The Thistle Doll

There was once a young girl called Dolly, because of her small stature. Her parents had died long ago, and she was in the service of a rich farmer. The world treated her ill. Everyone was unkind to her, and no one took her part. One night, when she was very sad, she went out into the garden. There she saw that in the cup of each of the flowers there

danced a pretty little fairy. "Come and dance with us!" cried the golden-haired fairy of the sunflower. "We are the spirits of the flowers." The girl needed no persuading, and she danced with them till morning light. From then on her heart was not so heavy. But the farmer began to wonder how it was that the girl was so tired every morning, and one night he kept watch in the porch. When the stars came out he saw Dolly slip out of the window, as quiet as a mouse. Right away he took hold of her roughly. But Dolly called on her friends for help: "Sunflower, golden Sunflower, come to poor Dolly's aid!" And at that the sunflower turned her into a prickly thistle, which tore the farmer's hand until it began to bleed. From then on little Dolly remained enchanted. When the thistle is in flower, out of it steps a little doll in a blue dress, and dances with the other fairies beneath the starry sky. She is no longer alone, and no one is unkind to her any more. And when the flowers are gone, the air

fills with thistledown, as if snow were falling. This is the thistle doll sending her messages of comfort to all sad, neglected children.

## 5 MARCH

# How to Cure a Sheep

The sheep was poorly. They gave her waybread and centaury, applied poultices of camomile and woody nightshade, but they couldn't find a way to cure her. In the end they had to take her off to the sheep infirmary. The doctor, an old ram, put his spectacles on his nose, pushed his stethoscope into his ears, and told the sick animal, "Put out your tongue and say aaah!" The sheep put out her tongue and said "baaah". "Now I know what the trouble is," said the doctor, gleefully. "This animal is deaf!" Everyone was amazed at the doctor's wisdom and skill. "Now, put out your tongue and say baaah," the doctor told his patient, a little more quietly. The sheep put out her tongue and said "baaah". "That's better," said the doctor, satisfied. "The devil himself would have to be in the matter, if I were unable to cure her." And he leaned over and whispered in the sheep's ear, "Now, my dear, you don't have to go to school tomorrow." The sheep

jumped like a fish. "Hurrah! No school tomorrow!" she shouted. The old doctor-ram simply smiled knowingly. "If you wish to cure a sick sheep, do not send it to school," he said. Maybe he was right.

## 6 MARCH

# The Shepherdess and the Chimney-Sweep

By the wall of the old parlour stood an ancient carved wooden cupboard. It was decorated with wooden roses and tulips, and in the middle frowned the ugly wooden face of a man with horns in the middle of his forehead, a goat's feet and a goat's long beard. The children used to call him "goatsfeet-in-chief and minor major-general", because it was difficult to say and sounded rather important. The horned fellow decided he would like to marry the little china shepherdess. She stood in her place on the little table under the mirror, next to the china chimney-sweep. Behind them stood the fat china Chinaman, who could nod his fat china head. He said he was the little shepherdess's grandfather, and when the goat-footed wooden man asked for her hand, he nodded

his head and said to the china maiden, "You would do well to marry the goat-footed general. You shall have a whole cupboard full of silver, and you will become madame goatsfeet-in-chief and minor major-general." But the shepherdess did not want to go into the cupboard, where the goat-footed man already had a dozen other china women, and in any case she was engaged to be married to the chimney-sweep. The two of them were in love. "Let us run away together," she begged the sweep, tearfully. So that night, when all were asleep, they set off.

## 7 MARCH

# The Shepherdess and the Chimney-Sweep

As the sweep and the shepherdess were climbing carefully down from the table, the goat-footed wooden general woke up, and called to the old Chinaman, "Wake up! They are escaping!" The fugitives were afraid, and jumped up on the window-seat. There was a puppet theatre there, and four card games. Just then there was a comedy on at the theatre about a young couple who were in love, but who could not be together. The playing-card queens were sitting in the front row, fanning themselves with tulips and applauding, but it made the shepherdess want to cry. Just then she turned and cried out: "The old Chinaman is coming!" Without delay, the chimney-sweep caught her by the hand and pulled her into the stove, up into the oven, and out into the

chimney. Higher and higher they climbed together, a black and terrible journey, until at last they reached the very lip of the chimney. The sky above them was full of stars, and the world around them appeared so infinitely great that the shepherdess burst into tears. "Let us go back," she begged. The sweep tried in vain to persuade her to change her mind. So they tramped silently back down the chimney, and when they reached the parlour again, they saw the old Chinaman lying smashed on the floor. When he had ambled after them on his fat little legs, he had slipped and fallen from the table; his head had gone rolling into the corner. The shepherdess felt sorry for him, but the chimney-sweep comforted her, saying, "Don't worry, the people will stick him back together again, and put a wooden peg into his head." Which is just what happened. Only the old Chinaman could no longer nod his head, on account of the wooden peg, and the next time the goat-footed general asked for the shepherdess's hand in marriage, he preferred to remain silent, rather than have to explain that there was something in his head which had no business there. So the sweep and the shepherdess stayed together, and if they have not got broken, they stand there under the mirror to this day.

## 8 MARCH

# The Gypsy Baron

One day the gypsies decided to teach the old ram to speak German. But the ram was stupid, and would not learn. The only thing he managed to say was baa, baa, baa. But the gypsies decided that was enough, dressed the ram up as a gentleman, put him a monocle in one eye and a top-hat on his head, and off they went to the tavern. They sat the ram down at a table and called out, "Hey, taverner, bring us food and drink, for we are travelling with the gypsy baron and his bride, a Hungarian princess." — "And who will pay the bill, you gypsy crew?" asked the taverner. "Why, the gypsy baron, who else?" called out the gypsies. The taverner turned to the old ram. "Well, will you pay, mighty lord?" he asked. "Baa, baa," the aristocrat replied, and turned his attention to a barrel of sauerkraut. The taverner was satisfied, and he brought the gypsies food and drink enough for a feast. When they had eaten and drunk their fill, one after the other they disappeared. When the taverner saw this, he turned on the baron angrily, "Let me see your money, lordship, or I'll give you what for!" And since the ram seemed to have no intention of paying, the taverner struck him across the face again and again, until his monocle fell in the sauerkraut tub. The ram was not going to stand for that. He took a run at the taverner and butted him right through the window onto the dung-heap. "Enough, enough, your lordship!" cried the taverner. And the ram said, "Baa, baa."

sparrows have been the cleverest in the world. Because they went to school, and even whispered the answers to the teacher's questions. And the lazy little boy? He has long since grown up, and they say he went abroad to a foreign country. And since he had never learnt anything worthwhile, they made him first minister there.

## 10 MARCH

## A Red Indian Tale

Wherever a man goes, he takes his shadow along with him, so he always has someone to

## 9 MARCH

## The Sparrow's Nest

In one of the towns along the River Rhine the cleverest sparrows in the world can be found. And this is how they came to be there. Once upon a time a naughty boy lived in that town. He had no wish to learn anything, his fingernails were always dirty, and his hair made a perfect sparrow's nest. One day an old sparrow saw this, and soon he moved in with his whole family. Thus it was that the sparrows began to go to school with the boy. One morning the teacher called the boy up to the blackboard and asked him, "What are one and one?" The boy pricked up his ears to see if anyone would whisper the answer, and heard a quiet little voice saying, "Cheep, cheep." "Cheep cheep," the boy replied. His teacher frowned fiercely, and asked, "How long did the Thirty-Years' War last? How much does a pound of feathers weigh? Which is further, from here to there, or from there to here?" The boy answered each question "Cheep cheep," for that was what the sparrows kept telling him. The teacher lost his temper, and the boy got nought out of ten for everything. But since that time the town speak to. Long, long ago, the stars used to hunt on the prairie with the Indians. They looked like beautiful Indian maidens, but because they were transparent, they did not throw a shadow like ordinary people. So their leader begged the sun-god to make them shadows by magic. But the sun-god did not hear her plea. "I shall ask the moon-god, sisters," said their leader. In the night she took a canoe and rowed over the endless lake to the place where it touches the sky. There she stepped out of the canoe and into the sky. "Give us shadows," she begged the moon-god, "that we may have a companion to speak to when we hunt alone." The moon heard her plea and said, "It shall be. But from now on you may hunt only in the sky, by the light of my beams. Call your sisters!" The leader of the stars looked down to earth and saw her own shimmering reflection on the surface of the lake. "What is that?" she wondered. "It is your shadow," replied the moon-god. "Because you are clear and sparkling, your shadow too is clear and sparkling." The star was delighted, and she called her sisters to her. And ever since then the stars have hunted only in the heavens.

## 11 MARCH

# Ow and Ouch

An old Chinaman caught a wonderful bird in his garden one day. Whenever it snapped its beak, gold pieces would fall out of it. But the richer the old man got, the meaner he got. Whenever his servants' wages were due, he would order them to go to the market to buy him ow and ouch. "If you come back without them, instead of wages you will receive a hundred strokes of the cane," he would say.

They always preferred to stay at home and lose their pay. Once he took a clever young boy into his service. When his wages became due, the old man sent him to market like the others. "If I bring you ow and ouch, will you give me your magic bird?" the boy asked. The old man grimaced wickedly, but he agreed. The boy ran into town. On the way he took two gourds, into one of which he put a wasp, in the other a bee. Then he hurried back to his master. "I have brought you ow and ouch," he called out. "Put your finger in the gourds, and you will see!" As soon as the old man did so, the angry wasp stung him. "Ow, ow!" he cried. "Did I not tell you, master, that I had brought you ow?" laughed the boy. "Put your finger in the other gourd, for there you will find ouch!" But the old man had had enough. He had to give the boy his magic bird, and he never sent anyone to market for ow and ouch again.

## 12 MARCH

# Aladdin and the Wonderful Lamp

Deep in the heart of Africa lived a powerful magician who had a magic ring. Whenever he turned it three times, a genie in a turban would appear, bow to the ground, and say: "I am the slave of the ring: your wish is my command!" One day the magician asked the genie of the ring who was the most powerful in the world. The genie answered him: "Far to the east there is an underground cave; in the cave, in an enchanted garden, burns an ordinary-looking old lamp. If anyone rubs that lamp, my brother, the genie of the lamp, will appear to him. He is a thousand times mightier than I. It is written in the stars that the only one who may enter the cave is Aladdin, son of a poor widow in a distant land to the east. But if he wishes to get out alive, he must wear on his finger your magic ring." When he heard this,

the magician at once ordered the slave of the ring to take him to Aladdin's home town. Then, one day, he dressed himself as a rich merchant, and went to visit Aladdin's mother. "I am the long lost brother of your dead husband," he told her. "For many a year I have wandered the world, but now I have returned to my native town to help your son, my nephew, to find his fortune. Put the boy in my care, and I shall make him a rich man." The poor widow was only too glad to agree, and so Aladdin set off into the world.

## 13 MARCH

# Aladdin and the Wonderful Lamp

As they wandered through the world, Aladdin and the magician came upon a range of high mountains. Here the magician muttered some secret spell, and there appeared before them the entrance to an underground cave. "Go down and bring me from the magic garden an old lamp you will find there," the magician ordered the boy. "But if you value your life, touch nothing else!" With these words he slipped the magic ring on Aladdin's finger, and the boy climbed down into the cave. Gold and pearls lay all around, but Aladdin took no notice of them, hurrying along the underground passages until he reached the enchanted garden, watched over by two stone dogs. He snatched the lamp from its niche in a wall, and hurried back again. But one or two precious stones got caught in his shirt as he brushed past the blossoming golden trees. When he reached the entrance, Aladdin called out: "Help me, please, uncle, I cannot climb up alone!" But the magician told him first to hand up the lamp. At that moment the boy noticed the evil look in the other's eyes, and was loath to give him the lamp. The magician grew angry and muttered some secret spell, whereupon the ground closed up over Aladdin's head. In a cloud of smoke, the magician flew back to Africa. Aladdin was a prisoner in the cave.

# Aladdin and the Wonderful Lamp

Aladdin sat in the dark cave and felt like crying. Suddenly, without knowing it, he rubbed the lamp with the palm of his hand, and there in front of him stood a terrible genie. He bowed to the ground, and said: "I am the slave of the lamp. Master, your every wish shall be fulfilled!" As soon as Aladdin had recovered from his amazement a little, he ordered the genie to take him home to his mother. No sooner had he finished speaking, than he found himself in the hallway of his home, where his beloved mother ran to embrace him. From then on Aladdin and his mother wanted for nothing. The slave of the lamp granted their every wish, and they lived in great style. One day in the city Aladdin caught sight of a beautiful girl, the sultan's daughter. He fell in love with her at once. "Go to the sultan's palace, offer him the gift of the precious stones I brought back from the enchanted cave, and beg his daughter's hand in marriage for your son," he told his mother. His mother hesitated, but in the end she went to the palace. When the sultan saw the jewels, he could not believe his eyes. "Your son must be even richer than I," he said. "Tell him he shall have my daughter's hand if he builds her a golden palace overnight." As soon as Aladdin heard this, he smiled, rubbed the old lamp with the palm of his hand, and ordered the genie to do as the sultan had asked. When dawn broke, beside the sultan's palace stood one of pure gold, such as no human eye had ever seen. And so the old sultan gave Aladdin his daughter's hand without further delay.

## 15 MARCH

# Aladdin and the Wonderful Lamp

Aladdin and his beautiful bride lived together in love and happiness. But one day the wicked African magician heard of his good fortune, and set off at once to try to get the magic lamp. When, one day, Aladdin had gone hunting, the magician dressed up as a peddler and called out beneath the palace windows: "New lamps for old!" When Aladdin's wife heard this, she remembered the old lamp which hung in her husband's chamber. She sent one of the servants to give it to the peddler in exchange for a new lamp. Now the magician had what he had yearned for so long.

At once he rubbed the lamp and ordered the all-powerful genie to carry Aladdin's palace with his beautiful wife away to his home in darkest Africa. When Aladdin returned from his hunting, he was overcome with grief, but he accidently turned the magic ring, and there before him stood the slave of the ring. "Your wish is my command," he said, bowing. Aladdin was filled with joy, and ordered the genie to bring back his palace and his wife. But the slave of the ring told him sadly, "Alas,

I cannot gainsay my brother, the slave of the lamp, for he is mightier far than I. But I shall take you to the magician's home. If you can take back the lamp, you shall have all you ask. Here is a phial of poison. Tonight the magician will celebrate his success. Have your wife drop the poison secretly in his wine. When he is dead, the lamp will be yours again." And so it came about. When the wicked magician fell dead, Aladdin took the lamp from under his cloak, summoned the genie, and ordered him to carry them together with the palace to his home. There he and his wife live happily to this day.

kingdom. "Do not worry, queen sheep," he said, "I shall count your subjects for you. When I have counted them, ring your golden bell, and the fairy tale will end." And he took his pipe and whistled, and all the black sheep and the white ones flocked into the meadow. The shepherd drove them on and on, until they reached a broad river. Across the river stretched a narrow footbridge. There the shepherd ordered the sheep to cross over the bridge, one by one. Can you see them? There they go, one after the other, and the shepherd counts them as they pass. We must keep counting until they are all over on the other side. You can count as well. One, two, three, four, five ... When you hear the bell ring, the fairy tale is over.

## 16 MARCH

# How the Shepherd Counted Sheep

Once upon a time there was a sheep kingdom, ruled over by a sheep queen, who had a golden bell around her neck. She had so many subjects that no one could count them, and this worried the queen a good deal. One day a little shepherd wandered into the

## 17 MARCH

# The Poor Mill-Hand and the Cat

There once lived an old miller who had no children. He had three mill-hands, and one day he called them to him and said, "I have no one to whom I can leave the mill. Go into the world, and whichever of you brings me the finest horse shall have the mill when I die." The mill-hands set off without delay. The youngest of them, Jack, was thought a fool, so the other two wished to get rid of him and, leading him into the deep forest, they left him

cats gathered around Jack, black ones, white ones, ginger ones, grey ones: they dressed him and fed him, and then their mistress, the tortoiseshell cat, set him to work. She gave him a silver axe, a silver wedge and a silver saw, and sent him into the forest to cut wood. Jack was no shirker, and it was not long before the whole forest was cleared. Afterwards the cat gave him a golden scythe, and told him to cut the meadow in front of the castle. He wasted no time, and before the sheep returned from the pastures he had the grass cut and dried. "You are a good worker, Jack," said the cat, pleased. "As your reward we shall dance together again." And so they did. But time was passing, and Jack was beginning to wonder when he would get what he had been promised. "When you have built me a silver house, all of silver beams," the cat told him. She handed him a broad-axe made of silver, and the young mill-hand set to work with a will. Soon he had built a little house as neat as neat can be. When the cat saw this, she

there alone. Jack was sad that they should use him so, but, out of nowhere it seemed, a tortoiseshell cat suddenly appeared. "I know well enough what troubles you," she mewed. "If you go with me to my cat palace and serve me faithfully for seven years, you shall have the finest horse in all the world." Since there was nothing else for it, as Jack could not find his way out of the forest alone, he went with the cat. They came to a castle which was occupied only by cats, each of which had a small spider as its footman. They welcomed Jack among them, sat him at the table, and began to make music and to dance. When Jack had eaten his fill, the cat invited him to dance. "Why not," the lad replied. And they danced and played the whole night long.

## 18 MARCH

# The Poor Mill-Hand and the Cat

As soon as the sun rose in the morning, all the

smiled with satisfaction, and mewed. "It is seven years to the day since you entered my service. Now put on your torn old clothes again and go back home. Tomorrow I shall myself bring you the horse you have earned." What was Jack to do? He obeyed her, and set off home.

## 19 MARCH

# The Poor Mill-Hand and the Cat

How they laughed at Jack when he returned to the mill empty-handed! The other two mill-hands, who had brought their horses long ago, wished him nothing but ill, and though they themselves had earned only lame jades for their service, they laughed at him fit to bust. The old miller, too, was far from satisfied. "What, have you not even earned a new suit of clothes in all these years?" he said, angrily. "Be off with you, you good-for-nothing, go and sleep in the goose-pen!" And so Jack had to sleep among the geese. But at the crack of dawn a golden coach came rattling along the track, and out of it jumped one cat after another; first ginger ones, then black ones, then white ones, then grey ones, and, last of all, the tortoiseshell cat. No sooner had their feet touched the ground, than they changed into beautiful maidens, and

the tortoiseshell cat into a beautiful princess. At that moment Jack thrust his head out from the goose-pen. "I bring you your horse," said the princess. And so she did! There, trotting behind the coach, was a horse which was a delight to behold. On it sat a dog, and on the dog a squirrel. These, too, leapt to the ground, changing into a footman and a chamber-maid. At once they dressed Jack in cloth-of-gold, and the princess drove him off to the silver house. They left the old mill to the envious mill-hands. Nor did it bring them any good. They soon sold it and drank away the money. But the little silver house became a grand palace, where Jack is king to this day.

## 20 MARCH

# How the Fool Freed a Princess

Once upon a time there was a cottager's son whom people called Jack Simple. He couldn't even count up to five, and his father would not even trust him to take their only cow to graze, in case he managed to lose her. Only his elder brothers were allowed to go to the pastures. Jack was sorry about this, and one day he told his father: "Father, let me take the cow to pasture, you will see that all will be well." At first his father would not hear of it, but in the

end he let Jack have his way. Jack took the cow on a piece of rope, and set off behind the cottage. But all they found there was thistles and nettles. "Only be patient, cow, I shall find you better fare," thought the lad, and he took the cow down to the river. No sooner had they reached the bank, than the cow jumped into the water and set out to swim to the other side. It was all Jack could do to catch her by the tail. "Stop, you stupid creature," cried Jack, angrily, but the cow took no notice, and dragged him along through field and hedgerow until they reached a fine castle. All things in it were of silver and gold, and the stables had the scent of fresh hay. The cow went up to a manger and began to munch contentedly. As soon as she had eaten her fill, she let Jack lead her home again. His father was amazed at how well-fed the cow looked, and he praised his stupid son highly.

on a golden throne. And so Jack Simple became king. Believe it or not, he even learnt to count to five in time! And he ruled wisely and well.

## 21 MARCH

# How the Fool Freed a Princess

From then on only Jack took the cow to pasture. His elder brothers were angry and envious, but to no avail. Their father was full of praise for how fat the cow was looking, as round as a beer-cask, and he would not hear a word spoken against his youngest son. One day, as Jack arrived at the golden castle with the cow, a little black dog ran up to them. Jack was about to drive the dog away, but she spoke to Jack in a human voice. "Tomorrow, when you come with the cow to my castle, bring with you an axe!" Jack asked no questions, and did as he was told. The next day, as soon as he reached the castle, the dog ran up to him and said, "Cut off my head!" Jack hesitated, for he had a gentle nature, but when the dog insisted, he did as he was asked. Scarcely had the blow fallen, when the earth trembled, and there in front of Jack stood a beautiful princess. She fell into his arms, and with tears in her eyes thanked him for releasing her from the spell. Then she took him by the hand and sat him down beside her

## 22 MARCH

# One-Eye, Two-Eyes and Three-Eyes

Once upon a time, in a certain cottage, there lived a woman who had three daughters. The eldest was called One-Eye, because she had a single eye in the middle of her forehead. The middle one was called Two-Eyes, because she had two eyes, just like other people. The youngest had an extra eye, and so she was called Three-Eyes. Two-Eyes had a hard time of it. Her mother hated her, and her sisters were unkind to her. They envied her because she was the most beautiful. They gave her the worst clothes, and all she got to eat was what was left over when the others had finished. Every morning the poor girl had to take the goat off to graze, and she was allowed to return only after sunset, when there was almost nothing left on the plate. No wonder she was always weeping! One day a strange woman met her in the meadows, and asked her, "Why do you cry so, Two-Eyes?" Two-Eyes told her of her troubles. Then the woman stroked her hair, and said, "Do not be sad, Two-Eyes! Whenever you are hungry,

over again: "One-Eye, now your vigil keeping, One-Eye, now so softly sleeping." It was not long before One-Eye fell asleep. Two-Eyes quickly asked the goat to lay the little table, and when she had eaten her fill she sent it away again. Towards evening she woke her sister up and they hurried home. One-Eye was forced to admit to their mother that she had slept, and had seen nothing at all. Her mother was very angry with her, and the next day sent Three-Eyes instead. Two-Eyes sat beside her in the grass, and in a while began to sing: "Three-Eyes, now your vigil keeping," but by mistake she sang, "Two-Eyes, now so softly sleeping." And so it happened that Three-Eyes seemed to fall asleep, but her third eye, which had not been mentioned in the song, she only pretended to close, and with it she saw all that took place. As soon as they got home, she told their mother how their goat had given Two-Eyes all manner of good things to eat.

just say to your goat: 'Dearest goat, as you are able, Fill with food your little table!' And you shall have whatever food you wish." Two-Eyes did as the lady told her, and in a trice a small table appeared, heaped with the most delicious foods. The girl ate her fill, and the unknown woman said: "Dearest goat, as you are able, Clear away your little table!" At that the table disappeared, and the strange woman with it.

## 23 MARCH

## One-Eye, Two-Eyes and Three-Eyes

From then on Two-Eyes was much happier. But it seemed curious to her sisters and her mother that she no longer ate hungrily what little they left her on her return from the pastures. So their mother sent One-Eye with her to the meadows. Two-Eyes soon felt hungry, and she wished to ask the goat for something to eat. But first she sat down next to her sister and said: "Sister, I shall sing you a pretty little song." And she sang, over and

## 24 MARCH

## One-Eye, Two-Eyes and Three-Eyes

When the girls' mother heard how the goat

had been treating Two-Eyes to such delicacies down in the meadows, she was so angry she had the poor creature's throat cut at once. Poor Two-Eyes was broken-hearted. But the kind woman appeared before her again, and said: "Do not cry, Two-Eyes. Take a horn from your poor goat and plant it beside the front door." At that she was gone again. Two-Eyes did as she had been told and, wondrous to behold, a beautiful tree bearing golden apples grew up there overnight. Her mother and her two sisters rushed to pick the fruit, but the branches slipped out of their hands as if they did not wish to be touched by them. But when Two-Eyes came up to the tree, the apples seemed to fall right into her lap. However, her mother and her sisters took them all away for themselves. One day, a handsome young knight rode by. Her mother and sisters shoved Two-Eyes under an old tub, saying that they were ashamed of her, and themselves bowed to the rider from afar. "Whose is that beautiful tree?" the knight asked in wonder. "I will give any reward you ask, if you give me a branch from it." The two sisters cried each other down, saying the tree was theirs, but the branches always slipped out of their hands. Then a golden apple fell from the tree and rolled straight to the upturned tub where Two-Eyes was hidden. The knight lifted the tub, and when he saw Two-Eyes beneath it, he asked her for a branch from the tree. This she was happy to give him. "Now I know to whom the tree belongs," he said, and to the disgust of the wicked mother and sisters, he took the beautiful Two-Eyes off with him to his castle. And the magic tree? That uprooted itself and followed her to her new home, where it bears golden apples to this day.

## 25 MARCH

# The Two Musicians

Two poor musicians were wandering through the world. One played the trumpet and the other beat the drum, until the glass rattled in the windows. One day their wanderings brought them to a woodland spring. Fairies were dancing around it. "Play for us, musicians," begged the fairy queen. The trumpeter began to play a merry dance. But the drummer refused to play, saying he would not beat his drum for nothing, and that anyway he was so hungry he could scarcely raise his arms. He lay down in the grass and went to sleep. The fairies danced to the trumpeter's tune, and when they had danced enough, their queen said: "Now you shall both have your rewards." She touched the trumpet with a golden primrose, and beat the drum with a dry thistle. "You may keep such a reward as this," said the drummer, turning up his nose. But the trumpeter smiled warmly at the fairies and said, "You have rewarded me well. I am well satisfied if your feet keep time to my music." And the musicians went their way. They came to a village where a festival was in progress. The trumpeter blew into his

trumpet and the drummer twirled his drumsticks, and — what do you suppose? From out of the trumpet gold pieces began to fall, and they went on tinkling to the ground as long as the trumpeter played. But a swarm of wasps flew out of the drum, and drove the drummer up hill and down dale, away out of the village.

## 26 MARCH

# The Two Musicians

The worthy trumpeter stayed on in the village and married the mayor's daughter. Never did he turn a poor man from his door, and he trumpeted on his way any beggar who came along and gave him a couple of gold pieces for his journey. But for the drummer things went from bad to worse. He threw the accursed drum away, and was left with no way

of making a living. One day he happened to wander by the woodland spring again. Suddenly, the fairies appeared. "Play for us as we dance," they begged him. "If you were to give me a magic trumpet such as you gave my companion, I should play for you from morning till night," he said. The fairy queen only smiled, plucked a reed from the waterside, and struck it with a dry thistle. The reed turned into a golden trumpet that was a delight to behold. The musician snatched it up and, before the fairies could change their minds, made off. After a while he could wait no longer, so he stopped by the wayside and blew a few notes. But what an unpleasant surprise! Strange things began to happen to him. His whole body was suddenly covered in hair; claws grew out from his fingers and toes, and his nose got longer and longer, until it was like a bird's beak. The musician looked at himself in a lake, and almost fainted with horror. He had turned into a horrible spectre. Ever since then, on a moonlit night, a strange hooting can be heard from the woods. People say it is the tawny owl, but do not believe them! It is the selfish musician, playing his trumpet as the fairies dance, and waiting for them to take pity on him.

## 27 MARCH

# The Iron Box

One day a poor peasant went into the forest to gather firewood. Among the roots of an old tree he found a locked iron box. "Whatever could be inside?" he thought to himself. At that moment an old woman appeared from nowhere beside him. "The box is full of thalers," she told him. "They belong to me, but you may take them if you wish. Only you must speak to no one about it, otherwise it will go ill with you!" And with these words she was gone. The peasant hurried home with the box and smashed it open with an axe. The old woman had, to be sure, told the truth. The peasant rushed off to tell his wife. "But you must tell no one!" he warned her. The woman promised, and went off to buy meat and flour; then she baked, and roasted, and fried. Soon there was such a wonderful smell of cooking from the cottage that the neighbours' mouths watered. "What good things are you cooking?" asked one. The peasant's wife had never kept a secret in her life, and soon she told the whole story. "My husband found a box full of money: I am cooking him a meal to celebrate. Mind you, you must tell no one!" The neighbour promised, but because he was related to her, she didn't really count the gravedigger, so she told him. He told the sexton, and the sexton told the parson. The parson at once ran off to tell the judge while the news was fresh.

## 28 MARCH

## The Iron Box

The moment the judge heard from the parson of the peasant's new-found riches, he sent for the man and began to question him harshly. "Listen, you cunning fox. I hear you have stolen a pile of money somewhere or other. Your own wife said so. Now, tell me where you stole it!" But the peasant would admit

nothing. "Your honour should not set such store by a woman's words," he said. "My wife is a little mad."—"Mad, is she?" the judge retorted. "Then I shall have her brought to court in fourteen days' time, and we'll see how mad she is!" The unfortunate peasant racked his brains for a way out of the mess he was in. Then he had a bright idea. He bought pretzels and cakes from all the bakers in town, took them home and scattered them about the garden, throwing a few onto the roof; then he called to his wife in the kitchen. "A poor housekeeper you are, wife! It has been raining cakes and pretzels, and you do not even come to gather them up!" The woman was filled with amazement, but she wasted no time, and soon she had a sackful of pastries. The next day her husband said, "Hurry, mother, hide under the washtub! The king's soldiers are coming to the village. They have long iron beaks instead of mouths, and they peck almost to death any woman they see!" Without delay his wife crawled under the washtub, and waited to see what would happen.

## 29 MARCH

## The Iron Box

While the peasant's wife was crouched beneath the washtub, shivering with fear, her husband poured a sackful of corn over her and let the chickens into the yard. They ran up and pecked at the corn, tap, tap, tap!—until it was all gone. Only then did the peasant lift up the tub and call out, "Come on out, mother, the soldiers have gone!"—"Thank the lord," the woman sighed with relief. "How scared I was when they were pecking at me with their iron beaks!" The peasant just smiled quietly to himself. In two weeks' time the judge summoned her to court. "Tell me about the money," he ordered. The woman answered fearfully that her husband had brought a box full of thalers from somewhere. "Do not believe her, my lord!" cried the peasant. "Can't you see that she is mad?" And he asked his wife, "When do you say I brought the money?" His wife answered, "Do you not remember? The next day it rained pretzels, and the day after that the king's soldiers came with their iron beaks, and I had to hide from them under the washtub. Even now I shake with fear when I recall how their beaks pecked at me, tap, tap, tap!" The judges decided that she really was crazy, and they let the peasant go free.

## 30 MARCH

# The Foolish Bride

There was once a miller's daughter who was so foolish that the young men from miles around kept well out of her way. One day a farmhand was passing by the mill. "Better a poor husband than none at all," thought the girl's mother, and she invited the young man to eat with them. They got talking, and by and by the lad promised to marry the miller's daughter. Her mother sent her to the cellar to draw a jug of ale with which to seal the bargain. The foolish girl set the jug on the floor, turned the tap, and began to look around her aimlessly. She noticed an axe wedged in a beam. "Mercy!" she cried in horror. "What if we should have a baby, and the axe should fall on his head! What a misfortune!" And she burst into tears. The beer was lapping about her ankles. Just then her mother arrived. "What is the matter?" she asked in surprise. Right away the girl told her of the terrible misfortune which threatened the miller's future grandchild, and the mother, too, began to cry. The beer foamed around their knees. Before long the miller himself came on the scene. As soon as he heard the fearful tale, the miller sat down beside them and began to mourn the poor child. Just then the farmhand came to see what was keeping them. They all spoke at once, telling him of the danger that threatened his unborn child. The lad began to laugh: "Better wed to poverty, than such a stupid wife," he said, and moved on.

## 31 MARCH

# Father Gold, Mother Silver and Son Copper

Far across the sea there lived two brothers—one poor and the other rich. One day the poor man found a silver piece by the wayside. He took it to his rich brother. "Brother, I bring you a bride for your gold pieces," he said. "If you put one of them in my care, I shall marry him to my silver piece. When they have a child, I shall bring you the whole family." The rich man hesitated, but because he was greedy, he finally agreed. By and by his brother brought him one gold piece, one silver piece and one copper piece. "See," he said, "our coins are blessed with a copper son. A pity that both were not gold, for you might have had more gold pieces." The rich man could not believe his eyes. "Brother," he said, "I shall give you all my gold pieces; marry them off, and let them have an abundance of children!"—"Why not?" the poor man agreed, taking the gold pieces and going his way. When he did not return for a long time, his brother went to see him. "Where is my money?" he asked. "My condolences," said the poor brother sadly, "all your gold pieces have passed away." "Fool," fumed the rich man. "How can money die?"—"If it can have children, then why should it not die?" smiled the clever brother, and the local judge laughed, and had to agree. So it was that a rich man became poor, and a poor man rich.

# APRIL

## 1 APRIL

## The Cat and the Mouse Join Forces

Once upon a time there was a cat who managed to persuade a mouse to come and live with her. "It will be just like a wedding breakfast," she told the mouse. "We shall play and dance together, eat, drink and make merry." The mouse decided it might really be a good idea, and so she moved in with the cat. So as not to go hungry in the wintertime, they put a pot of dripping aside for a rainy day. "But where shall we hide it?" asked the cat. The mouse thought of putting it under the altar in the church, saying that it was sure to be safe from thieves. The cat agreed. But after some time she took a fancy to a little dripping. "Dear mouse, my cousin has a baby son," she lied. "I must go to the church for the christening." "Have a good time," the mouse told her, kindheartedly. The cat ran along to the church and licked the top of the bowl of dripping clean away. "What is your godson's name?" asked the mouse when the cat came home. "Er—Topgone," said the cat, hurriedly. "What a strange name," said the mouse, raising her eyebrows. "Oh, what's in a name," purred the cat. "Anyway, it is no stranger than Crumbscavenger, as your godchildren are called." And she curled up, and slept, and slept.

## 2 APRIL

## The Cat and the Mouse Join Forces

Before very long the greedy cat thought up another christening, and this time she ate a full half of the dripping. "What is the baby called this time?" asked the mouse. "Halfgone," the cat told her. The mouse shook her head. By and by the cat again had to go to the church to be godmother. This time she licked the bowl clean. "What is the baby's name?" inquired the mouse, as usual. "Allgone," mewed the cat. "Allgone? Never in my life have I heard such a name!" the mouse said in wonder, but the cat just smiled secretly to herself. When winter came along they had nothing to eat, and the mouse, remembering the bowl of dripping, set off for the church with the cat. But the bowl was quite, quite empty. Suddenly the mouse realized what had been happening. "So that's it! You have eaten it all yourself," she chided the cat angrily. "First the top gone, then half gone . . .!"—"Keep quiet," hissed the cat, "or I'll eat you up too!" But it was too late for the mouse to stop herself from finishing what she wanted to say: ". . . and then all gone!" she squeaked. No sooner had she said the last word, than the cat pounced on her and swallowed the poor mouse at one gulp. There you are, you see: if the cat the mouse befriend, the mouse shall rue it in the end!—anyway, that's what the dog says.

## 3 APRIL

## The Ram's Head

A father sent his greedy son to market to buy a roast ram's head. The boy hurried along, anxious to please his father. But on the way back he did not walk so fast. The roast meat smelt so delicious, it made his mouth water. He dillied and dallied, and, being greedy, pulled off pieces of meat all the way, until

only the bones were left. In the end he brought home a bare ram's skull. "What is this you have brought me?" his father asked in surprise. "Why, a ram's head, of course," his greedy son replied. "And where are its eyes?" asked his father. "Oh, father, the ram was blind," the boy told him. His father frowned like thunder. "Then where are its ears, my clever lad?" he said, gruffly. "Oh, father, the ram was deaf," the boy persisted. "And its tongue?"—"Father, the ram was dumb, too!"—"Why has it no skin on its head?" his father asked, angrily. "Father, dear father, the ram was quite bald!" the greedy boy replied, and dashed off to his mother to beg a cake.

## 4 APRIL

## The Waterman Who Couldn't Sleep

In a lake below the forest lived an old, bad-tempered waterman. A mischievous fish had once stolen his sleep, and since then he had been unable to sleep a wink. One night a merry journeyman passed by the lakeside. The waterman thrust his green fingers out of the water and grabbed the traveller by the leg. "I've got you!" he croaked. "Unless you tell me where I can find sleep, I shall take you to the bottom of the lake!" The journeyman was frightened, but he quickly recovered himself. "You cannot sleep at night?" he asked, pretending to be surprised. "Then, what kind of water do you place beneath your head?"—"Why, water from the spring," the waterman said. "Ah, then that's it! You must make your bed with marsh water, for spring water is much too hard," the clever journeyman told him. The waterman thanked him for his advice and let him go. That night he made his bed with marsh water, but again he did not sleep a wink. One day he caught the journeyman again as he was passing by the lake. "You gave me bad advice," he said, "I shall drag you to the bottom!" But the journeyman was undismayed. "Then I'll tell you what to do," he said. "Call together all the frogs and watermen to sing you a lullaby!" The waterman allowed himself to be persuaded, and the next evening all the frogs and watermen made music enough to crack the eardrums. It was a terrible croaking and wailing, but the waterman in his willow tree felt his eyelids grow heavy, and soon he dropped off into a deep sleep. Ever since then, on a moonlit night you can hear the waterman's choir croaking its harsh song down by the waterside.

## 5 APRIL

# How Foolish Jacob Learnt to be a Robber

In the dark forest over the hills lived an old robber and his foolish son, Jacob. One day the old man said to his son, "Son, my eyes are beginning to fail me, and I can no longer shoot straight, it is time you learned my trade. You must earn your own living soon!" So what was Jacob to do? He yawned widely, pulled his feathered hat down over his eyes, and, so as not to have to walk, rolled down the hillside into the valley. A penniless vagabond was just passing that way, pockets so full of holes the wind whistled through them, and they wouldn't have known what a farthing was if they had seen one. "Your money or your life!" shouted Jacob, just as his father had taught him. The vagabond was startled, but he soon recovered himself. "Most esteemed robber," he said, bowing. "I have but one life and, little as it is worth, I should rather hang on to it, but you may have all the money I have in my pockets. Only have a care, for it is wind money, which I was given by the wind king. If you were to take it from my pockets to put into yours, it might blow away—feel how it flies about in there! It were better to change your clothes with mine." The foolish Jacob liked the idea, so he put on the vagabond's rags, leaving the clever fellow his fine robber's clothes. You can imagine the welcome he got when he came home!

## 6 APRIL

# Little Pip

In a far-off land there lived a small fellow who went by the name of little Pip. His parents died, so Pip set off into the world on his pony to seek his fortune. On the way he wandered into a beautiful city. In it there lived an old woman who had a house full of cats and dogs. She took little Pip into her service, and told him to look after her animals well. He was happy there, and before long all the animals liked him. His greatest friend was a lame little dog. One day the dog led little Pip into a secret chamber. The only things in it were a large pair of slippers and a strange stick. "The stick is magic," the dog told him, in a human voice. "Wherever there is gold to be dug, the stick will tap the ground three times. If it taps twice, you will find silver beneath." Little Pip thanked the dog and started to leave, but the dog said to him, "Do not forget the magic slippers. If you turn on your heels in them three times, they will carry you wherever you wish." The dog had spoken truly. Before long Pip had more gold and silver than he could carry. One day, he turned his pony loose, put on the magic slippers, turned three times on his heels, and ordered the slippers to take him to the royal palace. There he offered his services to the king as the swiftest runner in the land.

# 7 APRIL

# Little Pip

When the king saw little Pip, he burst out laughing. But Pip pleaded so touchingly to be allowed to take part in the next races that in the end the king took pity on him. The next day there was a great celebration at the palace. When the feasting was over, all the best runners in the world gathered in the royal gardens for a race to see who was the fastest. With a smile, little Pip put on his magic slippers, turned on his heels three times, and before the other runners knew what was happening was at the finish. The king could not believe his eyes, but when he had got over his surprise he appointed little Pip his chief runner and messenger. But the boy's happiness was short-lived. It was not long before envious folk noticed that the strange little fellow had all the gold and silver he might wish for, and they began to spread tales about him throughout the city. At first Pip thought he could silence them by his generosity, but the more he gave away, the more his rivals hated him. Finally, word came to the king that Pip's riches were stolen from the royal coffers. The king was enraged, and had Pip thrown in gaol.

## 8 APRIL

# Little Pip

Poor little Pip. He believed the king to be a just man, and thought that if he revealed the secret of the magic stick and slippers he would be set free. But, alas! The ungrateful king kept the magic gifts for himself and drove Pip from his palace without a penny to his name. He wandered miserably about the world for a long time, until he came to a secret forest where beautiful fig-trees grew. But no sooner had the hungry Pip eaten a few mouthfuls of the fruit, than he found that he had grown enormous ears and a long nose. He began to cry. Bemoaning his cruel fate, he carelessly chewed the fruit of another fig-tree, and to his amazement his nose and ears returned to their usual size. This gave Pip an idea as to how he might revenge himself. He returned to the royal city and offered the palace cook the fruit of the first fig-tree. The moment the king tasted the figs after his supper, he thought he would die of shame! Not even the royal

elephant had such a nose and ears. What lamentation there was in the royal household! Then along came Pip, dressed as a doctor. "Sire, I will rid you of your unsightly ornaments, if I may choose from your treasures whatever I will," he told the king. The king agreed, and led him to his treasure-house. There Pip spied his magic slippers and stick. Quickly, he picked up the stick and put on the slippers and called out, "For your treachery you shall keep your ass's nose and elephant's ears, ungrateful king!" And with these words he turned three times on his heels and disappeared, no one knows where. Perhaps somewhere his faithful pony was waiting for him.

## 9 APRIL

# Cinderella

There was once a rich merchant who had all he could wish for; money to burn, a good and beautiful wife, and an even more beautiful daughter. But misfortune often strikes where least expected, and one day his beloved wife died. His daughter visited her mother's grave every day, day after day, and wept long and bitterly at their sad loss. The merchant thought it wrong that one so young should grieve so long, and, so that she might not grow up without a mother's care, he took a second wife. The stepmother had two pretty daughters of her own. They looked like a pair of rosebuds, but their hearts were filled with envy and hatred. The moment their stepfather left the house, they would turn on their new sister. "Just look at the proud little princess! How finely she dresses! But from now on you shall earn your bread in this house." They took away all her beautiful clothes, gave her a pair of old wooden shoes, and made her wear a tattered smock. Then they shut her up in the kitchen and gave her all the most unpleasant tasks to do. And as if that were not enough, they would drop peas and lentils in the ashes, and make the poor little girl pick every last one out again. Even when her dreary day's

work was ended they gave her no peace, and instead of her feather bed, she was made to sleep among the ashes in the fireplace. Because the poor girl was always smutty, they started to call her Cinderella.

## 10 APRIL

# Cinderella

Poor Cinderella! She was afraid to tell her father, in case her stepmother and the two wicked sisters mistreated her even more. One day, as the merchant was setting off into the city, he asked his stepdaughters what presents he should bring them. They asked for fine robes and jewels, necklaces, bracelets, and all manner of vanity. But Cinderella told him to bring her the first twig to catch against his hat as he was returning home. This happened to be a hazel twig, and he brought it to Cinderella as she had asked. She planted it on her mother's grave and watered it with her tears. In the twinkling of an eye a splendid hazel bush grew up, and on it alighted a little white bird, which said, "Cinderella, I shall grant your every wish!" But the modest child wanted no more than to remember her poor mother. One day, she came home from the churchyard to find her stepmother and two wicked sisters getting ready for a grand ball at the royal palace. It was to last three whole

days, and the young prince was to choose himself a bride there. Cinderella begged them to take her with them, but her stepmother only laughed and, tipping a bowl of lentils into the ashes, said, "If you can pick them out again in one hour, we shall see!" Cinderella ran into the garden and begged the birds to help her. The birds set to with a will, and soon all the lentils were back in the bowl. But the stepmother was only angry with her, and shouted, "You shall go nowhere, you would only bring shame on us, you ragamuffin!" So the poor girl had to stay at home.

## 11 APRIL

# Cinderella

As soon as her stepmother and the wicked sisters had set off for the ball, Cinderella ran all the way to her mother's grave, and begged the hazel bush: "Give me a gown to please a prince's eye, dear hazel." The bush shook itself, and the little white bird threw into Cinderella's lap a gold and silver gown and a pair of velvet slippers. Quickly, she changed her clothes and set off for the royal castle. All the guests at the ball were astounded at her beauty, and even the stepmother and the wicked sisters could scarcely take their envious eyes off her. Whoever would have thought that this beautiful princess could be

their poor Cinderella? As for the prince, he would dance with no other the whole evening. But as midnight approached, Cinderella slipped from his arms and hurried off home again. The prince galloped after her on his horse, but Cinderella was as swift as a bird, and when she reached the courtyard of her father's house she hid in the dovecote. Just then her father arrived home from his travels, and the prince told him of the beautiful girl who was hiding in his dovecote. "Could it be Cinderella?" her father thought to himself, and he threw the dovecote to the ground and chopped it to pieces with an axe. But Cinderella? She was already asleep among the ashes, smiling in her dreams. The prince returned to his castle empty-handed.

## 12 APRIL

# Cinderella

The next day the hazel bush gave Cinderella an even lovelier gown and a pair of silver slippers, and again the prince danced away the whole evening with her. Towards midnight she slipped away again, and this time she hid in the crown of an old pear tree. But before the prince could climb up after her she jumped down and curled up among the cinders.

On the third evening the prince had the palace

73

steps spread with gum, and when Cinderella, this time in golden slippers, again ran away from him, one of the slippers remained stuck to the steps. The prince picked it up, and at once made straight for Cinderella's house. He bowed to the wicked stepsisters, and said, "Whichever of you the slipper fits, shall become my wife." Cinderella was nowhere to be seen. The two sisters tried every way they could think of to get the slipper on, but to no avail. Then the younger one, taking her mother's advice, chopped off one of her toes, and managed to get her foot inside. The prince would have taken her back to his castle with him, but at that moment a white dove appeared and began to coo:

*"Has not the bride a toe too few-oo-oo,*
*Who cut the foot to fit the shoe-oo-oo?"*

The prince had a look, and sent the cheating sister away in disgrace. Nor did the other stepsister come off any better when she sliced off a piece of her heel. She, too, was given away by the dove. Then Cinderella appeared, and asked to be allowed to try on the shoe, and to the wonder of all those present it fitted like a glove. The prince took a good look at the ragged girl, and recognized his lovely dancing partner. "She is the one I shall marry, and no other!" he cried, and he took the smiling Cinderella off to his royal palace.

## 13 APRIL

# The Magic Merry-Go-Round

Once upon a time there was a little boy who had a kitten he loved more than anything in the world. But one day the kitten wandered off somewhere and did not come back again. The little boy was heartbroken. He cried, and cried, and could not be comforted. Some time later an old man with a merry-go-round came to the village, ringing a silver bell and calling out: "Come and take your seats! My magic merry-go-round will take you wherever you please!" The children had lots of wishes, one of them wanting to go to America, another to a gingerbread cottage; but our little boy wanted only to go to his little lost kitten. No sooner had he wished, than the wooden horse he was sitting on galloped away with him. Before very long, they arrived in a strange land. There were many people and animals there, but they all looked like shadows. Suddenly, along came the little kitten. "Where am I?" asked the boy in wonder. "In the land of memories," replied the kitten in a human voice. "All those who are sadly missed in the world come here. But they may live only so long as someone remembers them." The boy would have taken his kitten home with him, but the kitten told him, "I cannot go with you. But if you call my name before you go to sleep, I shall come to you in your dreams." The boy played with her for a while, then he jumped back on the merry-go-round horse, and before he knew it he was standing on the village green. Strange to say, the magic

merry-go-round had disappeared from sight. When the boy told his mother of his journey, she did not believe him. But when he called the kitten's name before he went to sleep, she came to him in his dreams. And he never forgot her.

## 14 APRIL

# The Tale of the Wicked Goat

In a little painted cottage lived a kind old woman. One day a wicked goat came along and begged to be allowed to warm herself in front of the fire. But as soon as the old woman let her in the goat attacked her with her horns and drove her out of the little house. In tears, the old woman turned to the brave donkey for help. He rapped on the door with his hooves, and called out, "Open up, you stupid goat, or I shall trample you underfoot!" The goat stuck her head out of the door and butted the donkey so hard his bones rattled. The unhappy woman appealed to the bear, but he came off no better. To this day the forest spiders are busy mending his fur. Now the old woman did not know what to do. She wept and wandered about, and came across a little hedgehog. "Dry your tears, old woman," said

# The Old Flower-Seller

In a far-off kingdom, long ago, ruled a foolish and capricious king. One day he made a law that all his people must be happy. It was forbidden for anyone to cry. From then on everyone had to smile, even if there was nothing to smile about at all, and if anyone was sad, he had to hide away in a corner somewhere until his tears were dry. But the more people smiled, the sadder their hearts became, and the saddest of all was the king. One day an old flower-seller set up her stall beneath the palace windows. On it were the most beautiful of flowers, but all of them sad and drooping. "Why are those flowers not smiling?" roared the king from one of the

the hedgehog, "I shall see to the goat!" He knocked gently at the cottage door, and rolled up into a ball. When the goat charged at him she pricked herself so cruelly on his sharp spines that tears came to her eyes. Bleating with pain, she took to her heels. Overjoyed, the old woman moved back into her cottage, and she gave the bold hedgehog a bowlful of apples as a reward.

windows. "Do you not know that all creatures in my kingdom must be happy?" The old woman shook her white head. "Happiness is not made by royal decree, my lord! Whoever wishes to know true joy must be able to cure a sad heart with tears. My flowers languish because they lack the very thing you have forbidden, human tears." Just then one of the flower-buds began to sing. It sang so sweetly and plaintively that tears came to the foolish sovereign's eyes, and when his subjects saw this, they, too, began to cry. All at once they could feel their tears washing a heavy burden from their hearts, and soon their faces broke into the first real smiles they had smiled for years. All the flowers opened out in wondrous beauty, but the wise old woman had vanished like a summer breeze.

## 16 APRIL

# King Wren

Long, long ago, everything on earth could speak, and every sound had a meaning. So when the blacksmith brought his great hammer down on the anvil, the hammer would call out over and over again, "Stand! Stand! Stand!" and the anvil would reply, "Swing! Swing! Swing!" The carpenter's saw would exhort its master, "Rip—through, rip—through!" And as the mill-wheel began to turn it would boast, "Forty sacks a day, forty sacks a day!" In those days the birds, too, had their own language, and everyone understood them well. At that time the birds decided to choose a king from their number. From field and forest alike, all feathered creatures came flying to the meeting: the eagle and the finch,

the owl and the crow, the sparrow and the lark, the cuckoo and the hoopoe, and one tiny bird who did not even have a name. Only the lapwing was not too happy with the idea of having a king, and flew off in the opposite direction in search of peace and quiet. "We'll see, we'll see," she called, disdainfully, finding herself a lonely spot in the marshes, away from them all. Meanwhile, the birds warbled and chirped and debated, until they decided that whichever of them could fly the highest should become their king. The hen was somewhat hard of hearing, and kept asking the cock: "What? What? What, Co-Co-Cock?"—"What to do, to do," the cock explained, and told her how the matter was to be decided. "Hurrah! Hurrah! Hurrah!" exclaimed the crow, who couldn't wait for the fun to begin.

## 17 APRIL

# King Wren

Early the next morning, a flock of birds like a great black cloud rose slowly up to the sky. Each tried his utmost to win the crown, but soon one after the other fell back, exhausted, until at last the eagle soared high above them all. "You shall be our king," the others called to him, "for none has flown higher than you."—"Only I," piped a thin little voice, and there above the eagle circled the little bird without a name. The cunning creature had hidden among the eagle's feathers and ridden high above the clouds. Now he flew on up towards the sun, where not even the eagle could catch up with him. "Not fair!" screeched the other birds, angrily, and decided to have a new contest, in which the winner should be the one who went deepest into the ground. But the clever little bird found a mousehole, and called out from inside: "I win, I win, I win!"—"A mite like him king?" chirped the other birds in disgust, and they resolved that they would sooner starve him to death. So that he might not escape, they set the owl to watch over the mousehole through the night. The owl grew sleepy. First one eye winked shut, then the other, then both closed together and, hrrr! the little bird was gone. Since then the owl dare not show his face in the daytime, for fear of being set upon by the other birds. And to this day the little bird hides away in briar and hedgerows. His name is the wren—or, as some people call him, the hedge-king.

little wren," the wolf told him. "He claims to be the king of the birds, and so some call him the hedge-king." The bear was avid with curiosity to know what the palace of a bird-king might be like. So they waited awhile, until Their Majesties the king and queen were pleased to fly off in search of food, and then the bear peered gingerly into the wren's nest. It was full of cheeping youngsters. "What sort of a royal palace is this?" growled the bear. "It is more like a beggar's palace! Your nest is a disgrace!" What a stir he caused! The baby wrens set up such a racket that the bear and the wolf ran off in dismay. The moment the father wren returned to the nest, his children twittered to him excitedly about how the bear had slighted the honour of his royal house. "Just you wait and see, Bruno!" said the wren, angrily, and right away he flew off to the bear's den and declared outright war, to begin the very next day.

18 APRIL

# King Wren and the Bear

One day, the bear and the wolf were walking through the forest. "Who is it that sings so sweetly?" asked the bear in wonder. "Why, the

19 APRIL

# King Wren and the Bear

The bear wasted no time, and no sooner had dawn broken, than he summoned all four-legged creatures to a council of war.

Meanwhile the wren had called to arms everyone that flies in the air, even the flies, the wasps and the mosquitoes. One of the mosquitoes flew off at once to spy on the enemy. He settled beneath a leaf on a nearby tree, and heard the animals choose the most cunning of all the foxes to be their general. "Very well," the fox agreed, "I shall lead you into battle. But first we must decide on a signal. I have a fine, thick tail. If I hold it proudly aloft, charge and have at the foe! But the moment I hang my tail, flee for all you are worth!" The mosquito hurried back to report all this to the wren. The moment the armies drew up for battle, the clever wren dispatched a hornet to sting the fox just below his tail. The fox yelled with pain and tucked his tail between his legs. As soon as the other animals saw this, they took to their heels and scattered throughout the forest. Thus it was that the wren defeated the bear in war. Then one little warrior bird perched on the bear's head and led him by the ear to the wren's palace. There the mean old bear had to apologize to the young wrens and beg their forgiveness, and even dance for them. They laughed and laughed!

## 20 APRIL

# The Dragon Band

A ten-headed dragon had moved into the kingdom. "Confound the beast, and damn his twenty eyes!" raged the king. "Now I suppose he'll go and ask for my daughters for his wives!" And he was quite right. He sat on his throne and began to cry. Just then the royal bandleader, Señor Tarara, came shuffling up.

"Your Majesty," he said, waving his arms in distress, "all the royal bandsmen have left the kingdom, because, if you please, Their Highnesses your daughters will insist on pulling the royal cats' tails, and the cats, if it please Your Majesty, make a noise no musician can put up with!"—"Señor Tarara, how can you speak to me of cats' tails, when a ten-headed dragon has taken up residence in my kingdom? Have a heart!" "A dragon?" exclaimed the bandleader. "A ten-headed one? What a piece of luck!" And Señor Tarara loaded all the instruments on a cart and set off for the dragon's lair. "Here you are," he said to the dragon. "Here's the drum, here's the bass, there you have the clarinet, the tuba and the piccolo; and now, play, my ten-headed friend!" And the bandmaster raised his baton, which, as everyone knows, is magic; whoever it is waved at must play to the bandleader's time. The dragon did play—like a whole band. And all the people danced, even the king himself. Unless they have stopped, they are dancing there to this day.

## 21 APRIL

# The Grain of Millet

Once upon a time there was a poor boy whose parents died, leaving him only a single grain of millet. Taking it, he set out into the world. Towards evening, he knocked at the

door of a peasant's cottage to ask for a bed for the night. Before going to sleep, he laid his grain of millet down in the porch, saying, "It is all I have in the world; I pray no one may steal it!"—"You may sleep soundly, my boy, for I shall not rob you," the peasant assured him. But early the next morning the cock awoke and pecked up the millet. "My cock has eaten your grain of millet," said the peasant. "You must take the cock instead." The boy thanked him, and went his way. That evening he asked another peasant for a roof over his head for the night. He was afraid for the cock, but the peasant calmed his fears. "You may sleep soundly," he said. "I shall not rob you." But in the morning the peasant's pig bit the cock in the throat. "I'll tell you what," said the peasant. "Take my pig instead of your cock." The boy was pleased. He tied a piece of string round the pig's neck, and went on. That night he slept in another farmer's cottage, but there a cow gored his pig to death. "Take the cow instead," said the farmer. The boy thought himself lucky, but in another village a stallion kicked his cow to death. Its owner was generous. "Take the horse for your cow," he said. This time the lucky lad swung himself into the saddle and made straight for a glass mountain to free a beautiful princess. And so it was that the poor boy became a king. Don't you think he was lucky? As you see, a little grain of millet may in fact be a great fortune!

## 22 APRIL

# The Poor Country Boy and the Cat

In a deserted mill lived an old cat, who thought she was mistress there. One day a country lad wandered up to the mill. The cat arched her back and hissed: "Go away, this is my mill!" The boy looked her up and down, and said: "Pussycat dear, what use to you is a mill? Come, let us exchange our worldly goods! I shall give you my magic spectacles. Whatever you look at, they make it twice as

big." The cat tried on the glasses and—indeed it was so! A little mouse which ran by was twice its size. "Very well," said the cat. "If you give me your bundle of oatcakes as well, then you may have the mill." The lad agreed, and the cat took the glasses and the bundle and set out into the world. After a while she met a wolf. "I shall eat you up!" he cried, but the cat was not afraid. "Take a good look at me first!" she said, putting the glasses on his nose. The wolf took one look and ran off in terror, his tail between his legs. Never before had he seen such a huge cat! The cat just managed to take the glasses back again. Now she really puffed herself up with pride. "I am the strongest creature in the world," she sang, and she went back to the mill and told the country lad to give it back to her, or she would swallow him up. "Just take a good look at me!" she mewed, boldly, setting the glasses on the lad's nose. The boy smiled contentedly and gave the cat a good clout. "That is for your foolishness and vanity," he said. And so the proud cat lost everything she had.

## 23 APRIL

# Little Violet and the Midnight Flowers

In a forest full of violets, on the bank of a violet-covered hillside, was a little cottage, and in that little cottage lived a woodcutter and his wife. They wanted nothing more in the world than a little baby boy or girl, but none was born to them. Sometimes it made them very sad indeed. Then, one day, there was a gentle knocking on the door, and a little girl in a dress made of leaves walked in. She wore a garland of violets in her hair, and when she stood on tiptoe she was no taller than the flame of a taper. "I am Little Violet, maid of the meadows," she said, with a bow. "My queen has sent me to you, so you can bring me up as your child. You need not feed me; it is enough if you water me sometimes." The woodcutter and his wife were overjoyed, and

they watered the meadow maid so generously that she soon grew into a fine little girl. How happy they were in the little cottage! But autumn came, then winter, and the flower-maid fell ill. They gave her herbs, and they gave her spices; they coaxed her and they stroked her, but all to no avail. One day she said to them sadly, "My sisters in the meadows have long since dropped their petals. I pine for them, and I shall surely die." But one night at midnight Jack Frost went by the little cottage. He heard weeping from within, so he breathed on the window and drew his lovely midnight flowers there. The moment Little Violet saw them the next morning, she began to smile, and soon she felt much better. The icy flowers brought her joy right through until springtime. One day they disappeared, but by then the first little snowdrops were pushing up through the snow, and Little Violet was quite well again. Since then she has not been afraid of winter; she knows she will not be the only flower left, even when her sisters have finished blooming.

## 24 APRIL

# The Bird That Wanted to be King

In a bird-catcher's garden, an empty cage hung from the branch of a tree. It was all of gold, and the door hung open. On the bottom

of the cage stood a trough full of food, and above it hung a perch, also of pure gold. Two birds came flying by. One of them was called Proudfeather, the other one Wingloose. Proudfeather saw the cage first and twittered, "See! A golden palace! And what rich foods are on the table! And look at that golden throne! They are surely all waiting for a king. I shall fly inside and hold sway from my golden palace." Wingloose warned him, "Do not be tempted by luxury; for us birds the best thing is a nest of feathers and twigs, freedom, and the blue sky above our heads!" But Proudfeather would not listen; he flew into the cage, and straight away the bird-catcher slammed the door shut. Ever since that day Proudfeather has sat upon his perch like a golden throne cheeping mournfully: "I am king! I am king!" and gazing longingly at his brothers as they fly free.

## 25 APRIL

# His Majesty the Donkey

Long, long ago, the animals lived together in peace and contentment. One day the old king of the lions died, and the lions held a council to decide on a successor. Quite by chance an old donkey came wandering into their group. "Why should you choose a king from your number?" he asked. "You are all the same, with nothing to mark you one from the other. What sort of a ruler is he who is not distinguished from his subjects by his appearance and his great beauty? Look at me, bold lions! I have hooves on my feet and an

ass's ears on my head. How many of you have ass's ears? Take my advice, make me your king!" The lions put their heads together and in the end they decided the donkey might be right. So they elected him king. No sooner had he sat down on his throne, than he began to make laws. But they were donkey laws. He decreed that the lions should eat grass and thistles, bray, and, all in all, behave like donkeys. But one day a young lion the donkey had ordered to bray lost his temper. "My tongue is that of the lions; my honour is a lion's honour, and lion's blood flows in my veins, foolish donkey!" he cried, and choked the donkey to death. Since then the lions eat the flesh of other animals, so that no one may ever rule over them again.

## 26 APRIL

## The Blue Lamp

There was once a soldier who served his king faithfully. But when the war was over, the king sent him home again without so much as a word of thanks. What could the soldier do? His pockets were empty, his stomach even emptier, so he set out into the world. He walked until he came to the cottage of an old witch. The soldier was not afraid, and he asked her for something to eat and a roof over his head for the night. "Even a wandering soldier must earn his keep," the old witch croaked. "Dig my garden and chop my firewood!" The soldier did so for two days. When he had finished, the old woman told him, "You may stay here another night if you bring me back my lamp from the bottom of the old well behind the cottage. It burns with a blue flame which never goes out."—"Why not?" the soldier replied, and in the morning, when he had slept well, the witch threw a rope down into the well, and the soldier climbed down and took the lamp from the bottom. Then he gave a signal to the hag to haul him up again. When he was almost out of the well, the old woman told him to pass the lamp out to her. But the soldier felt that something evil was afoot, and he refused. The witch flew into a rage, and let the soldier fall back into the well.

## 27 APRIL

# The Blue Lamp

When the soldier fell to the bottom of the well, he was unhurt. Strange to tell, the blue flame of the lamp had not even gone out. But to what avail? The soldier would surely never get out alive. As he sat and considered his fate, it occurred to him that he could have a last smoke before he died. He took hold of the lamp and lit his pipe, but he had scarcely sent the first puff of smoke floating up the well shaft when, from out of nowhere, he saw standing in front of him a strange, grubby little imp. "What is your command?" he asked, with a bow. "I must do all that you ask of me."— "In that case," said the soldier, "get me out of this well, then find me some money!" No sooner had he said this, than he found himself outside again. Then the little man showed him

the treasures the old hag had hidden around her cottage. The soldier wasted no time in filling his pack with gold pieces, but as he was doing so the witch came riding up on a black cat. The soldier ordered the imp to bind her and carry her off to court. Before you could count to five, the little man was off, with the witch bound hand and foot. Before long he returned. "I have done as you ordered. The old hag already hangs from the gallows," he said. The soldier told him he had done well, and for the moment let him go.

## 28 APRIL

# The Blue Lamp

Now the poor soldier lived like a lord. He had more money than he had ever dreamed of. He had fine suits of clothes made, and he moved into the best inn he could find and told the innkeeper to spare no expense. When he had eaten and drunk his fill, he lit his pipe with the blue lamp and called up the magic imp. "What is your wish?" the little man asked. "Late at night, when the king's daughter is asleep, go to her bed and bring her to me. She shall work for me like a servant-girl, for her father never rewarded me for my faithful service!" And so it was. At midnight the door flew open, and the little imp entered, carrying the sleeping princess. "Hey!" shouted the soldier. "Take the broom like a good girl, and sweep and scrub the floor!" The sleeping princess did as she was told. Then she had to pull off his boots, do the polishing, wash his shirts and starch his collar. As soon as the cock crew, the little imp carried her back to the palace. "Oh, what a strange dream I have had," sighed the princess, when she woke up and she told the king how she had been obliged to serve a strange soldier in her sleep. The king looked at her hands, which were all dirty, and said to himself, "That was no dream." And he pondered what he should do about it.

# The Blue Lamp

That evening, as the princess went to bed, the king hung around her neck a bag with a hole in it, which he filled with peas. He supposed that the fallen peas would lead his soldiers to the bold fellow's house. But the little imp

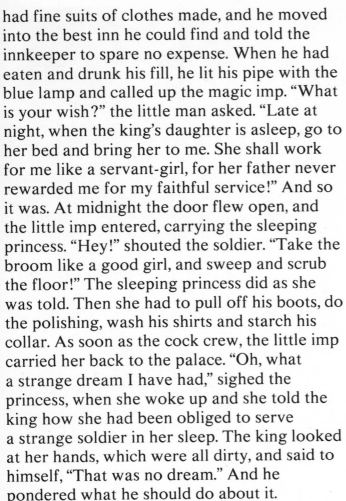

noticed the bag, and he scattered a whole sackful of peas around the streets. The next morning the princess was all aches and pains when she awoke, but the king's soldiers returned empty-handed. "The next time it happens," the king told his daughter, "you must kick one of your shoes under the rascal's bed." She did as she was told, and the next day the king ordered all the houses in the city to be searched. The soldiers found the shoe where the princess had left it. The poor soldier was thrown in gaol, and the royal judges sentenced him to death. As he stood beneath the gallows, he begged to be allowed to have a last smoke of his beloved pipe. The king graciously agreed, but no sooner had the soldier taken out the blue lamp and lit his pipe, than the little imp appeared with a cudgel and laid about the unjust judges. The king was so afraid that he pardoned the soldier and offered him his daughter as his wife. Nor did she regret it.

# Why Cats Catch Mice

The cat in the picture is just telling grandfather this cat fairy tale: Once upon a time, long, long ago, the king of the cats declared war on the king of the dogs. The war lasted a thousand and one years without either side winning it, so in the end they made peace. They drew up a solemn treaty on a piece of parchment, where it was written that cats and dogs would no longer squabble with each other; the cat king unsheathed his claws and scratched his signature, and the dog king cocked a leg and signed himself as dogs do, and that was it! The pact was sealed. And so that no one might steal that solemn treaty, they hid it in the attic in a bag of oats. But one day a wandering dog returned from his travels. He did not know that the cats and dogs had made peace, and he bared his teeth savagely at the first cat he set eyes on. "You fool, don't you know that we have signed a treaty of eternal peace?" hissed the cat in dismay. "Show me the treaty!" growled the dog. So the cat led him to the attic, but, alas! The mice had got into the sack of oats and chewed the treaty to pieces. "You liar, just you wait!" the dog barked angrily, and flew at the cat. Ever since then dogs have growled at cats because they consider them liars. And cats have caught mice—because it was the mice who tore up their peace treaty.

# MAY

## 1 MAY

### The Frog Czarevna

There was once a Czar who had three sons. One day he called them to him and said, "On the wall of the armoury hang an old musket, a crossbow and a longbow. Choose each of you his weapon from these, and shoot once in any direction you please. The girl at whose feet your shot shall fall, shall be your wife. That is my will." The czarevitches promised to obey. The eldest loaded a copper ball into the musket and fired; his shot fell at the feet of a peasant's daughter. Then it was the turn of the middle son. He took the crossbow and fired a silver bolt, which landed in front of the beautiful daughter of a rich duke as she sat in her father's castle. The czar was pleased with the match. Then the youngest of the brothers took the longbow and drew it. His golden arrow shone like a streak of lightning as it whistled through the air, and disappeared over the horizon. The czarevitch saddled his horse and went to find it. He rode and rode, until at last he came to a bottomless marsh. There, beneath a burdock leaf, sat an ugly frog, holding his golden arrow in her mouth. Czarevitch Ivan was dismayed, and turned to

run away, but the frog croaked out, "Will you go against your father's will, czarevitch?" Ivan was ashamed, so he wrapped the frog in a cambric scarf, and set off home again.

## 2 MAY

### The Frog Czarevna

How they all laughed when czarevitch Ivan returned to the palace with his frog bride. "Throw the foul creature away!" they shouted at him. At this the poor frog began to cry. When the czarevitch saw this, his heart was moved to pity. "The word of a czar's son shall not be broken!" he proclaimed, and led the frog straight off to the altar. By and by the Czar called his sons to him again and said: "I wish to know how my daughters-in-law keep house. Let each of them bake me a loaf of white bread by morning!" Czarevitch Ivan sadly gave the frog the news, but she only smiled and said, "Do not worry; tomorrow is another day." And she sang him to sleep with a sweet lullaby. Then she filled the

kneading-trough with flour, poured on water from a bucket, and poured the mixture into the hearth. Through a crack in the door a servant-girl sent by the elder brothers' wives was watching to see how the frog mixed the dough, and she saw everything. When the girl told them what she had seen, they did the same as the frog, but their dough burnt to a cinder, blacker than a hussar's boot. Meanwhile the frog took a big drum and beat it, and from all the puddles far and wide green frogs came hopping along and set to work. In a little while they had baked a loaf whiter than snow.

## 3 MAY

# The Frog Czarevna

The old czar praised the frog's bread, but the blackened cinders that the others brought he threw to the dogs in a rage. Then he told his sons that their wives must weave him silk carpets by the next day. The frog only smiled at the czar's order, cut up some silk thread and threw it out of the window into the field. When the other wives heard of this from the servant-girl, they tried to copy her, but the wind blew the silk about, mixing it with straw and brambles, so that when the women finally

got down to weaving, their carpets were a sorry sight! But the carpet which the frogs had woven in the night shone with pearls and precious stones like the sun on a rippling lake. The czar could not take his eyes off it. Then he said: "Tomorrow I shall give a grand banquet. I wish my sons' wives to dance with my guests there." When the youngest czarevitch heard these words, he trudged off sadly to tell his frog. "Do not be sad, czarevitch Ivan!" she comforted him. "Go tomorrow to the czar's palace, and wait for me at the oak table." The czarevitch did as she asked. Scarcely had he taken his place at the table, when a golden coach was heard to draw up in the courtyard, and out of it stepped a young girl so beautiful that all the guests gazed at her in wonder. "I am the wife of czarevitch Ivan," she proclaimed, in a clear voice; and she took to the floor and danced.

## 4 MAY

# The Frog Czarevna

All were filled with joy, and drank to the czarevna's health; but czarevitch Ivan crept into her chamber unseen and burnt the unsightly frog skin which was lying on her bed. At once there was a clap of thunder, and the golden coach again drew up in the courtyard. "Alas, Ivan!" he heard her call. "If only you had waited till morning, I should have been yours forever. But now I must return to the palace of the evil magician,

Thainan the Immortal!" And the coach was gone. The unfortunate czarevitch leapt on his horse and galloped after it. He reached a dark forest, where a strange cottage was turning round and round on a moth's leg. Looking out of the window was the old witch, Yagga the Hag, an ugly bag of bones. "Feed my servants, the bear, the eagle and the pike," she whined. Czarevitch Ivan tore a piece of meat from his own leg and threw it to the animals. "You have acted wisely," said the hag, "and I shall reward you. Not far from here is the castle of Thainan the Immortal. Before it stands a tall oak tree. On the tree is a golden casket; in the casket is a golden duck, and in the duck a golden egg. In the egg a rusty needle is hidden. If you break off the point of the needle, the wizard will die, and you will win back your wife for ever." The czarevitch rode off in the direction the witch had shown him, and soon he came to the tall oak tree. Out of nowhere a huge bear appeared and tore up the tree by its roots. A golden casket crashed to the ground and burst open. Out flew a golden duck. Suddenly a fierce eagle plunged down from the sky and pounced on the duck; but the duck dropped the golden egg into a deep lake. Then a pike thrust its head out of the water and gave the egg to the czarevitch. Without delay he broke it open, took out the rusty needle which lay inside, and broke off its point. There was a sudden tremendous thunderclap; the castle of Thainan the Immortal crashed to the ground and there, in front of the czarevitch, stood his beautiful wife. They returned together to his father's palace, where they live happily to this day.

# 5 MAY

## The Three Recruits and the Giant

Once upon a time there were three young fellows who were not too fond of work. "Let us go and join the army," said the oldest of them one day. So they lined up like soldiers and off they marched. Left, right, left, right!

Soon they were in the deep forest. They came to the bank of a great lake. In the middle of the lake was an island, on the island a huge house, and from the window of the house an enormous giant looked out. The men saluted him like real troopers, and marched on. On the edge of the forest they found some soldiers encamped. The three heroes strutted right up to the captain and offered their services. The captain twirled his moustache, and said: "He who would be a soldier must know no fear. Whichever of you brings me the giant's mirror shall earn his soldier's tunic." The smallest of the three volunteered, turned about, and marched off to the giant's house. At the bank of the lake he made himself a boat, and when he reached the island he slipped quietly into the house. He hid in a stove until nightfall, and when the giant was sound asleep he took up the mirror and hurried back to the camp. The captain praised him highly and dressed him in a soldier's tunic.

# The Three Recruits and the Giant

The next day the second young fellow went to the captain for his orders. He was told to steal the giant's bedsheet. He, like the first, hid in the stove until night-time. Then he crept up to the giant's bed and pulled at the sheet. He pulled, and pulled, but he could not pull the sheet away. On it, beside the giant, lay two huge lumps of amber. Only when the young man laid these on the floor was he able to take the sheet. The captain could hardly believe his eyes, and he made the new recruit a sergeant-at-arms. Now it was the turn of the third hero. "If you go to the giant's house and bring me back the giant himself, then you will become captain of the troop," he was told, and in addition the captain promised him a house with eight parlours and eight tables. The lad saluted, and off he went, left, right, left, right, to the giant's house. He took with him a bugle. When he reached the island, he saw the giant sitting on a rock and bemoaning the fact that someone had stolen his mirror and his bedsheet. The young hero blew on the bugle and called out: "Do you hear, giant? The day of judgement is at hand. I am come to make you a coffin, so that you may have somewhere to lay your bones." The giant was dismayed, and agreed at once. He himself helped the lad fell a linden tree and make the coffin. When it was ready, the young man told the giant: "Try the coffin for size!" The stupid giant lay down inside the coffin, and in a flash the young man had shut the lid and nailed it down. He dragged the coffin with the giant inside back to the captain. "Upon my soul, I have never seen such courage!" said the captain, and fulfilled his promise.

# The Brave Little Tin Soldier

One little boy got a box of tin soldiers for his birthday. There were twenty-five of them, almost all as like as two pins. Indeed, they

were all brothers, for they had been cast from the same tin spoon. Only one of them was not quite like the rest; he had only one leg, for he had been the last to be made, and there was not quite enough tin left. The little boy played with the soldiers, placing them on the table and giving them orders like the king himself. There were lots of other toys on the table, but the most beautiful of all was a paper castle. In front of it there were little paper trees, and a crystal mirror that was supposed to look like a little lake shone all around. There were wax swans swimming on the lake, their white forms reflected in it. But loveliest of all was a little paper doll which stood in the middle of the castle gateway. She looked like a dancer. Her arms were stretched over her head, and she had one leg kicked so high that the little tin soldier thought that she, too, had only one leg. "She would be the wife for me," he thought to himself. "But she is far too noble—she lives in a castle, not in a poor paper box," he sighed, and he lay down behind the snuff-box, and dreamed of the little paper dancer.

## 8 MAY

## The Brave Little Tin Soldier

When evening came, the other tin soldiers went back to their box, and the people in the

house went to bed. The only ones who did not move were the one-legged soldier and the little dancer. The clock struck midnight, and the lid of the snuff-box suddenly flew open. Out of it peeped a little imp. He saw how the tin soldier was gazing lovingly at the paper dancer, and began to make fun of him. "Mind you don't stare your eyes out, tin soldier!" he said. But the soldier pretended not to hear. "Just wait till morning, my proud fellow, and you'll get what you deserve!" threatened the imp. Nor was it an idle threat. Early next morning the children placed the one-legged soldier on the window-sill. Whether it was caused by the little imp or the wind, no one will ever know, but suddenly the window swung to, and the little soldier fell headlong into the street below. It was a terrible fall, and his cap and bayonet were thrust right into the ground. He wanted to cry and call for help, but since he was a soldier, he did not make a sound. It began to rain, until streams of water were running down the street. Then two little boys came along, and they picked up the tin soldier and put him in a paper boat in the gutter. Oh! What a voyage that was. The little boat pitched and rolled as though it were on the open sea, but the soldier stood bravely on his one leg, and held on to his rifle more firmly.

## 9 MAY

## The Brave Little Tin Soldier

On and on the little soldier sailed, until suddenly his boat plunged into a long, dark tunnel. A large rat which lived nearby came running up, bared its teeth and called out, "Have you paid·the toll for passing under my bridge?" The tin soldier knew nothing about tolls or bridges, but he thought that a horrible rat had no right to tell him what to do. He gripped his rifle even more firmly, and stood on his one leg without batting an eyelid, for a soldier must be brave, however afraid he feels. "Catch him! Catch him!" squealed the rat, but the current grew stronger, and shot

# The Brave Little Tin Soldier

It was even darker in the fish's stomach than it had been in the rat's tunnel. But the soldier lay with his rifle in his hand and did not move a muscle. Suddenly, there was a blinding light above him, and a voice said: "Look at that! A tin soldier." For the fish had been caught, taken to the kitchen, and cut open with the cook's sharp knife. Believe it or not, for

the little boat like an arrow out into the daylight again. The little soldier was beginning to rejoice at his deliverance when all of a sudden the boat spun around beneath him, dipped steeply, and was whirled into a huge waterfall. "This is all the little imp's doing," the soldier thought to himself, but he stood firm on his one leg, even though his boat was sinking deeper and deeper beneath him. "What can my dear paper dancer be doing?" he wondered. Then the paper boat burst apart, and the soldier was hurled into the raging flood. In a flash he was swallowed by a large fish.

stranger things happen it this world, the cook picked the soldier up in her fingertips, and put him down in the room where he used to stand. There were the same toys, and the same children, and even the same castle with the paper dancer. She was still dancing on one leg, with the other held high in the air, and she smiled at the little tin soldier. Suddenly, who knows why, one of the little boys picked up the soldier and threw him into the fire. The wicked little imp must have whispered in his ear. The soldier felt a terrible heat; his paint cracked and his tin body began to melt like wax. He knew it was the end of him, but he went on holding his rifle bravely, looking sadly at the paper dancer. At that moment a draught caught her up, and the paper doll flew like a butterfly into the fire beside the tin soldier. She burst into flames and was burnt up. And when the servant came the next morning to clear the ashes, all that remained of the brave soldier was a little tin heart. All that was left of the little dancer was her lovely silver star; but she was burnt to a black cinder.

11 MAY

## The Hunter and the Swan Maiden

Once upon a time there was a young hunter. One day, his wanderings in search of game brought him to the banks of an unknown lake. As he gazed across it, three snow-white swans came flying down to alight on the shore; they shed their feathers, and there before the astounded young man stood three lovely maidens. With a whooping sound they disappeared into the waves. Without hesitation, the young man picked up the feathers of the youngest and most beautiful of the maidens, and hid them beneath his coat. When the maidens had swum to their hearts' content, they wanted to change back into swans; but the youngest could not find her feathers, and began to cry. The young hunter came out of hiding and began to comfort her.

"Do not cry, beautiful maiden; I have taken a liking to you, and want you to be my wife. Come home to our cottage with me." When he had spoken these words, he led the swan-girl off to his mother's cottage, hid the swan's feathers in a chest, and put the chest away in the attic. So the swan maiden had to stay with the hunter. She liked him, too, and it was not long before a wedding was being prepared. Guests came from all over the land, and all the birds of the forest came to sing for the swan-bride. Shortly after the wedding, the young wife was looking for something in the attic, when she came across the chest with her swan-feathers. She put them on and soared up into the sky, calling down to her husband, "If you want to see me again, you must find me inside the glass mountain, for I am an enchanted princess, and to that mountain I must return!" And with that she was gone.

12 MAY

## The Hunter and the Swan Maiden

There was no holding the unhappy hunter. He packed up his bundle and set off to look for his lost swan wife. After journeying for many days he came to a great wilderness, where three brothers lived as hermits, far away from each other. The hunter came to the dwelling of the first old man, and begged him to tell him how to get to the glass mountain. "Never in my life have I heard of a glass mountain," the hermit told him. "But if you ask my elder brother, he may be able to tell you more." And he gave the traveller a piece of a gold coin. The second brother knew no more than the first, and he sent the hunter on to the oldest of the three, giving him a piece of gold like the first, and telling him to put the two together when he felt tired. The hunter wandered endlessly through the vast desert, and whenever his strength began to fail he placed the two pieces of gold together, and soon felt strong again. One day he came across the carcase of an ox in the middle of a thicket. A lion, a hyena, an eagle and an ant were quarrelling over how they should divide up their spoil. "Fools! To argue so," the hunter chided them. "Hyena, you shall take the bones and the fat. Eagle, you shall have the offal, since you like to rummage among your food. The lion has powerful jaws, so he shall have the meat. And as the ant would like to live in his larder, he shall have the head!" The animals put their heads together and conferred.

## 13 MAY

# The Hunter and the Swan Maiden

When the animals had considered the hunter's words carefully, they said to him, "We are all satisfied with your suggestion, and shall reward you well." The lion and the hyena each gave the hunter a hair from his coat. The eagle gave him a feather from his wing, and the ant his torn-off leg. "Whenever you rub our gifts in your palm, you'll turn into one of the

95

animals yourself," the lion told him. The hunter thanked them, and went his way. After many more days he reached the hovel of the oldest of the hermits. He showed the old man the pieces of gold, and the hermit was filled with joy. "I am happy that my brothers are still alive," he said. "I shall be glad to help you in return for your good news." And he showed the hunter the way to the enchanted glass mountain. The young man thanked him and set off once more. This time he had not travelled far when he saw, in the far distance, a shining peak. He rubbed the eagle's feather in his palm, whereupon he instantly turned into an eagle and flew high into the clouds. In the glass at the mountain top he spied a tiny hole. Rubbing the ant's leg in his palm, he turned into an ant and crawled inside the mountain. Everything there was made of glass, even the people. By the window, like a transparent statue, stood the king, with two glass daughters at his sides. But his youngest daughter, the hunter's wife, sat in another chamber on a glass throne. The ant settled down in her glass hair. He began to feel sleepy.

# 14 MAY

# The Hunter and the Swan Maiden

As soon as the little ant woke up, he heard sad voices. "Father, who will set us free?" sighed the glass princesses. The king shook his head sadly. "If you had not allowed yourself to be caught," he said to his youngest daughter, "we should long since have been released from the spell. As it is, we must wait until someone we cannot see enters the glass mountain and takes my advice. Then he must slay the twelve-headed dragon. From the last of the dragon's heads a hare will spring. If the hare is slain, a dove will fly out of it. In the dove's head is a stone. Our deliverer must throw the stone through a hole into the glass mountain." As soon as the ant had heard these words, he

crawled out of the mountain, changed back into an eagle, and flew off to the dragon's lair. There he changed into a terrible lion. Three days and three nights he struggled with the twelve-headed dragon, until at last he tore off the last of its heads. Out leapt a hare: the lion changed into a hyena and throttled it to death. From out of the hare's head flew a white dove. Now the hyena became an eagle, which caught the dove in its talons and tore the stone from its head. Then it flew back to the mountain and dropped the stone through the hole. There was a crash like thunder, and the glass mountain shattered, releasing the enchanted king and his daughters. The hunter and his wife were reunited joyfully, never again to part. And the old king? He settled down comfortably on his velvet throne. But do

you suppose he bothered to rule anybody?
Not a bit of it; he spent his days greedily
licking honey from a golden spoon!

## 15 MAY

# Which is the Strongest of All the Birds?

There was once a mother bird who had six
sons, all little brother birds. All of them would
shout at once, boasting that they were the
strongest birds in the world. One day their
mother saw a worm poking its head out of the
grass. She caught it in her beak and pulled,
and pulled, but she could not pull it out. "Wait,
mother, I'll help you," twittered her eldest son,
"for am I not the strongest bird in the world?"
They pulled, and pulled, but they could not
pull the worm out. Her second son came
flying up. "Wait, mother, I'll help you. I am
stronger than the strongest of my brothers,"
he boasted. They pulled, and pulled, but they
could not pull the worm out. The third, fourth
and fifth brothers all flew up, and they pulled,
and pulled, but they could not pull the worm
out. "What heroes you are," mocked the
youngest of the brothers. "You will see that
I am the strongest in the world." He stood at
the end of the line, and they all pulled, and
pulled, but they could not pull the worm out.
Then a little fly caught hold of the last bird's
tail. He was so small that they could not even
see him. He took hold of a feather, and they
all pulled and pulled, and pulled the worm out,
and fell back onto the ground. "I am the
strongest in the world!" shouted all the birds
at once. Do you think they were right?

## 16 MAY

# The Imp in the Box

In an old ring-box lived a wicked little magic
imp. He had an enchanted mirror which
swallowed up anyone he pointed it at, and
would not let them go. They became a little
glass picture. You would not believe how
many people and things the magic mirror had
imprisoned. There was a king with the whole
of his palace, a princess with a golden star on
her forehead, a phoenix, a blue parasol, and all
manner of other things. One day the ring-box
was found by a little glass doll from the
kingdom of glass. The moment she opened the
box, the wicked imp peeped out and pointed
the magic mirror at her. But since she was
made of glass, and was clear and quite
invisible, the mirror could not see her, and
could not swallow her up. "Oh, what beautiful
little glass pictures there are there!" she cried,
excitedly, as she looked into the mirror. And
she put her hand in and, one by one, drew
them all out to safety. The imp lost his temper,
and wanted to destroy the mirror. But when
he turned it round, the mirror swallowed him
up. He became a little glass picture. Now that

picture hangs in a glass palace in a certain fairytale kingdom. The ruler of the kingdom is the little glass doll. Why don't you go and see her sometime?

## 17 MAY

# The Bearskin

Back in the days when the rivers ran uphill and the rain fell from the earth to the sky, an old soldier was wandering about the world. At noon one day he was resting under an old oak tree and trying to recall what army rations tasted like. Suddenly there was a rustling in the branches, and an acorn came tumbling to the ground. No sooner had it landed, than a strange, strange little man leapt out of it. He had a short green coat and a hoof on one leg, and looked a little like a water sprite. "Afternoon; and who the devil might you be?" the soldier asked. "Might be, might not be, but the devil I am, in disguise," said the little fellow, gruffly. "My compliments," said the soldier, "and how might I be of service?" The devil grimaced as if he had bitten on an aching tooth. "Well," he said, "I really can't imagine what the likes of you might do for me. But I may be of use to you. First, though, you must show that you are not afraid. Take a look over your shoulder!" The soldier looked round, and what should he see! A huge bear was

lumbering toward him. Without hesitation he levelled his rifle and laid the creature to the ground with a single shot. "I see that you are no coward," said the demon. "Come to the oak again tomorrow, and we shall sign a devil's contract. Now I must go to hell."

## 18 MAY

# The Bearskin

The next day the soldier sat beneath the old oak tree and waited. Before long an acorn fell to the ground, and out crept the little green man. "Hear me well, old soldier," he said. "I shall give you my green jacket. Whenever you reach in the pocket, you will find a handful of gold pieces. In return you must wear the same clothes for a full seven years. You must not wash, shave, or cut your hair. And for a cloak you must wear the skin of the bear you shot yesterday. If you can do this for seven years, you'll be free. Otherwise I'll carry you off to hell." The soldier needed no second asking. He put on the green jacket, skinned the bear, and flung the skin across his shoulders. As soon as he put his hand in the pocket of the green jacket, he felt a pile of gold pieces there. "Now I shall have a fine time!" he hooted. And indeed he did. But not for ever. Before a year was out, he had changed beyond all recognition. Unwashed and unkempt, claws on his hands and feet like a wild animal—what a sight he was! Wherever he went, people ran away from him; children threw stones at him, and he had nowhere to lay his head. True, he had money to burn, but what use was it to him, when everyone shouted at him: "Be off with you, you old bearskin, don't you dare show your face here again!"

## 19 MAY

# The Bearskin

For more than two years the old soldier had roamed the world in his bearskin. Winter came and the frost bit, and the poor fellow knocked desperately at a cottage door. A peasant with tears in his eyes opened it; he was at the end of his tether. The soldier asked him for shelter. "Poor wretch," the peasant moaned. "What a refuge you have found! Here you will not get a bite to eat, for we are starving to death ourselves. The waters carried away our crops, and if I do not pay my master what I owe on the morrow, I shall be thrown in gaol. But if you will make your bed on the bare boards, you are welcome beneath our roof. Indeed, you seem still less fortunate than I." The soldier thanked him, and huddled in a corner of the parlour. When they arose in the morning, the soldier dipped his hand in the pocket of the devil's coat and strewed a pile of gold pieces in front of the peasant. "Go and pay your debts," he told him, "and you shall have enough for a good living besides!" The peasant could not believe his eyes. When he

had come to his senses, he said: "I thank you, kind sir! But I shall repay this debt. Take whichever of my three daughters you please to be your wife." And he led the soldier in his bearskin off to meet his daughters.

## 20 MAY

# The Bearskin

When the peasant's daughters set eyes on the beast in the bearskin, they almost fainted with horror. They did not want to hear of marrying him. But in the end the youngest of them took pity on him, and promised to be his bride. Then the soldier broke a golden ring in two and said: "There is time enough for marrying; I must first go out into the world again. Whoever brings you half of my ring four years from now, you shall take him as your husband." With these words he left them. He had a harder time of it than ever in the wide world, but finally the seven long years were up, and the soldier returned to the old oak tree. An acorn fell from the tree, and out jumped the little green man. "You have kept our bargain, soldier," he said. "Now I must fulfil one more wish for you." With a laugh the soldier told the devil to wash him, shave him, and to cut and comb his hair. What else could the little devil do? He set to work at once. And as soon as the soldier had again turned into a handsome young fellow, he set off for the home of his bride-to-be. On the way he got himself a fine suit of clothes, and he knocked at the peasant's door looking a fine gentleman. The moment he showed his loved one the ring, she threw herself in his arms—and they were married and lived happily ever after.

## 21 MAY

# The Forgetful Elephant

Deep inside the jungle lived a foolish elephant. He was so forgetful that he would forget to get up in the morning, and forget to go to bed at night; he didn't remember to wash himself, or when to eat his meals. The monkeys would laugh at him and shout: "Brother elephant, where have you left your head again?" The angry elephant would suck up a trunkful of water and spray the

mischievous monkeys from head to foot. The monkeys tried to think of a way to get their own back on him. One old monkey had a bright idea. "Brother elephant," he called out from the branches, "why not tie a knot in your trunk, so as to remember what not to forget?"—"A good idea," the elephant thought to himself, and he asked the monkey to do it for him. But no sooner was the knot tied, than the monkeys began to laugh at him again, and dropped coconuts on his head. "Why have you a knot in your trunk, brother elephant?" they shrieked. "I don't know," said the poor elephant, "I can't remember." And he began to cry noisily. In the end the monkeys took pity on him and untied his trunk. "But you must promise not to splash us with water," they told him. "Of course, of course, I promise," said the elephant, and he sucked up a trunkful of water and sprayed the monkeys until they nearly choked. You see, he really was a forgetful elephant: he had already forgotten his promise.

## 22 MAY

# The Two Fishermen

Long ago, in a poor hut by the sea shore, lived a fisherman. Though he cast his nets from morning till night, he was unable to catch anything. He almost died of hunger. One evening he was sitting on the shore, sadly pondering his fate, when he saw a flame shoot out of the water. "Might there not be some sunken treasure there?" he thought to himself. "But I want nothing to do with it; upon my faith, the devil's hand is in such a thing!" And he turned on his heels and walked quickly towards his hut. But a voice behind him said: "Do not go away, fisherman!" The young man turned round. A strange figure with long blue hair and wearing a tail-coat was stepping out from the sea. His arms were stretched out in front of him, as if he could not see where he was going. "Andrew," the stranger addressed the fisherman, "I know you are troubled by poverty and hunger. If you wish, I shall help you. Take my brass ring and come here again tomorrow at midnight. You will see a flame on the sea. Go straight to it. Beneath it you will find three upturned pots. Lift the middle one, and you will release the soul of a drowned man; but you must speak to no one on the way. You will see how your fortunes will change." But the fisherman thought that Lucifer himself was tempting him, and he rushed home to his hut.

## 23 MAY

## The Two Fishermen

No sooner had the fisherman reached his bed, than he became ill, and he was ill the whole year. He had to sell his boat and nets, and even his poor wooden hut. He was left with only a beggar's staff. Exactly a year later, on St. Andrew's eve, he was again sitting sadly by the shore, when a flame suddenly shot out from the waves. From out of the flame the strange man appeared again. "It is a year since we spoke together, Andrew," he smiled. "Will you not change your mind?" The fisherman, thinking that even hell could be no worse than his present plight, promised to return at midnight the next night to release the soul of one of the drowned. The stranger slipped a brass ring on his finger and disappeared into the sea. The next day at midnight the fisherman set off into the waves. Far off over the sea he saw a mysterious light, and he headed towards it. He thought he would have to swim, but the water came up no higher as he walked, and in a while, to his amazement, he came upon a beautiful meadow. There were mowers there, merrily scything the grass and singing with joy. The fisherman recognized people from the villages around his home who had been drowned at sea, but he did not stop to speak to them. Nor did he stop at a beautiful house from which a young girl was calling to him. Instead he hurried on to the upturned pots, and set free from the middle one the soul of a drowned man. At that moment all the mowers ran towards him, shouting and wailing. The fisherman thought his hour had come, and he fainted with terror. When he awoke, he was lying on the beach, his whole body aching and sore. To his astonishment he saw that he was covered in scales, and that the scales were of pure gold. From that moment he never knew want again.

### 24 MAY

## The Two Fishermen

The news of the sudden good fortune of fisherman Andrew soon spread up and down the whole coast. One of those who heard the tale was Peter the fisherman. He was a lazy, envious fellow, and to make matters worse he had a wicked, nagging wife. So he drank away what he earned down at the local tavern. One day his neighbour came rushing into the tavern to tell him his wife had drowned in an accident. "What God gave, he has taken unto his own," thought Peter. "But if golden scales were to grow on me, like on fisherman Andrew, I should have a merry time of it now, without my nagging wife." And towards evening he set off down to the sea to look for the mysterious flame. It was not long before a flame leapt up, and out of it stepped the curious stranger. "I, too, should like to free the soul of a drowned man," fisherman Peter grunted at him. The stranger threw a brass ring at his feet without a word, and disappeared into the waves. The next day at midnight, Peter set off into the waves. The sea parted in front of him, and before long he had reached the beautiful meadow, where the mowers reaped and sang merrily in the green grass. At the edge of the meadow stood a fine house. "That would be the place to live," thought Peter to himself, and he knocked at the door. Rat-a-tat-tat! Who do you suppose will come and open it?

### 25 MAY

## The Two Fishermen

As soon as the fisherman knocked, the door flew open, and there stood a giantess, grinning from ear to ear. "Good lady," stammered the fisherman, "do you not know where I might find three upturned pots?"—"Just you wait, I'll show you," shrieked the giantess. "Marry me"

102

you will not, but bang and make a racket, that's what you like to do!" And she chased after the fisherman, followed by the mowers, who came running as if summoned. The fisherman took to his heels. He ran like the wind; then, suddenly, he saw in front of him three upturned pots. Straight away he turned over the nearest of them, and at that moment it seemed as if the sky fell in on him. "This is the end of me," thought Peter to himself, and he fell into a dead faint. When he awoke, he was lying on the beach, aching all over. He felt his skin quickly, and what do you suppose? There were scales on his body, all right, but not of gold! They were quite ordinary fish scales. "Perhaps I shall have some gold pieces at home, at least," he thought, and set off for his cottage with tears in his eyes. He saw something shining from the window, and he thought it must surely be the gleam of gold. But when he reached his doorstep, what should he see but his nagging wife, waiting for him with her arms folded. You can imagine the welcome he got! He remembers it to this day.

## 26 MAY

# The Singing River

On the banks of a crystal river a young Indian maiden lived. She was called Morning Dew. When the sun rose in the morning, Morning Dew began to sing, and she sang so sweetly that every day the chief of all the gods would stop all life on earth for an instant to listen to her song. Since then there has always been a moment of sacred silence just before daybreak. Morning Dew loved the most courageous of all the Indian braves, and she had promised to become his squaw. But one day the young man took his canoe down the river and forgot to greet the powerful god of the waters. The river grew angry, overturned the canoe, and dragged the young brave to the bottom. There he turned into a rainbow trout. Morning Dew, in tears, begged the river to give her back her loved one, but the river just

flowed quietly on down to the distant Lake of Shadows, and the waves did not reply. So the maiden flung herself into the water, and tearfully begged the crystal waters to take her life. The spirits of the waters took pity on her for her grief, and changed her into a white waterfall. Every year a rainbow trout swims up to the waterfall, basks in its waters, and whispers with its eddies. Since then the crystal river has sung a song at daybreak. Its voice is like that of Morning Dew.

## 27 MAY

# The Clever Schoolmaster and the Stupid Shark

In a certain fishing village there lived a wise schoolteacher. He read old books, and could do many strange things. He knew how to

count to five, sleep on his left ear, speak underwater, and sneeze into a handkerchief. The strangest thing of all was that he wore a hat on his head even when it was not raining. The people of the village used to say that perhaps he even knew magic. One day, he was passing the time by sunning himself in a little boat near to the shore. Along came a shark, turned the boat over, and dragged the teacher by the leg to the bottom of the sea. His hat was left floating on the surface. "What a foolish shark you are," said the schoolmaster, beneath the waves. "Can you not see that my head has floated away? Why, that is the best part of me—it is a full of good things: my eyes, my ears, my nose and my brain." The shark looked up, and, sure enough, something was floating on the surface of the waves. He left the schoolmaster behind and shot off to catch his head. Meanwhile, the clever teacher swam to the surface and made quickly for the shore. Now he tells everyone the story of the stupid shark. People laugh and say it is a very tall story indeed. But what if it is true? If you ever see a shark wearing a hat, it might be that one, looking for the schoolmaster whose head floated away.

## 28 MAY

# The Princess and the Pea

There once lived a prince who wanted only a real princess for his wife. So he went out into the world to seek his bride. There were princesses everywhere he looked, like flowers in the meadows, but none of them seemed to the young prince to be quite the real thing; each and every one of them had at least some little fault. He returned home sadly. Then, one evening, in the midst of a terrible storm, somebody came knocking at the palace door. The queen opened it. On the doorstep stood a beautiful young girl, soaked from head to foot like a flower the gardener has just watered. If she had wrung out her clothes, it would have left her standing in a proper little lake. She asked the queen for a bed for the night. "Who are you?" asked the queen. "A princess," the girl replied, "a real princess." All in the palace were overjoyed to hear that a real princess had arrived, but the queen was not just going to take her word for it. She took a little pea and placed it on the princess's bed. On it she laid twenty mattresses and twice twenty cushions, and then she bade the princess good-night. The next morning, she asked her how she had slept. "Oh," sighed the princess. "Oh, my poor back. I did not sleep a wink all night; there was something so terribly hard in my bed!" Then they all knew that she was a real princess, and it was not long before a grand wedding was celebrated at the palace.

## 29 MAY

# The Danced-Away Shoes

There was once a king who had twelve daughters, each of them lovelier than the next. They all slept in the same bedchamber, and every night the king locked the door with seven locks, to make sure that his daughters did not stray from their beds. But it was all to no avail; every morning the princesses' shoes were worn down, as if they had danced the night away somewhere. One day the enraged king proclaimed throughout the land that he would give one of his daughters and his whole kingdom to anyone who could discover where the princesses went to dance every night. Princes and knights began to assemble from all around to watch over the king's restless daughters. Each of them took his place by the door of the princesses' bedchamber, but the moment the clock struck midnight, it was always the same story. Each of the royal suitors would mysteriously close his eyes, and sleep, and sleep, and sleep. In the morning, the princesses' shoes would be danced away as before. One after the other, the king had the careless sentries banished from the land, and he sat on his throne and lamented until all the servants and courtiers stopped up their ears. Once a poor soldier was passing that way. As he walked beneath the palace windows he heard the royal groans, and said to himself: "Why should I not try my luck? I shall go and guard the restless princesses; anyway, I have nothing better to do." And he set off for the palace gates.

30 MAY

# The Danced-Away Shoes

On his way to the king, the soldier met an old woman. He gave her a friendly greeting, and the woman smiled and said to him: "A kind word is like a mother's caress. I shall reward you for your greeting. I know where you are going, soldier! When you go to guard the princesses' chamber, you must not take the wine they will offer you! If you heed my words, you will not blink an eye till morning. But you must pretend to be asleep. Take this magic cloak. If you throw it across your shoulders, you will become invisible, and you may watch secretly to see where the princesses wander at night." The soldier thanked her kindly, and went to seek an audience with the king. The servants dressed him in splendid clothes, and when evening came they sat him down by the door of the princesses' bedchamber. "If you fail in your task, you will lose your head," the king warned him. But the soldier only smiled. When, just before midnight, the youngest of the princesses offered him a goblet of wine, he pretended to drink it; but he poured the wine into an old sponge which he wore around his neck. Then he lay stretched out on the floor and snored until the windows rattled. When midnight struck, the eldest of the princesses lit a candle and knocked three times her bed; the bed fell through the floor and, one after the other, the princesses climbed down through the hole into the ground. The soldier threw the magic cloak over his shoulders and went after them.

## 31 MAY

# The Danced-Away Shoes

As the princesses ran down a flight of underground steps, the invisible soldier accidentally trod on the last one's train. "Sisters, someone is following us!" she cried in dismay; but the others reassured her, saying: "It was only a nail in the floor!" In a while they came to an enchanted garden. Exquisite trees grew there, with gold and silver branches, and a little bird all covered in diamonds was singing on a glistening tree-stump. The soldier snapped off a twig from each tree he passed, so that he might prove his story to the king. "What is that crackling behind us?" asked the princesses, nervously. "It is probably the enchanted princes firing a salute in our honour," their eldest sister said, soothingly. They hurried on to the banks of a broad lake. There twelve princes stood waiting with twelve little boats; they took the princesses aboard, and sailed towards a rainbow palace in the middle of the underground lake. "Princess, why are you so heavy today? You quite weigh my boat down," declared the prince who had the extra passenger, hidden by his magic cloak. At last they reached the palace, and began to dance. The invisible soldier danced along with them, and if one of the princesses happened to be holding a goblet of wine, he would drain it at a gulp. "What strange magic is this?" wondered the princesses. This went on all night; then, just before dawn, the princes took their partners back across the lake, and the girls hurried back to their chamber. But the soldier got to the palace first, and went to tell the king. He told the girls' father everything, and showed him the splendid twigs and a wine-goblet he had kept as a souvenir. The grateful king had the enchanted passage walled up, married the soldier to the most beautiful of his daughters, and found the rest of them soldiers for husbands, too. And the enchanted princes? They dance with the midnight fairies in their rainbow palace, and I daresay they don't even want to be set free any more.

# JUNE

## 1 JUNE

# The Magic Flower

Once upon a time there was a king who resolved to find out how his soldiers lived and what they thought of him. So he dressed as a beggar and knocked at the door of his trustiest corporal, asking for a bed for the night. "To be sure, you may make your bed here in the straw," the young man agreed. But the king had scarcely closed his eyes, when the soldier shook him awake again. "I can see, old man, that the world has not treated you too well," he said. "Come along with me to the town square. I have a magic flower, which opens all locks." The king was curious, and he agreed at once. They came to a shop; the soldier opened the lock with his magic flower, and took all the money out of the shopkeeper's strong-box. He counted it carefully, and divided it into three piles. "This pile is the money the shopkeeper paid for his goods," the soldier explained. "The second pile is money honestly earned. But the third pile we shall keep, for it is money the shopkeeper obtained by cheating his customers." They continued thus until they had been to all the shops in the square, and then the soldier led the king to the royal treasury itself. The king

pretended to fill his pockets greedily, but the soldier gave him such a slap in the face that his ears rang. "This money goes to the keep of all the king's soldiers; you must not touch it!" he scolded. "Take your share of what he spends on his extravagant courtiers." And the soldier was as good as his word. Afterwards they parted. The next day the king summoned his corporal and revealed all. The soldier thought it was the end of him, but the king said to him: "Soldier, I pardon you, for you are a just man. In return for an honest slap in the face, I shall make you general of all my forces."

## 2 JUNE

# The Parrot's Story

Once a young man bought himself a parrot in the marketplace. He knew how to tell stories, and this is one of them: When I was small, a young parrot scarcely fledged, I lived in a golden cage, in the chamber of a certain proud princess. She was so beautiful that all the flowers bowed to her as she passed, and even the most splendid peacocks in the royal gardens would hide themselves in shame behind their splendid fans. But she was as

cruel and capricious as she was beautiful. There was not a jewel that was precious to her, nor did the finest gifts earn her gratitude. She wore a robe embroidered with stars, a veil of butterfly wings, and sparkling slippers hollowed out from huge diamonds. She bathed in the tears of her chambermaids, and slept beneath a gossamer bedspread spun from maidens' hair. Her father, a powerful king, granted her every wish. One day, just before dawn, the proud princess went out into the garden, so as to enjoy the sunrise for the first time in her life. The grass and flowers were covered in dew. Then the sun sprang up over the horizon, and at once the dewdrops glittered like rainbow diamonds. It was so bright and beautiful that the princess had to close her eyes so as not to be blinded by the dancing, dazzling colours. When she came to herself again, she ran off, calling, "Father, I must have a diadem of morning dew, or I shall die!"

## 3 JUNE

# The Parrot's Story

No sooner had the king heard his daughter's wish, than he summoned all the goldsmiths in the city and ordered them to make the princess a diadem of dewdrops by the very next day, or he would have their heads cut off. The jewellers made their way sadly back to their homes. They knew that none of them could fulfil the princess's wish. The next day, before dawn, as they stood before their ruler with tears in their eyes, they had already in their hearts taken leave of this life. "Have you brought the diadem of dew?" the king asked them sternly. They shook their heads mournfully. Just then the voice of an old stranger was heard from a corner of the chamber. "I shall make the princess the diadem she desires; but first she herself must gather the most beautiful of the diamond dewdrops." When she heard this, the princess ran out into the garden, ready to catch the gleaming drops in her palm. But the moment

she touched them, they disappeared beneath her fingers. "Do not require of others what you cannot do yourself," the old man said, and was gone in an instant, like the morning dew itself. The princess was ashamed, and ran tearfully into the palace, where she rewarded the frightened jewellers with gold and precious stones. From then on, she was proud no more.

## 4 JUNE

# The Lucky Shepherd

Once a shepherd was grazing his sheep when a naughty little lamb wandered off from the flock. The shepherd followed him into the forest. Suddenly he saw a cooking-pot in a tree. A wonderful smell came from inside it. The shepherd did not hesitate, but took a mouthful from the pot with his wooden spoon and tasted it. It was meat, but it wasn't meat; it was pudding, but it wasn't pudding: all he knew was that he had never tasted anything so good in all his life. Suddenly, there was a rustling in the bushes; the shepherd took fright, and hid in the branches of the tree. He was sure that robbers were coming. But it was only an ordinary cat! The cat looked into

he would have been piling up trees to this day. When all the trunks were stacked in a heap, the cat told him to set light to it, and to throw her on the fire. When she insisted, the shepherd did as he was asked. All of a sudden, there in front of him stood the loveliest princess you have ever seen. "Thank you for setting me free," she said with a smile. "Now, come with me to my castle and become my husband."—"Why not?" said the shepherd, gladly. And off they went. On the way they met a rider on a horse. The stranger jumped down and said to the shepherd: "Hold my horse till I return, my lad." The shepherd did as he was asked, but as soon as the man had disappeared into the forest, he leapt on the horse with the princess and galloped away to her castle. They came to a river, where the shepherd cut off the horse's tail and threw it in the water. Then they rode to the other side. Meanwhile, the stranger was looking for his horse. He ran to the river, saw the horse's tail,

the pot, then up into the branches, and said, "So, my fine shepherd, you have been stealing from my cooking-pot!" The shepherd was so astonished he could not even reply, so the cat smiled and said, "Come down here, I have work for you. If you can chop down the whole forest by nightfall, I shall give you twelve hundred gold pieces!" Well, that is not the sort of money you find lying in the street, so the shepherd set to. He felled trees for half the day, but it always seemed that there were still as many as before. "Wait a moment, shepherd; I'll help you," said the cat. She took the axe, and in a twinkling trees began to fall like corn beneath a scythe. Before long the whole forest lay on the ground. "Now we shall sleep," said the cat, "but tomorrow you'll pile the trees up. Then you will receive another twelve hundred pieces of gold."

# 5 JUNE

## The Lucky Shepherd

Early the next morning the shepherd went to work again, but if the cat had not helped him,

and thought that the shepherd and the horse had both drowned, so he went to look for a bridge across the river. The shepherd rode a little way, but then he remembered that he had left his cap on the opposite bank. He asked the princess to hold the horse for a moment, and went to look for the cap. While he was looking for it, the stranger spied his horse, leapt upon it, and rode off with the princess to her castle. But at least the shepherd found his cap!

may not be lonely, I am to keep house with you until he returns." The farmer's wife liked the tinker, and she gladly agreed. The tinker at once began to make himself at home. First of all he had the peasant's family cut down the two linden trees which stood in front of the cottage, saying they cast too much shade. Hardly had they done so, when the peasant returned with his flour. The pony recognized his home, but the peasant shouted at him, "Whoa, where are you going, you oaf? Do you not know where we live? There are two linden trees in front of the gates. This is not our farm. We must have wandered into another village." And with these words the peasant set off into the world to seek his home.

## 7 JUNE

## The Wise Peasant

As he rode, the peasant wondered how it could be that he could not find his home. When he grew tired of plodding along, he stopped at a wayside tavern. As he sat there,

## 6 JUNE

## The Wise Peasant

A certain peasant was once riding to the mill on his pony. In order to take weight off the pony, he slung his bag of grain over his shoulder. On the way he met a clever tinker. "Hey, farmer," said the tinker, "that sack is heavy enough. Do you want to break your pony's back? Why do you not walk, and leave the pony to carry the sack?" "Fool," said the peasant, "can you not see that I am carrying the sack, and not my pony?" The tinker saw at once that the peasant was a little short of sense, and decided to play a trick on him. As they went, he asked where the peasant lived, and made straight for the cottage. He said to the peasant's wife, "Mother, your husband sends greetings and a farewell kiss. He has had enough of his ungrateful family, and wishes to see the world a little. So that you

111

a cottager came running up to him. "Help me, good fellow," he said to the peasant. "My fine mare is lying in her stable, and will not get up." The peasant allowed himself to be persuaded, and he hurried off to look at the mare. He knelt down beside her and whispered, "If you are tired of life, then there are plenty of dogs which will be glad of your meat. But if you want to live, there is grass enough for you to eat." The mare was not sick, but only lazy. As soon as the peasant began to speak of feeding the dogs, she jumped up and began to canter. The cottager's mouth fell open in wonder. "Who are you, that you can cure a horse just by speaking to it?" he asked in astonishment. Before long the tale of the wise doctor had spread to the king himself. He invited the sage to his palace. When the peasant arrived, the king happened to be sitting in his summer-house. The weather was close, for a storm was brewing, and the peasant waved away mosquitoes as he walked. The king thought the man was waving his hands at him, and went to meet him. At that moment a bolt of lightning flew down and struck the summer-house. "So that was why you were waving to me, oh greatest of sages!" said the king, delighted that his life had been saved. "You shall be richly rewarded for delivering me from the lightning." And he appointed the peasant his chief counsellor.

## 8 JUNE

# The Bagpiper

A young bagpiper was on his way to a village festival when a black egg rolled onto his path. "Let me out!" called a thin little voice. The piper cracked the egg open, and out jumped a little imp. "I shall reward you well, bagpiper," he promised, and he cracked a hair from his mouse's tail like a little whip, over the musician's pipes. As soon as he had done this he disappeared like the steam from a kettle. "Well, a fine reward!" thought the piper, and went to play in the village. The moment he

squeezed the bladder, out of the pipes leapt the little imp, and began to sing, "Ill-gotten riches, wherever you be, Fly from your masters and hurry to me!" No sooner had he said this, than the gold and silver of the grasping landlords, dishonest merchants and crooked dealers of the village jumped from their pockets and purses, came rolling and tumbling along to the feet of the startled piper, and leapt into his enchanted pipes. "Stop, thief!" cried the scoundrels who had paid for this wonderful entertainment, and they tried to run after their money; but they

stood on the spot as if enchanted, unable to lift a finger or a foot. "The thief cries: stop, thief," grinned the imp. "It has ever been so in this world." The piper frowned. "I see you do not have too good an opinion of people," he said, and he tipped the money onto the ground and gave it away to the poor. "Let the money be returned to those it rightfully belongs to," he added. "You have done the right thing, piper," the imp told him, approvingly. "If you had kept dishonest money, you would have sold your soul to the devil." The piper smiled, squeezed the bag of his pipes, and played until every foot began to dance. Perhaps he is playing to this day.

## 9 JUNE

# The Green Goose

Long, long ago, in times beyond memory, there was a cottager who had twelve daughters, whom he and his wife were scarcely able to keep. One day the cottager was out in the forest with his eldest daughter, gathering firewood into bundles so that they might at least warm themselves, even if their stomachs were empty. Suddenly a golden carriage appeared before them, and out from it leaned a beautiful maiden, green all over like a frog. "I know of your troubles, good fellow," she said. "But if you will put your eldest daughter in my service for seven years, you shall have a larder full of food and drink, which will never grow empty." The cottager did not know what he was to do, but when his daughter beseeched him to do as the green maiden had asked, he unwillingly agreed. The maiden took his daughter into her coach and, before the cottager knew it, they were gone. When he returned home, he told his wife, "Bring from the larder our best food and drink!" The poor woman burst into tears, thinking her husband had gone off his head from want and hunger; but in the end she went to look in the larder. She almost fell down the steps with wonder and joy! The larder was stacked from floor to ceiling with food and drink fit for a king. From then on they lived in the little cottage like lords.

## 10 JUNE

# The Green Goose

Meanwhile, the green maiden took the cottager's eldest daughter to a golden palace on a silver pillar. There were more rooms in the palace than cherries on a tree. The maiden stroked the poor girl's hair and said: "Here are the keys to all chambers; for a whole seven years you shall dust the rooms and clean them and make the diamond-studded beds. But do not enter the last of the chambers, or it will go ill with you." The girl promised, and set to work, as she had done since she was a small child. Six years passed like six months, and in all that time the cottager's daughter never met a soul in the palace: but each morning the beds were crumpled, as if they had been slept in. As the seventh year drew near, the girl was overcome with curiosity, and she opened the door of the forbidden chamber just a crack, and peeped inside. She saw there a huge golden hall with an enormous pond in the middle; on the pond a green goose was swimming. The moment she saw the girl, the goose called out sadly, "Alas! You hapless child; if you had obeyed, I should have been released from the spell. Now I must wait another hundred years." Before the astonished girl had come to her senses, she was again standing in her poor cottage home. All the good things had disappeared from the larder, and again the cottager and his family were as poor as church mice.

## 11 JUNE

# Tall, Broad and Sharpsighted

Once upon a time there was an old king who only had one son. One day he called the young man to him and said, "My son, it is time for you to choose a bride. Take this key and go to the thirteenth chamber, where you will find the portraits of all the most beautiful princesses. Whichever of them you choose shall become your wife." The prince obeyed, and when he entered the secret chamber he found twelve magnificent gold frames. Eleven of them contained the portraits of princesses, each more lovely than the next, but the twelfth was covered over with a black drape. The prince was curious, and drew back the cloth. The beauty of the face beneath took his breath away. But the girl's face was as pale as wax, and her eyes shed real tears. "This one, and no other!" breathed the prince, enchanted by her beauty. At these words the sad princess

smiled, and the portrait disappeared. When the prince told his father of his decision, the old man was saddened. "You have not chosen wisely, my son," he said. "Your bride is a prisoner in the castle of the Black Wizard. Many a brave knight has tried to set her free, but none has returned." But the young prince was not to be deterred. He quickly took leave of his unhappy father and set out into the world to seek the sad princess.

## 12 JUNE

# Tall, Broad and Sharpsighted

For a long time the prince roamed the world, not knowing where to turn. Then, in a deep forest, he came across three strange fellows. One was as tall as a fir tree, the second as round as a pumpkin, and the third wore a black scarf across his eyes. "Hold fast, noble prince! Take us into your service," called the tall one. "Who are you, and what can you do?" asked the prince. "We are called Tall, Broad and Sharpsighted," replied the lanky fellow. "I am able to stretch myself up to the clouds. Broad can drink up the whole sea, and when he has taken his fill, his stomach flattens all living things around him. Sharpsighted can see to the end of the world, and if he takes the

114

scarf from his eyes, his very glance can crack open the hardest rock." And the three strange fellows at once showed him their skills. "Very well," said the prince, impressed by their tricks, "I shall take you into my service, if you tell me where I may find the Black Wizard's castle." At this Sharpsighted peered all around; the rocks cracked open, and soon he called out: "Now I see it; but we should not reach it if we walked to the end of our lives, were we to go on foot. Tall shall take us all on his shoulders!" And so it happened. Tall stretched himself out until his head disappeared into the clouds, and off they went, the others sitting on his shoulders. A score of miles he strode with every step, and before evening they were standing before the castle of the Black Wizard.

## 13 JUNE

# Tall, Broad and Sharpsighted

Inside the gates there was a deathly stillness. The only things to be seen in the courtyard were the strange statues of knights in full armour, looking as though they had suddenly been turned to stone. One held a half-drawn sword, another's mouth was open wide, while a third looked as if he had just stumbled, but had not yet fallen to the ground. But the prince and his companions went on boldly into the banqueting hall, and sat down at the great oak table. Strange to relate, at that moment the empty plates were filled with delicacies, and the pewter goblets contained good wine. Putting all else out of their minds, the weary travellers set to with a will. No sooner had they finished their meal, than with a bang and a flash the wall parted and into the hall stepped the Black Wizard himself. He had a long black beard, and around his waist he wore an iron band. He was leading the sad princess by the hand. "I know why you have come," he snarled. "If you are able, oh prince, to guard the princess in this hall until daybreak, she is yours. Otherwise you shall all be turned to stone!" He led the girl to the

centre of the room, laughed fiendishly, and was gone in a puff of smoke. The prince tried in vain to speak to the maiden; she lay as if asleep, but with tears glistening in her eyes. Then Tall stretched himself round the room like a belt, Broad blew himself out in the doorway like a great barrel, and the prince took the beautiful princess by the hand. They promised each other that none would sleep a wink, but before many moments had passed they all fell into a deep slumber.

## 14 JUNE

# Tall, Broad and Sharpsighted

When, just before dawn, the prince awoke from his sleep, the princess was nowhere to be seen. "Have no fear," Sharpsighted assured him, "I shall soon find her." He looked out through the window into the world, gazing until the rocks cracked open; suddenly he

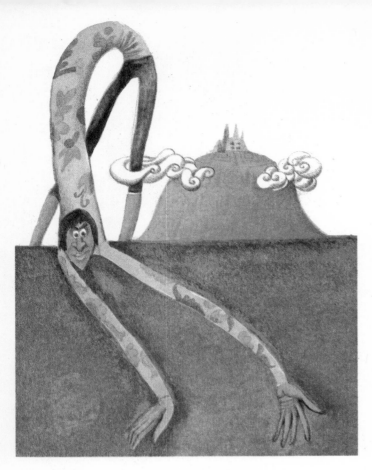

stony knights came alive, and led the prince and princess in triumph to the prince's castle. Only Tall, Broad and Sharpsighted went their own way, off into the world again to help good people everywhere.

## 15 JUNE

# The Swede

There once lived two brothers, one of them rich and the other one poor, as is the way of the world. Both of them served in the army. But the poor brother soon tired of a soldier's life, and he turned to farming instead. He dug a tiny field and sowed it with swedes. Before he knew it, a swede had grown up so large that he could only pull it up with the help of a pair of oxen. "What am I to do with such a monster?" said the poor man in dismay. "I shall not eat it as long as I live, and no one will buy it from me." Then an idea came to him. "I shall give it as a present to the king!"

cried, "Now I see her! Far away from here, on the bottom of a black sea, lies a golden ring, and that ring is the enchanted princess." At this Tall took Broad and Sharpsighted upon his shoulders, stretched himself out, and off he went. Thirty miles with every step, and soon they reached their goal. But alas, however Tall stretched himself on the shore of the black sea, he was unable to reach the ring. Then Broad puffed himself up like a huge cask, and with a single draught he drained the sea. Now they had no difficulty in getting the ring, and soon Tall had again taken them on his back and set off for the castle. But Broad was now so heavy that he had to put him down again, and the sea ran back out and down to where it had come from. At that moment the first rays of dawn began to appear in the sky. Without delay Tall reached out and dropped the golden ring through the window of the Black Wizard's banqueting hall. The moment it touched the ground it changed into the beautiful princess. When the wicked magician saw this, he roared with anger, the iron band around his waist snapped in half, and he changed into a raven. Immediately, all the

he said to himself. And so he did. When he saw the giant swede, the king was astonished. "You must have been born under a lucky star, that your fields give you such a harvest," he told the man. "Indeed not sire, for I have known only hunger and want since my childhood," was the reply. "But my brother, the captain—there is a lordly fellow. Gold pieces fall into his lap!" The king took pity on the poor man. "If you are indeed so poor, then take what gold you can carry from my coffers!" he told him, and gave him a fine piece of farmland as well. When his brother heard of this good fortune, he said to himself, "If the king gave my brother such riches in return for an ordinary swede, then I shall bring him far richer gifts, and shall surely have a much greater reward!" He bought jewels and rings, loaded them on fine black horses, and took them off to the palace. The king shook his head over the gifts. "Whoever can offer such gifts must be richer than the king himself, and wants for nothing," he said. "But I shall reward you." And do you know what he ordered his servants to bring? Why, the huge swede, of course. It took the rich captain weeks to roll his present home!

## 16 JUNE

# Lazy Hans

There was never a fellow as lazy as Hans. So that he should not have to take the goat to pasture, he preferred to marry fat Trina. He thought she would look after the goat for him, and at first that is how it was. Trina would take the goat to graze, and Hans would lie in his bed till mid-day, in order not to waste good food on breakfast. But Trina was not too fond of work either. One day she said to Hans, "Let us exchange the goat for our neighbour's beehive. Bees do not have to be taken to the pastures—they fly there on their own. And we shall have a pot full of honey." Hans liked the idea. "Anyway, honey tastes better than goat's milk," he piped in, and went to change the goat for the bees. By autumn they had a pot full of honey. Trina put it down by the foot of the bed with the hive beside it, so that no one might steal their honey, and the two of them lazed among the bedclothes all day long. "Dear me," said Hans one day. "Trina has a sweet tooth; she is sure to eat all the honey herself, and there will be none left for me. Let us rather exchange it for a goose and goslings."—"Very well," Trina replied, "but not before we have children, for who is to take the geese to grass?" Hans frowned. "Children are no good at working," he said. "They will only go chasing butterflies." "Let them try," said Trina. "I should soon smack their bottoms for them! Like this!" And she caught up a stick, swung it down, and, crash! The pot of honey smashed to pieces. "Well, that is the end of our goose and goslings," said Hans. "Now no one will have to look after them. How well we have settled the matter!" And they licked the honey from the pieces of the pot, and went to bed. There was nothing for them to do anyway.

## 17 JUNE

# The Loaf and the Flask

A miser and a generous man were travelling through the world together. Neither of them had two coins to rub together, but the generous man always divided the little he had with anyone who cared to share it, while the miserly fellow would not have given a flea from his head. One day they found they had just three crusts of bread left in their bundle. Suddenly, a white-haired old man appeared beside them. "Give me a little of your bread," he pleaded. "Not a morsel has passed my lips for three whole days." — "Why should we?" the miser said to him roughly, and he quickly ate two of the crusts, to make sure he did not go short. But the generous one shared the last crust with the old man. "I shall reward you both well," the stranger told them, as they prepared to go their way. "Here is a loaf of bread and a pocket-flask. Whoever swallows a piece of the loaf, the mouthful will turn into pure gold. In the flask is the water of life. It is able to cure any ailment. You may share the gifts as you wish." — "What are the sick to me?" thought the miser to himself. "I shall take the magic loaf." The old man only smiled, and disappeared. The miser at once began to eat. He swallowed greedily; the bread turned to gold in his throat, until he could not even stand up, and had to roll along instead. He

rolled onto a bridge, but it gave way beneath his great weight, and the gold dragged the miser to the bottom of the river. The fellow with the generous heart wandered the world, curing the sick everywhere he went with his wonderful water. In the end he cured a beautiful princess, and so became king.

## 18 JUNE

# Beautiful Vasilisa

There once lived a beautiful girl called Vasilisa. There was not another maiden for miles around whose beauty could compare with hers. She wanted for nothing. But one sad day her dear mother lay on her deathbed. Before she died, she gave Vasilisa a little doll. "Care for her as if she were your very own child," her mother told her. "Whenever times are hard for you, give her food and drink, and she will comfort you." With these words she gave up the ghost. Vasilisa cried until she had no tears left to cry; but misfortunes never come singly, and before long her father brought home a stepmother and two ugly stepdaughters. They hated Vasilisa so much that they would have starved her to death. They gave her all the most unpleasant work to do, and beat her frequently. Whenever her heart was heavy with sadness, she would feed her doll with milk, and the doll would sing her her mother's song to comfort her. But one day her father left home to go on a journey. The stepmother and her daughters lay in bed all

day, and Vasilisa had to wait on them hand and foot. She had so much to do that she let the fire go out. "Off with you to Yagga the Hag herself to get fire!" the women shouted at her. "But don't you dare come back from the old ogress without it!" What else could the poor girl do? She set off into the dark night to visit Yagga the Hag.

## 19 JUNE

## Beautiful Vasilisa

Poor Vasilisa walked, and walked, until she came to a black forest. A black rider on a black horse rode past her, and human skulls shone white from all the trees. Terrified, Vasilisa began to run, until she arrived, breathless, at a gate made of human bones.

Beyond the gate stood a birch tree, and on the other side of the tree a strange cottage was turning around on a chicken's leg. Out of it jumped a black dog and a black cat, their jaws covered in blood and their claws glowing like hot coals. They rushed towards Vasilisa, ready to tear her throat out. But just then a black-eyed dwarf-girl looked out of the window and called the beasts off. "What are you doing here, poor child?" she asked Vasilisa. The hapless girl told her tearfully why she had come. "Dear me, child, I really don't know if you will leave here alive," sighed the black-eyed girl. "Yagga the Hag, my mistress, lives on human meat and dresses in human skins." But at that moment there was a roar in the air like the draught up some dark chimney, and Yagga the Hag herself came flying up astride a broomstick, sweeping black clouds behind her. "What are you doing here, you skinny little worm?" she asked, with a snivel. Vasilisa begged the hag on her bended knees to give her a little fire, saying that she must not go home without it. "Very well," said the ogress. "If you serve me well, you shall have what you ask. Otherwise I shall roast you for dinner." And she made Vasilisa a bed for the night in a black mousehole.

## 20 JUNE

# Beautiful Vasilisa

When Vasilisa got up in the morning, Yagga the Hag tipped a sackful of peas and poppy seed on the floor in front of her and told the girl: "If you have not picked out the peas

before a red rider on a red horse passes by my gate, you shall not leave here alive!" With these words she flew off on her broomstick, making a terrible roar. Poor Vasilisa started to cry. "I shall not finish this work till the end of my life," she wailed. And she took her little doll on her knee, gave her a little milk, and poured out her heart to her. "Do not be afraid," the doll said. "Everything will be all right." Then the doll called all the birds of the forest, and in no time at all they had picked out the peas from the poppy seed. When Yagga the Hag returned, she could hardly believe her eyes. "Very well," she muttered. "I have a still harder task for you. Before a black rider on a black horse passes by my gate, you must shell all my nuts." And she tipped thirty sacks

of golden nuts on the floor in front of Vasilisa; then she flew off again. Again the girl wanted to cry, but the doll helped her again. She clapped, and sang, and all of a sudden the cottage was full of mice, and before evening all the nuts were shelled. By that time the black rider was on his way, and Yagga the Hag was flying home. When she saw that Vasilisa had again finished her work, she scowled with disappointment and sent the child off to her mousehole.

## 21 JUNE

# Beautiful Vasilisa

In the night the hag woke up her black-eyed servant and told her to light a fire under the oven so that she might roast Vasilisa for breakfast. Then she stretched out on her bed, laid her broomstick over herself, and was soon fast asleep. But Vasilisa had heard the ogress, and she pleaded with the black-eyed dwarf, and said, "I'll give you my silk scarf if you set me free." The dwarf-girl had a kind heart, and she agreed. The dog and the cat ran after Vasilisa, and would have torn her to pieces, but Vasilisa threw them a piroschek and hurried towards the gate. There the birch tree wound its branches into her hair, and the gate slammed in her face. She tied the branches back with a silk ribbon and greased the hinges of the gate with butter. The tree and the gate thanked her and let her go free. She ran as fast as if she had wings. So that she could find her way, she stuck a skull with shining eyes onto a long stick, and was able to see the path in front of her as she ran through the dark forest. In the morning, when Yagga the Hag awoke and found Vasilisa gone, she turned angrily on the black-eyed dwarf, the poor animals, the tree and the gate; but they replied that in all the years they had served her faithfully she had never given them anything, while Vasilisa had rewarded all of them. The hag was so angry that she fell into the ground and was swallowed up. When Vasilisa got home, her stepmother and the two sisters gave her a warm welcome. "Where have you been so long?" they shrieked at her, and would have punished the poor girl. But the skull turned its glowing eyes on them, and the wicked women were burned to ashes. After that Vasilisa lived in the little house in happiness and contentment. One day a young prince passed by, and was so enchanted by her beauty that he carried her off to his castle.

## 22 JUNE

# The Lad Who Wanted to Learn to Fear

There were once two brothers, one of them clever and the other foolish. But the clever brother was a terrible coward. "If he has to cross the yard at night, he shakes with fear!" people would say. "What a wise fellow my brother is, that he is able to shake with fear," the foolish fellow complained sadly to his dog. "How I should like to know how to do it!" The sexton heard him say this, and he told the simpleton to come to the church belfry at midnight to ring the bells. That night the sexton dressed in a white sheet, thinking he would scare the fellow to death. But it was no use; the lad just shouted at him, "Go away, you silly old ghost. I haven't time for you—I must ring the bells so that I may learn to shake with fear!" But when the sexton went on howling and wailing, the foolish lad gave him such a clout across the ear that he rolled down the stairs and broke all his ribs. In the end the lad gave up in disappointment and went home. His father gave him a good scolding when he heard what he had done to the sexton. He put a purse with fifty thalers in it in the boy's hand, and sent him out into the world so that he might not bring disgrace on the family. As he went on his way the foolish fellow said to himself aloud, "I should have to be the devil himself not to be able to fear in the wide world!" A passing wayfarer heard these words and, smiling to himself, led the young man to a gallows. "Stay here till morning," he told him, "and you will soon know what fear is." And he went his way.

## 23 JUNE

# The Lad Who Wanted to Learn to Fear

The simpleton sat down beneath the gallows and lit a fire. The night was cold; seven corpses swung from the beams until their bones creaked, and shadowy bats flitted past.

"Dear me, those fellows will catch their deaths of cold," thought the lad, and since he had a good heart he untied the corpses and sat them down beside him round the fire. In a little while their rotten clothes began to smoulder, but the hanged men did not move a muscle. "Stupid fellows, must I do everything for you?" the boy scolded them, beating sparks from the glowing cloth; and he hung his silent companions back on the gallows. The wayfarer again came by in the morning. "Well, my good fellow, have you learnt to be afraid?" he asked, with a smile. "It was no good," said the simpleton. "And even those fellows up there did nothing to help, though I sat them down beside me." The wayfarer was astonished. "Never have I seen such a fearless lad," he said. And he took the boy off to see the king. The king listened to the tale of the young fellow's heroism, then said, "So you wish at all costs to learn to shake with fear? Very well! Not far from here is a haunted castle. Demons guard a great treasure there. If you can stay there for three nights, you shall have my daughter for your wife. But you may take only three things with you."

### 24 JUNE

# The Lad Who Wanted to Learn to Fear

The next day the simpleton ordered the servants to bring along a vice, a spokeshave and a lathe, and they set off for the haunted castle. Night fell, and the lad lit a fire in the hearth and waited to see what would happen. Midnight struck, and into the chamber rushed a dog with bloody fangs and a cat with fiery eyes. They spoke fiercely, saying, "Come and play cards with us. If you lose, we shall tear you to pieces!"—"Why not?" said the lad. "But your long claws might tear the cards. First I must trim them a little with the spokeshave!" The dog and the cat obediently put their paws in the vice; the simpleton screwed it down on their claws, and cut both their throats with the spokeshave. Then he went contentedly to bed.

But the bed began to toss and turn like a stick in a stream, spinning round first one way, then the other, and finally overturned in a tub of grease. "Phew, what a ride that was!" the lad said with satisfaction, and slept like a log. When the king came the next morning he thought the young fellow was dead. But then he opened his eyes and said, "I wonder if I shall learn to shake with fear tomorrow at least!" And that evening he set off for the haunted castle again.

122

## 25 JUNE

## The Lad Who Wanted to Learn to Fear

At midnight there was a rattling in the chimney, and out of it fell, first a pair of man's legs, then a head, then the trunk to go in between them. Soon the apparition had put himself together, and without invitation he sat down at the table. In a while came a second, then a third and a fourth. Ghost after ghost! They began to throw human skulls from one to the other. "Come and play skittles with us!" they whined at the young man. "Why not?" he answered. "But the balls are not quite round; I must grind them a little." And he put the skulls in his lathe and made them nice and round. They began to play, and when the cock crew the ghosts disappeared. "Oh dear, shall I never learn to shake with fear?" grieved the simple lad. The next night there was again a terrible noise in the chimney, and down came a coffin containing the body of a bearded old gaoler. "My, how cold you are,

old man," said the boy, feeling sorry for him; and he laid the corpse beside him in his bed. As soon as the body warmed up a little, it came to life, and the old man grabbed hold of the boy. "Come and try your strength with me," he grunted. "If you do not shake with fear, you shall die!"—"Indeed, that is why I am here," replied the lad. The corpse led him off through secret passages to the dungeons. There it thrust an iron pillory into the ground with a single blow. "I can do better than that," smiled the lad, and he swung an axe and caught the old man's long beard in the pillory. At once there was a noise like thunder, and in the place where the old man had stood was a huge, sparkling heap of gold and diamonds. When the king came the next morning he could not believe his eyes, and he gladly gave the young man his daughter's hand. Believe it or not, she taught him to shake until his teeth rattled. How? Every morning she poured a bucket of icy water into his bed. Thus it was that the lad finally learned to do what he had wanted to for so long.

## 26 JUNE

## King Ragbeard

A certain king once held a great tournament in order to choose a bridegroom for his proud daughter. Princes, knights and even kings gathered from all corners of the earth to joust and win the favour of the beautiful princess. But the proud young lady only laughed at them all. One was too short, another too tall; this one too thin, that one too fat—and so it went on. But most of all she mocked the young king who was the boldest and most handsome of all, for, while hunting, he had been wounded on the cheek by a savage bear. He defeated all his rivals in the tournament; but that was not enough for the princess. "Dear Heavens, not to save my life, would I become that ragbeard's wife!" she giggled, and from then on the name stuck, and the unfortunate king was known as Ragbeard. In the end all the suitors were so insulted that

husband wherever you will," he told her. "But do not show you face here again." The princess walked along miserably behind her husband, up hill and down dale, until they came to a beautiful country with rich forests, fields and meadows. Not far away they could see a royal city, sparkling proudly in the sunshine. "What is this lovely country?" the princess asked, sighing. "It is the kingdom of King Ragbeard," her husband replied. "Alas! If only I had known; I might have sat upon its throne," the princess sobbed. "You are my wife, proud princess; I will not have you lamenting for another!" the minstrel rebuked her sternly, and he led her to a poor little cottage, so low that she had to crawl into it on her hands and knees. "This is our home," the minstrel told her. "From now on you must work your fingers to the bone so that we may have enough to eat." And he began at once to teach her to weave baskets, knead bread and clean and tidy the cottage. But soon her soft hands were torn and bleeding. "You are no use at all," her husband said with a scowl. "Go at least to market to sell a couple of earthenware jugs!" She did as she was told, and laid out her

they left in disgust. The king was angry with his proud daughter, and said to her, "I shall punish you for your pride. You shall become the wife of the first wandering vagabond who comes to the palace gates." At that very moment a poor minstrel struck up a tune beneath the windows of the royal chamber. He sang so beautifully that the soft notes smoothed away the anger from the monarch's brow. "That is the husband for you, proud child," he exclaimed, and he had the wedding made ready without delay.

## 27 JUNE

# King Ragbeard

The princess wept bitterly, and begged her father to take pity on her, but to no avail. The moment she was married, he sent her away from the royal castle. "Go with your poor

wares at the corner of the market square. But suddenly a drunken hussar appeared on his horse, and trampled the jugs to smithereens. "You good-for-nothing!" her husband shouted at her when she came home. "You would do better to wash the dishes in the royal kitchens." And so it was to be.

## 28 JUNE

# King Ragbeard

Now the princess really had a hard time of it. She was rushed off her feet from morning till night, and had never a kind word from the royal cook. But she managed now and then to save a few poor scraps in a pot she carried tied beneath her apron, so they did not go hungry, anyway. One day, the chief steward ordered the cook to prepare a great feast. The young king, whom the princess had never set eyes on since she came to the palace, was to bring home his bride. That day in the kitchen she didn't have time to turn round, but when evening came, and she was setting off home, exhausted, with her secret jar of food full to the brim, she could not resist just a peep into the banqueting hall through a crack in the door. Just then a pair of arms caught her around the waist from behind; she turned, and

could not believe her eyes, for it was none other than King Ragbeard himself, and he took her in his arms to dance. He tripped and whirled with her so gaily that the jar of food came unfastened, and all the scraps she had hidden went flying across the floor. The princess nearly died of shame, and wanted to run away, but the king held her fast and said, kindly: "Do you not recognize your own husband from the poor cottage? Your father and I wanted to punish you for your pride. The hussar whose horse stamped upon your jugs—that was also I! But because a kind heart beat within your proud bosom, you have passed the test. Now we shall never again be parted." And the princess fell into his arms.

## 29 JUNE

# A Little Mouse Story

Once upon a time there was a mouse kingdom, in which there lived a mouse who was never satisfied. Nothing was to her liking: she turned up her nose at everything. One day she decided to go out into the world. She crept quietly past the guards and peeped out of the mousehole at the world outside. Not far away in the grass she could see a bird's nest. "Ah, what a splendid palace! I should like to live there," she whispered. Just then a little bird flew out of the nest and up into the sky. "That is surely the king of the birds himself—what fine robes he wears!" sighed the mouse. "How much more splendid they are than the dirty grey coat worn by the mouse-king." And

before you could blink an eyelid, she had jumped into the nest and was making herself at home. "Now I am queen. Don't you dare disturb me!" she said to the astonished birds. They flew off to tell the falcon. "A fine state of affairs," said the falcon, angrily. "A mouse, queen of the birds? I'll show her!" But as soon as he came into sight above the nest, the mouse called out, "There he is, hunter: aim your gun and fire!" The falcon took fright and flew away. Just then a little boy went by; he saw the mouse and mewed softly like a cat. The mouse was off down the nearest mousehole as if the devil himself were after her. The birds were so pleased to see the last of her that each of them dropped the little boy a feather into the grass.

## 30 JUNE

# The Thief Robbed

There once lived a foolish country lad, who was so lazy that he would have ridden to church in his bed if he had been able. "Begone from my sight, lazybones!" his father roared at him one day. "If you cannot do an honest day's work, then go and learn the highwayman's trade at least!" The lad was not against the idea. He took his grandfather's old pistol from the chest in the attic, thrust a rusty knife into his belt, and crouched beside the old well at the end of the parish field. He was in luck right away. The merchants and farmers were just making their way home from market, and when the lad called out in his best robber's voice "Your money or your lives!", they pacified him with gold pieces. Before long he had money by the sackful. Then along came

the king himself in his coach. "Your money or your life!" cried the stupid lad. But the king was no fool. "Dear me; all I possess is yours, Most Esteemed Highwayman," he said. "But all my riches are hidden in this old well, and neither I nor my coachman can swim. Why do you not go into the well yourself to bring out the treasure?" The lad did not hesitate, but took off his clothes, filled with stolen gold, and leapt into the well. The king laughed until his sides ached. "You fool; did you not know that the king is always the greatest robber in the land?" he chuckled, and he picked up the highwayman's booty and was gone.

# JULY

## 1 JULY

# The Cobbler and the Devil

There once lived a poor cobbler who had a nagging wife. One day he had had enough, and he packed up his belongings in a bundle and set out into the wide world. He walked and walked, until suddenly a flame sprang up in front of him, and out of it leapt the devil himself. "Where to, my friend?" he shouted at the cobbler. The henpecked husband told the devil his troubles. "Well, I see that your plight is the same as my own," the devil told him. "I too had to run away from a fiendish wife who made my life hell. She would complain from morning till night, saying that there would be the devil to pay if I did not mend my ways, and even when I fell exhausted into my bed at night she would put a crucifix under my pillow just to make sure I didn't sleep a wink. I tell you, not even Old Nick himself could put up with it." The cobbler was sympathetic, and the two were soon friends. They set off to see the world together. One day they wandered into a strange kingdom. "I'll tell you what, my friend," said the devil. "I shall go and possess the king's daughter. When the doctors are unable to cure her, you will dress up as a sage and make her well again. The king is sure to reward you well." And he was as good as his word. The princess, possessed by the devil, went right out of her senses, and none of the

learned men in the kingdom was able to help. Then the cobbler came along in disguise and announced himself to the king.

## 2 JULY

# The Cobbler and the Devil

As soon as they led the cobbler into the princess's chamber, the devil flew out through the chimney, and the princess smiled and was as healthy as ever. The king gave the cobbler a great pile of gold, which he shared out equally with the devil outside the city walls. And so they continued the length and breadth of the world, with the devil possessing princesses and the cobbler making them well again. But one day the devil said to the cobbler, "I am tired of all this tramping around. You have all the gold you could wish for. Get along home and spend it, and I shall possess one more princess; then I shall carry her soul off to my fellows down in hell. But mark my words, don't you dare come to cure the princess, or you'll end up along with her in hell!" The cobbler promised that no such thing would even cross his mind, took leave of the devil like an old friend, and went home to his wife. Now that he had so much money, she was a good deal more pleasant to him. But one day the king's soldiers came banging at

the door. The king himself had sent orders for the cobbler to come and cure his daughter, who was possessed by the devil. If he refused, the soldiers were to shoot him on the spot. The cobbler did not want to go, of course, but what else could he do? The moment he entered the princess's chamber, the devil began to shout at him: "Did I not tell you to mind your own business?" But the cobbler whispered to him: "It is all up with us, my friend. Our wives are looking for us: they want to put a halter round our necks and make us plough the fields!" When the devil heard this, he flew out through the chimney, and that was the last that was ever seen of him. The cobbler returned to his wife and said, triumphantly: "There you are; you see what you women are like! The devil himself cannot put up with your ways!"

## 3 JULY

# The Golden Goose

Once upon a time there was a peasant who had three sons, all of them different. One was clever, one was lazy, the third was dreamy as a daisy. Their father and mother treated the first two well, but never had so much as a kind word to spare for the third. They thought him a little short of sense, and the whole family called him Noodle. One day their father sent the eldest son into the forest to cut firewood. His mother made him a pancake and gave him a bottle of sweet wine to put in his bundle. No sooner had the lad reached the clearing, than he began to eat. Just then a strange, white-haired old man appeared, not much bigger than a toadstool. "Share your food with me, young fellow," he begged. "Why should I?" said the young man, harshly. "I should have to go short myself." The old man waved a threatening finger at him and disappeared. The moment the lad began to chop, he cut his finger with the axe, and had to hurry home. The second son set off to do the work instead; but he was no more polite to the old man than his brother had been, and he had scarcely

taken the axe in his hand, when he chopped himself in the leg. So it was the turn of the youngest of the three. Do you suppose he will get on any better?

## 4 JULY

# The Golden Goose

When Noodle set off to cut wood, instead of a pancake his mother baked him a piece of dry soda bread in the ashes, and instead of wine he was given sour beer. He had hardly reached the forest when the little old man appeared and begged for a share of his food. "Take as much as you like," the kind-hearted lad said, "but you will eat simply, for I have only a piece of dry soda bread and a bottle of sour beer." But when he untied his bundle he found the sweetest of wine and the finest-tasting pancake he had ever eaten. The old man thanked him kindly, and said, "You shall be rewarded for your generosity. Cut down yonder dry tree. Take what you find beneath it, and go out into the world. Good fortune will come your way, you'll see!" The young man did as he had been told. Among the roots of the tree he found a goose with feathers of pure gold. It gleamed like the sun. Noodle took the goose under his arm and set off to see the world. He met three peasant girls. One of them wanted to pull out one of the golden feathers without his knowing, but—oh! when she touched the goose her fingers stuck to it like glue, and she could not get them free.

A second girl ran to help her, but she became stuck to the first. The same happened to the third girl, and to a peasant who caught her by the skirt. Then the parson got stuck to the peasant, the sexton to the parson, an old woman with a goat to the sexton, a whole wedding party to the goat, and finally a thief who tried to take the bridegroom's silver watch out of his pocket. The thief was pulling a stolen pig along on a string; a band of gypsies came running up, thinking they would cut the pig loose, and they were soon caught as well. Noodle and his whole procession headed for the royal city.

5 JULY

## The Golden Goose

Just at that moment the sad princess happened to be gazing out of the palace windows. The king had proclaimed that whoever made the princess smile should have her for his wife. The minute Noodle appeared in the courtyard with his strange train, the princess burst into such a fit of laughter that she nearly split her sides. But the king tried to

get out of his promise. He was not keen to have a village lad as a husband for his daughter, so he told Noodle that he must first find him someone who would drink all the wine in the royal cellars at one sitting, and eat a whole mountain of cakes on top of it. "Very well," said the lad, and he plucked from his goose the golden feather which the peasant-girl was holding on to; right away the motley band of followers went their separate ways like startled crows. Noodle took his goose and went back to the spot where he had

met the enchanter with the long white beard. "Perhaps he will help me again," he said to himself, and he laid the goose back in the tree-roots. At that moment there stood in front of him a man as stout as a cask. "I know what troubles you," he said to the young lad. "But I shall be glad to help you. I have eaten but a dozen oxen since morning, and drunk only a score of buckets of wine, and my stomach is rumbling with hunger already." So off they went together to the royal city, and the stout fellow set about eating and drinking his way through the king's wine and cakes. He ate, and ate, and if the king had not quickly promised the young man his daughter's hand, he would probably have eaten up the whole kingdom. But at that moment the glutton changed into the little old man; he gave the couple his blessing, and disappeared.

## 6 JULY

# Rumpelstiltzkin

There was once a miller who had a daughter so beautiful that the king himself got to hear of her loveliness. He was unable to contain his curiosity, and set off for the mill to see her for himself. "Gracious, how lovely she is!" he sighed, the moment he spied her. The miller thought that the king himself might not be a bad match for his daughter, and in the hope of enticing him he lied: "What of her beauty, My Lord? My daughter can spin gold from straw!" The king could scarcely believe his ears. "Bring her to my castle tomorrow," he ordered the miller. When he had gone, the miller's daughter was dismayed. "Why did you say that, father?" she said. "What a fool I shall appear before the king tomorrow!" But the miller told her that it would all turn out well in the end, and the next day he took her off to the royal palace. There the king shut her up in a room full of straw. "You must spin all this straw into gold by morning, or I shall have you pilloried!" he told her. The girl began to cry. At that moment the wall in the corner cracked like an eggshell, and into the room

leapt a manikin, dressed in clothes of straw. "What will you give me if I spin a roomful of gold by morning?" he asked. The girl promised him her ring, and the manikin sat down at the spinning wheel; by morning he had spun all the straw into gold. The king was astonished, and the next evening he shut the poor girl up in an even larger room with an even bigger pile of straw.

## 7 JULY

# Rumpelstiltzkin

The moment the king had turned the key in the lock, the manikin appeared, and asked the miller's daughter for some present. So she gave him her necklace, and the little creature spun and spun; in the morning the king was overjoyed to see his new-found riches, but ever greedy for more. The third night the poor girl had nothing to give the little man. The manikin frowned darkly, and said: "Very well; I shall spin for you tonight also—but you must promise me the first child that is born to you!"

The unhappy girl promised, thinking that there would be time enough before it came to such a thing. The manikin set to work. When the king saw the pile of gold the next morning, he delayed no longer, and took the miller's daughter as his wife. Before a year had passed, a little son had been born to the royal couple. He had a golden star on his forehead, and little alabaster arms. The joyous queen did not want to leave her child even for a minute. But one night at midnight, the wall beside his cot cracked open like an eggshell, and into the chamber stepped the manikin. "Give me the child!" he screamed. The queen burst into tears, and cried, and cried; she begged the little man not to take away her son. "Very well," he said in the end, with a frown. "If in three days you can guess my name, you shall keep your child. If not, I shall take him away!" With these words the little man disappeared from sight.

## 8 JULY

# Rumpelstiltzkin

The moment the sun set the next day, the manikin appeared again. "Guess what I am called, oh queen!" he chuckled. "Peter? Paul?" she tried. "Matthew? Giles?" she went on, but the little man only grinned fiendishly, hopped on one leg, and said, triumphantly, "Dear, dear, nowhere near!" As midnight struck, he

disappeared again. The queen did not sleep a wink, trying to think what the little man's name might be, but when the little fellow appeared again the next evening, she ran through all the names in the calendar in vain. "Dear, dear, nowhere near!" the manikin screeched over and over again, and at midnight he again disappeared like a whiff of smoke. The evening of the third day was drawing near, and the queen was beside herself with grief. Then a shepherd arrived at the castle. "I saw a strange sight in a woodland glade today," he told the queen. "Two spectres were warming themselves before a fire; a third, a strange little man, was dancing on one leg and singing: 'The day before yesterday I ate gruel, yesterday a sweet breadroll, and today I shall roast myself a prince! What a feast for Rumpelstiltzkin!'" No sooner had he told his tale, than the grinning little man stepped into the chamber. "I have it!" cried the queen. "You are Rumpelstiltzkin!" The goblin scowled like thunder, as if he had bit on a sore tooth. "The devil himself must have given it away!" he screamed, and he caught hold of both his legs at once and tore himself apart with rage. And that was the end of Rumpelstiltzkin.

## 9 JULY

## Puss in Boots

In an old mill lived a miller with his three
sons. They had only an old donkey and
a tomcat, which, even as a kitten, liked to sleep
in the miller's boots. And since the miller was
said to have more sense in his boots than in
his head, the cat managed to pick up more
than his share of worldly wisdom. He even
learnt to speak. When the old miller died, he
left the mill and the donkey to the two older
brothers, while the youngest inherited nothing
but a hungry tomcat. "Are we both to go
short?" the young man said to the cat one day.
"I should do better to kill you and roast you
for supper!" The cat was startled, but at once
began coaxing his master cleverly: "I should
not be more than a couple of mouthfuls for
you, and as for my skin, why, it wouldn't even
make a decent hat! I'll tell you what. I've like
high boots since I was a kitten. Why don't you
buy me a fine pair, with spurs at the heels, and
a hat and feather to go with them, so that
I may look like a gentleman? I'll make you
your fortune, you'll see." The miller's son
smiled at the idea. "Why not?" he said to
himself. "It will be fun, at least." And he
borrowed the money to fit the cat out as he
had wished. The cat dressed up like a rather
strange courtier, and set off for the king's
palace.

## 10 JULY

## Puss in Boots

On the way to the castle the cat caught
a whole sackful of partridges and hares. He
laid these before the king. "A present, Your
Majesty, from my master, the Marquis of
Carabas," said the cat, bowing low. The king
thanked him graciously, rewarding him with
a handful of gold pieces. From then on the cat
often brought presents of game to the palace,
always being sure to convey greetings from
his master. In this way the miller's son was
able to live well enough on the gold the cat
brought home. One day, the king went riding
in a coach, accompanied by his beautiful
daughter. When the clever cat saw this, he at
once ran off and told his master, "Take off all

133

your clothes and jump into the river!" The miller's son did as he was told, and the wise tomcat ran to meet the king's carriage. "Your Majesty, help my master; as he was bathing in the river, robbers stole his clothes!" he called out. The king, remembering the generous gifts of game, at once ordered his footmen to dress the miller's son in his own fine garments, and graciously offered him a seat in his coach. There the beautiful princess was unable to take her eyes off him, so dashing did he look, dressed as a noble marquis.

## 11 JULY

## Puss in Boots

Wherever the king, his daughter and the miller's son went, the people stopped their work for a moment and called out, respectfully, "Long live our gracious lord, the Marquis of Carabas!" And when the king

leaned out of the window of his coach to enquire to whom the beautiful fields and pastures they were passing might belong, the peasants replied, "Why, to the Marquis of Carabas, our master, of course!" All this was because the clever cat had gone ahead of them, telling the people what to say, and giving gold pieces in return. Finally, he ran up to a golden palace. It belonged to a wicked giant, but the cat was not afraid. He bowed low, and said, "Honourable giant, I have heard that you are a great magician. But I should dearly like to see with my own eyes that you are a greater one than I." The wizard laughed scornfully, and changed himself in a trice into a huge monster with long claws and sharp teeth. The cat shivered with fear, but he pretended not to be afraid at all. "For such a giant it is no great feat to change into something so large," he said, cunningly. "But I wonder if you are able to turn into a small creature, say a mouse?" The stupid giant took up the challenge, and in a flash the cat had pounced on the mouse and killed it. At that moment the king's coach came rumbling into the courtyard. "Whose is this fine palace?" enquired the king. "Why, it belongs to my master, the Marquis of Carabas," said the cat, welcoming the royal visitors. At this the king lost no time in preparing a magnificent wedding for his daughter and the miller's son. I was there, too. I ate, drank and made merry, and when I enquired about the clever cat, I was told that His Excellency the Minister was busy in the royal cellars, catching the most esteemed royal mice.

## 12 JULY

## The Stupid Octopus and the Clever Fish

Once upon a time, long, long ago, the fish of the sea made an octopus their king. He boasted that he would catch them as much food as they could wish for in his huge tentacles, and the fishes believed him. But they

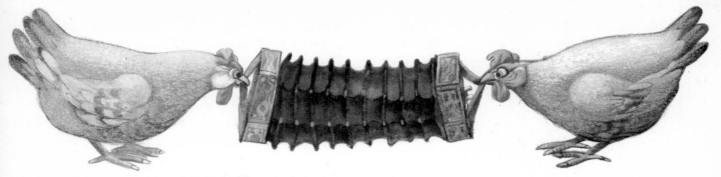

were making a great mistake. The octopus was stupid and capricious. The sharks, the eels, the swordfish and the other predators of the sea tried their best to make him happy, bringing him all manner of fine treasures, but the king was never satisfied. Then, one day, a clever little fish found an old umbrella in a sunken wreck, and brought it to the sea-king. "What use is it?" he asked, surprised. "It will keep the rain off you as you sit on the sea-bed," the fish said with a smile: The octopus was delighted. "Never have I had such a fine present," he told the little fish. "I appoint you my first minister." The little fish almost burst with pride. He told all and sundry how clever he was, and laughed at the king behind his back. But one day he was caught on a line by an old fisherman. "Set me free!" demanded the fish. "I am the king's first minister!" And he began to boast of his cleverness. The fisherman laughed at the tale. "When the king is a fool, then the clever ones prosper," he said. "But all of them get caught in the end." And he roasted the little fish and ate it.

## 13 JULY

# The Cock and the Hen

On the rubbish-heap behind the barn the musicians played, and the cock and the hen danced the polka together. When they had danced to their hearts' content, they went for a stroll. The hen found a grain of corn, the cock a letter. "Listen, hen," the cock said, proudly. "It is written in this letter that I am to go to Rome and become Pope."—"Then I shall go with you and be the wife of the Pope," replied the hen. So they set off together for Rome. On the way they met a magpie. "Where to, where to?" asked the magpie, inquisitively. "Oh, to Rome," the cock told him, casually. "I have found a letter in which it is written that I am to become Pope. The hen will become the Pope's wife."—"Take me with you," the magpie implored them. "I shall be your treasurer." So they took him along. They walked, and walked, until they met a sparrow. The cock boasted, "Sparrow, we are off to Rome! I have found a letter where it is written that I am to become Pope. The hen will be the Pope's wife, and the magpie will be our treasurer."—"Pope? Pope? Pope?" cheeped the sparrow in wonder. "Then I shall go with you; I have a good voice, and will be your sexton." And he joined them. Then they met a fox. "We are going to Rome," they called to her. "The cock has found a letter, saying that he is to become Pope. The hen will be the Pope's wife, the magpie his treasurer, and the sparrow his sexton."—"But it is late," grinned the fox. "Come and sleep in my house, and tomorrow I shall show you the way to Rome." So they all went off to the fox's house.

## 14 JULY

## The Cock and the Hen

No sooner had the door of the fox's little house closed behind the cock and his companions, than the fox ordered: "Now, cock, you will sing me a song!"—"But I do not know any," the cock replied. "Then I shall sing one myself," said the fox. "Listen well: when I was in the service of a cruel mistress, I never slept properly on your account. You would crow in the morning, and I had to get up. For that I shall bite off your head." And so she did; then she turned on the hen. "Now you will sing me a pretty song!"—"Dear me," said the hen, "I cannot sing at all." "Then I shall sing you one," the fox told her. "When I was in the service of the cruel woman, you laid eggs that no one could find. My mistress thought I was stealing them, and would reward me with blows. For that I shall bite off your head." And she did as she had promised. "Now you will sing for me, magpie!" But the magpie said that he sang out of tune. "Then I shall sing you my song," said the fox. "Listen! When I was in the

service of a cruel mistress, you always laughed at me when I was beaten. For that I shall bite off your head!" The fox pounced, and that was the end of the magpie. "You at least must sing for me, little sparrow!" said the fox, scowling. "With all my heart," replied the sparrow. "But I must have fresh air to fill my lungs. Open the window, please." The foolish fox did as she was asked, and the sparrow flew out onto the branch of a tree and sang, "Why should I sing for a fox in her lair, when I may wing through the free forest air?" And away he flew!

## 15 JULY

## The Goose-Girl

In a dandelion kingdom, long, long ago, lived and ruled a widowed queen. She had only one child, a daughter, but she was so very, very beautiful that there was not a painter in the land whose portrait could do her justice. When the princess had grown up, her mother came to her one day and said in tears, "Dearest treasure, it is time for us to part. For while you were still in your cradle, your father and I promised your hand in marriage to a prince in a far-off kingdom. Now the day has come when you must set out on your journey to your husband." And she dressed the girl in her finest robe, made of butterflies' wings, and ordered two horses to be brought, one for the princess and one for her maid. The princess's horse was named Falada, and he was no ordinary steed, for he could speak in a human

voice. As her daughter was leaving, the queen gave her a little white handkerchief. "Care for it like the eyes in your head," she told the girl. "There are three drops of my blood upon it; it will protect you on your journey from all evil." With great sadness, the princess took leave of her mother and set out on her long trek. The day was hot, and soon she became thirsty. She told her maid to bring her a little water in a golden cup; but the maid answered, haughtily: "I am tired of serving you—go for the water yourself!" So the princess bent down by the stream and drank the water from her cupped hands. But, without her noticing, the handkerchief her mother had given her fell into the stream and floated away. Now her mother's magic could protect her no more.

## 16 JULY

# The Goose-Girl

The wicked maid had taken good note of how the handkerchief had fallen in the stream, and when the princess went to mount her horse, Falada, again, the servant-girl shouted at her: "I will ride Falada, and you shall sit on my horse!" Then she made the unfortunate princess take off her royal robes and put on her own. She had to promise to tell no one who the real princess was, or the maid would have killed her on the spot. Then they journeyed on, and the princess had to serve her maid all the way. When they reached the foreign kingdom, the prince at once led the maid in the princess's clothes into the palace. The hapless princess herself was sent to take the geese to grass with the little gooseherd, Conrad. But the false princess was afraid that the faithful horse, Falada, would reveal to the prince what had happened on the journey, and she ordered the butchers to make an end of him without delay. They nailed the poor beast's head to the city gate through which the princess drove the geese to and from pasture every day. When she saw the head, she wept bitterly, saying: "My faithful steed, Falada, come to such a plight!" But the head replied:

"And what price now, princess, your royal beauty bright? For if your noble mother were to be here now, her heart would break to see her daughter sunk so low!" Conrad the gooseherd thought it strange that the girl should speak to a horse's head, but he said nothing and drove his flock to pasture.

## 17 JULY

# The Goose-Girl

In the meadow the princess sat down, loosened her long golden hair, and began to comb it. Conrad admired the shining curls so much that he tried to cut himself a lock. But the princess laughed, and called out: "Fling Conrad's cap upon the ground, good Wind, that he may run, and have to chase it all around, until my toilet's done!" And the breeze grew stronger, caught up the lad's cap, and

sent it dancing about the meadow. Conrad had to run after it. But when they returned to the palace, the boy went to tell the old king, the prince's father, how the strange goose-girl had magic powers. The next day the king secretly followed them to the meadows. He heard for himself that she spoke to the horse's head at the gate, how the head answered, and saw how she turned to the wind for help. That evening he had her summoned to his chamber, and asked her who she was. But the princess was afraid to speak, so the king said to her: "If you will not tell me, then tell at least the old stove; you are sure to feel better for it." When the king had left the room, the princess indeed opened the door of the stove and told it the whole story. But the wise old king was listening at the chimney in the room next door, and heard everything. He sent at once for the false princess, and asked her, "What punishment would you mete out to a deceiver who pretended to be the daughter of a royal house?" And the false princess replied: "She would deserve no less than to be flung by the servants from a high bridge." — "You have pronounced your own fate," said the king, sternly, and he ordered the sentence to be carried out. Then the beautiful goose-girl found happiness at last.

## 18 JULY

### The Four Clever Brothers

Once upon a time four brothers set off into the world to find out what life was about.

Soon they came to a crossroads where the paths went in all directions. They began to discuss which way they should go. An old owl heard them. "Each should go his own way," it advised them. "When all of you have learnt something, you may meet here again." The brothers did as the owl had suggested, and each went in a different direction. The first of them met on his wanderings a master robber. "Come and learn our trade," the robber said to him. "It is not the most honourable of callings, but if you learn it well, you may have that which others cannot, and without ever being caught." The young man allowed himself to be persuaded, and he was soon such a master of the trade that there was no robber in the land to compare with him. The second brother became apprenticed to an astronomer. When he had learnt the names of even the tiniest of stars, his master gave him a telescope. "In it you will see all that goes on in the heavens and on the earth, and nothing shall be hidden from you," he told him. The third brother learnt to be a hunter. As they parted, his master gave him a rifle which always shot true to remember him by. And the fourth of the brothers became a tailor. From his master he received a parting gift of a needle which was able to sew everything in the world, though not a stitch was to be seen. In time all the brothers met again at the crossroads; they embraced each other and set off home.

hunter aimed, and BANG! The shells flew in all directions. The tailor gathered them up and sewed them back together again with his magic needle, so that there was not a stitch to be seen. Then the thief returned them to the nest. The bird did not even notice. Soon they hatched into healthy little birds, though each of them had a red stripe on its neck. "You will always find work in the world," their father told them. And indeed they did.

## 20 JULY

# The Four Clever Brothers

Before many days were out, there was a great weeping and wailing throughout the kingdom. An evil dragon had carried off the king's only daughter. The unhappy king announced that he would give his daughter in marriage to anyone who could set her free. "This is work for us," thought the brothers, gleefully. "At least we shall find out what we have learnt!" The astronomer looked through his telescope, and right away called out, "I see her already! Far away from here there is a rock in the middle of the sea, and it is there that the dragon guards his prey." Before long the robber had stolen a ship from the harbour, and off the four brothers sailed. On and on they sailed, until at last they came to the rock.

## 19 JULY

# The Four Clever Brothers

Their father greeted the four brothers with open arms, and at once asked them how they had got on in the world. Each of them boasted of what he had learnt. "Very well," said their father, "I shall try your skills. Over yonder is a tree; in the tree is a bird's nest, and the bird is sitting on its eggs. Tell me, astronomer, how many eggs are there!" "Five!" answered the astronomer, the moment he glanced into his telescope. "And now, robber! You must steal the eggs, without disturbing the bird," the father ordered. This was no trouble to him at all. As soon as he had brought them, the father placed one at each corner of the table, and the fifth in the middle. "Can you shoot all the eggs with a single shot?" he asked the hunter. The

The princess was sitting on a stone, and the dragon had his head in her lap; he had his eyes wide open, but he was snoring so loudly that the waves of the sea raged and roared. The hunter aimed his rifle, but then he lowered it again. "I cannot kill the dragon without shooting the princess as well," he said. "Then I must try my luck," said the robber. He crawled up to the dragon and stole the princess from him so skilfully that the monster did not even notice. The brothers set off on their return voyage. But soon the dragon woke up, saw the ship on the open sea, and gave chase. The hunter raised his weapon and shot the beast right through the heart. But as luck would have it, the dragon fell right on top of their ship, and smashed it to pieces. Then the tailor took out his magic needle, and sewed, and sewed, until the ship was as good as new. Then they sailed home to the royal city. Which of them do you suppose married the princess? Why, none of them. She was so ugly she was fit only to be a scarecrow! All four of them found themselves much prettier brides.

# The Sharp-Eyed Princess

Beyond seven rivers and seven hills lived a princess who had an enchanted chamber. It had as many windows as there are parts in one bee's eye. When the princess looked through the first window, she saw everything that went on in the palace gardens. If she looked through the second, she was able to observe every last little movement in the royal city. And if she looked through the other windows, she could see even with her eyes closed all that happened or did not happen on earth, and beneath the earth, and above the earth, and in front of her nose, and behind her nose, and where else everywhere nobody knows. And how proud she was of her powers! One day she had it proclaimed throughout the land that she would take as her husband any man who could hide himself away somewhere where she could not see him. But woe upon him whom she did find! He would be shorter by a head. There was no lack of young men willing to try their hand, but the princess spotted them all in an instant, and the headsman was kept so busy he hardly had time to sharpen his axe. But when there were no longer any suitors bold enough to try, a young archer arrived at the palace, a fresh-faced fellow, little more than a lad. "I have come to play hide-and-seek with you," he told the princess. "Twice shall be for practice, the third time for real."—"Very well," agreed the princess; so the archer went off to look for a place to hide.

## 22 JULY

## The Sharp-Eyed Princess

The young archer looked around for somewhere to hide in the palace gardens, but he could not find a place. Just then a little bird came flying out of the crown of a tree. The

archer drew back his bowstring, but the little bird called out: "Do not shoot: one day you may have need of me!" The young man put the arrow back in his quiver and left the bird alone. From the palace gardens he went down into the city. A broad river flowed through the city, and as he walked beside it the archer saw a large fish leaping there. Again he took aim, but the fish begged the archer to spare him, and he agreed. Then he passed on to the deep forest, where a fox crossed his path, limping, for he had a thorn in his paw. The archer slipped an arrow in his bow, but then he took pity on the poor creature. "Wait, fox!" he called. "I shall take the thorn out of your paw." The fox thanked the young man and said, "I shall never forget this; when you have need of me, remember me." Then the young man returned sadly to the castle. "A fine day I have had, indeed," he thought to himself. "I have shot nothing with which to win the princess's favour, nor have I found a hiding place." The princess was waiting for him. "Well, go and hide somewhere!" she called to him. The unhappy archer sat down beneath a tree in the palace gardens, and felt near to tears.

## 23 JULY

### The Sharp-Eyed Princess

As the archer was sitting mournfully under the tree, what should appear before him, but the

little bird he had taken pity on. "Have no fear; I shall help you," she twittered. She brought one of her eggs, pecked it in half, and hid the young man inside; then she put the two halves of the shell together again and sat down on the egg. "Ready?" called the princess. "Ready!" shouted the young man. The princess ran to her magic chamber, and she only had to glance into the first window to see the archer hiding in the bird's egg. "This time you are forgiven," she told him with a smile, and she sent him to find a better hiding-place. The archer wandered sadly down to the bank of the river which ran through the royal city. "If only I could dive to the bottom," he thought to himself. Just then the big fish stuck his head out of the water and said: "Do not worry, I shall help you!" And he stretched his jaws wide open and swallowed the young man as if he were a worm. Then he plunged to the bottom of the river. "Ready?" called the princess. "Ready!" was the reply from inside the fish's stomach. But as soon as the princess

looked out of the second window, she saw the archer hunched up inside the fish. She ordered the fishermen to catch the fish in their nets, and then told the unhappy fellow: "I forgave you the first time, and I forgive you a second time; but next time your head will roll!" The archer trudged sadly away from the castle. Where do you suppose he will get to?

## 24 JULY

### The Sharp-Eyed Princess

As the archer wandered aimlessly along, he

He hurried back to the palace to the princess, and she had to marry him, like it or not. In the end she did like it. Indeed, they made a fine couple!

## 25 JULY

# The Two Butchers in Hell

There was a certain rich butcher who had a poor brother. One day he sent for him to help him make sausages. There were piles of meat, but when they had finished the rich man gave the poor man only one little sausage. "A fine reward, indeed!" sighed the poor brother. The rich butcher flew into a rage and threw another sausage at his brother. "Here you are, you fool!" he cried. "And now, go to the devil!"—"If you say so, then to the devil I shall go," said the poor fellow; and he ate one of the sausages, hung the other on his staff, and strode off to find Hell. It was not until early the next morning that he arrived at the gates.

came to the deep forest. Suddenly the fox came running out of the bushes and said to him, "The princess can see into all the hiding-places in the world; but do not be afraid—I shall help you." Then the fox jumped into a woodland pool, plunged three times beneath the water, and came out in the guise of pedlar, such as sell animals in the market-place. He told the young man to do the same; the archer obeyed, and when he came up for the third time he had changed into a little monkey. The pedlar set him upon his shoulder and hurried off to the palace. The moment the princess saw the monkey, she liked him so much that she threw the pedlar a sackful of gold pieces, and kept the monkey as a pet. "As soon as the princess goes to the window, hide quickly under her hair!" the pedlar told the enchanted archer in a whisper. This time, when the princess called "Ready?" the fox answered for the young man in a human voice. The princess ran to her magic chamber, the monkey hopping after her. When she went to the window he hid inside her plaits. The princess looked out of the first window, and saw nothing. She looked out of the second, but the archer was nowhere to be seen. When she could not see him even in the third window, she stamped her foot, and grew so angry that she even drove the monkey away from her. He dashed off to the pool in the forest, plunged into it three times, and was again turned into the dashing young archer.

In front of them sat Lucifer's own grandmother with her knitting. The pauper greeted her politely and said, "My brother the butcher sent me here with this sausage." The old woman thanked him and let him inside. In a few moments the devils came flying through the air. "You must hide under the bed," said the old woman, "or my grandsons will tear you to pieces." He stayed there all day, and towards evening, when the devils flew off again, she gave the poor man a devil's hair to take home with him. But before he reached his cottage the hair had grown, and grown, until it was the size of a beam; and, believe it or not, it was made of pure gold. When the rich brother heard of the pauper's good fortune, he took the longest sausage he could find and marched off to Hell to try his luck. He did not even bother to greet the old woman, but went in and sat in the middle of hell, waiting for the devils to arrive. As soon as they flew in, they began to shout, "We are hungry!" And they tore the rich man to pieces. His kindly brother inherited all his riches.

honoured to make Your Majesty a magic suit of clothes. But take note: whoever is a fool, or not worthy of his office, will not be able to see such clothes." The emperor could not wait to have a magic suit. He set aside a chamber for the two tricksters, and had gold, pearls, diamonds and fine silk sent there, as they requested. When the pair of them had stuffed these riches away in their baggage, they sat down in front of an empty loom, and pretended to weave.

## 26 JULY

# The Emperor's New Clothes

There was once a little girl whose grandfather gave her a magic piano for her birthday. When she played the white keys, out of the piano jumped a little white cat, and began to purr little white fairy tales. When she played the black keys, a little black cat would jump out and begin to read little black fairy tales. She is just reading one now. Listen!
Once upon a time there was a proud, extravagant emperor. All day long he did nothing else but dress up and prance up and down in front of a mirror like a peacock. One day a couple of rogues arrived in his realm. They put their heads together, and then asked for an audience with the emperor. "We are tailors and weavers from a far-off land," they introduced themselves with a bow. "We are able to weave magic garments. We should be

## 27 JULY

# The Emperor's New Clothes

The emperor could hardly sleep, so curious was he to see his new suit; but he was afraid to go and see how the work was getting on. What if, God forbid, he could not see the clothes? Just to make sure, he sent his First Minister to have a look. The minister peeped into the chamber through a crack in the door, and saw the two rogues threading invisible thread and cutting out invisible cloth. "Good Heavens!" he thought to himself. "Am I then a fool, or unfit to hold my office?" So he had to describe to the emperor how fine the invisible robes already looked. It was not long before the two tailors sent word that the clothes were ready. All the lords of the land, the ambassadors and ministers, and the whole of the emperor's

# The Tale of Grandma Toadstool

Once upon a time there was a lazy old man who lived in a little moss cottage with his little black cat. How untidy it was in there! There were cobwebs in every corner, dust on the floor thicker than in the grinding room of a mill, and the bedsheets looked as if a chimney-sweep slept there. "We cannot go on like this, pussy," sighed the old man one day. "We must look around the world for a grandmother to clean and tidy the parlour for us." So off they went into the world together. The cat mewed, the old man whistled, and the miles passed quickly. They met an old goat. "Hey, granny goat, how would you like to tidy our cottage for us?" they called out to her. "Who, me-e-e?" bleated the goat. "What a lazy goat!" scowled the old man and the cat, and on they went. They saw a scarecrow in a field, looking like an old hag. A rook was standing on top of it. "You there, old hag, come and clean our parlour for us; we'll sing you a pretty song," they promised. The old man pulled the cat's tail, and the cat sang such a song that the rook nearly jumped out of his skin. "What a rack- rack- racket!" croaked the rook, and off he flew. "Did you ever see such a lazy old hag?" grumbled the old man, and since they were good and tired by now, they lay down in a meadow and went to sleep.

court gathered in front of the throne to see the marvellous suit. Suddenly, the doors of the hall flew open, and in came the rogues with a great flourish, holding their arms outstretched as if they were carefully carrying a rare and beautiful suit of the finest royal clothes. The emperor and all his court were filled with horror, because, of course, they could see nothing at all. Then they all began to speak at once, calling out: "How beautiful they are! See how finely cut is the cloth! How gorgeous the colours, how skilful the stitching!" Then the confused emperor had them dress him in his new robes, and he paced proudly up and down in front of the mirror as if he had never worn such beautiful clothes in his life. Then he set off with the nobles and courtiers to the city to show off his new clothes to his subjects, with a couple of pages walking behind him, carrying his invisible train. All the people shouted: "Praise and glory to our emperor and his new clothes!" For they were afraid to admit that they could see nothing. But suddenly one little boy called out, "Mother, the emperor is quite naked!" Everyone burst into uproarious laughter, and the emperor ran all the way home to his palace and hid under his bed in shame. And the two rogues? They had gone as suddenly as they had arrived!

broom, and swept all the dust out of the door. The others swung the cat by her tail and dashed about the room sweeping away the cobwebs from every little corner. The cottage was soon as clean as a new pin, but the old man and the cat were quite out of breath. They quickly slammed the door of the toadstool cottage and carried it off back to the woods. Nor did they ever again go looking for a grandmother to clean their home for them.

## 30 JULY

# The Lake of Tears

Now I'll tell you a secret I heard from a golden dandelion. Not very far away from here is an invisible crystal lake. Stars fall into it, and the moment they touch its surface they change into pink water-lilies. There is as much water in the lake as there are human tears in the world. Whenever anyone is sad enough to cry, a little water nymph awakes from her sleep, takes out the stopper made of rainbow fish scales, and lets out the hundreds of tiny rivulets that flow into people's eyes as tears. Then the nymph herself begins to cry. Clear

## 29 JULY

# The Tale of Grandma Toadstool

As the old man and the cat lay there in the field, they heard a thin little voice call out: "Let me out! Le me out!" The old man looked around him, but the only thing he could see was a big red toadstool. "Who is calling?" he asked in a startled voice. "It is I, Grandma Toadstool," replied the voice. "The wind has blown the door to, and I cannot get out of my little house!" The old man took a look at the toadstool and, what do you think? There was a little door in it just like in a real cottage. He and the cat pulled at the handle; the door flew open, and inside they saw, sitting in a spotless little parlour, a tiny old woman the size of a man's thumb. She had a little red hat with white spots on it and wore a clean white dress, and altogether looked like a little toadstool herself. "Now we have caught you, grandma!" called the old man. "You shall come along with us and tidy our cottage!" And he and the cat picked up the toadstool, carried it home with them, and planted it in a flowerpot on the windowsill. What a surprise they were in for! For no reason at all the handle of the bread-knife began to rap, and from all corners of the cottage there appeared little men in toadstool hats. They pushed a broom of birch twigs into the old man's hands, jumped down his shirt, and tickled him and tickled him until he danced around the parlour, waving the

little teardrops trickle down her cheeks, tinkling against the still surface of the lake and turning into softly iridescent rings. So it is that the water in the lake never goes down, just as the tears of the world never lessen. Then, from somewhere in the depths, a smiling little waterman comes forth, tunes his enchanted violin, and starts to play a soothing, silvery melody, as kind and gentle as a mother's caress. He goes on playing until the tear-nymph's eyes close in peaceful sleep, and a soft smile lights her face. Then he quietly puts back the stopper in the lake: the trickling little streams dry up, and out of the pink water-lilies tiny white clouds go floating up to the sky. Each of them contains a single little tear that has been shed.

## 31 JULY

# How the Mouse and the Frog Fell Out

Once upon a time a mouse and a frog lived together by a woodland spring. They would sleep all day long in their little cottage, and only when the moon rose in the evening would they come out to sit in the porch and tell each other fairy tales. One evening the frog took a kingcup flower down to the spring to get water. The water was sparkling with stars, like precious jewels in some royal treasure house. "Mouse, see how rich we are!" the frog cried out. The mouse came running up, and could not believe her eyes. Then she fell into thought. "Frog," she said, after a while, "you and I must take turns to guard our treasure, so that no one can steal it."—"You are right," said the frog. So they took turns to watch over the spring until morning. The last watch fell to the little mouse. Who knows what happened—perhaps the mouse dropped off to sleep for a while—but in the morning there was no sign of the sparkling treasure in the well. "Frog!" the mouse cried. "You have stolen our treasure!"—"I?" said the frog, angrily. "You are the one who had the last watch—you must have stolen it!" And the mouse and the frog began to argue so, that in the end they parted company and went to live separately. Fools! That evening the spring was again full of stars.

# AUGUST

## 1 AUGUST

## The Clever Peasant-Girl

There was once a poor cottager who had nothing in the world but his beautiful and clever daughter. "If only the king would be pleased to give us a little piece of land, so that we might not die of hunger!" he sighed one day. Who knows how the king came to hear of it, but he did, and he granted the poor man's wish. The peasant set to work joyfully. Suddenly something rang out beneath his mattock. The man bent down and, what

should he see but a golden mortar! "I shall take it as a present to the king in return for the field he gave us," said the poor cottager. But his clever daughter warned him: "Father, if you take the king the mortar, he will want a pestle, too; you would do better to keep it!" But the man took no heed of his daughter's words, and carried his rare find to the royal castle. "Where is the pestle to go with this mortar?" asked the king, sternly. And, though the cottager solemnly swore that he had found no pestle, the king would not believe him, and had him thrown in gaol. How the poor fellow wept and wailed! "Why did I not heed my daughter's words?" he lamented. One day the king himself heard his groans, and had him summoned again. "Why do you call on your daughter so?" he asked. The cottager told him everything, and the king pondered awhile and then said, "If your daughter is indeed so wise, then send her to me here. If she can guess my riddle, then I shall take her for my wife."

## 2 AUGUST

## The Clever Peasant-Girl

The next day, when the cottager's daughter came to the castle, the king said to her: "I shall fulfil my promise and take you for my wife if you come to me tomorrow, not dressed, not naked, not on horseback, not on foot, not in a cart, not by road, and not by field." The girl only smiled. The next morning she took off her clothes, so as not to be dressed. Then she put on a fishing-net, so as not to be naked, and tied the net to the donkey's tail. Then the donkey dragged her along the ditch to the king's palace. Thus she went neither on horseback, nor on foot, nor in a cart. She travelled neither by road, nor by field, but in between the two. When the king saw her from the window, he smiled and said: "Indeed you are a wise girl; you deserve to be queen. But, mark my words, you are not to meddle in affairs of state!" And so before very long the cottager's daughter was sitting on the throne beside the king.

148

hands, and pretended to catch fish. "Fool!" called the king from the window. "How can you catch fish here?" But the peasant replied: "If a pair of oxen may have a foal, why should I not catch fish in the street?" The king smiled, but then he said sternly, "This was not your own idea; who told you to do it?" At first the peasant would not tell, but after being given a sound beating he gave the queen away. The king flew into a rage, and told the queen: "You have not kept your promise. Tomorrow you shall return to your home. You may take with you from the palace whatever is dearest to you." The clever queen got the king to drink with her that evening for the last time, and made him drunk. In the morning she put him on a handcart and took him off to her cottage. When he woke up, she smiled and said to him: "You are dearest of all to me, so I have brought you with me." The king laughed heartily at her cleverness and took her back to the palace with him. From then on the king always took his queen's advice, and they lived happily ever after.

## 3 AUGUST

# The Clever Peasant-Girl

One day there was a great market in the royal city. During the night a fine foal was born to a certain farmer's mare, but it wandered off and lay down between a couple of oxen. In the morning, when the owner of the oxen found the foal, he wished to keep it for himself. He and the rightful owner argued for so long that the king himself heard of their quarrel. "The foal belongs to him with whose beasts it lay!" was the judgement of the king. When the queen heard this unjust verdict, she secretly called the wronged peasant to her, and said to him: "If you tell no one, I shall advise you how to get your foal back again." Then she whispered something in his ear. The next day the foal's owner sat down in the middle of the road in front of the palace with a rod in his

## 4 AUGUST

# The Three Magic Gifts

A soldier was returning from the wars. All he had been given by the emperor in return for his brave and faithful service was five groschen. As he was walking along he came across a large fishpond. On its surface stood a table, and round it sat four watermen, green and ghostly. "Be a good fellow, and take pity on us," they croaked. "We are out of tobacco, our wine-jug is empty, and for our fish-scales

we cannot even buy a piece of dry cheese! Give us just a groschen!" The soldier scratched his ear. "This is a fine thing," he said. "But what am I to do with you, my good fellows! Here is a groschen for each of you, that you may drink to my health." The watermen thanked him kindly, and the eldest of them said to him, "Since you have such a kind heart, my son, we shall grant you three wishes." The soldier scratched his ear again for a moment, then said, "Well, if that is to be, then give me a pipe which is always full, a pack of cards with which I may always win and . . . and a sack to which I may say only 'In you go!' and into it will fly anything or anyone I wish to get rid of!" The watermen smiled and gave him what he asked for, and the soldier went his way.

## 5 AUGUST

## The Three Magic Gifts

The sun was soon sinking in the west, and the soldier looked around him for a place to lay his head for the night. At length he came to an inn. He said to the innkeeper, "Here you have

my last groschen—let me sleep here tonight." But the innkeeper frowned and said, "Whatever are you thinking of? Every night, just before midnight, the devils come to my inn. I myself always run away at night. But if you will, you may stay here for nothing." The soldier thanked him, and when the innkeeper had left, he lay down on a bench in the taproom and fell fast asleep. Scarcely had the clock struck eleven, when down the chimney and into the room swept a whole swarm of devils. "Come and play cards with us, or we shall tear you to pieces!" they screamed at the soldier. "Why not?" grinned the soldier, taking out his magic cards; and the game began. Soon the soldier had all the devils' gold piled in front of him on the table. The devils lost their tempers. "We'll carry you off to hell for this!" they threatened him. "Just you try, you ill-mannered louts!" said the soldier with a smile, and he pulled out his magic sack and called out, "In you go!" In a brace of shakes

the devils were wrapped and tied in the old sack. When the innkeeper came home in the morning, he was astonished to find the soldier still in one piece. But the soldier just smiled, and told the innkeeper to give the old sack a good beating with a stout stick. You should have heard how the devils squealed and yelled! And when the soldier finally took pity on them and let them out of the sack, they did not so much as stop for breath until they reached the gates of hell.

## 6 AUGUST

# The Three Magic Gifts

The soldier went on wandering the world for a while, but then he bought himself a nice little farm with the devils' gold, and lived there in peace and happiness. But time does not stand still, and by and by the soldier grew old. Then, one day, whom should he see sitting in the pear tree in the garden, but Lady Death herself, looking like a great black bat. "I have come for you," she croaked. But the soldier was none too keen to leave this world for the next just yet, so he grabbed his magic sack and cried: "In you go!" And Death was in the trap. The soldier took the sack and threw it down the well, then filled the well with stones just to make sure. That very day one of the village lasses went to cut the goose's throat in the back yard; but no sooner had she drawn the knife across the bird's neck, than the goose's head jumped back into place, and off it flew. Just then the butcher came running by, waving his arms and shouting: "Save us! A slaughtered pig is chasing me!" To cut a long story short, nothing died any more, and before very long people were swarming about the world like flies, and it was a wonder they did not start to eat each other up. "It's no good, this can't go on," said the soldier to himself, and he went and set Death free again; no sooner was she out of the bag than she grabbed the soldier, and that was the end of him. The moment he was dead he made straight for heaven, but St. Peter did not want to let him in, saying that he had been a drinker and a gambler and heaven knows what else.

What now? The soldier had no wish to try his luck in hell, for the devils had surely not forgotten their beating at the inn; so he was relieved to bump into the village parson. "Reverend," he begged him, "would you mind taking this old sack to heaven for me?" The parson had no objection, but he had scarcely taken three paces when the soldier pointed a finger at himself and said: "In you go!" And in he went. The parson was quite out of breath by the time they reached the pearly gates, but the soldier got to heaven all right in the end.

## 7 AUGUST

# Smuttikin

Smuttikin the urchin lived in the forest with a stag who had golden antlers. Who knows how Smuttikin got there; maybe one day the

golden-haired wood-nymphs set him down on the doorstep, but no one can remember any more. The important thing was that he was happy there. When he was at home on his own, he would play the violin, and all the birds of the forest would sing along to the tune. Or else he would ride around the parlour on his tame squirrel's tail. During the day the stag would go to pasture, and he always reminded Smuttikin sternly not to open the door to strangers. But one day there was a knocking at the door and silky little voices from outside called to him, "Smuttikin the urchin, open up the door; we would only warm our fingers before your parlour fire." Smuttikin felt sorry for the soft-spoken strangers out in the cold, but he remembered the stag's warning and did not open the door. "It was well done," the stag praised him when he heard the boy's tale that evening. "Those were evil fairies, the Cavies. If you had opened the door to them, they would have carried you off to their den and roasted you for supper." Smuttikin cuddled up happily against the stag, and the stag told him a fairy tale.

## 8 AUGUST
### Smuttikin

The next morning the stag with the golden antlers again set off somewhere to pasture, and to pass the time Smuttikin began to play

the violin. Then he heard from the other side of the door voices even softer than those of the day before. "Smuttikin the urchin," they called. "Open up the door; we would only warm our fingers before your parlour fire." Smuttikin would so have liked just to see the Cavies, but he did not open the door. Then the fairies outside the door began to cry; they shivered with cold and moaned softly until Smuttikin felt so sorry for them that he forgot the wise stag's warning, and opened the door just a crack. The Cavies pushed their fingers through the door, then their hands, and before he knew it they were in the parlour. They grabbed hold of Smuttikin and ran off with him into the forest. But the boy began to play a sad lament on his violin: "From o'er the hills and far away, among your pastures green, come hither, golden stag, to me, and save your Smuttikin!" The stag with the golden antlers heard this plea and came thundering through the forest like a gust of wind; he took Smuttikin up on his antlers and carried him to safety. When they reached home, the lad got a good scolding. "Never open the door to strangers again!" the stag told him, angrily. Do you think Smuttikin will obey him?

## 9 AUGUST

### Smuttikin

Not many days had passed before there was again a whimpering at the door: "Smuttikin the urchin, open up the door; we would only warm our fingers before your parlour fire!" The boy tried to pretend not to hear, but when the wicked fairies began to weep and wail, and promised to play with him and give him nice things to eat and drink, he relented and opened the door again. Quick as a flash, the Cavies grabbed hold of him and ran off into the forest. Smuttikin wept bitterly and called to the stag, but he was grazing far off in the valley and did not hear the boy's cries. So the fairies took him off to their woodland lair. At first he had nothing to complain of: they gave

him all manner of good things to eat to fatten him up before roasting him. When he seemed nice and plump, they laid him in a dish and carried him to the oven. But Smuttikin begged them in tears to let him play his violin once more before they ate him; when they heard his plea, he again struck up his sad song: "From o'er the hills and far away, among your pastures green, come hither, golden stag, to me, and save your Smuttikin!" Before he had finished there was a pounding of hooves; out of the trees charged the stag with the golden antlers, drove the wicked fairies this way and that, and carried the boy off home. But what a scolding he had this time! He remembered it for the rest of his life, and he never, never opened the door to a stranger again.

## 10 AUGUST

# Goldenhair

There was a king who caught a strange and exotic bird in his garden one day. Under its wing the bird held a golden key. The king tried in vain to think what the key might fit. Then one day the bird laid a golden egg, and in that egg was a keyhole. The king tried the golden key in it, and as if by magic the egg flew open and out stepped a bearded little manikin. In his hand he held a fish on a tray. "Sire, I am the servant of the queen of the fishes," he said. "If you eat this fish, you will understand the language of all the animals."

And with that he disappeared without trace. The monarch told Jack, the young cook, to fry the fish for his lunch. "But mind you, you are not to taste the fish!" he told him. What sort of a cook could prepare a dish without even tasting it? When no one was looking, the lad slipped a small piece of the tail into his mouth. Just then a couple of flies flew by. "Leave some for us, leave some for us!" they pleaded. Jack was amazed that he could understand what they were saying. "So that is the dish which the king is to eat," he said to himself. He took another mouthful and hurried off to the king with the fish. After lunch, the king ordered the young cook to accompany him in his hunting. As they were riding through a grove of oaks, Jack's horse neighed merrily: "How light are my hooves today! I could leap over hill and dale." But the king's horse replied, gruffly: "It is all very well for you; but if you had on your back such a fat fellow as I, you would speak differently. If only the old fool would fall and break his neck!" The king frowned darkly, but young Jack laughed gaily at the horses' talk. The king looked at him suspiciously, and at once gave orders that they should return to the castle.

## 11 AUGUST

# Goldenhair

The king resolved to find out why Jack had laughed. "I shall make a test to see whether he tasted the fish," he said to himself, and he ordered Jack to fill his goblet with wine. "But if you spill the wine, or do not fill the cup to the brim, it shall cost you your head," he told him. Then he opened the window and let two small birds into the chamber. One was holding in its beak three golden hairs. "These are the hairs of Princess Goldenhair," it twittered. "Show me, show me," chirped the other, curiously, and chased the first all around the chamber. Jack listened with a smile as they squabbled, watching them flying about, and — the wine ran over the brim of the goblet. "So! Your head is forfeit!" cried the king. "But I shall show you mercy. If you bring to my palace the golden-haired maiden, you will be pardoned." And there was nothing for it but for Jack to set off into the world. Before very long he rode into a dark forest. There, beneath a tree, he found a couple of young ravens that had fallen from their nest. "Help us, good fellow," they beseeched him. Jack willingly picked them up and put them back in their

nest, and the birds croaked, "When you have need of us, think of us." Jack waved to them and went his way. He came to the shore of a black sea. Two fishermen were arguing over a little fish. "Sell it to me," he told the men. He gave each of them a golden ducat and threw the fish back in the sea. "When you have need of me, think of me," called the fish, and disappeared into the waves. And Jack rode on boldly.

## 12 AUGUST

# Goldenhair

Jack wandered far and wide, until at last he came to a lakeside palace. It was the palace of King Little, who was no bigger than a thimble. He had twelve daughters, each of them prettier than the next; but the most beautiful of all was Goldenhair. When King Little heard why Jack had come, he said to him, "Very well, I shall give my golden-haired daughter in marriage to your master, but first you must carry out three commands. This morning, as Goldenhair was bathing in the sea, she lost her gold ring. Go, and bring it to me!" Jack wandered sadly down to the seashore, an looked out over the dark waters. "If only the little fish were here," he thought to

154

himself, and before he knew it the little fish had poked its head out of the water, and was holding the gold ring in its jaws. King Little was pleased, but he said, "Before you may win the golden-haired maiden, you must bring from the spring at the end of the world the waters of life and death." "How am I to get to the end of the world?" sighed the unhappy Jack. "Unless, perhaps, my little ravens were to fly there." Scarcely had he thought this, when a whole flock of ravens came flying up, bringing him the waters of life and death in two little phials. Jack turned back merrily towards the lakeside palace. On the way he saw a spider, about to make a feast of a golden fly that was caught in its web. The young man sprinkled the fly with the water of life, and when it had come back to life again he set it free. "When you have need of me, think of me," it called to him. Jack waved to the fly and hurried back to King Little.

## 13 AUGUST

# Goldenhair

"You are a bold young fellow," King Little told the lad. "But if you would take away my Goldenhair, you must first pick her out from among my other daughters." And he led Jack to a chamber where twelve maidens stood, covered from head to foot in white sheets.

"Which is she?" asked the king. Just at that moment the golden fly whose life he had saved came buzzing around Jack's head. "Not that one; not that one; not that one either," it whispered to him. "This is she!" cried Jack triumphantly, as the golden fly alighted on one of the girls' veils. And it was indeed Princess Goldenhair. Now there was nothing for it but for King Little to bid farewell to the dearest of his daughters. When Jack brought Goldenhair back to the king, his master was so taken with her beauty that he almost forgot to breathe. Then he said to Jack with a cruel smile: "Since you have served me well, they shall cut off your body instead of your head!" And the executioner carried out the king's order without delay. But at midnight Princess Goldenhair came to where they had laid his body and sprinkled it with the water of death; as soon as she had done so the head grew back onto the body. Then she sprinkled him with the water of life, and Jack opened his eyes and sat up as healthy as ever, only twice as handsome as before. "Oh, how deeply I have slept!" he said in wonder. When the old king saw how Jack had come to life, looking younger and more dashing than ever, he had them cut his own head off, but then they found that the phials of wonderful water were empty. And so it was that the bold Jack himself became king—for did he not have the most beautiful of princesses at his side?

## 14 AUGUST

# The Giant Pig

Once upon a time a farmer found a china pig on the rubbish heap. As a jest he laid it down on some straw in the pigsty and told his swineherd to put some acorns in its trough. As soon as people got to hear of this, they laughed at the farmer: "The old miser! He wants to fatten himself up a china pig!" But, believe it or not, the pig grew, and grew, and was soon so big that it knocked down the whole sty. The farmer drove it into the parlour and filled the washtub with acorns for it. But the pig ate and ate, until soon it brought the whole farmhouse tumbling down, chimney and all. "See what a fine fellow he is growing into!" said the farmer gleefully, and he drove it into the barn. Then he brought it a cartload of potatoes. The pig munched, and crunched, and it was not long before it brought the whole barn crashing down around it. Now the farmer had nothing but the pig, so he called the butcher to come and make china sausages of it, but the pig gobbled up the butcher like a raspberry. Then it swallowed the swineherd, the milkmaid, a hunter, and a whole regiment of dragoons. In the end the royal artillery had to come, and the gunners fired their cannon all day and all night, until at last they blew the pig to pieces and let all the poor folk out. All the farmer had left was a huge pile of broken china. Believe it or not, in the middle of it he found a little china pig. But this time he isn't feeding it; he is saving up his money in it to buy a new farm.

## 15 AUGUST

# The Biggest Fool in the World

There was once a merry kingdom where the king laughed at everything, and was forever thinking up new jokes, games and pastimes.

He would sit on a throne made of lemon cheese, sleep in a whipped cream bed, and go around wearing a suit of curds. One day, the king decided to give his only daughter in marriage to whomever brought him the biggest fool in the world. A certain trickster heard of this, and said to himself: "Why should I not try my luck? I shall go into the world and look for the biggest fool: he is sure to cross my path some day." And go he did. At one crossroads he came to he saw a fellow who was harnessing a horse to a cart back-to-front. "Whatever are you up to, you dunce?" laughed the trickster. "Simple," the other returned. "I must go back home, for I forgot to wish my wife good day." "Then why do you not turn the whole cart around?" asked the young man in surprise. "Indeed, I had not thought of that," the stupid fellow replied. "Thank you for your good advice. So that you may know I am not ungrateful, I shall give you my horse and cart in return and I shall go on foot." The trickster laughed. "Surely he is the biggest fool in the world," he thought to himself, and told the fellow: "If you insist, then I shall take your horse and cart: but sit in the back—for your kindness I shall drive you home." With tears of gratitude in his eyes the fool thanked him and sat down.

## 16 AUGUST

# The Biggest Fool in the World

The trickster had not driven far when he came upon a strange sight. Beneath a big oak tree a man was trying to teach his pig to climb up. "Fool!" called the trickster. "Why do you vex the poor creature so?"—"Am I to let it die of hunger?" replied the man, gruffly. "He must climb the tree and feed on the acorns there!"—"Why do you not shake them down to the ground?" asked the young man. "Indeed, I had not thought of it," the fellow said with a grin. "Thank you for your good advice, stranger!" The trickster laughed until his sides ached. "He must surely be a greater fool than the first," he thought, and he invited the fellow to sit down in the cart, saying he would take him to see the king. Before they had gone very far, they saw a fisherman in a boat on the river. Each time he caught a fish on his hook, he took off his clothes, held his nose, and jumped in to get the fish. "Why do you not haul it in on the line?" asked the trickster. "Indeed, I had not thought of that," the fisherman replied. "Thank you for your good advice."—"I shall not find another such fool in a hurry," thought the young man, and he invited the fisherman to come along with them to see the king.

## 17 AUGUST

# The Biggest Fool in the World

On the way to the king's palace, the trickster and his companions strayed into a queer city. The trees there were planted roots upwards, and the houses built with their roofs pointing down. Just at that moment there was a great to-do in the town square, with people putting their bottles, buckets and pots out in the sun and then carrying them off into the town-hall. One old citizen explained to the youth what

was happening: "We have built a new town-hall, but we must carry the sunshine inside; for some reason or other it is quite dark in there!"—"Fools!" cried the trickster. "You have forgotten to make windows in it. Knock them through, and you shall have all the light you could wish for!"—"Indeed, we never thought of that," said the old man in surprise. "Since you are so wise, young stranger, tell us how to move the town-hall a little to one side, for we have built it right in the road."—"That is a simple matter," said the trickster. "You must all push on one side of the town-hall; I shall place my coat on the other side, so that we may see how much it has moved." So all the citizens went to the other side and pushed. In a little while the trickster secretly folded his coat in half. "See," he called out, "it is moving already, for half of my coat is under it." The people spat on their hands and set to again with a will. Meanwhile, the young man slipped his coat into the cart. "Enough!" he cried. "My coat has quite disappeared beneath the building." All the citizens embraced him, and the trickster said to himself: "The world is full of fools: why should I seek the biggest of them? It would be better to stay here and become mayor of the city. Fools are easily governed." And so he never returned to the merry kingdom. To this

day he is mayor of that city. Do you want to go and see him? You must go to the end of the world on the train that brings the fairy tales.

## 18 AUGUST

# The Fearless Princess

Once upon a time there was a village lad called Jake, for whom life was no bed of roses. His parents had long since died, leaving behind them only the poverty they had always known. None of the village girls would so much as look him over, for who in her right mind would take on such a penniless fellow for a husband? So poor Jake lived by himself in his little turf cottage by the wild rose bush. So that he would not be lonely, he tamed a little mouse, and carried him around in his pocket wherever he went. One day his godfather called the lad to him and said:

"Young fellow, I can no longer bear to see how poorly you live. Take my old cornet and go out into the world to seek your fortune. It is no ordinary cornet. When you blow it, all who hear it must follow you wherever you lead them." Jake thanked him, took the cornet, and set off into the wide world. When he played it, people came running up to him and walked behind him like a procession. "A fine thing my godfather has given me," thought Jake to himself. "Am I to wander about the world with folk treading on my heels, as though I were some general or other? I had better stop playing the devilish instrument." So stop he did; at once the people ran off in all directions to their homes, and Jake stretched himself out in a clearing in the forest, and fell fast asleep.

around him on all sides; but young Jake looked straight ahead of him and set off briskly towards the castle with his ghostly train.

## 19 AUGUST

# The Fearless Princess

When Jake woke up, it was just on midnight. At that moment little fires appeared all over the woods, and weird spectres began to enter the clearing from all sides. Goblins and werewolves, hullabaloos and will-o-the-wisps, fiery-eyed bats, pixies with mouse's tails, strange animals with human heads, watermen, trolls and flibbertigibbets and all manner of other horrible creatures. Jake began to shake with fear, until the little mouse's teeth rattled in his pocket. The demons began their council. "I wonder if you know," croaked a waterman, "that there is a princess in the castle beyond the haunted wood who is not afraid of the devil himself? They have tried a seven-headed dragon on her, a headless horseman and a horseless headman, but she only laughs and says that ghosts don't exist. She says that anyone who can frighten her may have her for his wife." Jake listened without moving a muscle. "I should dearly like to become king," he thought to himself. And at once he had an idea. He put the cornet carefully to his lips and began to blow with all his might. As soon as the spectres heard this, they gathered

## 20 AUGUST

# The Fearless Princess

The fearless princess was just listening to her suitors reading a frightening tale about a terrible ogre. "That's nothing to be scared of!" she laughed. "If he were to come to me, I should give him a nice kiss. But I should have to stand on tiptoe!" The young men racked their brains for something to frighten her with. It was then that young Jake appeared in the chamber with his procession of assorted apparitions. "I'll scare you all right, princess!" he called out, and he blew his cornet until the forest had emptied all its most horrible creatures into the princess's chamber. They gave out a wailing and hooting and hullabalooing and shrieking, rolled their heads around the marble floor, spat fire, and all in all played every demonic trick they knew, until all the princes and bold knights ran and hid themselves inside, under and behind anything they could find. But the princess only laughed and clapped her hands. "Oh, what dear little creatures!" she cried. "I never saw such a fine thing in my life." Now even young Jake did not know what to do. But suddenly the princess's necklace burst with her laughing, and one of the little jewels rolled under her gown. Jake's little mouse spotted it at once as he peeped out of the lad's pocket, and quick as a flash he was after it. "He-e-e-lp! A mouse!" screamed the princess in horror, and fainted quite away. When she came round, she could hardly catch her breath. "Oh, Jake, how you frightened me!" she gasped. "You shall be my husband." And she flung her arms round his neck. So it was that poor Jake became king. But first of all he had to have his pocket sewn up, so that his little mouse could not get out.

## 21 AUGUST

### Hansel and Gretel

In a cottage by the forest there once lived a poor woodcutter. His wife had died, leaving him alone in the world with their two children, Hansel and Gretel. So that they might have someone to look after them, one day he brought home to their little cottage a stepmother. That year a great famine came upon the land, and it was not long before the woodcutter and his family were down to their last loaf of bread. As they were going to bed that night, the stepmother said to her husband: "Unless we do something, we shall all die of hunger. Let us take the children into the forest tomorrow morning and leave them there: Providence will take care of them." The woodcutter did not want to hear of it, but

when his wife continued to pester him, with tears in his eyes he finally agreed. The children were so hungry they could not sleep, and they heard all that their parents were saying. Gretel began to cry bitterly, but Hansel whispered words of comfort, "Do not weep, dear sister, I shall think of something." And when the adults were asleep, he crept quietly out of the cottage and filled his pockets with shiny pebbles. Then he slipped back inside. No sooner had dawn broken, than the stepmother roughly shook the children awake, gave each of them a slice of dry bread, and told them to make ready to go into the forest. "We shall go to gather firewood," she lied to them. "But do not eat your bread all at once, for you will get no more today." And off into the forest they went, the woodcutter, the stepmother, and the two children.

## 22 AUGUST

### Hansel and Gretel

As they walked into the forest, Hansel kept stopping and turning round. "Hansel, why do you tarry so?" his father scolded him. "I am looking at my little white cat, sitting on the roof of our cottage and watching me," the boy told him, but he was really dropping the pebbles from his pockets on the path. "It is not

your cat, but only the morning sun shining on the chimney," said his stepmother, sharply. On and on they walked, until at last, deep in the forest, the woodcutter made a fire and told the children to wait there until he and their stepmother came back again. To pass the time Hansel and Gretel began to pick strawberries, but when their parents did not return, they sat down by the fire and waited. They thought they could hear the blows of an axe in the forest nearby, but it was only a dry branch which their father had hung from a tree, banging in the wind. Before long the children's eyes grew heavy, and they dropped off to sleep. When they awoke, it was night-time, and the forest was pitch-dark. Gretel burst out crying with fear, but just then the moon came out, and they saw the pebbles shining along the path; they glistened in the moonlight like pure silver. Hansel and Gretel took each other by the hand, and the silver trail led them safely back to their cottage. How angry their stepmother was to see them safe and sound!

## 23 AUGUST

# Hansel and Gretel

It was not long before the children, as they lay in bed, heard their stepmother telling their father to lead them even deeper into the woods the next day. "We have only half a loaf of bread in the cottage," she wailed. "If we do not rid ourselves of the children, we shall all die of hunger." In the end the unhappy woodcutter again agreed. The moment their father and stepmother had fallen asleep, Hansel stole out of bed and went to fetch some more pebbles. But, alas! The door was locked. Gretel again began to cry, but Hansel comforted her once more, "Don't be afraid: by morning I shall have thought of something." Early the next morning their stepmother again got them ready to go into the forest. This time she gave each of them an even smaller piece of bread. Hansel crumbled the bread in his pocket, and kept turning round and dropping the crumbs onto the path. "Why are you

stopping and looking round?" his father asked, crossly. "I am looking at my little white dove, sitting on the roof of our cottage and watching me," said the boy. "That is no dove, you foolish child, but only the morning sun shining on the chimney!" snapped his stepmother. And when they came to the darkest part of the whole forest, she told the children to wait by the fire until she and their father returned. Hansel and Gretel lay down in the grass, and they were so tired from their long walk that they soon fell fast asleep. When they woke up, black night had again descended on the forest. "Do not be afraid, Gretel," Hansel again soothed his sister. "When the moon comes out we shall find the breadcrumbs, and they will lead us back home."

## 24 AUGUST

# Hansel and Gretel

The moon rose over the dark forest, but the breadcrumbs were nowhere to be seen. The woodland birds had pecked them all up! "Don't be afraid," Hansel told his sister. "We shall find our way without them." But this time it was no easy matter; they walked all night, and all the next day, too. Evening was falling once again, and the end of the forest was nowhere in sight. Finally the children huddled together among the ferns and cried themselves to sleep. No sooner had they woken up the next morning, than a beautiful white bird appeared. It flew in front of them as if to show them the way, and sang so sweetly that the children ran after it. Soon they came to a clearing, and in the clearing stood a cottage. Now, the cottage was quite different from its owner: how beautiful it looked, and how wonderful it smelled! "See, Gretel, the walls are made of bread and cakes!" gasped Hansel. "And the roof of marzipan! And the windows of clear sugar crystals!" cried Gretel. Hansel had an idea at once. "I'll eat a piece of the roof, and you break off a piece of the shutters!" he told his sister. And straight away he began munching marzipan, while Gretel stood beneath a window and crunched away at the sparkling sugar, licking her fingers and smacking her lips. What a feast they had! Suddenly they heard a voice from inside the cottage say: "Are those little teeth I hear, nibbling at my cottage dear?" And the children replied: "It is only the wind as it blusters and squalls, tearing the gingerbread down from the walls." And they went on eating as if nothing had happened.

## 25 AUGUST

# Hansel and Gretel

The children were having the time of their lives nibbling away at the sweet-tasting

cottage, when the door flew open, and there in the porch stood a wrinkled old hag. She was leaning on a stick. "Well, well, and how did you get here?" she asked in surprise. "Come along inside, you will like it here." She took the children by the hand and led them to the table, where she fed them on all sorts of goodies; then she put them to bed under a soft eiderdown. But before they could rub the sleep from their eyes the next morning she grabbed hold of Hansel and shoved him into a little wooden pen to fatten him up for the oven. From then on Gretel had to take him the finest of foods, but she got only a few poor scraps that were left. Every day the wicked witch went to the pen and called to him, "Hansel, put out your finger, that I may feel how fat you have got!" But each time the clever lad pushed only a dry old bone through the bars of the pen. In the end the witch could wait no longer. "Fat or thin, I shall roast you anyway," she said, and ordered Gretel to light the fire under the oven. "Get inside the oven to see if it is hot enough, my dear," the old hag

told her; but Gretel made excuses, saying she did not know how to get in, that the door was too small, and such, until at last the witch lost her temper. "I shall show you, foolish child," she said, and pushed her head inside the oven. Then Gretel gave the old hag a good push, and into the oven she went. Right away the girl opened the pen to let her brother out; then they broke off a few mouthfuls of gingerbread, filled their pockets with jewels from the witch's chest, and hurried off home. They would never have got there, if a kindly white duck had not carried them across an enchanted lake; but at last they arrived at their own little cottage, where their father greeted them joyfully. Their wicked stepmother had died while they were away, and so they lived happily with their father again. They sold the witch's jewels, and built themselves a gingerbread cottage out of the proceeds.

## 26 AUGUST

# Waterman William

There once lived a lazy waterman called William. During the day he would sleep

soundly on the bottom of the woodland lake with frothy water for an eiderdown, dreaming his watery dreams. And what sort of dreams were they? Well, they were as dumb as fish; they even had fishes' scales, and up above them little rings of ripples spread across the water. For a waterman dreams as many water dreams as there are rippling rainbow rings on the surface of the lake. When evening fell and the moon slid out into the sky, daddy waterman would send sleepy waterman William off to school. And where was the school? Why, up in the old willow tree on the bank of the little lake. The waterman would sit there, open his waterman's reading book and study his waterman's ABC. There he would find everything, right from A to Z. How to stop the miller's water-wheel, how to light will-o-the-wisps, how to make mist over the water, why dogs bark and cats climb, how to tie ribbons on a willow wand, how to guard people's souls under upturned pots after drowning them, how many fingers there are on a hand and jars in the larder, and all manner of other things. But William was not very good at his lessons. One night, as he was sitting sadly in the willow, he heard a thin little voice in the grass down below saying, "Teach me to read! Teach me to read!" William looked down and, what should he see! A little maiden in a frog's skin, with frog's eyes and a frog's smile. And what sort of smile is that? Why, from ear to ear! The waterman liked the little maiden, and promised to teach her to read the very next day.

## 27 AUGUST

# Waterman William

Believe it or not, the frog maiden learnt her lessons as if there were nothing easier in the whole world. Daddy waterman himself thrust his head out of the water and said to himself, "Now, that would be a fine wife for my son! All green, soft as the grass—in a word, a real beauty!" When he suggested it to his son, the

lad was willing. Why should he not marry? Why, he was three years, three months, three weeks and three days old, and that was the best age of all to be marrying. So the next time the frog maiden came for her lessons he told her he would like to have her for his wife. The maiden smiled a smile like when the dew tinkles on a snowdrop, and said, "I should be glad to be your wife, if you fulfilled one wish for me." And she reached in the pocket of her apron and pulled out three hazel nuts. "Take the darkness out of these nuts and sew it into a coat that will keep out the cold when I am under the water," she said. Waterman William grew sad. "How on earth do you get the darkness out of a nut?" he thought, puzzled; then he took a stone and cracked open one of the nuts. But the darkness was gone without trace. "Maybe there is something about it in the waterman's reading book," he thought to himself, suddenly. And he began to study until his head ached, and soon knew the waterman's ABC back to front and better than all the other watermen put together. But he could find no mention at all of how to get the dark out of nuts. He was so sad he could have cried.

## 28 AUGUST

## Waterman William

The frog maiden frowned when the young waterman told her he couldn't fulfil her wish. "You must have slacked at school," she told him. "Go out into the world and open up your eyes, lazybones! Otherwise I shall not marry you." So the waterman went. He met a little mouse and told her of his troubles. "If you help me carry grain into my hole, I shall tell you how to get the dark out of nuts," promised the mouse. But as soon as the work was finished the mouse laughed at the waterman. "Fool! No one in the world can learn the impossible. It is clear that you are still very stupid," she told him. The disappointed waterman met a hedgehog. "If you help me clean out my hole, I shall tell you," he offered. But when the waterman had worked his fingers to the bone and the job was done, the hedgehog laughed at him, too. The same thing happened when he visited the fox, the squirrel,

the goat and the horned stag. He helped them all, but they only laughed at him. In the end he went back to the frog maiden and told her: "I can do everything in the world: carry grain, clean and tidy, get the seeds out of pine-cones, dry hay, feed stags—but I cannot get the darkness out of nuts. It is quite impossible." The little maiden smiled at him and said: "I shall take you as my husband, since you have learnt the greatest wisdom of all: Let alone the impossible and learn at least the useful." And so waterman William at last married the little frog maiden. By and by two little water-children were born to them, and grandfather waterman taught them the waterman's ABC.

## 29 AUGUST

# The Three Spinstresses

There was once an old spinstress who had a very lazy daughter. She would not take to spinning, no matter how her mother tried to persuade her. One day the old woman lost her patience and began to beat the lazy child. The girl began to shout and scream terribly. Just at that moment the queen herself happened to be passing by the cottage. "Why do you beat the poor child so?" the queen chided the spinstress, sternly. The woman was ashamed to admit how lazy her daughter was, and she lied instead. "Why should I not beat her, when she will not stop working? She spins and spins all day; where is a poor woman to get so much flax?" The queen comforted the poor girl, and told her; "I like to see the spinners at work; the whirr of their wheels is like music to my ears." And she asked the girl's mother to let her take her daughter back to the castle with her. The woman was only too glad to see the back of the lazy child. When they got to the palace, the queen led the girl to three chambers, filled from floor to ceiling with the finest flax. "If you spin this flax for me as quickly as you can, you shall have my eldest son for your husband, for a woman's industry is more than any dowry." The girl was dismayed. She would never spin so much flax if she worked till the day she died. She went over to the window and began to cry.

# The Three Spinstresses

As the girl stood by the window and wept, down by the palace gate she spied three strange old women. One of them had a foot the size of a mill wheel; another had a lower lip so long that it hung below her chin; the third had a thumb as thick as tree-trunk. "Why are you weeping so?" they called through the window to the unhappy spinstress. She told them of her troubles; the old women smiled and said to her: "If you promise to invite us to your wedding and not to be ashamed of us, but own us as your aunts and sit us down beside you at table, we shall spin the flax for you right away." The girl was happy to promise, and she let the three strange women into the palace. No sooner had they sat down in the first chamber than the spinning-wheel began to sing its merry song: "Tittity, tittity, tittity-tee; the spokes they shall turn and the bobbin shall spin, and the beautiful spinster be wife to a king!" The old woman with the huge foot smiled and stepped on the treadle; the one with the great lip smiled and wet the yarn, and the one with the thick thumb wound it up and tapped it against the table. Whenever she did so a skein fell to the floor, and the yarn on it was as fine as gossamer. They spun and spun the whole night through.

## The Three Spinstresses

Before the sun rose the next morning, the flax in all three chambers was spun. The three old women said farewell to the girl. "Do not forget your promise," they reminded her. "It shall be to your profit." Then they disappeared. The moment the queen saw the pile of yarn she had the wedding prepared without delay. The prince, too, was delighted that he should have such a beautiful and hard-working wife. He praised her to the skies. Then the girl said, "I have three aunts who have been of great service to me, my lady, and I should like to reward them. Might I invite them to sit beside me at table when the wedding feast is held?" The queen and the prince agreed. When the ceremony was over and the banquet had begun, into the hall came the three spinstresses, dressed in clothes that must have been older than the Ark. "Welcome, dear aunts," called the bride, but the prince frowned. "What ugly creatures are these?" he wondered, and at once he asked the first of the women, "Why is your foot so broad?"—"From working the treadle of the spinning-wheel," she told him. "And why is your lip so large?" he asked the second. "From wetting the thread," she told him. "And my thumb is so thick from spinning," the third woman told him. The prince was astonished, and said right away, "From this day on my beautiful wife shall never touch a spinning wheel again!" Do you suppose his bride was disappointed?

# SEPTEMBER

## 1 SEPTEMBER

# The Boy Who Was Looking for His Eyes

Once upon a time there was a little boy who was always crying, even though there was nothing to cry about at all. In short, he liked it when everyone was sorry for him and tried to comfort him. The more they spoiled him, the more plaintively he wailed and tried his poor mother. One day she lost her patience with him, and said, "Just you be careful, little cry-baby! He who cries for nothing will cry away all his tears. Then the little goblins will come creeping up in the night, steal the eyes from his head, and take them far, far away to the secret forest spring which is guarded by the snake with an enchanted elder sprig. The snake touches the eyes with the sprig, and they turn into precious stones and fall to the bottom of the deep water. There they stay until someone comes along to fill them again with tears. But first he must outwit the wicked snake and take away his enchanted sprig." When his mother had finished telling him this, the boy began to cry louder than ever. He cried and cried, until the Dream Maker awoke and locked up his tearful eyes with a golden key. Then he laid the key on the pillow, where it was found by the goblins from the far-off land of springs and sparkling pools. They opened up the boy's eyes with the key and carried them off to the snake sentry of the pool.

## 2 SEPTEMBER

# The Boy Who Was Looking for His Eyes

The next morning, when the boy awoke, he felt the warm sunbeams on his cheeks, but all around him was as dark as the bottom of a well. "Mother, I have no eyes!" he called out, and tried to burst into tears, but there were no tears to cry any more. His unhappy mother tried her best to comfort him, but she did not know what to do. From then on the boy was blind, and grew sadder day by day. Then, one day, he took courage, wrapped a scarf around his empty eye-sockets, and when no one was looking he slipped out into the world to go searching for the enchanted well. He felt with his hands in front of him, and stumbled along through the black, black darkness, and he would surely have not got very far at all, had he not suddenly heard a quiet little voice say: "Ow! You are standing on my foot!" The boy bent down, and there, at his feet, he felt a little frog. "Do not hurt me," he begged. But the blind boy took the frog gently in his hand and blew his poor little leg better. "You have a kind heart, my boy," said the frog. "For that I shall reward you." When the boy told the frog of his troubles, the frog leapt from his hand and under a burdock leaf, and pulled out a ball of blue string. "Take the end of the string in your hand and hold it tight," the frog told him. Then he flung the ball down the bank and croaked: "Froggy skip and froggy hop, down the stream and never stop." At these words the string turned into a babbling brook, which seethed over stones and through hollows and led the blind boy and his friend the frog right to the snake's pool.

## 3 SEPTEMBER

# The Boy Who Was Looking for His Eyes

On the way the frog said to the boy, "When we get to the spring, tell the snake you have brought him food, and throw me in front of him. When he opens his mouth to swallow me, the elder sprig will fall from it. You must throw it into the water without delay."—"I cannot do such a thing, for you have been so good to me," the boy told him, but the frog insisted. When at last they reached the spring, the snake reared up in front of them and hissed: "Hsss, hsss; my sharp fangs' poison, in a trice, will turn you to a block of ice!" But the boy was not afraid, and said: "I have here food for you, sentry-snake!" and he threw the frog to the ground. The snake dropped the elder sprig and pounced on the frog; but in an instant the frog changed into a white-hot pebble, and as soon as the beast swallowed this he burned to a cinder. The blind boy felt for the elder sprig and threw it into the spring. There was a brilliant flash of light, and the water began to bubble and seethe with human eyes turned into precious stones. One by one

the boy took them out and tried them until he found his own. Then he burst into tears of joy, but because he was not crying for nothing this time, his eyes grew brighter and more beautiful than ever, and the tears on his cheeks turned to pearls. The little frog was nowhere to be seen. The boy filled his scarf with jewelled eyes, and gave them to all the blind children he met on his way home.

## 4 SEPTEMBER

# The Little Glass Fairy

When I was quite, quite small, I had my own little brittle glass fairy which none of the grown-ups could see. She was clear and colourless and quite invisible. A little glass butterfly sat in her hair, and a red glass heart beat quietly in her breast. Pink, pink, pink tinkled that little red heart. The fairy lived in our garden inside a little glass tulip. We liked each other very much. One day we were playing together underneath the dog-rose bush which knew how to speak. I don't know where he had learnt it; maybe from the little children who used to pass by our garden fence, because he had a terrible lisp. The glass fairy would tease him about it; she told him he had a knot in his tongue, and laughed at him. "Briar, dear briar, say 'the seething sea ceaseth'," she would nettle him. "I am not a briar, I am a rothe," the proud and prickly

169

bush would snap back. "And I than't thay anything for you, tho there!" The glass fairy put her hand on her little glass heart and promised not to laugh, but the dog-rose was adamant, and would not be friends with us at all. Just to spite him, the fairy picked his most lovely flower, the one of which he was so proud. She ran across the grass with it, and planted it at once beside her own little glass tulip.

## 5 SEPTEMBER

# The Little Glass Fairy

When the little glass fairy picked the most beautiful flower on the briar rose-bush, the rose-bush lost his temper: "I'll tell on you, you little thcamp!" And since mother came into the garden at that very moment, he wasted no time in telling her all about it. Only mother couldn't hear him. I don't know why it is that grown-ups can never hear the voices of the flowers, or of the birds and the animals, or of toys. How sad the world must be for them. But

this time I was glad my mother couldn't hear, because she would have been cross with me and that would have upset me. So I pulled a face at the rose-bush, and the glass fairy and I joined hands and danced around the rose. "Little Tommy Tell-Tale," we chanted. The bush began to cry, until his leaves shook with sobbing. Then he dried his tears in the sun and began to whisper with someone. "Shhh, shhh, shhh," whispered the bush. Full of curiosity, the glass fairy stretched out her ear, but she could understand not a word. So she crept nearer and nearer, holding a hand against her glass skirt so that it would not jingle, though now and again her glass hair did tinkle softly. The bush pretended not to hear, and just went on whispering "shhh, shhh, shhh" importantly to someone or other, maybe the bees.

## 6 SEPTEMBER

# The Little Glass Fairy

As the dog-rose went on with his secret whispering, out of the bush flew a magpie, the bird which steals everything it sees which is small and shiny. "Run!" I shouted to the glass fairy, but she was frozen with fear. It was a wonder her little glass heart did not stop beating; little glass tears began to run down her cheeks, shattering on the stones as they fell to the ground. Ting, ting, ting they tinkled as they smashed. The thieving magpie almost had the little fairy in her beak, when the glass butterfly in her hair woke up. "Get off, you thieving devil!" it screeched at the magpie, and brrrh!—off it fluttered into the sky. How its little glass wings glittered in the sun! When the magpie saw this shimmering splendour, she left the fairy alone and flew off after the butterfly. Both of them soon disappeared in the distance. I wasted no time at all and, snatching up the little glass fairy, I hurried off with her to the glass tulip. There I sat her down in her parlour in the cup of the flower and begged the glass petals to shut over her as if dark were falling. Then I sat down by the tulip to keep watch.

## 7 SEPTEMBER

# The Little Glass Fairy

As I sat watching over the glass tulip, a soft sobbing came to my ears. "Why are you crying, little glass fairy?" I asked. "O-o-o-oh," she moaned from her little glass parlour, "I am not beautiful any more!"—"Why ever not?" I asked. "Because the glass butterfly from my hair has flown away," she whimpered. "Then I shall catch you another—a real live one," I promised, but she would not hear of it. She wanted nothing but to die of a broken heart, she told me, and other such things. This upset me. If my little glass fairy were to die, I should

never be able to imagine another one, since she was the only one I loved. I looked round the garden unhappily. Suddenly something glinted like a rainbow across the other side. What else but the glass butterfly! There it was, playing with its live companions, as if nothing were the matter at all; now bobbing up and down on a rose, now licking away from the cup of an acacia flower, flitting here, there and everywhere—just like any butterfly! "Come back at once, you rascal!" I called to it. "Don't you know the little glass fairy is crying for you?"—"Indeed!" the butterfly replied. "But I am not tame any more, and I want to play here with the others!" The little glass fairy peeped out of the tulip. "Does it mean nothing to you that I am not beautiful any more?" she asked. "Nothing at all," replied the butterfly, and dived straight into a peony. The glass fairy burst into tears again. Can you hear her tears falling? Ting! Ting! Ting!

## 8 SEPTEMBER

# The Little Glass Fairy

Everyone tried to comfort the little glass fairy. The golden pheasant from the gamekeeper's lodge brought her a pretty feather for her hair, and gave the thieving magpie a good

scolding. The little hedgehog brought her the most beautiful water-lily he could find, and the green frogs came hopping along with a fiery poppy, which they first had to quench in the water so that it would not burn her. But the glass fairy could not be comforted. When she had cried away all her little glass tears, though, she flew into a rage, caught up her little glass skirt and leapt straight out of her little glass parlour into the grass. Off we went to chase the butterfly. But the butterfly only laughed, flitted on his glass wings from flower to flower, and made funny faces at us. The glass fairy was soon in tears again. Then a golden spider called out from the dog-rose, "Don't cry, glass fairy, I'll catch your butterfly for you!" And he set to work busily. He spun, and spun, until he had spun a huge web over the rose-bush. It was as clear and invisible as the glass fairy herself. Then the rose-bush said, "Forgive me, little fairy, for thending the wicked magpie to get you; I'll never do it again." The fairy forgave him gladly, and the bush called out to the butterfly: "Come here, you rathcal; I shall give you the sweetest of honey to drink." The butterfly did not wait to be asked twice, and flew straight into the bush's branches. Before he knew it, he was fluttering hopelessly in the spider's web.

## 9 SEPTEMBER

# The Little Glass Fairy

The glass fairy thanked the rose-bush and the spider kindly, tied the little glass butterfly back in her glass hair, and said: "You just wait, you little scamp: I'll soon have you tamed again!" But the butterfly replied: "I was getting homesick anyway, and I am glad that you are beautiful again." I ran to fetch my mother, so that she might look at my little glass fairy, but she just let down her own honey-coloured hair in the sunshine, smiled, and said, a little sadly: "I can't see your little glass fairy, I'm too big." And she gave me two sweet-smelling rhubarb tarts. "One for you and one for your fairy," she said, stroking me on the head. I took the fairy her tart. "Mmmm, that's good," she said, licking her lips with her little glass tongue until they tinkled. "It is strange, but big people often can't see the purest things in the world. Just remember that. Then they are always sad. But then you too will stop seeing me one day, though I shall always be here with you." I did not believe her, then. We spent many happy days together. But one day I came into the garden, and the little fairy and the glass tulip had disappeared as though the ground had swallowed them up, though to this day, when white birds wing their way across the sky, I sometimes hear the beating of her little glass heart, somewhere near to me. Pink, pink, pink.

## 10 SEPTEMBER

# The Tale of a Circus

One day the circus came to town. Elephants and monkeys strolled through the streets, and acrobats in golden suits turned somersaults on horseback. What a fine sight it was! "Come to the circus, see the magic and the wonders!" called the clowns, tears of laughter streaming down their cheeks and glowing red smiles on their lips like many-coloured butterflies. In the town there lived a little boy who longed to go and see the wonderful circus. He begged his mother for the money to buy a ticket, but before he reached the big top the coins had fallen out of a hole in his pocket and rolled away somewhere. He stood miserably outside, peeping enviously now and then through a hole in the canvas. It was marvellous! High above the ground slender fairies danced on a silver thread, shining like snowflakes and flying through the air like glistening strands of gossamer. Beautiful princesses in colourful costumes rode along on white horses with flying plumes, and frowning wizards swallowed fire, leapt through flaming hoops, or had steel swords plunged into their breasts. "If only, just for a moment, I could enter the forbidden world of magic," thought the boy. Then a wonder came to pass!

## 11 SEPTEMBER

# The Tale of a Circus

As the boy was gazing wistfully at the prancing horses, a strange old man appeared before his eyes. He had big paper boots and a red paper nose on his face. On his white-painted face there was the orange glow of laughter, like the flame of a candle. He stroked the boy with a transparent hand and said, "I am Pepe the conjurer. I see that you would like to visit the world of magic and wonders. If you like, I shall change you into an elephant, and you may walk through the sawdust ring like the king of the jungle." — "I would rather you conjured up the money for me to buy a ticket," said the boy, who was not too sure he wanted to be turned into an animal. But the old man replied, "It is easy to turn small things into larger ones, but it is much more difficult to make small ones from

173

big ones. There are many folk who make small deeds into something wonderful, but few know how to make trifles of great deeds. It is the same with magicians. Choose what you would like to be, but do not ask me to make you smaller than you are." The boy did not understand the old man's words too well, but just then the roar of a big cat could be heard coming from the tent. "I should like to be a tiger-tamer," he said, softly. And before he knew what was happening he was standing in the middle of the ring in a splendid braided uniform with a goad in one hand and a whip in the other. All around him huge striped cats were creeping menacingly.

## 12 SEPTEMBER

# The Tale of a Circus

As the boy stood in the middle of the floodlit ring of sawdust, surrounded by bloodthirsty tigers, his heart sank with terror. The big cats bared their fangs at him, and great bloodied tongues hung from their jaws. "Pepe, Pepe the Magician!" he called out desperately. "Turn me into something huge, so that I need not be afraid!" But the old man in the paper shoes and the red paper nose replied, "There is nothing as enormous as fear. Only you can make yourself bigger!" The tigers roared fiercely and clawed the air. The boy glanced

miserably up towards the roof of the big top, and there he saw a tiny, beautiful princess, dancing high above the ground on a flying trapeze. In her hand she held a white parasol. Suddenly her delicate little foot slipped, and the slender princess came floating down on her parasol like a snowflake, right into the middle of the snarling beasts. The strange white shape annoyed the tigers. They roared fearfully and leapt towards her. At that the boy overcame his fear; he cracked his whip and goaded the animals into their cage. He could hear a great clapping and cheering, but he hardly noticed anything but the delicate arms that were flung around his neck. "It was nothing," he said. Just at that moment Pepe the Magician, the man with the paper shoes and paper nose, clapped his hands, and the boy found himself at home in bed. Beside him lay a little doll with a white parasol.

## 13 SEPTEMBER

# The Sleepy Bear

In a certain forest there lived with his mother a certain little bear. He liked nothing better in the world than eating honey and sleeping in the sun. One day his mother told him a story about the kingdom of honey. It is ruled over by the queen bee, and anyone who is disobedient must for his punishment eat a whole pot of honey, sleep in the sun, and listen to fairy tales. "Oo, how I should like that!" thought the little bear, and when his mother wasn't looking, he set off to look for the kingdom of honey. He walked, and walked, until he came to the shore of a great sea. Close at hand a fisherman was mending his boat. "Good day," the bear greeted him. "Do you by any chance happen to know how one is supposed to get to the kingdom of honey?" Now the fisherman was a sly old fellow, and it occurred to him at once that he might put the young bear to work for him. "Why, of course I know," he said. "If you untangle this big ball of twine and find the end

# The Little Big Prince

for me, I shall show you how to get there." And he showed the bear what to do. The ball of twine was huge, and the little bear did not feel a bit like working so hard. "Why should I ravel and twist for nothing, when every piece of string has an end at both ends," he thought to himself, and he caught the end that was at the beginning between his teeth. Then, since the sun was shining so brightly, he curled up and fell fast asleep. When the fisherman came back, he said crossly: "A fine worker you are! Where is the end of the string?"—"Why, here, of course," replied the clever bear. "I found it right at the beginning." The fisherman smiled. "Very well," he said. "Come with me; I shall take you to the kingdom of honey." He led the bear to a beehive, gave it a good bang with his fist, and ran off. You should have seen how the bees chased that poor little bear! He ran back to his mother in tears, and did not even want to hear fairy tales about the kingdom of honey any more.

Once upon a time there was a tiny little prince. He was so small that even on tiptoe he could see no further than the end of his nose. Everyone laughed at him. While the rest of the princes fought with seven-headed dragons, delivered enchanted princesses and pulled the tails of the palace cats, Prince Little, as they used to call him, could not even face up to a mouse. Instead of a horse he would ride on a grasshopper, and instead of a sword his mother gave him a rusty old needle. One day he was sitting sadly in the palace gardens on an upturned thimble and watching the birds pecking away at the ripe poppy heads. One of the little poppy seeds fell and rolled to the prince's feet. He picked it up and ate it, and, what do you think? Suddenly he felt his body stretching out, and before he knew it his head was high above the clouds. When he looked down and saw how tiny everything on the ground seemed from up there, he had to burst

out laughing. But it was not long before he felt anxious. "How am I to live like this?" he thought. "Feet on the ground, head in the clouds! I should rather be tiny, as I was before!" Scarcely had he thought this to himself, when he shrank back to his former size. "It must have been the poppy seed that did it," he thought, and he quickly picked up some more and put them in his pocket.

## 15 SEPTEMBER

## The Little Big Prince

Now that the little prince had found out how to be big when he wanted to, he decided to go out into the world like the other princes. He saddled his grasshopper, sharpened his rusty needle, and with a "gee-up, there!" went riding out of the palace gates. On the way he met some boys who were racing on their hobby-horses. "Who will be there first?" he

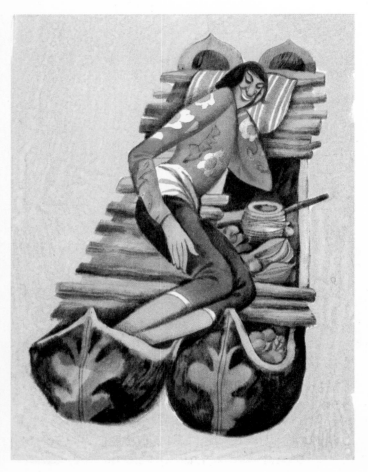

called to them, and spurred on his mount. The boys shot after him as fast as they could, but Prince Little beat them all and was there first. Where? They hadn't the slightest idea. There were iron trees and stone flowers growing there, and a troop of wooden soldiers marching along the road. "Halt!" called their leader. "What will you here?" Prince Little replied boldly that they were seeking their fortune in the world. The soldier was pleased, and took the prince and his friends to see the king right away. The king was also made of wood, and every time he took a step he creaked like anything. "I am glad," said he, in his wooden voice, when the soldier had made his report. "I have a daughter named Fortune. An evil wizard has taken her off to a paper island on a paper sea. He put her on a paper rose, which has grown to the sky. There she sits and weeps and waits for her deliverer. She is afraid to jump down lest the paper island should give way beneath her." — "Have no fear," said Prince Little, "I shall have her free in no time at all." And he and the boys went off to the paper sea.

## 16 SEPTEMBER

## The Little Big Prince

Beside the shore of the paper sea two small boats were rocking at anchor. They were sisters, and they held hands all the time. "How are we all to get in?" said the boys on the hobby-horses. "Just wait and see!" laughed Prince Little. He lay across both the boats and swallowed a grain of poppy-seed; at that he began to stretch out, and the boats with him, until they made a wooden bridge to the paper island. The boys rode across, and then Prince Little and his army banged on the door of the wizard's paper castle. "We are come to free Princess Fortune!" the prince called out sternly. "Help yourselves!" chuckled the magician. "She is sitting up there in the paper rose." Prince Little stretched out his arm, but he could not reach the top of the rose. So he quickly swallowed another grain of poppy-seed, and at once was twice as tall as before. Then he took Princess Fortune in his hand and lowered her gently to the paper island. They and the boys set off at once for the opposite shore, with the wizard following. But the moment they had reached dry land the prince thought to himself, "Let me be as small as before!" At that the bridge again shrank into a pair of little boats again. These could not bear the wizard's weight, and sank in the paper sea, taking the evil magician with them. Strange to say, Princess Fortune was also no bigger than your little finger, so she and the prince were wed; but when he wanted to tease her, he would eat a grain of poppy-seed and grow to the sky.

## 17 SEPTEMBER

## The Table, the Ass and the Cudgel

Long, long ago there lived a tailor who had three sons. Every day one of them would take the goat to pasture. One day the eldest brother took her to the cemetery, where the grass was as soft as silk, and left her to eat her fill. When evening drew near, he asked her: "Well, goat, have you had enough?" And the goat replied, "Master, even if we stayed, I could not eat another blade." The lad was pleased, and led the animal home. But after supper his father went and asked the goat, "Well, goat, how did you eat today?" And the goat replied, "Master, how was I to eat, when instead of pastures sweet, I was grazing all the day, in among the tombstones grey?" The tailor flew into a rage and turned his eldest son out of the house. The next day the middle son took the goat to pasture. He led her to a meadow full of sweet clover. Before long she had munched it bare. "Well, goat, have you had enough?" the second son asked her towards evening. "Master, even if we stayed, I could not eat another blade," the goat

replied. So the young man took the creature home again; but his father did not trust him, and went to ask the goat, "Well, how did you eat today?" "Master, how was I to eat, when instead of pastures sweet, I was grazing all the day, in a field of stones and clay?" The tailor was again enraged, and drove his middle son away, too.

## 18 SEPTEMBER

## The Table, the Ass and the Cudgel

On the third day the youngest son was sent to pasture the goat. He found her a spinney where the leaves were green and juicy, and as evening fell the goat told him how well she had eaten. But the moment they got back home, the goat complained bitterly to the tailor: "Master, how was I to eat, when instead of pastures sweet, I was grazing all the day, where the fallen leaves decay?" As soon as the tailor heard this, he sent the youngest son out into the world to fend for himself. The next day he set off to take the goat to pasture himself; he took her where all the most luscious goat delicacies grow, and she munched away greedily. When evening came she said contentedly, "Master, even if we stayed, I could not eat another blade!" The tailor led her home jauntily and tied her up in

177

the shed. "Well, goat, at last you have eaten your fill!" he said to her. But the mischievous goat replied, "Master, how was I to eat, when instead of pastures sweet, I was grazing all the day, where the grass was dry as hay?" Then at last the tailor realized how he had been taken in by the deceitful creature. He gave her a good beating with a stick, and shaved her head till she was quite bald; but what good did it do? It would not bring his sons back again.

## 19 SEPTEMBER

# The Table, the Ass and the Cudgel

Meanwhile the three sons were not doing too badly for themselves in the world. The eldest became apprenticed to a carpenter, and so skilfully did he work, that his master soon took a liking to him. When his apprenticeship was over, the carpenter gave him as a parting gift a little wooden table. "It is no ordinary table," he told him. "If you tell it 'Table, be laid!', it will fill itself with whatever foods you fancy." The young man thanked him and set off home. When he grew hungry, all he had to do was to give the order to the table, and it was at once full of the most delicious titbits. On the way home the lad stopped by at an inn. The inn was full of guests, but the landlord had run out of food and drink. So the young man set the table down in the middle of the dining-room and ordered it: "Table, be laid!" Soon all the guests were eating and drinking as though it were Shrove Tuesday. Among them sat a band of wandering gipsies. They ate so well that when they had finished they spread themselves out around an empty cask in front of the inn, and fell fast asleep. "I should dearly like to have such a wooden cook," thought the innkeeper to himself, and when the lad, too, had dropped off, he changed the table for another just like it. In the morning the young man set off for home with the innkeeper's table under his arm. His father greeted him with open arms. "I have learned the carpenter's trade," his son told him proudly. "Invite all our relations, and you shall see how I shall wine and dine them," he bragged. When all the relatives arrived, the eldest son placed the table in the midst of them and ordered it: "Table, be laid!" But, of course, nothing happened at all! How ashamed the young man was!

asleep, he swapped the ass for another. It was this other animal that the young man led home to his father, who welcomed him with tears in his eyes. "What have you brought me, son?" he asked. "Wait and see, father," the middle son told him. "You must invite all our relations, and I shall give them more gold than they have seen in their lives!" When the family was assembled, he said, "Ass, give me gold!" But the only thing the ass could offer was something that was nothing at all like gold. What a scandal there was again!

## 21 SEPTEMBER

## The Table, the Ass and the Cudgel

The youngest son learned the turner's trade. His master gave him a wooden cudgel in a sack as he was leaving. "If you tell it 'Cudgel, out you come!', it will jump out and beat your enemies soundly," he said to the lad. The young man thanked him, and because his brothers had written to tell him how the innkeeper had swindled them, he made straight for the fellow's inn. There he got talking to the landlord. "Here in this sack I have a prize far more precious than any bountiful table or golden-mouthed ass," he told the greedy fellow, casually. When the lad had eaten his fill, he lay down on a bench and put the sack under his head. Soon he pretended to be fast asleep. The innkeeper crept up on tiptoe and tried to get the sack from him. But the youngest brother shouted out "Cudgel, out you come!" and the wooden cudgel set about the dishonest landlord until he was black and blue. The lad would not call the cudgel off until he had returned the magic ass and table. What a homecoming it was when the youngest son arrived at his father's house! They invited all the relations once more, laid out a great feast, and gave them all as much gold as they could carry to take home with them. From then on life was like a fairy tale.

## 20 SEPTEMBER

## The Table, the Ass and the Cudgel

The second son became apprentice to a miller. When his time was served, the miller rewarded him for his service with an ass. "But it is no ordinary ass," he told him. "If you say to it 'Ass, give me gold!', it will drop gold coins from its mouth faster than you can gather them up." The boy thanked the miller and set off home, leading the ass behind him. Soon he chanced to arrive at the same wayside inn where his brother had been robbed of his magic table. He tied the ass up in the stable and went to ask for a bed for the night. "First you must pay!" the landlord told him. "I am not having you making off in the morning without paying." So the young man borrowed a tablecloth from the innkeeper, saying he would fetch some money. The innkeeper was puzzled, and secretly followed the boy to see what he was up to. He saw the ass fill the tablecloth with gold pieces. "I should dearly like to have such a money-mint for myself," he thought, and that night, when the lad was

## 22 SEPTEMBER

# The Table, the Ass and the Cudgel

Now it only remains to be told what happened to the mischievous goat. When the tailor beat her with his stick and shaved her head with his razor, she was so ashamed that she ran off into the woods and hid herself in a fox's lair. When the fox came home, a pair of huge eyes shone from her lair, a pair of horns creaked at her, and a set of hooves beat the ground menacingly. The fox ran away in tears. "Why are you crying, sister fox?" the bear asked her. "Why would I not cry, when the devil himself has moved into my lair, with his fiery eyes, his goat's horns and his satanic hooves!" the fox told him. "Dry your eyes, sister fox," said the bear. "You shall see how I get the rascal out of there." And he went straight to the fox's lair. But when he saw the fiery eyes himself, he, too, took to his heels. He met a little bee. "Why so sad, Bruno?" asked the bee. The bear told her all, and the bee smiled. "A fine couple of heroes you are!" she said. "I'll show the fellow!" She flew into the lair and stung the goat on her bald head so terribly that she bleated with pain and ran off into the trees. That was the last that was ever seen of her.

Do you know where I heard this tale? It was told by a father starling to his little ones, and before he had quite finished they were all of them fast asleep.

## 23 SEPTEMBER

# The Tale of the Mouse

Once I met a little boy who was holding in his hand a little brown mouse. When he saw me, he put the mouse down in the grass and said, "Help me build a mountain of pebbles. When it is finished we shall climb to the top with my little mouse and see what it is like up there, high above the clouds. Perhaps my little sister will come up afterwards, but she can't just yet, because she is poorly. What do you suppose the sky is made of? Won't we fall through it?"—"I don't know," I told him, "I have never been there. Perhaps it is a great big meadow with stars growing on it."—"Meadows are green," he said, wisely. "You never know," I said. "Maybe some meadows have grass that is quite, quite blue. There are little white sheep grazing there, and round their necks they have little glass bells. When the bells ring the sun comes up, and it is morning."—"Why is it morning?" he asked, curiously. "Because the flowers have dropped their petals."—"Why do they drop their petals?"—"Because they only

flower at night." "Why do they only flower at night?" he asked. "Why? Because!" I said, crossly. "You keep on asking questions as though you had nothing better to do. You had better grow up soon. Grown-ups are not surprised at anything."—"Why aren't they?" he wondered. I told him I should rather help him build his pebble mountain than answer his questions. While he worked, he told me the tale of his little mouse.

## 24 SEPTEMBER

# The Tale of the Mouse

Once upon a time there was a little mouse. One night he slipped out of his hole and began to gnaw at some sweet ears of corn. Suddenly he heard a whispering, and all at once a tiny voice called out, "Let us be, you are ruining our house!" "Who can it be?" thought the mouse in surprise. "We are the little grain fairies. One of us lives in each grain, and we look after the ears. If you do not harm us, we'll show you a magic footpath." The mouse promised to leave them alone, and out of the grains of corn jumped little fairies in white caps and white lace aprons. In their hands they held dandelion-down parasols, and floated down to the ground on them like little snowflakes. They sat on the mouse's tail and showed him how to get to the magic footpath. "There it is!" they shouted, when they came to

a grassy ridge. And indeed it was. A tiny little path stretched out like a stream of tears between the stalks and bushes, over field and through forest, and at the end of it the great full moon was shining. "Where does it lead to?" asked the mouse. "We don't know," said the grain fairies, but it wasn't true. They had heard that whoever sets out on that path wanders far into the wide world. And since they did not want the mouse to come back and chew their ears of corn again, they had decided to show him the enchanted footpath. Now, where do you suppose it will lead to?

## 25 SEPTEMBER

# The Tale of the Mouse

The mouse walked and walked, and was just beginning to feel sad and lonely when he met a little frog. "Where does this path lead to?" he called out. The frog started, but when he saw that it was only a little mouse speaking, he took heart, and replied, "I don't know; I have been hopping along it for a long time, but it seems to have no end. Perhaps it leads to the sky itself. If you like, we may go together, so that we won't be afraid." The mouse agreed. Soon they reached the kingdom of marsh-marigolds. The king sat in a golden flower with a tame bee on his lap. He was giving her honey from a crystal goblet, and the bee was fanning him with her wings.

With one hand the king was turning the pages of a great book, made of marsh-marigold leaves bound together. "Halt!" the king ordered the mouse and the frog. "Whoever enters the kingdom of marsh-marigolds by the enchanted path shall at once, immediately and without delay be turned into a marsh-marigold! Thus it is written in the book of marsh-marigold laws. Here, you may see for yourselves!" The mouse and the frog took a courteous peep. "We cannot read, Your Majesty," they said. "Oh, what a pity!" sighed the king of the marsh-marigolds. "I was hoping you would read the rest of this book to me, for I am tired of reading it. But if you cannot read, then get out of my sight. Where are you going to, anyway?" — "To the sky," replied the mouse. "This way, please," said the king, and pointed towards the moon. So that was the way they went.

## 26 SEPTEMBER

# The Tale of the Mouse

The mouse and the frog could scarcely put one foot in front of the other, but they seemed to be no nearer the sky. "I wonder what the sky is like," said the mouse. And the frog said, "I suppose it is like a great puddle, with a beautiful water-lily floating on it. On the water-lily sits the queen of the frogs, looking after the little star-frogs. She has one silver eye and one golden one. She looks through one of them at night and the other in the daytime. When she closes her eyes, it is dark here on earth." — "Oh, no," said the mouse, shaking his head. "The sky is sure to be as dry as a mouse's hole." — "Then why does it rain from there?" asked the frog, a little crossly. "It is a great puddle, I tell you!" They would probably have fallen out altogether, if something had not hissed beside them in the grass, and a pair of devilish eyes had not shone at them out of the dark. One of them was silver, the other golden. "Hurrah, we're here," shouted the frog. "I told you so!" He wanted to jump forward, but he couldn't even move. The mouse, too, was fixed to the spot. It was as though they were both turned to stone. For out of the grass poked a hideous snake's head, its forked tongue swishing through the air. The snake opened his mouth wide and hissed, "Just you come along into my splendid jaws, and make yourselves at home. Whoever would get to the end of the path of wandering must pass through my stomach." Just then the shadow of an owl fell across the path, and the snake's bright eyes dulled with fear. The mouse and the frog waited for nothing and dashed to safety.

## 27 SEPTEMBER

# The Tale of the Mouse

The two animals plodded along that enchanted path, and began to feel very sorry for themselves. "Are we nearly there?" asked the frog. "Is it far now?" he panted. But there were no words of comfort for the little mouse to offer. Then they came to a great lake. The whole of the night sky was reflected in its water, the stars glittering on its surface like tiny bits of mother-of-pearl. "Hurrah, we're here at last!" cried the frog, joyfully. "I told you the sky was a great puddle." And before the mouse could say a word, the frog had leapt into the lake and disappeared into the depths. The mouse waited, and waited for the frog to come up again, but there was no sign

# The Tale of the Mouse

Luckily, mice are not the least bit helpless under the ground. As soon as the little traveller had got over the shock of being thrown in a bee-dungeon, he began to dig and scrape, until at last he dug his way right out of the bees' nest. But there again was the endless lake, and the mouse began to cry hopelessly. "I shall never find out what the sky is like," he wailed. Just then a little boat made of a walnut shell came floating up in the breeze. The mouse begged it, "Take me with you, far, far away to where the sky is."—"I was just about to go there anyway," said the little boat, which knew how to talk and sing. "The two little children have sent me to see how far it is to the sky. But I have been sailing ten days and nights, and the clouds just run away from me. Come with me if you wish: at least we shall not be lonely." The mouse was pleased, and curled up contentedly in the bottom of the shell. It was a lovely day, and the sun shone so pleasantly that the mouse was soon sound asleep. Suddenly he was woken up by piercing cries. A flock of seagulls was circling over the little boat, and their king called out angrily: "Whoever values his life stays away from the kingdom of the water birds!" And he snatched at the little mouse with his beak. But the boat puffed out its sail and shot across the water like an arrow, until the birds were lost from sight.

of him. "Perhaps there is one sky for frogs, and another for mice," he thought to himself. Suddenly he felt very homesick. As he turned around, he suddenly saw nearby a little passage like a mousehole. "Maybe I shall find a friendly mouse there who will take me in," he thought to himself, and stuck his head in the hole. But out of the passage came a buzzing sound, which grew louder and louder, then out of the hole flew a swarm of angry bumble-bees. They settled all around the poor wanderer, and the queen said angrily, "How dare you disturb our kingdom? As a punishment we shall shut you up in the underground cells!" And they drove the poor creature down the passage and walled it up with earth and wax.

## 29 SEPTEMBER

# The Tale of the Mouse

Who knows how long the mouse and the little boat bobbed up and down over the waves; but the sky was always as far away as ever, and they never, never reached the place where it meets the water. In the end a fierce storm drove them back to the shore. There were two small children standing there, a boy and a girl. "Look!" called the boy. "Our little nutshell boat has come back again." The children were surprised to find the half-dead mouse inside, and they took him in their hands and warmed him gently. Then the little mouse told them how he had set out on the enchanted path to the sky, so as to find out what it was like up among the stars. Then the boy said: "I, too, should like to know what it is like up in the stars. I shall build a high mountain of pebbles, so high that it will reach into the sky. Then I shall go and become king of the stars. I shall rule wisely and fairly, and teach grown-ups to believe in miracles." — "Then take us with you," begged the little girl and the mouse. "We, too, should like to go higher and higher, to climb up with you along the magic pathway to the blue realm of the stars." — "I'll take you," said the boy. It was the same little boy I helped to build his pebble mountain. When it is finished, I'll tell you what it is like up there in the sky. But if we should grow old, and never manage to finish it, then you must go on building it,

dear children. Perhaps there are even people like us living up there, and waiting to throw their arms around us.

## 30 SEPTEMBER

# The Inquisitive Fish

There was once a little fish who just had to be everywhere, and hear everything. Her mother would say to her, "You know, curiosity killed the cat!" But the little fish would not listen, and swam hither and thither about the sea, so as to miss nothing. One day she came across a clump of sea-plants on her travels. "Clack, clack, clack," she heard from inside. An old crab was sharpening his claws. "Whatever can it be?" thought the curious little fish, and for a while she swam round and round, since she was a little afraid. But her curiosity got the better of her fear. When the tapping did not stop, she turned and swam up to the mysterious clump, just to take a peep. Now that was a mistake! The old crab did not take kindly to inquisitive visitors. He stuck out his pincers and, snap! He nipped the curious little fish on the nose until her eyes watered. You should have seen how she hurried home to her mother, weeping and wailing. True, her mother put a sticking plaster on her sore nose, but then she gave the little fish a good smacking with her fin, to teach her that it doesn't pay to be inquisitive. What about you, children? Are you inquisitive? You had better watch out; not only for crabs, but also in case a blackbird should come along and peck off your nose!

184

# OCTOBER

# 1 OCTOBER

## The Selfish Fox

Once upon a time a fox went to visit her godmother. She carried a sack of poppy-seed on her back, so that they might bake poppy-seed cakes. She met a little hedgehog. "Give me a handful of poppy-seed," begged the hedgehog, "so that I may bake a cake for my children. If you give it to me, your sack will grow heavier and heavier. If not, it will get lighter with every step." The selfish fox frowned. "Why should I want the sack to be heavier, when I have such a long journey before me? And what are your children to me, foolish hedgehog!" And she went on. The hedgehog hurried quietly after her, and slipped in front of her on the other side of the woods. He rolled himself up in a ball, until he looked like a little tree-stump. When the fox saw him, she said to herself: "I have walked long enough; now I shall have a rest." So she sat down in the grass, and rested her sack on the tree-stump. But the hedgehog stuck out his spines and pricked the sack all over. When the fox had rested, she set off again. She did not even notice the poppy-seed falling out of the sack, grain by grain. "The foolish hedgehog was right," she thought, in a little while. "The sack is growing lighter step by step. A good thing I didn't give him so much as a grain of the seed." But before she got to her

godmother's, the sack was quite empty. There were no poppy-seed cakes that day. But the woodland birds had a fine feast, and thanked the hedgehog from their hearts.

# 2 OCTOBER

## The Magic Arrow

A young Indian brave went out hunting one day. Suddenly he saw a splendid bird in a tree nearby. Instead of feathers, it was covered in wild roses. Right away the young hunter drew back an arrow in his bow. "Do not shoot!" called the bird. "I shall reward you." The Indian put back his arrow, and the bird said,

"It is well that you did not shoot, for had you killed me, you would have met with ill-fortune. Go to your tepee and you will find there a magic arrow. Whenever you seek something, loose the arrow into the sky, and it will show you the way." The bird had spoken truly. When the brave returned to his home, he found in his tepee a beautiful arrow, covered in wild roses. The days went by, and then the young brave fell in love with the witch-doctor's beautiful daughter. One evening he summoned up his courage, and went to ask her father for her hand. "I shall give you my daughter in marriage, if you can three times find her where I hide her," said the witch-doctor. The young man agreed. The next day he set out into the prairie to look for his loved one, but though he wandered back and forth he could find the young maiden nowhere. Then he remembered his magic arrow. He shot it up in the air; the arrow turned around and flew like a bolt of lightning into the throat of a little red bird. As soon as the bird hit the ground, it turned into the medicine-man's daughter.

### 3 OCTOBER

# The Magic Arrow

When the young brave led the witch-doctor's daughter back to her father, the powerful magician was astonished, and said, sternly, "The second time you will not find her." But in the morning the young man did not hesitate, and shot his magic arrow straight for the sun. It flew for a long time, and as it flew it sang an Indian love-song, so that the young man might not lose sight of it. It fell into a deep lake, and soon a beautiful silver fish popped up out of the water. The arrow was stuck in its eye. The young brave pulled it out, and at once there stood before him the smiling beauty he loved. The witch-doctor frowned with anger. "You have not won her yet," he said. "If you do not find her a third time, I shall turn you into a wild wolf." The young man only smiled, undaunted. But when he shot his magic arrow

the next day, it soon fell back at his feet. He drew his bow again, but again the arrow fell to the ground. "I cannot find your bride," it said in a human voice. "You must give me your blood to drink." The young man did not hesitate, but shot the arrow through his own leg. Then he again loosed it to the clouds. As it flew, it sang a sad song. Then it fell and pierced a dry white flower. The young man picked the flower, but nothing happened. "Pour your blood over it," said the arrow, and when the brave had done so, it turned into the beautiful Indian maiden. They embraced, and were never parted again.

### 4 OCTOBER

# Sleeping Beauty

Once upon a time there lived a king and queen, who would say to themselves, day in,

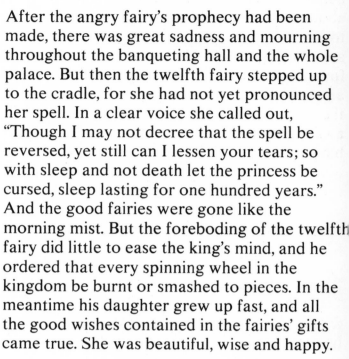

# Sleeping Beauty

After the angry fairy's prophecy had been made, there was great sadness and mourning throughout the banqueting hall and the whole palace. But then the twelfth fairy stepped up to the cradle, for she had not yet pronounced her spell. In a clear voice she called out, "Though I may not decree that the spell be reversed, yet still can I lessen your tears; so with sleep and not death let the princess be cursed, sleep lasting for one hundred years." And the good fairies were gone like the morning mist. But the foreboding of the twelfth fairy did little to ease the king's mind, and he ordered that every spinning wheel in the kingdom be burnt or smashed to pieces. In the meantime his daughter grew up fast, and all the good wishes contained in the fairies' gifts came true. She was beautiful, wise and happy.

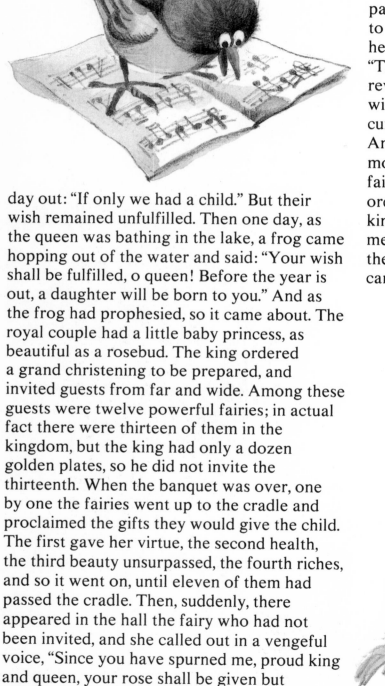

day out: "If only we had a child." But their wish remained unfulfilled. Then one day, as the queen was bathing in the lake, a frog came hopping out of the water and said: "Your wish shall be fulfilled, o queen! Before the year is out, a daughter will be born to you." And as the frog had prophesied, so it came about. The royal couple had a little baby princess, as beautiful as a rosebud. The king ordered a grand christening to be prepared, and invited guests from far and wide. Among these guests were twelve powerful fairies; in actual fact there were thirteen of them in the kingdom, but the king had only a dozen golden plates, so he did not invite the thirteenth. When the banquet was over, one by one the fairies went up to the cradle and proclaimed the gifts they would give the child. The first gave her virtue, the second health, the third beauty unsurpassed, the fourth riches, and so it went on, until eleven of them had passed the cradle. Then, suddenly, there appeared in the hall the fairy who had not been invited, and she called out in a vengeful voice, "Since you have spurned me, proud king and queen, your rose shall be given but summers fifteen, wherein she may grow, and in loveliness bloom; till the prick of a spindle shall spell out her doom!" All those present were struck dumb with horror; before they could recover themselves, the fairy was gone.

She grew into a lovely young maiden. It happened by chance that on the very day of her fifteenth birthday the king and queen had to leave the palace, and the princess stayed behind on her own. She began to wander about the castle, until she reached an old tower. There she found a strange little door, and, turning the rusty key in the lock, she found herself in a tiny chamber. There she saw an old woman sitting by a spinning-wheel with the spindle in her hand, and spinning merrily away. The princess could not take her eyes off her.

## 6 OCTOBER

# Sleeping Beauty

"Good day, old woman," said the girl at last. "What a fine game you are playing; I should dearly like to try it." And at once she put out her hand towards the spindle. But the moment she touched it she pricked her finger, and fell onto a golden couch which stood beside the wheel, slipping into a deep, deep sleep. With her all else in the palace slept too: the king and queen, who had just returned; the courtiers; the horses in the stables; the dogs in the yard, the doves on the roof, the flies on the wall, even the fire in the hearth. Even the cook, who was about to clout the kitchen-boy, dropped off, as did the girl who was plucking a chicken for the royal supper. The very wind which was gently blowing past the palace at the time settled down in the bushes and went to sleep. Only the thick briars which grew around the castle walls were not still; these grew and grew until the whole palace was covered with an impenetrable layer of thorny branches, and then a great silence descended on the place. Many a bold knight or prince tried to cut his way through the prickly mass, but all were caught up in the terrible briars and none returned alive. The years came and went like passing dreams, and the people from the countryside around the palace began to tell the story of the sleeping princess to their children, though none knew what was really

happening inside the palace. Then, one day, just one hundred years later, a handsome young prince happened to be passing through that land; he heard an old man telling his grandchildren the tale of the enchanted palace, and decided to see for himself.

# 7 OCTOBER

## Sleeping Beauty

The young prince threw himself at the thorny thicket with drawn sword; but the briars parted to let him by, and wherever he passed beautiful roses burst into flower among the thorns. When he reached the palace, however, the prince could not find a single moving creature, for all was steeped in the deepest of deep sleeps. The astonished prince wandered from one chamber to the next, until at last he reached the old tower. There, lying upon the golden couch, he saw a princess so beautiful that it quite took his breath away. He leaned over and kissed her gently. "Awake from your dreams, o sleeping beauty sweet, and open your eyes, that they and mine may meet!" he breathed. Then the princess gave a long, deep sigh, opened her eyes, and smiled at the prince. "I have been dreaming of you," she said. "Ah, what a long and beautiful dream it was!" And at that moment everything in the palace awoke. The wind rose and shook the flags, the fire shot out red tongues of flame, the girl finished plucking the chicken, the kitchen boy got his clout over the head from the cook, the horses in the stables gave a merry neigh, the doves flew down from the roof, and the flies began to buzz around busily. The king and queen and all the courtiers rubbed the sleep from their eyes and called on everyone in the kingdom to acclaim the bold young prince. Nor was it long before they were celebrating a glorious wedding, and all twelve of the good fairies were there. The thirteenth had moved off to another kingdom, and only the birds would sometimes bring news of her.

## 8 OCTOBER

## The Pot of Gruel

In the treasury of a certain kingdom the most precious treasure of all is a rusty old pot. The

old queen walks about the palace and tells all who stop to listen the tale of the pot of gruel. Long, long ago, there lived a miller who had fallen upon hard times. As if that were not enough he had a nagging wife, so that his only joy in the world was his beautiful daughter. When, one year, a famine came upon the land, even the mice in the miller's corn-loft started to go hungry. One day, the miller's wife cooked a pot of gruel from the last few handfuls of flour, set it down on the table, and said, "When we have eaten it, we may take our leave of this life, for this gruel is all we have in the world." When the miller heard this, he grabbed a wooden spoon, anxious to taste a last morsel before he set about the business of starving to death. But his quarrelsome wife would not let him near the pot, afraid lest he should leave none for her daughter and herself. When they had fought over the gruel for a long time, she suddenly grabbed the pot, put it on her head, and ran out of the mill. Waving the wooden spoon, the miller chased after her. When their daughter saw them, she did not even stop to put on her shoes, but took them in her hand and went after her parents. But they had disappeared from sight. Then, to cap it all, the poor girl dropped one of her shoes on the way, and couldn't find it again. She sat down on a bank and began to cry.

## 9 OCTOBER

# The Pot of Gruel

Scarcely had the girl wept her last tear, when there beside her an old woman suddenly appeared. "Why were you weeping so?" she asked, kindly. The girl told her everything that had happened, and the old woman smiled at her. "Here you have another shoe," she said and, reaching into her bag, pulled out a slipper all of gold. "Go through the forest until you come to the king's castle," she told the miller's daughter. "Knock on the gate and ask for some clothes. But take only silk ones. If they ask you why, tell them you have worn silk all your life." When she had said this, the old

woman disappeared. The girl did as she had been told, and when the servants had brought her silken robes, she looked like the most beautiful of princesses. The moment the prince saw her, he fell in love with her. The old king liked the girl too, and so a great wedding was prepared. While the cakes were being baked, the girl looked out of the window at the birds as they twittered to the parrot in his cage. Suddenly, she saw her mother running across the fields with the pot of gruel on her head and her father chasing after her with the wooden spoon. She could not help bursting out laughing. "What are you laughing at?" asked the prince in surprise. She told him a tale, since the truth was much too shameful. "Oh," she said, with a laugh, "I was just thinking how small this palace is for such a wedding. Wherever are we to put all our guests?" The prince fell into thought. What do you suppose he will think of?

## 10 OCTOBER

# The Pot of Gruel

When the prince had thought for a long time and thought of nothing, he asked his bride, "Have you then a bigger palace than ours, that this one makes you laugh so?"—"Why, of course!" the miller's daughter told him proudly. The prince was glad to hear this. "Then we shall put the wedding off for a week, and invite the guests to your palace." And he rushed off to tell the king. His bride suddenly grew sad, and was sorry she had boasted to the prince so foolishly. Then, before her very eyes, the bird in the golden cage changed into the little old woman. "I heard all," she said. "But do not fear; next week you shall set off on your journey. A little dog will be waiting outside the city gates. No one will see him but yourself. He will lead you and the royal train to a great palace." Then the old woman disappeared again. And all was indeed as she had said. No sooner had the royal procession left the palace gates, than a little dog ran out of the bushes, and led the

miller's daughter to a magnificent castle. "This is my palace," said the bride to her guests, and they all went inside, sat down at a huge table, and ate, drank and made merry. Then the doors flew open, and into the banqueting hall ran a woman with a pot of gruel on her head. "Help! He will beat me!" she called out. The king, the queen and all the guests burst into roars of laughter, and in the end the young bride smiled and admitted that these were her dear parents. They all rejoiced, ate the gruel with the wooden spoon, and then placed the pot in the royal treasury.

## 11 OCTOBER

## The Tale from the Zoo

There was once a beautiful zoo. There must have been animals there from all the world. They all liked it there, because no one did them any harm, they had plenty to eat, and the children and the adults would gaze at them admiringly all day long. One day a bold African lion was brought to the zoo. They shut him in a cage and gave him his breakfast. But the lion would not touch his food, frowned, and roared at the top of his voice, "I don't want to go to prison; I haven't done anything wrong." — "Don't be silly," the keeper told him. "This is not a prison, it's a zoo. Now you will be the most important of all the lions. You will get a fine-sounding name, like Julius Caesar or Jack the Ripper, the Count of Monte Christo or Harry Hawkins, and you will show all the children what a real, unstuffed lion looks like." The lion was flattered. "That's more like it," he

said. "I know all about looking like a real lion; just as long as you don't want me to look like a real anything else, that will be all right. And you can call me Harry. I like that name." So they called him Harry. The children crowded round his cage, and the lion was proud enough to burst. But before very long there was a terrible mess all round his cage. The naughty children threw their rubbish on the ground, and the keeper could not clear it up fast enough. "Now that was all I needed," thought the keeper to himself, and he sat down to think.

## 12 OCTOBER

## The Tale from the Zoo

When he had done all the thinking he intended to, the keeper said to the lion: "Dear, golden lion Harry; it seems to me we shall have to send you back to Africa again. The minute the children see you, they throw down their ice-cream cornets, sweet packets and lemonade cups, and come over to talk to you. Who is supposed to sweep all that lot up after them? It's not as if you knew what to do with a broom yourself." Harry the Lion grew very sad. He liked the zoo; he was pleased with all the attention he got from the children, and didn't much fancy going back to Africa. So he, too, began to think, and suddenly he said to the keeper: "What are those strange animals over there?"—"Why, kangaroos, of course," the keeper replied. "They have a pouch on their stomachs to carry their children."— "I know!" said the lion, brightly, and he whispered something in the keeper's ear. The keeper's face lit up, and he went off to get a brush and some paint. On either side of the lion's cage he placed a kangaroo, painted on his stomach the word "rubbish", and smiled with satisfaction as the children threw their junk into the kangaroos' pouches. When they were full, the kangaroos went off and emptied them, and then stood by the cage again. From then on the zoo was as spick and span as mother's back garden. And Harry the Lion was as pleased as Punch that he did not have to go back to Africa.

## 13 OCTOBER

# Annie the Monkey, Chico the Parrot and Wally the Bear

Once upon a time there was a sailor who had sailed in a ship through all the seven seas. He had seen many strange countries and all the wonders of the world. But still he was sad and lonely, for he was all alone; he had no wife or children, and there was not a port that he could call home. One day, as he was sailing across the open sea, the ship ran into a huge storm. The waves towered over the ship like terrible mountains, and it bobbed up and down like a nutshell. Suddenly a giant wave washed over the deck, sweeping away the whole crew, along with the captain himself, all except for the sailor. Luckily the captain was smoking his pipe at the time, and the sailors swam after the puffs of smoke, until they all reached America safely. There they wrung out

their clothes, dried their boots, and went to the cinema. Maybe they are there to this day. The sad sailor was quite alone on the ship. He was tossed here and there by the storm, until at last he arrived at an unknown island. "What am I to do without the captain and the crew?" he lamented, but just then a parrot alighted on a branch nearby and called out: "I am the admirrral! I am the admirrral!"—"Well, if I haven't got a captain, I shall have to make do with an admiral," thought the sailor to himself, and he took the parrot on board.

## Annie the Monkey, Chico the Parrot and Wally the Bear

The parrot was called Chico, and he knew as much about sailing as a cock does about laying eggs, but he was as stern and as self-important as the most captain-like of captains. All day long he would sit on the flagstaff and call out: "I am the admirrral, I am; full steam ahead as fast as you can!" The poor sailor had his work cut out to stoke up, draw water, swab the decks, cook and darn. "We can't go on like this," he said to himself one day. "We shall have to find a deck-hand somewhere." They were just coming to an unknown shore, and in a while they spotted a little bear collecting honey. "We have plenty of honey aboard!" the sailor shouted to him. "If you like you can have a white sailor's cap and you may work as a deck-hand." The bear liked the idea. "My name is Wally," he said, as he came aboard. It was merrier right away with three of them, but Wally the Bear was not one for hard work. He liked nothing better than snoozing or licking the dishes and

snooping around looking for pots of honey. The sailor had to do everything else. "This is no good," he said to himself. "We must at least find ourselves a cook." And he steered for a nearby island.

## Annie the Monkey, Chico the Parrot and Wally the Bear

On the island they found a little monkey swinging from the trees. "What's your name?" the sailor called out, but the monkey did not reply. The sailor pulled a face at the impolite creature; the monkey did the same. The sailor put out his tongue; so did the monkey. Well, being a monkey, it could only monkey about. But the sailor took it aboard just the same. They started to call her Annie. They gave her a little white apron, and she became their cook. She was not the least bit lazy, but whatever the sailor wanted her to do, he first had to do it himself. Then the monkey would do it. That way they always cooked the same food twice; first the sailor, then the monkey. They ate so well that they always fell asleep on the spot; the parrot on the flagstaff, Wally the Bear in a tub of marmalade, Annie the Monkey hanging by her tail from the pendulum of the clock, and the sad sailor in a barrel of salted herrings. Once, as they were sleeping like that, their ship was spotted by pirates. They sailed closer, but could not see a soul on board. "Let us board her and plunder her, then we shall send her to the bottom," said the pirate chief. "Have at them!" he called, and the pirates began to hurl kegs of gunpowder aboard the other ship. Boom! Boom! Boom! they went.

## 16 OCTOBER

## Annie the Monkey, Chico the Parrot and Wally the Bear

The first to wake up was Chico the Parrot. He blinked one eye and called out: "I am the admirrral, I am; full steam ahead, as fast as you can!" The pirates were startled. "Could it be the admiral's flagship?" they wondered. Then Wally the Bear crawled out of the marmalade tub. "He-e-elp!" cried the pirates. "A sea-devil!" At that Annie the monkey woke up, swung along on her tail and, seeing the pirates hurling kegs of powder at their ship, began to copy them and threw at them everything she could lay her paws on. Finally the sad sailor hauled himself out of the barrel of herrings. He was covered all over in fish-scales, and had a herring between his teeth. The pirates thought it was Neptune himself, and they were so scared they leapt into the water, and before they could swim ashore they were eaten by sharks. Then the sad sailor and his crew sailed to the pirates' island and raised their flag triumphantly. They

found chests full of gold there, and sweet nuts and pots of fine honey. They built themselves a cottage and the sad sailor scrubbed it from top to bottom. When the monkey saw this, she grabbed a hedgehog and tried to scrub the floor with that, but she pricked herself so badly on its spines that she never touched a scrubbing-brush again. They are living there together happily to this very day. Now the sad sailor has found himself a home port, and we have a secret island to send messages to by carrier pigeon.

## 17 OCTOBER

## Why

In a far-off land to the east lived a ruler who loved to set his subjects riddles. One day he summoned the greatest sages in all the land and said to them: "Tell me, tell me, why has the camel got a hump? If you cannot answer in three days, you shall lose your heads." The learned men went off sadly. It had never occurred to them to wonder about such an obvious thing as that, and now they could not answer their monarch's riddle to save their lives. They hurried to their libraries to consult their learned books, but they could not find the answer. So they turned to the stars, but they were no help either. In the end the eldest of the sages called up powerful magicians, using ancient spells and incantations; they put their heads together, and gazed into their crystal balls, magic mirrors and fiendish flames, but all to no avail. After three days the ruler summoned the sages again and said: "Well, tell me why the camel has a hump!" The wise men stood in silence and secretly took their leave of this life. Just then a little boy ran into the chamber and called out, "Because its back is not straight!" "Indeed, I should not have thought of that myself!" laughed the ruler; he set the wise men free and gave the boy a splendid glass marble. So you see that there is nothing magic about cleverness!

## 18 OCTOBER

# Woodkin

Long ago in a little cottage on the edge of the forest there lived a carpenter and his wife. They prayed in vain to the Lord to give them a little child. Then one day the woman forgot herself and cried out in her bitterness, "If the Lord will not give us a child, then may the Devil at least!" That evening her husband brought home from the forest a little tree-stump. It looked for all the world like a little baby; all he had to do was trim it a little and carve two holes for the eyes. The woman wrapped it in an eiderdown and began to rock it in her arms. "Rock-a-bye, baby Woodkin!" she sang. Then the wooden child opened his eyes and shouted, "Mummy, I'm hungry!" The joyous woman hurriedly cooked a pan of gruel, but before she could turn around the child had eaten it, pan and all. "Mummy, I'm hungry!" he called, as if he were starved to death. The woman sent her husband for a loaf of bread, but Woodkin swallowed it like a raspberry. "Mummy, I'm hungry!" he shrilled, growing before their very eyes at

a tremendous rate. Before long he was as big as a well-fed pig. The carpenter rushed off to the shed to milk the goat, but when he got back there was no sign of his wife. "Where is Mummy?" he asked. "I've eaten a pan of gruel, a loaf of bread and Mummy, and I'll eat you up too!" called Woodkin, and he had scarcely finished speaking when he opened his mouth like a barn door and swallowed the carpenter, milk-jug and all.

## 19 OCTOBER

# Woodkin

Now Woodkin was bigger than the old stove. Since there was nothing left to eat in the cottage, he set off for the village. On the green he came across a girl with a handcart. "My, how swollen your stomach is!" she cried. "Whatever have you eaten?" — "I have eaten a pan of gruel, a loaf of bread, a jug of milk, my mummy and daddy, and I shall eat you up too!" he cried. And before the girl knew it she, too, was in his stomach. Just then a farmer went by with a load of hay. "My, my, lad, what a stomach you have! What have you been eating?" said the farmer. "I have eaten a pan of gruel, a loaf of bread, a jug of milk, my mummy and daddy, a girl with a handcart, and I shall eat you up too!" said Woodkin, and with a glug! the farmer was in his stomach. As he went along he also ate a whole flock of

sheep, along with the shepherd and his dog. Then he rolled along to a field where an old woman was digging beet. "Well, well, my lad; you have a fine stomach indeed! What have you been eating?" she asked in wonder. "I have eaten a pan of gruel, a loaf of bread, a jug of milk, my mummy and daddy, a girl with a handcart, a farmer and his hay, a shepherd and his sheep, and I shall eat you up too!" said Woodkin. But the old woman did not wait to be swallowed, and she ripped his stomach open with her mattock. You should have seen the procession that came out! But it was the last time the carpenter's wife called on the devil. The owl told me this tale, to-whit, to-whoo; if you go and ask him, he'll tell you one too.

## 20 OCTOBER

# Why the Ostrich Cannot Fly

Once upon a time, long long ago, the ostrich could fly just like all the other birds. It was in the days when the sun laid golden eggs and hatched out golden chickens from them. The chickens ran off across the sky in all directions; then people began to call them stars. The sun sent a little bird with a letter to the moon asking it to come and be godfather to the chickens. The little bird dashed over hill and dale to get to the moon before it hid behind the clouds, but soon his wings began to ache. Then he saw an ostrich down below on the ground. "Ostrich, dear ostrich," the little bird called. "Please would you carry me and my letter to the moon! My wings are aching so, I am sure they will drop off soon." The ostrich scowled, "Well, then, if your little wings are aching, what about me? I am much bigger and heavier, and it is terribly far to the moon. But if you like, you may sit on my back, and we shall go there slowly on foot. We are sure to get there in the end, anyway." And so it was. The ostrich had long legs, but they seemed to get no nearer their goal. Long before the moon got the letter, the christening

was over. "You lazy ostrich!" cried the sun, angrily. "If you are too lazy to fly, then from this day forth your wings shall be but an ornament!" And since then the ostrich has had to walk.

## 21 OCTOBER

# The Pen That Told Tales

There was once a naughty little girl. She obeyed nobody, never said good-day to anyone, and at school she read fairy tales underneath her desk. When the teacher asked her, she couldn't even say A, B, C, let alone all of the rest. But she knew how to tell lies all right. One day she lost her pen. At school she told the teacher someone had stolen it. "Are you sure?" her teacher asked, but she insisted that one of her schoolmates had taken it. The teacher smiled, and gave her a beautiful new pen, such as none of the children had ever seen before. When the little girl got home, she hurriedly scribbled her homework and ran out into the garden. She didn't even read her homework over. She was naughty all afternoon, and that evening she quarrelled with her little brother. The next day at school the teacher called her name. "Read me your homework!" he told her. The girl began to read, but soon she started to blush like a ripe cherry. The magic pen had written, instead of her homework, all the mischief she had got up to. From then on the little girl was much better behaved. She was afraid the magic pen would tell on her again.

## 22 OCTOBER

# A Bull in a China Shop

Once upon a time a great kingdom stood on the point of a needle. The king had one daughter, as pretty as a picture. He wanted to marry her to the most powerful man on earth. Suitors came and went, but none was to the old king's liking. Then one day a mighty magician came along. He knew all there was to know about magic, and right away he threatened to turn the kingdom into a pool full of frogs if the king did not give him his daughter. The old king was no fool. "Very well," he said. "I shall give you my daughter and all my kingdom, if you can conjure up a china shop in which there shall be a fine black bull, and that bull shall dance the

two-step in the china shop." The magician laughed, waved his magic wand, and said "abracadabra", and at once a shop full of fine china appeared. He waved his wand a second time, and in the middle of the shop a great black bull appeared. But before the magician had time to order the bull to dance the two-step, the restless animal had turned and shifted once or twice, and the beautiful china was smashed to smithereens. "You clumsy fool!" laughed the king at the magician, and the great conjurer was so ashamed that he hid himself away in his own pocket and disappeared to where he had come from. Since then, when people behave clumsily, we say that they are acting like a bull in a china shop.

## 23 OCTOBER

# The Three Satchels and the Purse

Once upon a time there were four brothers. Three of them were strapping young lads, but the youngest of them scarcely reached halfway up to the front-door handle. Everyone

with their bridegrooms. The tiny courtiers were clapping in time to the dance and calling, "Hurrah, hurrah!"—"Here we have our brides!" grinned the brothers, and they would have taken the peapod away. But at that moment Halfling caught up with them. "I want a bride too!" he called. What were they to do now? Bridegrooms all over the place, but only three brides to go round.

## 24 OCTOBER

# The Three Satchels and the Purse

used to laugh at him, and he often felt sorry for himself. But what he minded most of all was that his brothers called him Halfling. One day their father called them to him and said, "Go out into the world and seek your brides. Whoever brings home the most beautiful girl shall have the cottage and a field to go with it." So off they went. Halfling called vainly after the others to wait for him; they only laughed and lengthened their stride. In a while they came to a field of peas. From one of the pods they heard a great clamour and rejoicing. "Whatever can it be?" wondered the brothers. They cracked open the pod and peeped inside; they were astonished at what they saw. Inside the peapod was a whole kingdom. There on a golden throne sat a tiny king; beside him was an even tinier queen, and beneath the throne three tiny princesses were dancing

While the brothers were arguing over which of the pea-princesses they should each have as their brides, the tiny king said: "Gentlemen, what use would such tiny wives be to you? If you leave us in peace, I shall give you three magic satchels. The first contains plenty, the second more than enough, and the third a profusion." The greedy brothers agreed. But then Halfling spoke up: "There is no satchel for me, so I should like a bride at least. I am small, she is small; we shall want for nothing, and at least she will not bully me!" The king smiled, and said: "If you do not mind a tiny bride, then, very well. Here is a magic purse. It contains four painted eggs. Give them your broody hen to sit on when you get home; she will hatch you a bride, you shall see." Halfling agreed, took the purse, and hurried after his brothers. You should have seen how they laughed at him all the way! When they got home, the three elder brothers opened up their satchels with great excitement; but out leapt little green imps with cudgels, and began to beat the brothers mercilessly. One of them got plenty, another more than enough, and the third a profusion. But Halfling gave the painted eggs to the hen to hatch. From the first there hatched a golden castle; from the second a golden throne; from the third he got a golden crown, and from the fourth a lovely little half-girl hatched. The two of them were married, and to this day they live happily together in their little golden castle.

## 25 OCTOBER

# The Goblin Iwouldeat

There was once an old woman who used to go into the forest to gather firewood. One day, when she had filled her shawl with brushwood and dry pine-cones, she sat down in a clearing to rest. She took out a piece of dry bread and began to eat. Suddenly, an acorn came tumbling to the ground in front of her, and out jumped a tattered little dwarf. "I am the goblin Iwouldeat!" he shrieked at the old woman. "Give me some food, or I shall eat you instead!" The old woman had only a crumb left over, so she threw it to him; but the goblin flew into a rage and said, "Do you not know that I cannot bear to eat bread? I shall eat you!" And he opened his mouth wide and moved towards the old woman; but she took to her heels. For a long time she did not dare to set foot again in the forest, but in the end her cottage grew so cold that she had to set off to gather wood again. When her shawl was full, she sat down to rest. Then the little goblin again leapt out of his acorn and screeched, "I am the goblin Iwouldeat! Give me food, or I shall eat you up!" The old woman quickly took out a jar of honey from her apron, and the goblin plunged his head into it greedily. The old woman turned the jar over on top of him and hurried off home. Since then the honey-pot has leapt about the forest, with a voice inside it saying, "I would eat, I would eat." If you value your life, be sure you don't turn it over!

# The Rajah's Bride

Far away in the middle of the jungle lived a foolish and lazy rajah, ruler of the Forgotten Empire. He would lounge all day on a cushion of bird-of-paradise feathers and let himself be fanned. One day he decided he would get married. He sent his counsellors and missives to all the corners of the earth to find him a bride; all of them were every bit as stupid as he was. "I want only a bride who can walk on the ground and fly through the air; one who looks like a human being, but does not look like a human being; one who has four hands and four feet," he ordered them. The envoys went sadly along until they met a wild boar. "Your Porcine Excellency," they addressed him, respectfully, "we are seeking a wife for His Magnificence the Rajah." And they told the boar what was required. "An easy matter," the boar told them. "You must take him a monkey. She will be just the bride he has asked for." The rajah's men did as he suggested: they caught a monkey in the jungle and took it back to the rajah. "Fools!" roared

the rajah. "It is an ordinary monkey!"—"But Your Royal Highness," replied the counsellors, "it is the only creature in the world which looks like a human being and does not look like one, which can fly through the air from tree to tree and walk on the ground, and which has four hands and at the same time four feet. Indeed, it is the very bride you asked for!" There was nothing for it for the rajah but to keep his word and to marry the strange creature. People would laugh at him behind his back and say: "See what a monkey of a wife he has!"

# The Gossamer Veil

Long, long ago, there lived a queen who had magic powers. Out of a thimble she conjured up a live doll, Gretel, so that she might have someone to play with. But because the queen was cruel and wanton, she teased the little doll, and set her impossible tasks. One winter's day she told Gretel she must weave her a veil of gossamer which would make her invisible. The poor girl wandered sadly through the

frosty night, not knowing where to turn. All at once, a sturdy stag was standing in her path. "Tell me what troubles you, little girl," he said. When Gretel had told her sad tale, the stag just tossed his head, saying: "Don't worry, everything will be all right." Then he shook his antlers and, lo and behold, the snow suddenly thawed, and the trees were covered in blossom. Again he shook his antlers, and the trees were hung with fruit. He shook them a third time: the fruit ripened, the leaves began to turn yellow, and gossamer drifted through the air. Overjoyed, the girl gathered it up, and wove the magic veil. But instead of taking it to the queen, she threw it over herself, and at once became invisible. Then she returned to the palace. "Cruel queen, your days are numbered!" she cried out, in an eery voice. "Who speaks to me?" asked the witch. "Your sister, Death," replied Gretel. The queen was so startled that her wicked heart broke. So it was that little Gretel became queen, and from time to time the kind stag pays her a visit.

## 28 OCTOBER

# The Bad-Tempered Admiral

Once upon a time there was a bad-tempered admiral. He and his ship sailed the seven seas and all the rivers, lakes, ponds and puddles of the world, and wherever he went he ranted and roared until earthquakes shook the land and volcanoes spewed out streams of lava and more ash than Granddad's pipe. The admiral's poor sailors could stand his endless bawling no longer, for their heads ached fit to split, and the only way to sleep was lying on both

ears, and, as every sailor knows, that is no easy matter unless you happen to have both ears on the same side of your head. So one day they put their heads together, and when the admiral was sitting on shore and drinking his tenth keg of admiral's rum, they weighed anchor and made full steam ahead for the horizon. At that very moment the admiral happened to glance from the tavern window seaward, and he could not believe his eyes—there was his very own ship sailing off somewhere, straight along the equator. "Octopuses, sharks and anchovies!" he roared, turning purple with rage. "Why, stone the crows, they've made off with me ship, and me admiral's cap to boot!" And off he ran after it, sea or no sea, dashing over the waves to catch his ship. Since it was right on the equator, where the earth is fattest of all, he had a good long way to run, but he had nearly caught up with his ship when, from out of the crow's nest, the voice of Jack, the ship's boy, called, "Look out, Mr. Admiral sir, you're running across the sea!" The admiral looked down at his feet and, shiver his timbers, so he was! He got such a shock that he fell in the water and, since he couldn't swim, he altogether drowned. Well, he wasn't much of a sailor, anyway!

## 29 OCTOBER

# The Starlings

In a certain city, where the houses grow up to the sky, an ordinary starling nesting-box hung from a tree. One autumn, when the starlings were flying off to the south as usual, the city fathers met down at the town hall, and pondered over why the starlings did not want to stay in the winter. "Who would want to stay in such an old-fashioned nesting-box," said the Civic Engineer. "We shall build them a modern starling housing-estate, and I shall be most surprised if they still fly away in winter." And so they did. In spring, when mother and father starling came back from their holiday in Africa, they were quite taken

the south. "Hold on!" the people called to them from the town-hall. "Why are you flying away?" Father starling waved a disdainful wing: "Central heating," he said, scornfully. "Playing up again." And with a mocking laugh they both flew away. Don't worry; when the warm sun returns, then so will they. But who knows, they may find themselves an ordinary nesting box again.

## 30 OCTOBER

# Baron Redbeard and the Dog

Once upon a time there was a baron named Redbeard, who was stronger than the strongest of his subjects. All were afraid of him, for he was cruel, and mistreated both men and animals; most of all he liked to tease cats and dogs. One day he was walking through his domain when he came to a peasant's farm. A skinny little dog was tied up beside its kennel. "Listen, Baron Redbeard," the dog barked out suddenly. "If you can carry me on your back to your castle, I shall serve you faithfully for seven years without food. If you cannot, then you shall watch over my kennel for seven years." The baron laughed. "Very well," he said, and tried to lift the dog up on his shoulders. But the dog turned round on

aback. "Good heavens, which floor do we live on?" said daddy starling. "Right at the top, I think," replied the mother starling. "There is a good view from here, and we are nearer the sun."—"That is all very well," said the father. "But what if the lift breaks down?" And so they argued and quarrelled, and since they could not agree, they decided to move into the middle. They liked it there very much. But summer passed and autumn came along, and once more the starlings got ready to leave for

his tail three times, and before the baron could catch his breath, there in front of him stood a dog the size of barn. He tried in vain to lift the creature. Then he ran off to his castle as fast as he could. He had the blacksmith make him a pair of iron boots, the tinker a suit of iron clothes, and ordered the servants to chain him to an iron bed. He was afraid the dog would carry him off to his kennel. In a little while he fell fast asleep. But the moment he shut his eyes, there in the chamber stood the gigantic dog. It bit through the iron chains as if they were paper, and made off with the baron, iron suit, iron boots and all. When the dog got to its kennel it tied the baron up, with a collar round his neck, and the wicked fellow had for seven years to serve the farmer who lived there. And since he was covered in iron from head to foot, by the end of the seven years he had quite rusted away.

## 31 OCTOBER

# The Boats with Dewdrops Aboard

There was once a little boy who was building a mountain of pebbles so as to reach the sky. He went on building, and building, and when he was tired, he and his little sister went to play on the bank of a nearby lake so as to have a rest. Most of all he liked to sail little boats made of nutshells or pieces of pine bark. This time, too, he carved two pretty little boats and gave each of them a little paper sail; then he and his sister shook a tiny dewdrop into each of the little vessels. It was all the riches they possessed. "Sail away, little boats; as you voyage, find out what our pearls are worth in the world," said the boy. The boats sailed away obediently on a long voyage. It was a long time before they returned. They anchored quietly in the creek and called out, "Your pearls are like human tears, and so they are worth nothing. There are too many of them in the world, for there is a shortage of compassion." The boy thought for a moment, then said, "Very well! I do not know what compassion is, but when I grow up I shall find out. Then I shall spread it among people, so that they may know the value of tears." Then he saw that his little sister was crying. "Don't cry," he told her. "I love you." And the boats said, "You already know what compassion is. It is the wealth of the kind-hearted." And they quietly filled their sails and sailed away.

# NOVEMBER

## 1 NOVEMBER

## The Lad Who Learnt to Understand the Birds

There once lived a peasant who had a bright young son. One day he said to himself, "It would be a pity for such a clever lad to spend the rest of his life on the farm; I shall send him to get an education, so that he may wear shoes on his feet like a lord." His wife was willing, but she said, "What trade do you suppose he may learn?" The peasant scratched his head, but he could think of nothing. Then a little sparrow perched on the chimney and began to twitter some piece of news to the other birds. "Now I have it!" cried the peasant. "We shall send him to town to learn the language of the birds!" They gave him a sixpence to pay his fees, and bade their son farewell. By and by the lad returned to a joyful welcome. "Father, I have finished my studies," he said. "Now I can understand what the sparrows on the roof are chirping about!" he added, grinning from ear to ear. His father and mother put on their best wooden clogs as if they were going to church, and sat the boy down at the table they had spread to welcome him home. His father was impatient with curiosity. "Well, then, tell us what the sparrows are saying!" he said, excitedly. The lad stretched out his ears until they were longer than those of their old

donkey, listened for a while, and said with a smile: "Believe it or not, father, the sparrows are telling each other how one day you will fetch me water in a copper basin, and how mother will dry my hands on the best tablecloth." The peasant almost burst his buttons with rage, and shouted at his son: "You mealy-mouthed good-for-nothing! Fine airs and graces you have taught yourself in the world! Get out of my house, and never come back again!"

## 2 NOVEMBER

## The Lad Who Learnt to Understand the Birds

What was the poor lad to do? He wandered the world, offering his services everywhere. "What can you do?" they would ask him. But when he told them the truth, that he could understand the birds, he got short shrift. "Whoever needs to know the latest bird gossip!" they would say to him. In the end he became apprenticed to a poor cobbler. "At least I shall learn a proper trade," he thought. One day he was sitting on his shoemaker's stool patching up a pair of old boots, when a flea jumped into his shirt. "I'll show you, you cheeky little beast!" cried the lad, and laid his cobbler's strap square across the flea's head. The creature lost its appetite at once. It fell to the floor and lay there with its legs in the air. "My, what a beauty!" cried the lad gleefully; he measured the flea from head to toe and from toe to head, and then skinned it and sewed a fine pair of shoes from the hide. They

were so big that a band of dwarfs might have played skittles in them. "Only the king himself can have such feet," said the shoemaker's apprentice to himself. "Not for nothing is it said that where he has trod no grass grows for seven years!" And he loaded the shoes on a handcart and set off to take them to the king.

days three ravens have been flying beneath my windows, and I do not know what they want of me." The lad stuck his head out of the window, stretched out his ears until they were as long as a sexton's cold, and at once began to translate the ravens' cries: "The birds are a father, a mother and a son. Last year, when food was scarce, the mother left the youngster to die of hunger. But the father took care of him and brought him up. They are asking you, my lord, to whom the son belongs." — "Why, that is simple," replied the king. "To the father, who brought him up." When the ravens heard this judgement they stopped crowing and flew away. "You are the wisest of the wise, my son," said the king. "I shall give you my daughter's hand in marriage. She is quite stupid, and you have brains enough for two." — "Why not?" the lad agreed, and right after the wedding he set off in the royal carriage to his parents' cottage. When his mother and father saw their noble visitor they fell over each other to do him honour. They invited him inside; his father brought him water in a copper basin and his mother dried his hands with the best tablecloth. "There you are, you see, the birds were quite right," said the boy with a smile. Only then did they recognize their son, and how ashamed they were for having turned him away from their door. But the lad was not angry with them, and took them off to the palace in the royal carriage.

## 4 NOVEMBER

## The Clockmaker Imp

There was once a very, very old town, in which there were thousands of towers. In the tallest of the towers, inside the big old clock, lived the clockmaker imp. He always made sure the clock was neither fast nor slow, wound it up, oiled it, and looked after its bells. Ding, dong, ding, dong the clock would strike contentedly, and the clockmaker imp would give a smile of satisfaction. But one day some

## 3 NOVEMBER

## The Lad Who Learnt to Understand the Birds

The shoes fitted the king like a glove. "You are a clever lad," he said to the boy. "Can you do anything else?" The boy told him proudly how he could understand the song of the birds. The king's face lit up like the summer sun. "What a piece of luck," he said. "For three

little boys passed by the clock tower on their way to school. They looked up at the clock and started. "The school bell will ring any minute!" cried one of them. "We shall be late, and the teacher will put us in disgrace."—"All because we played hide-and-seek!" another boy said. But a third boy had a clever idea. "Let us ask the clockmaker imp to put back the hands," he said. So they knelt down in front of the clock-tower and called, "Clockmaker imp, clockmaker imp, help us please! If you put back the hands for us, we will bring you a bag of humbugs." The imp had a sweet tooth, and he gladly helped the boys. In a flash all the clocks in the world were a minute slow, and the boys got to school on time.

## 5 NOVEMBER

# The Clockmaker Imp

But the clockmaker imp in his tower waited in vain for his bag of humbugs. As soon as their fear was gone, the boys forgot all about their promise. This made the imp terribly angry. "So that is the ungrateful human race!" he scowled, and out of spite he began to turn the hands of the clock backwards. A fine mess that was! Everything in the world went back-to-front. People began to walk backwards instead of forwards; instead of

tomorrow there was yesterday; the dead rose up from their graves, the sun crossed the sky from west to east, spring followed summer, winter spring and autumn winter; night followed morning, evening followed night, and so on. The old folk were naturally pleased that they were growing younger day by day, but the forgetful boys were quite upset. Instead of the third class at school they found themselves in the second, then in the first, and they were surely soon going to be little babies wrapped in shawls again, or even disappear to wherever they had been before they were born. Luckily one of them remembered that they had promised the clockmaker imp a bag of humbugs. He took a quarter of a pound of the best and went hurrying to the clock-tower. He laid the bag of humbugs down under the great clock. The clockmaker imp got his temper back at once, put the clock right, and made everything in the world the way it was before. Don't you ever go upsetting the clockmaker imp, will you!

## 6 NOVEMBER

# The Stolen Tale of the Giant with the Golden Hair

There was once a little girl whose fairy godmother gave her a magic skipping-rope for her birthday. The moment she skipped over it there appeared in front of her a pair of terrifying robbers. They bowed right to the ground and said, "What is your command, most noble princess? May we have the honour of stealing something for you?" But the little girl waved her finger at them and said, "Stealing is wrong, you scoundrels! Think yourselves lucky I don't call a policeman. But since it is you, I shall let you steal a story for me from the realm of fairy tales. But be sure to take it back afterwards!" The robbers bowed and disappeared, but in a twinkling they were back again with a fairy tale under their arms. Which one? This one!

Long, long ago, a son was born in the cottage of a poor woodcutter. He was no ordinary boy. He had a golden star on his forehead, and what was more, he could lie on his tummy and on his back, wink his eyes, and yawn away like anything. Do you see? There he goes, yawning again. You'd better hide under the bedclothes before he swallows you up!

## 7 NOVEMBER

## The Stolen Tale of the Giant with the Golden Hair

Well, let us continue. Where were we? When that wonderful little boy was born, the wise old fairy from the foxglove wood came along to be his godmother. She looked at the mark on his forehead, then up at the sky, and nodded her white head. "It is written in the stars that your son will take the king's daughter for his wife," she said. Word of this spread far and wide, until it came to the ears of the king himself. He heard it on the very day that a girl as pretty as a picture was born to the queen. The king frowned. "My noble daughter the wife of a poor woodcutter's son?" he said to himself. "That shall never be!" Then he dressed as a rich merchant and set off for the woodcutter's cottage. "You have a fine son," he flattered the parents. "Give him to me to bring up; I shall make a noble gentleman of him!" The woodcutter and his wife were

unwilling, but in the end they agreed. The king took the cradle containing the little boy, and dropped it into a raging river from a bridge along the way. He was sure the child would be drowned in the torrent.

## 8 NOVEMBER

## The Stolen Tale of the Giant with the Golden Hair

Strange to relate, the seething waters suddenly became slow and gentle, and rocked the child in his cradle as softly and safely as if he were in his mother's arms. By and by they carried the cradle down to an old mill. A poor miller and his wife lived there. They had no children of their own, and when they found the little boy they were happy to take him in and treat him as their own. Because he had come bobbing down the river to their mill, they called him Bobbikin. He grew like a healthy spruce, and before they knew it he

here, if you value your life!" she called to Bobbikin. "If the robbers catch you here, it will go ill with you!" But the lad was so tired he could go no further, and in the end the girl hid him behind the stove. Before long the robbers arrived.

## 9 NOVEMBER

# The Stolen Tale of the Giant with the Golden Hair

As soon as the robbers arrived, one of them, who had a long nose, called out: "I smell a strange smell, like in the grinding-room of a mill!" And before he knew it, the long-nosed robber was dragging Bobbikin out from behind the stove. They would have killed him at once, but the girl beseeched them not to, so in the end they spared him. They went through his pockets, and found the letter from the king. When they had read it, they were angry at the cruel king's treachery. So they wrote another letter, saying that the queen was to marry her daughter right away to the man who brought the letter. Then they carefully put the king's seal on the new letter, and when dawn broke they sent Bobbikin off to the palace. When the queen read the letter, she was surprised, but, not daring to defy her husband, she did as she was asked. The marriage took place at once.

had turned into a fine young man, a pleasure to behold. When he was just sixteen, there was a great storm in the countryside thereabout. That day the king had been hunting in the forest close at hand, and he took shelter in the old mill. The moment he saw the young man with the golden star on his forehead, he asked whose son he was. The old miller, suspecting no evil, told the king how he had been brought to them by the river. At once the king guessed what had happened. Without delay he wrote a letter to the queen. In it he told her to have the head of the one who brought the letter cut off right away. Then he ordered Bobbikin to take the letter to the palace that very evening. The young man set off at once, but because the night was dark he got lost in the deep forest. Luckily he soon came to a strange cottage. A young girl, grubby and untidy, was looking out of the window; she was the daughter of a robber chief. "Go away from

When the king returned, he was horrified, and wanted to punish his wife severely. But she showed him the letter bearing his seal, and the king was at a loss to understand who might wish him such mischief. So as to get rid of his unwanted son-in-law, he summoned him to the throne and said, "I order you to bring me three hairs from the head of the giant Tellitall. If you fail, you shall lose your head!" So poor Bobbikin set off.

## 10 NOVEMBER

# The Stolen Tale of the Giant with the Golden Hair

For a long time Bobbikin wandered the world, until at last he reached a certain city. "Halt!" called the sentry at the city gates. "Where are you going?" Bobbikin said he was looking for the giant Tellitall, and the sentry told him joyfully: "If you promise to ask him why the spring of living water in our city has dried up, then you may pass." Bobbikin promised, and went his way. By and by he came to another city. There, too, the sentry stopped him, but when the lad had told him of his errand, he called out, "I shall let you pass if you promise

to ask the giant why our city's wonderful golden apple tree has ceased to bear fruit." Bobbikin gave his word, and the sentry let him pass. As he made his way onward, he came to a broad river. Sitting in a boat by the bank was a downcast ferryman. "Tell me, friend, where can I find the golden-haired giant Tellitall?" Bobbikin called to him, and the ferryman replied, "On the far bank of the river is the golden cave where the giant lives with his mother. If you promise to ask him how much longer I shall have to ferry folk across the river, I shall take you there." Bobbikin promised, and the ferryman took him to the other bank.

## 11 NOVEMBER

# The Stolen Tale of the Giant with the Golden Hair

The golden cave shone like the midday sun. Sitting in front of it, spinning golden thread, was a white-haired old woman. "What are you doing here, child?" she asked in surprise. "If you value your life, you will escape before my golden-haired son returns, or he is sure to make an end of you." But Bobbikin told her sadly that he had no choice. If he returned without three golden hairs he would be shorter by a head anyway. The old woman

took pity on him, and promised to help him. Bobbikin begged her to find out from the giant how much longer the ferryman had to carry people across the river, why the golden apple tree had ceased to bear fruit, and why the spring of living water had dried up. No sooner had he finished speaking, than the golden-haired giant came striding through the sky with huge steps. The old woman just managed to hide Bobbikin in the kneading-trough in time. "I smell human!" roared the golden-haired giant, but the old woman calmed him: "It is because you spend the whole day flying over men's dwellings." Then she laid his head in her lap and began to stroke his hair. Soon the giant dozed off. The old woman pulled out a golden hair. "Why do you wake me, mother?" asked the giant, irritably. "Oh, son, I fell asleep, and I dreamed of the ferryman; for age upon age he has had to ferry folk over the river." "He is a fool," laughed the giant, "for if he were to give someone the oars to hold and jump out onto the bank, then the other would have to take his place." And the giant was soon asleep again.

## 12 NOVEMBER

### The Stolen Tale of the Giant with the Golden Hair

The kind-hearted old woman soon plucked another hair from the giant's head, then another. Each time she told him she had had a strange dream; in this way she found out that the golden apple tree has ceased to give fruit because a poisonous snake was nesting in its roots, and that the spring of living water was being swallowed by a fat frog. Then she left him in peace. When he had had a good sleep, he set off once more across the sky with his giant steps. Bobbikin took the three golden hairs from the old woman, thanked her kindly, and set off for home. The impatient ferryman was waiting for him. "When you have taken me across, I shall tell you what you want to know," Bobbikin told him, and when he was safely on the other bank he called out, "You must give one of your passengers the oars to hold and then jump out onto the bank; he will have to ferry in your stead!" When he got to the first city, he told the sentry why the apple tree gave no fruit. Without delay the citizens slew the snake, and at once the tree burst into golden blossom. They rewarded Bobbikin with three carts full of gold. He fared just as well in the second city. As soon as the citizens had, on his advice, slain the frog, the spring of living water shot up to the sky. The grateful citizens gave Bobbikin ten carts loaded with diamonds and pearls. So it was that he arrived home richer than the king himself. When the envious king saw his great wealth, he himself set off to visit the golden-haired giant, but when he reached the dark river, the ferryman gave him the oars to hold and leapt onto the bank. To this day the wicked king has to carry people across the river. Bobbikin and his beautiful wife have lived happily ever since.

When the robbers had finished their tale the little girl thanked them and sent them back to the realm of fairy tales to return the story to where it belonged. They have never been back since.

## 13 NOVEMBER

# Baron Simple of Doltham

Once upon a time, beyond the dark forests, lived Baron Simple, Lord of Doltham. The baron was true to his name; he was so stupid that the sparrows on the roofs would twitter about his foolishness. Anyone who had any sense at all could catch him out with the simplest of ruses. No wonder he soon lost all that he owned to rogues and tricksters. What was left of his cloak just managed to keep the patches together. But the baron was as proud as any peacock, and thought himself the cleverest fellow in the world. One day a pair of poor old beggars came wandering up to his castle. The only thing they had in the world was a dog who had taken up with them along the road, knowing the beggars would treat him better than a rich master. The two old men banged on the blistered castle gate and asked the baron for alms. "Go away, you'll get nothing from me!" growled Baron Simple,

waving a rusty sabre and slamming the gate in their faces. The beggars pleaded with him to give them at least a roof over their heads for the night, but the foolish baron would not soften. "You wait, you old miser, we'll show you!" warned the old men. They begged some old bones from the cottages nearby and threw them to the dog. What he did not eat, he buried in the ground. With each of the bones the clever beggars placed a copper coin they had begged. Then they knocked on the baron's gate again.

## 14 NOVEMBER

# Baron Simple of Doltham

"You'll get nothing from me, I tell you!" shouted the baron again, when he saw the two beggars. "We have not come for alms," the old men said with a bow. "We have for sale a magic dog, which can find buried treasure. The first day he digs up copper pieces; the second day silver pieces, and the third day gold. We are too old now to run after him, but if you give us your poor domain, you may have our magic dog." The baron wanted to see for himself. The old men unleashed the hungry dog, and it began to scrabble away at the earth to uncover its buried bones. Every time it did so it dug up a copper coin. Baron Simple could not believe his eyes. "If tomorrow he

digs up silver, and the day after gold, I shall soon be able to buy a crystal castle, and shall be the richest noble in all the land," he thought to himself. Without delay he signed a contract with the two beggars, giving them his entire domain in return for their dog. Thus the two old men became the lords of Doltham. But it was in vain that the baron tried the next day to get the dog to dig up silver. In the end he had to beg the two old men to give him a roof over his head. They made him plead and beseech them, but in the end they took pity on him and relented. "You can keep your crumbling castle," they told him. "We shall make do with the blue sky above our heads." They took their beloved dog and went their way, and told everyone they met the story of the stupid baron.

## 15 NOVEMBER

### Red Riding Hood

There once lived a little girl whom everyone liked, but most of all her grandmother. She sewed her little granddaughter a pretty little riding hood of red velvet, and it suited her so well that after that she never wanted to wear anything else on her head. So they started to call her Red Riding Hood. One day her mother asked her to take a basket to her grandmother. "Take these cakes and this bottle of wine to Granny," she told her. "She has been ill, and they will give her back her strength. But, mark my words, do not tarry on the way or wander from the path! And do not forget to greet politely anyone you meet." Red Riding Hood promised, and off she went. Her granny lived in the forest up above the village, and it was a good way to her little cottage. Scarcely had she reached the edge of the forest, when she met a wolf; but she was not afraid, since she did not know what a wicked creature it was. He asked her where she was going, and Red Riding Hood told him everything. The wolf licked his lips greedily, and at once began to ponder how he might eat up the grandmother and the little girl in one go. He trotted along beside her for a while, and then said: "See what pretty flowers are growing all around. And how sweetly the birds are singing! Why are you in such a hurry?" Red Riding Hood looked around her, and saw that the wolf was right. "What a nice posy I can pick for Granny!" she thought, and she started to run here and there gathering the wild forest flowers. Meanwhile, the wolf hurried on to the grandmother's cottage.

## 16 NOVEMBER

### Red Riding Hood

When the wolf reached the cottage, he knocked at the door and called out: "It is I, Red Riding Hood!" "Lift the latch and come in, dear. I cannot get out of bed, for I am still weak from my illness," grandmother

answered. The wolf rushed inside and swallowed the old woman up. Then he put on her nightdress, pulled her night-cap down over his long ears, and lay down in her bed. Before long Red Riding Hood arrived. But what was this? The door was wide open, and her granny, lying there in bed, looked terribly strange. Red Riding Hood began to feel a little scared. "Good morning, Granny, what big ears you have today!" she said in surprise. "All the better to hear you with!" replied the wolf. "Dear me, Granny, what big eyes you have!"—"All the better to see you with!"— "And oh, what a big mouth you have!" said Red Riding Hood. "All the better to eat you

with!" roared the wolf, and he leapt out of bed and swallowed her up. Then he stretched out on the bed and began to snore loudly. A hunter happened to pass by the cottage, and he was surprised to hear the old lady snore so loudly. He peeped into the cottage, and recognized the wolf right away. "Just you wait, you old scoundrel!" he said to himself, and he quietly took a pair of scissors and cut open the wolf's stomach. Out jumped Red Riding Hood, and then Granny. "Dear me, how dark it was

in there, and how afraid I was!" cried Red Riding Hood, and all three of them were so glad it was all over that they set to and ate all the cakes from the basket. Then they filled the wolf's stomach with stones, and sewed it up again. When the wolf woke up, he tried to run away, but the stones were so heavy that he crashed to the ground and killed himself. And Red Riding Hood? Do you know, after that she always did as she was told, and never tarried or wandered from the path again.

## 17 NOVEMBER

# The Hare and the Fox

A certain deep forest was ruled over by a cruel fox. All the animals were afraid of him, and kept as far away from him as possible. On the edge of the forest, in a cosy little lair, there lived a clever hare. One day he got up early so as to go down to the fields for a taste of fresh cabbage. All of a sudden he found the fox standing in front of him, licking his lips greedily. "How dare you steal cabbages from another's field?" the fox snarled. "Take leave of this life, friend hare! For your impertinence I shall eat you!" The hare was frightened, but he soon recovered his wits, and said boldly, "Fool! Do you not know that these fields belong to my bride-to-be, the fairy of the lake? Just yesterday she sent for me; but I have no horse, as befits a rich bridegroom. If you carry me to her on your back, the fairy will reward you well." The foolish fox agreed. The hare smoothed down his coat like a noble gentleman, plucked a posy of flowers, and swung himself up on the fox's back. "Make way! I am on my way to visit my bride!" he called out, and he whipped the fox on until the hairs flew off his back. It was such a funny sight that all the animals rolled about with laughter.

## 18 NOVEMBER

# The Hare and the Fox

When they reached the lake, the fox, his tongue hanging out, growled, "Where is your lake-fairy, hare? I want my reward!" The hare replied: "Dip your tail in the lake and wait;

you will see that the fairy will hang something on it." No sooner had he said this, than he was gone. The foolish fox did as the hare told him, and waited, and waited. Days passed, then weeks, then months; winter came, and the lake froze over. "At last I have my reward," thought the fox, and he tried to pull his tail out of the lake, but it was stuck fast. "You have been too generous, lake-fairy," he whimpered. "I cannot lift your gifts; take some of them off!" But there was no fairy in the lake; it was only the clever hare's trick. In the end the dogs heard the cruel fox's cries, came running up, and tore him to pieces. From then on the animals of the forest had to put up with his tyranny no more.

## 19 NOVEMBER

# The Ungrateful Son

This is a tale the mother cat told her kittens. Listen: Once upon a time there was a poor widow who lived with her son on the shores of a great lake. The boy was called Si Angui. One day he asked his mother, "Mother, what is on the far side of the lake?" His mother sang to him: "On the far bank happiness abides, once he may cross over to our side." — "But, mother," said Si Angui in surprise, "does not happiness dwell with us? I have my own little cat and my own dear dog, my own mat to sleep on, and the tsai-tsai lizard; I have you to stroke my head when I am asleep." — "It was only a kind of fairy tale," his mother told him, hiding the tears of love behind her hand. So they lived happily. But as time went by, Si

216

Angui found himself more and more often sending his eyes like two little nutshell boats across to the far bank of the lake. "I wonder what the realm of happiness is like?" he reflected, and he grew more silent day by day. One evening, as his glance again wandered about the lake, he spotted against the starry sky a white sail. Nearer and nearer it sailed, shining like the smile of the sun, singing in the breeze like a reed flute. "Mother!" cried Si Angui, "happiness is coming to us!"

## 20 NOVEMBER

# The Ungrateful Son

They stood by the shore, waiting for happiness to reach their hovel. Si Angui could not imagine what happiness might look like; perhaps like a young girl with a skirt of leaves and a white spider in her raven hair. Or perhaps like an orchid on the River of Shadows. But when the boat reached the bank, out stepped an ugly, bald-headed old man in a parrot-feather headband. Si Angui could feel tears of disappointment welling up in his eyes. But the old man smiled warmly, and his face grew in beauty like a kindled flame. "I am the richest merchant in the island empire," he said to the boy's mother. "I have heard on my travels that you live alone with your son in humble circumstances—nay, in poverty. I have no heir to my fortune, so I would ask you, mother, to put Si Angui in my care. I shall teach him to sell salt and buy pearls; I shall reveal to him how to grow riches from cocoa beans. Mother, let your son sail with me to the other side of the lake!" The boy's mother hesitated. "You who wear bird feathers on your head," she said, "Si Angui is happy here." But then Si Angui cried out eagerly: "Why do you hold me back, mother? Let me sail across the lake and buy happiness! When I have become the richest man in the island empire I shall build a palace of pink coral, and then return for you and my dear animals." His mother began to weep, but then she knelt down and kissed Si Angui's feet.

"May the good spirits keep you on your journey, my son!" she said. And so Si Angui set out for the far side of the lake to buy happiness.

## 21 NOVEMBER

# The Ungrateful Son

For a long, long time Si Angui travelled from island to island with the old man. He came to know the glint of gold and the misty beauty of pearls, and piled up more and more wealth as the days went by. But he did not find happiness. The richer he grew, the more his heart turned to stone. The old man, his faithful teacher and guide, looked at him one day with sad eyes. "My days are numbered, Si Angui," he whispered. "But before I die, I want to tell

you that you are not the boy I thought you were. Riches and splendour have turned your heart to stone. I wished to teach you the knowledge that happiness cannot be bought; but you spurn wisdom as the night spurns the sun. You are the poorest fellow in the island empire, Si Angui the rich! If you would bring your heart back to life, fulfil the promise you made to your mother. Return to her. Your happiness is again on the other bank." The old man finished speaking, smiled grimly, and before Si Angui's astonished eyes turned into a heap of sparkling diamonds. Si Angui had forgotten how to cry. He disregarded the old man's words, and with a cry of joy grasped the fairy-tale wealth in his hands. When he had got over the thrill, he cried out, "I shall fulfil my promise; but first I shall build a palace of pink coral. Then I shall take my mother there and find happiness at last."

## 22 NOVEMBER

# The Ungrateful Son

Si Angui achieved his ambition. He built a splendid palace, and the rajah himself, the king of kings, gave him his beautiful daughter for his wife. So Si Angui became king. But his heart froze like an icy stone. One day he said to his wife, "Far across the sea and the jungle my mother lives alone, waiting for me. I have promised that one day I shall take her to my palace of pink pearl; it is time now to set off." His queen was happy to agree, and they set off at the head of a great procession towards the far-off lake. When they reached its bank, Si Angui whispered: "On the far shore happiness abides; once he may cross over to our side."—"What did you say?" whispered his wife. "It is only a kind of fairy tale," Si Angui replied. As their boats approached the far bank, a weak old woman in frayed old rags came out to greet them with open arms. Alongside her limped a scrawny cat and dog. "Si Angui, my son," she cried, and kissed the ground where he had trod. "Have you at last

found happiness?" At that moment Si Angui broke into tears. He bitterly regretted leaving his mother in such straits. He knelt and embraced her knees. "Forgive me, mother; forgive me, faithful animals," he said. "My happiness is here with you; here I have found that which I had lost, and have searched for in vain throughout the world." No sooner had he said this than the stony weight around his heart fell away. At last Si Angui was happy.

## 23 NOVEMBER

# The Magic Pot and the Magic Balls

There was once a sexton who was as poor as . . . well, as poor as a church mouse. One winter's day, when there was scarcely a scrap of food left in their cottage, he sent his wife to town to sell the last of the chickens, so that they might pay off their debts. The woman was soon exhausted from plodding through the snow, and she sat down on the edge of the forest to take a rest. Suddenly a bearded little man appeared before her. "If you wish," he told her, "I shall give you this magic pot for your hen. All you have to do is to cover it and say 'pot-belly, fill yourself'. The pot will at once cook whatever you happen to fancy to eat. But mark my words, you must never wash the pot, or it will go ill with you!" The woman believed him, and gave the little fellow the hen in return for his pot. The strange man sat on the bird, spurred it on, and rode off into the forest. When she got home the sexton was angry with her, but she set the pot down on the table and ordered it: "Pot-belly, fill yourself!" In an instant the pot was filled with the most delicious foods. From then on the pot would cook them anything they cared to think of. But the sexton's wife was unhappy that the pot was getting dirtier day by day, and one day she could resist no longer: she put it in the wash-tub and began to scour it with sand, until it shone like gold. All of a sudden something or other struck her such a blow on the head that stars swam before her eyes, and the pot went bouncing off into the woods.

## 24 NOVEMBER

# The Magic Pot and the Magic Balls

From the moment the magic pot disappeared into the forest, want and hunger came to the sexton's cottage again. One day the sexton led their lamb out of the shed and said to his wife: "I shall go and try my luck; perhaps I, too, may meet the little man." And off he went. On the edge of the forest he sat down on a fallen treetrunk and waited to see what would happen. Suddenly a voice said, "Welcome, sexton! If you wish, I shall give you this wooden ball in exchange for your lamb." The sexton turned, and saw standing behind him the magic little man. "A lamb for a wooden ball?" he wondered, but the little man smiled. "You will not be sorry, you'll see. When you get home, shut all the doors and windows carefully, place the ball on the floor, and tell it: 'bow politely, now'. You'll see what happens!" The sexton did not hesitate for long, and he gave the little man his lamb; the manikin sat on its back, spurred it on, and rode off into the forest. As soon as the sexton got home, he impatiently placed the wooden ball on the floor and ordered it to bow as the manikin had told him. The ball began to turn round and round, at first slowly, then

gradually faster and faster; then, suddenly, it split in half like an apple, and out leapt tiny little dwarfs. Some were carrying a tablecloth, others gold plates, dishes and cutlery, and others tureens full of food. The sexton and his wife and children feasted as if they were at a royal banquet. When they had eaten and drunk their fill, the little men cleared the table and disappeared again into the wooden ball.

## 25 NOVEMBER

# The Magic Pot and the Magic Balls

The sexton's good fortune was short-lived. The parson got to hear about his magic wooden ball. "It is surely the devil's work!" he cried, and took the magic ball away from him.

He promised to put up the sexton's wages, but he forgot to say when. As things grew worse and worse for the poor man and his family, he set off for the forest with their calf on a lead. Again the manikin appeared, and he gave the sexton for his calf another wooden ball, only

this time much larger than the first. When the sexton put it down on the floor, out of it jumped a pair of giants with clubs; they beat the unhappy sexton half to death, then disappeared back into the ball. The sexton had an idea. He took the wooden ball off to the parson. The parson had guests, and the little dwarfs could hardly keep up with their eating and drinking. "I have brought you something better!" the sexton told the parson. Filled with curiosity, the parson put the large ball on the floor, and ordered it, "Bow politely, now!" At his words out leapt the two giants and set about the parson and his guests without mercy. When they had finished, the sexton caught up both the balls and rushed off home. After that he and his family again wanted for nothing—but not for long. One day someone forgot to close the door; the magic balls rolled off into the forest, and were never seen again.

# The Boy, His Sister and the Little Mouse

A long time ago, it must be two or three days now, a little mouse came floating along to a little boy in a little boat. The mouse had been all the way to the sky. Quite by chance, the little boy was just building a mountain of pebbles so that he could get to the sky. He took the mouse in and promised that one day, when he was bigger, he and the mouse and his sister would climb up together among the stars. They had not managed it yet, but the boy said that did not matter. It might be more fun to long for something than to have it. He took the old flute out of Grandfather's chest and began to play this and that. It sounded wonderful. The little mouse listened and listened, and then said, "I shall never forget that you wanted to take me to the skies. Even if we never got there, what a beautiful journey it has been! More beautiful than a dark mousehole, brighter than a golden grain of rye. Thank you for playing the flute." And he disappeared down a mousehole.

## 27 NOVEMBER

# The Lost Letter

In a certain city the postboy was delivering the mail. There were sad letters and merry ones, ordinary ones and special ones, important ones and silly ones—in short, all sorts. Suddenly the wind blew the letters out of the postboy's bag. It wouldn't have mattered much, except for one little letter which was very important. It was written by a young prince who had gone out into the world, and it was to tell his princess that soon, very soon, he would return to make her his wife. The princess had waited in vain for news

of him, and she grew sadder day by day. No one was able to cheer her up. The young postboy was upset, too, that he hadn't delivered all the mail, the way a postboy is supposed to do, come rain or shine or earthquake. He was ashamed to go back to the postmaster, and he went off instead to look for the lost letters. He searched and searched, until finally he had found all those letters which were only ordinary, but not that one letter which was so important. It is a wonder the princess didn't cry her eyes out. But suddenly there appeared a carrier pigeon, carrying the letter in his beak. The postboy cried out with joy and took the letter to the sad princess; her tearstained cheeks burst into a smile like the cherry trees burst into bloom in spring. It was a stroke of luck, for otherwise the postboy would have had to roam the world back and forth to this very day. And what about the prince and the princess? Well, they got married, and sent letters to all good people to tell them.

## 28 NOVEMBER

## The Little Spark-Girl

A couple of little urchins were sitting by the wayside thinking to themselves, "If only we had a little fire, we might cook ourselves some sausages!" Suddenly, out of nowhere, a little spark appeared on the ground in front of them. "I am the Spark-Girl," she said politely, and bowed to the boys. "Will you play with me if I light a fire for you?" The lads were only too happy to promise. They brought some dry twigs and branches, then the Spark-Girl danced a merry dance, and the fire was soon blazing brightly. When the boys had roasted their sausages and eaten their fill, the Spark-Girl begged them, "Come and play with me now for a while!"—"Huh! We don't play with girls," said the lads, putting out their tongues at her. And they began to jump and play about the fire. Now if sparks could cry, the little Spark-Girl would surely have burst into tears with disappointment; as it is, they must not, or they would put themselves out. She just frowned crossly, spun her fiery skirt around, and called out: "Abracadabra!" Then, as the boys were dancing around the fire, a shower of glowing embers leapt out of it and shot into their trousers. You should have seen them run for the stream! They sat down in the water with a hiss; but that did not mend the holes they had burnt in their trousers. They got a good hiding at home on top of their scorching, and they would gladly have begged the Spark-Girl's forgiveness, but she never appeared to them again.

## 29 NOVEMBER

## The Queen of the Snakes

Once upon a time a young shepherd-girl found a snake under a briar. It was

221

half-starved, and its skin had been torn by the talons of some voracious bird. The girl took pity on the snake, tended its wounds, and even gave it some milk to drink from her cup. The snake soon recovered a little and crawled away. The girl went on with her work. Some time later a poor young farm-lad came to ask her father for her hand. But her father was a rich peasant, and did not want such a poor fellow for his son-in-law, so he showed the lad the door. The shepherdess cried and begged her father in vain; she could not get him to change his mind. So she ran out of the house and into the fields, and sat down beneath the briar. Then a snake came crawling up to her and hissed: "What ails you, child? I shall help you if I can."—"How can you help," sighed the shepherd-girl; but she told the snake all about her troubles, just the same. "Make me a garland of wild flowers," the snake said, when it had heard her sad tale. The girl did as she was told, and the snake at once had another request: "Kiss my forehead, good child; I am alone in the world, and no one loves me." The shepherd-girl shuddered with disgust, but when she saw the sad snake's eyes, she overcame her horror and kissed it. In an instant flames flew out of the earth and burned her father's farm to the ground.

## 30 NOVEMBER

# The Queen of the Snakes

When the young girl saw the terrible misfortune which had befallen her home, she wept more than ever. "You have rewarded me ill, ungrateful snake!" she complained, certain that it was the snake's doing. She ran home to offer at least words of comfort to her father; but words cannot make up for lost riches. The once-wealthy farmer had to set off into the world with his daughter at his side and a beggar's stick in his hand. From that time on he met with misfortune wherever he went, and at every turn a snake with a garland of wild flowers would appear before him. Meanwhile, the poor farmhand was getting on better every day, and before long he had become the richest farmer in the village. Folk told strange tales of him; they said that his fields were guarded by a fiery snake, and that it laid gold pieces on his doorstep at night. Before long the faithful young man came again to ask the now poor peasant for the hand of the beautiful shepherd-girl. This time the old man gave his blessing gratefully, and begged the young farmer for forgiveness. Before long there was a fine wedding in the village. When the celebrations were at their height, a snake came crawling up to their door, with a tiny fairy wearing a garland of wild flowers sitting on its back. "I am the queen of the snakes," she said to the bride. "I have rewarded you for your kind heart. Remember that it is an ill wind which blows no one any good. Only the want in which your father found himself softened his hard heart." Then the fairy smiled, and disappeared for ever.

# DECEMBER

## 1 DECEMBER

# The Tale from the Cottage in the Snows

Far away from here, in the midst of the deep snows, is a cottage where three little snowmen live. During the day they play just like other children, sledging, skating, and even bicycling into town for strawberry ice-cream; but the moment night falls and the moon lights up the icicles outside, they sit down at their snow-table and tell each other fairy tales from the land of snow and ice. I once went to visit them, so I can tell you one of those stories. Maybe this one:

Once upon a time there was a little girl called Nawarana. She lived in a little snow-house in a land far off to the north, where in summer the sun never sets and in winter it never even shows itself in the sky. Instead of the sun the sky is filled with twinkling stars, the moon shines, and the glimmering aurora thrusts out its luminous fingers. The long, crystal night holds sway. Throughout those endless winter nights Nawarana would sit in her snowy parlour, listening to tales of great polar bears that roam the skies, or of the white whale with the golden hair. Even though the frost outside was as keen as a knife, it was as warm and cosy in the little snow-house as in a feather-bed, and as Nawarana went to sleep, she would dream that the wise reindeer fairy had turned her into a beautiful snowflake, bringing people luck.

# The Tale from the Cottage in the Snows

Do you know who the reindeer fairy is? She is a kind, white reindeer hind who grants everyone's secret wishes. Nawarana knew this very well, which is why she dropped a glistening little tear into the flames of the fire every day. That was so that the reindeer magician in her silent realm of snow would hear the voices of people's dreams, as one wise old woman used to say. Nawarana was happy in her home made of frozen snow, and the only thing that troubled her was her mischievous elder brother. He was never up to any good. He would stick cold icicles in her hair and drop icy snow down the back of her reindeer-skin coat. Ow! How cold it was! Nawarana would have tears in her eyes, but she was afraid to tell anyone, in case her brother got his own back some way. One day, when their mother and father were out hunting on the frozen sea, her brother teased her so much that she could stand it no longer. She ran out in tears into the dark polar night, sobbing, "Reindeer fairy, reindeer fairy, take me off somewhere where my brother may no longer trouble me!" At that moment she thought she saw, far off across the tundra, the flash of a white reindeer hind. Around its head shone a veil of glimmering polar light.

## 3 DECEMBER

## The Tale from the Cottage in the Snows

Little Nawarana flew along towards the shadow of the reindeer fairy like a little bird. She ran through the crystal polar night, calling, "Reindeer fairy, reindeer fairy, wait for little Nawarana!" But the white wraith suddenly dissolved like a cloud, and the aurora that surrounded it was extinguished. Nawarana wandered, lost, about the endless snowy plains. How long she trekked across those icy wastes she did not know herself. But she suddenly found herself at the foot of a range of tall mountains. Up and up she climbed, until at long last she arrived on a broad plain. But, strange to relate, the ground began to shudder beneath her feet, like when the crust of ice on the sea begins to crack. Boom, boom, boom! she heard from beneath. Startled, Nawarana began to run across the plain, but another tall mountain rose up in her path. It was covered all over in thick forests; in the midst of the forest yawned a fearsome gorge, out of which a fierce wind howled, like when a storm is blowing up at sea. Terrified, Nawarana climbed to the very peak of the mountain, whose sharp point thrust up out of the forest. Then a terrible voice roared out: "What will you here, hapless child? Am I to swallow you up?" Nawarana looked round fearfully, but she could see no one. Who was calling?

## 4 DECEMBER

## The Tale from the Cottage in the Snows

When Nawarana heard that terrible voice, her knees shook with fear. "Who is calling me?" she piped up in a thin little voice. "Are you a good spirit, or an evil one?"—"Aah, foolish woman!" said the voice. "I am Kinak, the snow giant, and you are sitting on the end of my nose. It tickles so terribly that soon I shall sneeze!" And the giant gave such a sneeze that Nawarana just managed to hold on to a mole on the giant's nose, so as not to fall off. "You have been climbing over me for several days now," grunted Kinak. "You tickled me under the heart, and you crawled in my beard—just like a flea. Who might you be, anyway?" Nawarana told the giant who she was, and why she was wandering alone through the polar night. "I thought the reindeer fairy must have sent you to me," said Kinak. "She is my sister, and she knows well enough how lonely I am. I am so big that I cannot even stand up, so as not to trample on anyone, so I just lie here on my back the whole time, pining for someone I can be fond of. If you like, you may stay here; you can put up a tent right beside my nose. Only take care not to roll into my mouth!" It was only then that Nawarana realized that the terrible gorge from which the fierce wind was blowing was in fact the giant's huge mouth. But Kinak had such a kindly voice that she decided to stay.

## 5 DECEMBER

## The Tale from the Cottage in the Snows

Nawarana put up a tent of reindeer skins beside the giant's nose, and lived there for a long time with her herd of reindeer, which the giant caught for her in the palm of his hand. She had a fine time. She told the snow-giant fairy tales she had heard at home, and as a reward he let her catch fish in his eyes, which were as deep as a couple of lakes. But one day Kinak heard a quiet sobbing. "What is the matter, Nawarana, are you homesick?" he asked. "Very homesick," she admitted. "Perhaps father and mother are already crying for me." — "Well," grunted the giant, "it would be better if you were to go back home. Anyway, I cannot move on your account, in case I might crush you, and I cannot sneeze, for fear of blowing you away. You will be better off at home. And if your brother should bother you again, just you call me!" Then he took Nawarana carefully in the palm of his hand, blew with all his might, and sent her floating through the air like a snowflake, right down to the door of her snow-house. "Where have you been so long?" her brother snapped at her angrily, and he was just about to teach her a lesson when she called out: "Kinak, Kinak, help me, my brother wants to hurt me!" At that moment the distant giant sneezed so mightily that the wicked brother rolled for three days and three nights across the snowfields. When he finally got back home, he never troubled Nawarana again. He believed that she was hand-in-glove with the spirits of the snows.

## 6 DECEMBER

## The Waterman and the Dog

There was once a waterman called Walter. He loved to climb out of his stream at night

and go for a walk. His mother would warn him, "Don't you go wandering about on dry land, young man, you know very well that where there is no water it is no place for a waterman!" But Walter would not listen. One night he met a lonely little dog. "Let us be friends," said the dog. "I am quite alone in the world." The waterman took pity on the lonesome creature, and would play with him every night until his mother called him home. But one day some naughty boys saw him. "Look! A waterman!" they called. "Let us drive him away from the water; then we can tie him up with strips of bark and sell him to a circus!" And they ran after him. They drove him farther and farther from the water; the further away he got, the weaker he grew. He looked around desperately for some puddle or other, but there was not a drop of water in sight. He had given up all hope of ever being free again, when the faithful dog appeared, lifted his leg, and made a puddle. "Hurrah!" cried the waterman, wet himself all over, and dashed straight to the stream, where he splashed his way back home. But his mother had to give him a good wash. And you should have seen the scolding he got!

## 7 DECEMBER

## The Tale of the Lost Alphabet

A long, long time ago there was only one single fairy tale in the whole wide world; but it was so long that no one ever got to the end of it. All the fairy-tale stories that ever were fitted inside it. But one day a naughty wind came along and mischievously blew the fairy-tale alphabet off in all directions. Since then no one has been able to put the story together again. But whenever anyone comes across at least a letter of it, the letter tells him a little bit of that endless tale. Look, the dove, clever fellow, has just found the letter R. I wonder what the R will tell us?

Once upon a time there were a young mother and father who had seven sons, but no daughter. They so wanted to have a daughter, and when at last a little girl was born, they looked after her like a crock of gold. One day the father sent his sons to bring water from the well, wishing to bathe his daughter in her little gold bath. But the boys began to play down at the well, and did not return for a long time. Their father said angrily, "I wish you lads would be turned into black rooks for this!" Scarcely had he said these words, when seven black rooks rose up from the well and began to fly in circles around the countryside, wailing loudly. And how does the story go on? This letter won't tell us any more; we'll have to wait for another one.

enchanted brothers!" she called, but the sun did not answer and glared until her poor rags were burnt. She ran off in tears to see the moon, so that she might cool down. "Moon, kind moon, show me the way to my lost brothers," she begged. But such an icy blast of air came from the moon that the poor girl was changed into a silver snowgirl. At the end of her strength she just managed to reach the stars. But another letter will have to go on with the story now.

## 8 DECEMBER

# The Tale of the Lost Alphabet

Look, a scruffy little bird is scrawling the letter S on the blackboard for us. Let us ask how the story goes on. Like this? When the hapless father found that his careless curse had really turned his sons into rooks, he nearly died of grief. Luckily his lovely little daughter remained to assuage his sadness. She grew and grew, and when she grew up into a young woman, she was beautiful beyond compare. One day she found seven boy's shirts in an old trunk, and her parents had to tell her all about her brothers. When the girl heard the story, she decided to go out into the world to seek her brothers. First she went to the sun. "Sun, dear sun, tell me where I may find my

## 9 DECEMBER

# The Tale of the Lost Alphabet

Oh, look! The busy birds have turned up a magic letter C somewhere or other. We can go on listening now. When the girl got to the stars, the Morning Star smiled at her sweetly and said, "Dear child, your brothers are prisoners in the glass mountain. I shall give

you a little bone to take with you. When you get to the glass mountain, you must use the bone to open it." Then she showed the girl the way, and took leave of her. A rainbow stretched itself across the sky; the little sister stepped onto it and walked across it like a bridge until she reached the glass mountain. But when she looked in her bundle for the bone the Morning Star had given her, she could not find it. She knew at once what she must do; she cut off her little finger and used it to open the gate in the glass mountain. In the courtyard on the other side stood an ugly dwarf. "I know why you are here," he told her. "But if you wish to release your brothers you must with your bare hands pick glass nettles, spin from them a glass thread, weave the thread into cloth, and from that cloth sew seven glass shirts. If you cannot do this by morning, you too will become a black rook, and will remain enchanted with your brothers for ever more."

## 10 DECEMBER

## The Tale of the Lost Alphabet

See, that sooty little sparrow has found a magic letter K in the chimney. What story will it tell us? Maybe this one: The girl was not dismayed by the dwarf's words. With her bare hands she plucked glass nettles, paying no regard to the stinging pain; she spun glass thread, wove glass cloth, and sewed seven

glass shirts. She sewed and sewed all night long, and nearly went quite blind from peering at her work. The sun was slowly thrusting golden fingers over the horizon; but the girl had one more sleeve to sew on the last of the seven shirts. Then she heard the beating of wings above her head, and seven rooks appeared. "Hurry, dear sister," they called. "The sun is rising!" Without delay the girl threw each of them a glass shirt. At that moment there was a thundrous roar; the glass mountain changed into a golden palace, and there, in front of the girl, stood seven sturdy young men, her brothers. Only the seventh, whose sleeve she had not finished, had a black wing instead of one of his arms; but this did nothing to spoil their joy. They all joined hands and hurried home to their mother and father. Then they all went together to the golden palace. They live there happily to this day. The ugly dwarf had disappeared, no one knows where to, and the magic letter did not tell us. Why don't you have a look for some more of the magic alphabet?

## 11 DECEMBER

## The Otter Queen

In a certain woodland pool there once blossomed a lovely flower. It played and sang

228

such beautiful songs that all who passed that way had to dance whether they liked it or not, until the flower strummed a quiet lullaby. A young king heard tell of this flower, and wanted to bring it to his palace. He journeyed to the pool, jumped in the water, and swam to the deepest part of the pool. But the moment he touched the flower an old otter thrust her head out of the water. "How dare you steal flowers from my royal treasury?" she asked, angrily; she touched the king with a reed wand, and he turned into a beautiful pearl. This sank slowly to the bottom of the pool. "You shall lie here until someone has shed for you as many tears as there are drops of water in this pool," the otter told him, and disappeared in the murky water.

## 12 DECEMBER

## The Otter Queen

When the king did not return for a long time, his mother set out for the pool to seek him. The magic flower was singing a song about an enchanted pearl; when the king's mother heard the song, she sat down on the bank and began to weep. She wept until she had no more tears, but it was still not enough. Then drops of blood began to flow from her eyes. When she had cried away all the blood in her body, the old otter emerged from the water and dropped the pearl at her feet. It turned miraculously back into the young king. From the enchanted flower a beautiful young girl stepped out, swam to the bank, and kissed the dead queen. At that the queen opened her

eyes and began to smile. "Thank you, mother, for setting us free," said the king and the young girl. All three of them joined hands and hurried to the royal castle. "May you live in happiness!" the otter queen called after them. And they did.

## 13 DECEMBER

## The Clockwork Steamer

A little boy was once given a clockwork steamer by his grandfather. He filled the bath with water, wound it up, and off it steamed across the water. But what do you think? All of a sudden huge waves got up, and the little lake became the open sea. The toy steamer turned into a real steamer, smoke billowing from its funnel like from granddad's big cigar, and siren hooting fit to deafen you. The little boy clapped his hands gleefully at this wonder, and before you could count to five he had stepped aboard, strode up to the helm, and gave the order: "Full steam ahead!" The steamer leapt across the waves like a horse spurred on by its rider, and made for the horizon. Merry fishes scudded past in the water, seabirds wheeled above the waves, and the great ocean-going steamships greeted the steamer politely with their flags. "Where are you bound for?" the sailors called from the passing ships. The boy stood by the helm, saluted and proudly replied: "We are sailing to discover America!"—"Bon voyage!" called back the sailors, and waved them on their way. Then the steamer wound down, grew smaller and smaller, and once more became just an ordinary little toy steamer, and the great ocean changed back into an ordinary bath of water. What a pity! The boy would surely have discovered his America. No matter that Columbus has already discovered it long ago! Little boys will always discover it over and over again.

## 14 DECEMBER

# The Queen and the Knight

Once a little girl found an old chess set in the attic. All the figures had long since been lost, except for a knight on a lame horse and a sad queen. The little girl played with them, but the queen grew sadder every day, and the knight looked so unhappy that the girl herself burst into tears. "It is raining!" said the sad queen, and she opened a little umbrella over her

head. "Oh dear, raining," said the downfallen knight, and hurried to hide under an umbrella, too. The queen strutted up and down in the salty rain of tears, accompanied by her faithful knight, who reminded her of the good old days, when he and her lost husband would ride out into battle together. The more they remembered, the more abandoned they felt. The little girl did not know how to cheer them up. But one day she found the lost figures in an old cupboard, and laid them out on the squares of the chessboard. Soon there was the sound of joyful trumpet calls from the castle battlements; the queen smiled and she and the king embraced, sat down on their thrones, and ordered a magnificent tournament to begin. When the jousting was over, the old knight and the queen bowed graciously to the little girl, and gave her two little umbrellas as a keepsake. They never needed them again.

## 15 DECEMBER

# How the Animals Wanted to Build a House

In a certain zoo there lived a giraffe, a monkey, a parrot and a sparrow. "Let us build ourselves a house!" they said one day, and at once began to discuss what sort of a house they were to build. The giraffe said, "It must have a roof up to the skies, so that I may get my head inside it."—"But inside it there must be trees with nuts and thick branches, so that I may swing from them by my tail," said the monkey. Then the parrot said that it should swing in the air like a cage, and have a perch and a grain trough and all sorts of other things. "Oh, no," said the sparrow. "Our house shall be of grass and twigs, and small and cosy like a sparrow's nest, so that the wind cannot get in." In the end they decided to build a house which would suit everyone. They built and built, but they never managed to build that house. It was either too big, or it was too small, or it was too this, or it was not enough that. "There is nothing for it," sighed

sewed, and as she sewed she smiled sweetly to herself. She was looking forward to the baby that was soon to be born to her. It was winter, and outside the snow was falling and the little white flakes were settling on the black, black ebony window frames. Before she knew it, the daydreaming queen had pricked herself with the needle. She opened the window to cool the sore finger, and three little drops of crimson blood ran down into the snow. The queen smiled. "Oh, how I should like my child to be as white as the freshly fallen snow, with cheeks as red as blood and hair as black as ebony," she thought to herself. It was not long before her wish was granted. A little girl was born to her who looked just as she had hoped. They called her Snow White. But joy and grief go hand in hand in this world, and soon after the child was born her mother died. Before the year was out the king had brought a new wife to the palace. She was exceedingly lovely, but as she was beautiful, so was she cruel, proud and wanton. She knew spells and magic, and every morning she would look at herself in her magic mirror and ask it: "Mirror, mirror, on the wall, who is the fairest of us all?" And the mirror would reply: "Mistress, by my troth I vow, yours is far the fairest brow." And the proud queen would kiss the mirror.

the monkey at last. "Only children can paint a house like that for everyone. When the children come, we shall ask them to think up a house for us." And to this day they are waiting for someone to come along and paint them a lovely house that will suit them all. When you wake up in the morning, why don't you try and paint it for them?

## 16 DECEMBER

## Snow White and the Seven Dwarfs

Sitting beside the window, the happy queen sewed and sewed. Little coats and caps she

## 17 DECEMBER

# Snow White
# and the Seven Dwarfs

The years went by, and Snow White grew up into a lovely young girl. When she reached the age of seventeen she was as beautiful as a forest nymph, and far, far more beautiful than the queen herself. Then, one day, the queen again stood before her magic mirror and asked it with a smile: "Mirror, mirror, on the wall, who is the fairest of us all?" But the mirror darkened and said: "Mistress, by my troth I vow, Snow White is the fairest now!" The queen flew into such a rage that she could not sleep that night for envy and anger. The next day she called one of the royal hunters to her and ordered him to lead Snow White deep into the forest and to kill her there. "To prove that you have done it, you shall bring me her heart," she told him. What was the poor hunter to do? If he did not obey her, the queen would have his head cut off. So, like it or not, he had to lead Snow White off into the deepest and thickest part of the forest. The

beautiful child suspected nothing, and she drew such pleasure from the song of the birds, the scent of the flowers and the antics of the woodland creatures that the hunter took pity on her. He told Snow White what fate her stepmother had ordained for her, and warned her not to return home. Then he shot a fawn and took its heart back to the wicked queen. She threw it into the fire with an evil smile.

## 18 DECEMBER

# Snow White
# and the Seven Dwarfs

Poor Snow White wandered through the deep forest, not even able to see her way for tears. Finally she dragged her weary feet into a woodland clearing. In it stood a little cottage such as no human eye had ever seen before. It was all of moss and pine cones, and from the windows fireflies glowed. Snow White knocked gently, and when no one answered she tiptoed inside. How lovely it was in there! There was a tiny parlour, as spick and span as a gleaming new pin. In the middle of it stood a table, on which there lay a white tablecloth and seven little plates. Beside each plate was a golden knife, fork and spoon, and behind it a golden goblet. Over by the wall there were seven little beds with snowy sheets. The poor girl was so hungry and tired that she took a mouthful of food from each of the little plates, drank a sip from each of the goblets, so as not to leave anyone short, and then lay down in each of the little beds. In the seventh she curled up and fell fast asleep. When darkness fell, seven little dwarfs came

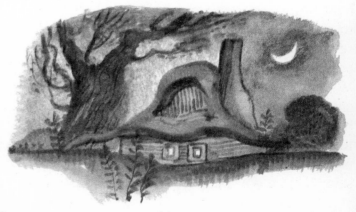

marching and singing into the cottage, and made straight for the table. Suddenly, they stood as if struck by lightning. Do you know why?

## 19 DECEMBER

# Snow White and the Seven Dwarfs

The dwarfs stood gazing at the table with their mouths wide open. "Who's been sitting on my chair?" wondered the first. "Who's been eating from my plate?" grumbled the second. "Who has broken a piece off my bread?" asked the third. "Who has been eating my vegetables?" said the fourth. "Who has been using my fork?" complained the fifth. "Who has been cutting with my knife?" cried the sixth, and the seventh exclaimed, "Who has been drinking from my cup?" Then the first dwarf looked round and saw his ruffled bedsheets. "Someone has been lying in my bed!" he announced. "In mine too, in mine too!" called the next five, one after the other, but the seventh saw Snow White still lying in his bed. The others gathered round him and shone their firefly lamps on her. "How beautiful she is!" they breathed, and so as not to wake her they crept quietly into bed. The seventh dwarf slept for a while in each of his companions' beds, and so they all slept well. When Snow White woke up in the morning she was startled to see the seven little men, but they looked at her so affably that she tearfully told them her sad story. The dwarfs put their heads together, and then the first one said: "If you will keep house for us, wash, sew,

cook and clean, then you may stay here. But do not open the door to anyone while we are out; your evil stepmother will soon find out that you have not perished in the forest." And so Snow White stayed on in the cottage of the seven dwarfs.

## 20 DECEMBER

# Snow White and the Seven Dwarfs

One day the proud queen again stepped in front of the magic mirror and said: "Mirror, mirror, on the wall, who is the fairest of us all?" But the mirror darkened, and replied: "Mistress, by my troth I vow, Snow White is fairer still than thou!" The queen knew now that the hunter had tricked her, and she fell into such a rage that sparks flew from her wicked eyes. Without delay she dressed up as an old pedlar-woman and set out for the cottage of the seven dwarfs. The enchanted mirror had told her the way. When she got there, she knocked on the shutters and called out to Snow White in a sweet, enticing voice: "Buy a pretty lace for your bodice, my dear." Snow White did not recognize her wicked stepmother, and in the end she let herself be persuaded. She bought a golden lace for her bodice, and the old woman willingly offered to tie it for her. When the trustful girl agreed, her stepmother pulled the lace so tight that the poor child could not breathe, and fell lifeless to the ground. There the dwarfs found her that evening when they returned home from their underground caverns.

## 21 DECEMBER

# Snow White
# and the Seven Dwarfs

When the dwarfs saw Snow White lying there in a deep faint, they quickly cut the lace of her bodice, and in a while she came to her senses. "Never open the door again!" her little friends warned her. Snow White was sure she would remember their advice. Meanwhile, back in the palace, the stepmother again asked the magic mirror who was the fairest. But again it told her: "Mistress, by my troth I vow, Snow White is fairer still than thou!" She was so enraged that her heart almost broke. She hurried to her magic chamber and prepared a silver comb covered in poison. Then she dressed up as a different pedlar-woman and set out for the cottage of the dwarfs. "Buy a pretty comb for your hair, my dear," she enticed her beautiful step-daughter. Snow White refused to open the door, but when the old woman coaxed her and cajoled her, she finally took the comb through the window and pushed it into her beautiful black hair. At once she fell to the ground and lay there motionless. When the dwarfs got home in the evening, they wrung their hands in despair over the poor girl. But the youngest and smallest of them found the poisoned comb in her hair and drew it out, and Snow White came to life again. You should have heard the scolding she got! In the meantime the queen had got back to the palace, and she rushed off to ask the mirror her question. But the mirror again replied: "Mistress, by my troth I vow, Snow White is fairer still than thou!" The queen turned white with anger.

# Snow White
# and the Seven Dwarfs

This time the wicked stepmother dressed up as a poor peasant woman. She took with her a basket of sweet-scented apples. Half of one of them contained a strong poison. When she got to the cottage she tried to persuade Snow White to buy the poisoned apple, but the girl was suspicious. "You need have no fear, my dear!" the envious queen told her, and took a bite herself from the good side of the apple. When Snow White saw this she was no longer afraid, and bit into the poisoned half of the apple. In an instant she fell dead. This time the dwarfs, do what they would, could not revive her; Snow White did not wake up. Weeping and wailing, the kindhearted dwarfs laid her in a silver coffin and placed a glass lid over it. Then they carried her to the top of a woodland mound, where the birds and animals of the forest guarded her night and day. One day a handsome young prince rode past, and when he saw the beautiful Snow White in her coffin, he begged them to allow him to carry the lovely creature off with him to his royal palace. The dwarfs would not hear of it at first, but finally they agreed. The prince's servants carried Snow White in her coffin along the forest paths. Suddenly, one of them stumbled over the root of a tree; the coffin fell to the ground, and the piece of

poisoned apple was jerked from Snow White's throat. She sat up and looked around her in astonishment. The prince and the dwarfs were struck dumb with joy. The prince led Snow White off to his castle, and before long a magnificent wedding had been prepared. Among those they invited was the wicked stepmother. She stood proudly in front of the magic mirror and asked who was the fairest. "Fairest is she who, though she died, now lives to be the prince's bride!" said the mirror. The queen was so furious that she hurled the mirror to the ground; at that moment her cruel heart shattered to a thousand pieces.

## 23 DECEMBER

# The Tree of the Abandoned Children

When the first flakes of snow begin to fall and the frost glazes over the rivers and lakes, in a certain silent forest a magic tree lights up. Its candles kindle, its ornaments glitter, and on each little twig a beautiful present grows for some abandoned child. Day and night the birds fly to and fro, carrying the gifts all over the world. As soon as they pluck from it one of the toys, another grows in its place. Once upon a time there lived, not far from that forest, a rich little boy. I don't know how it came about, but one day he wandered into the woods and happened to come across the magic tree. "Oh, how beautiful it is! It must be just for me!" he cried, and he ran home to fetch a saw; then he cut the tree down and planted it in the garden in front of his window. In vain did the tree beg him and beseech him. That year not one sad, abandoned little child got a present for Christmas. The wicked boy could not wait for morning, so that he might pick what he fancied from the tree. But what a surprise the next day, when he found the tree withered and without a single present on it! And, strange to relate, the little boy himself was as dumb as a fish. "You shall not get back your speech until you take me back into the

forest, and water me with your tears, so that I may grow green again," said the tree, sadly. The frightened boy carried the tree back into the forest and watered it with tears until its withered branches came back to life. At that instant he got back his speech. He hurried home to his mother and cried, "Mother, I do not want to be wicked any more!" And so once more the magic tree lights up in that forest every year. And every year the little boy comes along and hangs from its branches his own little present for the abandoned children.

## 24 DECEMBER

# The Three Carollers

Once upon a time there was a little boy who simply could not wait for that silent, holy night to fall on the snow-covered countryside, and for that warm wish, "Peace to men of good will" to go echoing from each and every dwelling up to the starry skies. He stood alone in his room and gazed out of the frosted window at the gently falling snow. Whenever he breathed on the window-pane, new frost-flowers would grow there, and glisten in the light of the snow-decked street-lamps. They seemed to the boy to be playing a delicate, tinkling melody, which rose high, high up to the heavens, like a breeze. He smiled a happy smile. "I shall go to Bethlehem and play the baby Jesus a lullaby on my violin," he thought, suddenly. So he waited until all in the house were asleep, then he opened the window and, with his violin tucked under his arm, slid out into the street. He did not know which way to go, but he followed the wind which drove the little snowflakes, and soon it led him into a large and silent park. There, on a stone plinth, stood the statue of a beautiful young girl, softly plucking with her frozen fingers the strings of a lute. "Where are you going?" she asked the boy. "To Bethlehem, to play a lullaby on my violin for the baby Jesus," he replied. "I shall go with you," said the statue, tucking up her skirts and stepping down from her plinth. So off they went together to Bethlehem.

# The Three Carollers

For a long time they walked through the endless, frosty night. The boy began to grow afraid; his fingers and toes were cold, and tears came to his eyes like two clear little icicles. The stone girl comforted him, saying, "Don't cry, we shall soon be there!" but she did not know herself how far it was to Bethlehem, or whether they were going the right way, so she lightly plucked the strings of her lute to drive away their fear. They passed by a big snowman with a shining new coat of fresh-fallen flakes; they tried to speak to him, but he did not answer, for he was dreaming of the land of the great white clouds where his forefathers had come from. He only sighed happily and smiled in his sleep. Then the two of them spotted a little frozen bird on a branch nearby. "Come along with us!" they called. "We are off to Bethlehem to play for the baby Jesus."—"With pleasure," replied the bird, "for I am alone and sad." And so they wandered the darkened streets, full of hurrying people; but no one took any notice of them, and no one was surprised to meet a girl made of stone playing the lute, for on the nights before Christmas Eve miracles may happen in the world, and people may believe in them. Then the three lone wanderers left the town behind them and turned their steps towards the place where, on the distant horizon, an exquisite star was blazing.

# The Three Carollers

The pilgrims were at once sad and deeply happy. They had no idea how long they had walked when they saw before them a little cottage covered in snow. There was the scent of hay all around, and out of a shed came the

the little boy curled up in his mother's arms. When he woke up in the morning, he found beneath the Christmas tree the last five fairy tales. They were all stories he had never heard before, and the boy was happy.

## 27 DECEMBER

## The Little Pine-Cone Sister

Once upon a time there were three little brothers. They were very fond of each other, but they were often sad just the same. "If only we had a little sister," they would say. One day they were walking in the woods, when a pine-cone tumbled down from one of the

bleating of lambs and the braying of an ass. Just then the flame of a candle blazed up in the window, and it seemed to the lonely travellers that out of the flame there stepped a tiny Virgin Mary with Baby Jesus in her arms. She walked towards them and smiled sweetly. The little boy and the stone girl fell down on their knees, and whispered to the little bird to bow his head. He did it so beautifully that he was proud of himself. Then the girl struck the strings of her lute, the boy drew the bow across his violin, and the little bird sang a lullaby in a voice so sweet and pure that the very stars were moved to tears. When it had finished, all the bells in the land rang out and Christmas trees lit up everywhere. Then the whole world began to sing:

*"Silent night, holy night ..."*

When the carol had died down, the pilgrims again bowed to the candle flame, and made their way home. The stone girl climbed back up on her plinth, the little bird went contentedly to sleep among the branches, and branches. "Here I am!" it called. The boys bent over and, sure enough, it was no ordinary pine-cone, but a tiny girl in a skirt of cone-scales. The brothers were filled with joy. "Would you like to be our sister?" they asked. "I should love to," said the cone-girl, so with cries of glee the boys carried her off home. They looked after her, played with her, carved her a little bed from the bark of a pine tree; but all to no avail. After a while their little pine-cone sister began to hang her head, to cry and to waste away. "I am sad for my tree," she wailed one day. The boys put their heads together, then they set off for the woods again. "Forest, dear forest, give us a tree for our little sister!" they called. There was a rustle and a swish, and a beautiful little tree thudded to the ground. The brothers carried it home, planted it in the garden in front of their window, and hung the little cone-girl from one of the branches. Right away the colour came back to her cheeks; the little girl clapped her hands, laughed, and began to sing songs. Then all the birds came flying up and sang along with her. Since then the three little brothers have had in their garden a tree which is always singing.

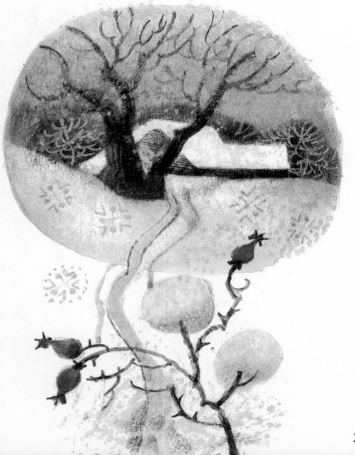

## 28 DECEMBER

# The Ice Bird

There was once a little cottage where a wise old woman lived. She had two granddaughters, Sally and Polly. Sally was a good and obedient child, while Polly liked best of all to dress up, and did not help the old woman with anything. She declared that she was the most beautiful girl in the world, and that one day a fairytale prince would come to fetch her. One year the winter was particularly hard, and the snow covered the little cottage right to the eaves. Then a little bird came and perched in front of the cottage. He was made all of ice, and he sang so sadly and beautifully that your heart would break. "Poor thing," said Sally. "He must have been put under the ice-queen's spell. We shall set him free!" She and her sister ran out and Polly took the bird in her hands. "Brrrh, how cold he is!" she cried, and threw the bird down in the snow. He sang so sadly that tears came to Sally's eyes. She took the bird into the cottage, lay down in her bed, and clutched the poor creature to her heart. He chilled like ice, and Sally seemed to be turning into an icicle herself. She almost wept with cold and pain, but in the end she fell asleep. When she woke up in the morning, a golden-haired prince was lying beside her in her bed. "Thank you for setting me free," he

said. "You warmed me at your breast, and for that service I shall never leave you." And so it was not the wicked Polly but the good Sally who married a prince in the end.

## 29 DECEMBER

### The Snow Princess

Long, long ago a poor potter lived all on his own. He had no one in the whole world, so on the long winter's evenings he often felt so sad he could have cried. One evening he went out onto the doorstep and watched the snow as it came tumbling down. He held out his hand, and one snowflake after another settled on his palm. The flakes quickly melted, but one of them suddenly changed into a beautiful little girl; she took hold of her white skirts and bowed politely. "I am the snow princess," she said, in a voice like tiny tinkling bells. "The winter queen has sent me to you, so that you may not be so lonely in the world." The potter rejoiced, and at once invited her into his warm parlour. "Oh dear, no!" she laughed. "If I were get just a little too warm I should melt away. Build me a little palace of snow; I shall live there, and you shall visit me every day. But don't forget your fur cap, so that your ears do not chap." The potter did as the snow princess asked, and he was no longer sad in the world. When spring came the snow palace melted in the sunshine, and the snow princess disappeared with it. But every year she returned, and she grew bigger and more beautiful every time. This went on for sixteen long years.

## 30 DECEMBER

### The Snow Princess

Word soon got about that the poor potter had the most beautiful daughter of any in the land. Even the king himself heard the tale. He had a team of horses harnessed to a sleigh, and set off to see for himself. Oh, what a ride it was. The sleigh-bells jingled, and wherever the royal sleigh went flying past, the people fell to their knees and called: "Out of the way, the king is passing!" The monarch pulled up beside the snow princess's ice-palace, and out

stepped a girl as white and gleaming as fresh-fallen snow. The king could not take his eyes off her. "I want her for my wife, and no other," he cried. The potter was taken aback. The king was old and ugly, and people said he was cruel and ill-tempered to boot. No wonder the potter tried every way he could to get her out of it. But the king would not be dissuaded. "I shall give you whatever you ask for your daughter," he said. "If you refuse, you shall lose your head." Then the snow princess whispered in the potter's ear, "Do not worry, father. Take the king's signet ring and tell him I should like to receive him in my snow palace." The potter did as the snow princess had told him. He took the king's ring, and the king stepped proudly into the princess's chamber. At once the palace shone with icy hoarfrost, snow began to fall from the ceiling, and soon the cruel king turned into an icicle. His courtiers searched for him in vain. When spring came the sun's rays melted the snow palace and the princess and the wicked king with it. Because the potter had the king's seal, he became king. And the snow princess? The next year she came back again, and she was more beautiful than ever. But what had happened to the wicked king she did not say. Perhaps he has to serve the winter queen for ever more.

## 31 DECEMBER

# The Dream Maker

Far, far away, in the starry realm of shadows, the Night Queen sits on her moon throne. In her clasped hands she holds, like a cup of holy water, a magic water-lily lake. The moment the sun has set on the Earth, the loveliest of the water-lilies spreads its petals, and on it there awake from their slumbers the Dream Maker and the kindly Night Fairy. Both of them are as transparent as a dewdrop, and

quite, quite invisible. The fairy's hair hangs in clear glass plaits, and her skirt is a crystal bell. The little Dream Maker will sprinkle stardust in her hair, or strike a tinkling note from her skirt with a slender moonbeam. Then the brittle melody rings out softly through the night, until sleep draws shut the eyelids of children the world over, as the Dream Maker croons his lullaby and stars drop from the heavens. Night is falling. The water-lily is spreading its petals. Can you hear? Out there in the distance someone is singing. The Dream Maker is calling you to his kingdom. Listen!

*Ting-a-ling starbells, faintly ringing;*
*Moonshine, silver bright.*
*Fairy voices, softly singing,*
*Far off in the night.*
*Hush now, children, close your eyes:*
*Before your dreaming's done,*
*Dewdrops, tinkling from the skies,*
*Will greet the morning sun.*